Sally Colin-James's love of character came long before her love of writing. The eldest of a large family from a regional seaport town, Sally grew up around sparkies and wharfies, miners and one-eyed football supporters, and hard-working Italian and Greek migrants. After being told by her school principal she should forge a career in pharmacy or economics and forget her dream of journalism, Sally found herself slumped in the plastic chairs of Adelaide University hoping that Statistics 1AC would help her calculate the chance of finding any joy in the situation. With a burning desire to 'write' and unable to transfer into journalism, she shifted gear and completed a degree in communications.

Following a globally successful corporate career in communications and event management, Sally returned to creative writing, gaining an Australian Postgraduate Award (APA) scholarship to complete a Doctor of Philosophy in professional writing. *One Illumined Thread* won the 2020 HNSA Colleen McCullough Residency Award, the 2020 Varuna PIP Fellowship Award and a placement with the Australian Writers Mentoring program. She has been the recipient of the Byron Bay Writers' Festival Mentorship Award and her work was shortlisted from over 2000 entries across 54 countries for the international 2021 First Pages Prize.

www.sallycolinjames.com

SALLY COLIN-JAMES

Fourth Estate

Fourth Estate
An imprint of HarperCollins*Publishers*

HarperCollins*Publishers*
Australia • Brazil • Canada • France • Germany • Holland • India
Italy • Japan • Mexico • New Zealand • Poland • Spain • Sweden
Switzerland • United Kingdom • United States of America

HarperCollins acknowledges the Traditional Custodians
of the land upon which we live and work, and pays respect
to Elders past and present.

First published in Australia in 2023
by HarperCollins*Publishers* Australia Pty Limited
Gadigal Country
Level 13, 201 Elizabeth Street, Sydney NSW 2000
ABN 36 009 913 517
harpercollins.com.au

A catalogue record for this book is available from the National Library of Australia

ISBN 978 1 4607 6210 3 (paperback)
ISBN 978 1 4607 1492 8 (ebook)

Cover design by Hazel Lam, HarperCollins Design Studio
Cover images by istockphoto.com and shutterstock.com
Author photograph by Kate Nutt
Typeset in Bembo Std by Kirby Jones
Printed and bound in Australia by McPherson's Printing Group

For D, my love.
Across how many lifetimes
has my heart found yours?
How many more to come?
Never enough.

A NOTE ON THE TEXT

While *One Illumined Thread* is a work of fiction, it is inspired by the real-life wife of a Renaissance artist and two women in one of her husband's more famous paintings. This is an invented narrative that draws on historical and biblical events. However, the artistic licence used in the rendering of characters and in the timing of inventions and events is an invitation to join me in the ongoing – and, in my mind, invaluable – enquiry into what we think we know about ourselves, each other and our worlds.

Aramaic was the language believed to have been spoken in the period set in Ein Kerem (Beit HaKerem). Please refer to the glossary and translation notes starting on page 333 for a guide to names and places.

I

The forms of bodies
could not be understood in detail
but for shadow.

LEONARDO DA VINCI

1

Adelaide, Autumn 2018

The girl in the mirror stares back at me and does not blink. It hurts to blink. Tears crest the balls of her cheeks and I clench against the desire to ache for her. She should know better. Why doesn't she know better? Although she is my exact image, she is not me. This is what I tell myself.

I reach my hand towards her, rest my fingertip on the purpling stain of skin around her eye. The coolness of the glass spares me from her flesh and blood heat. And she won't flinch because of the tenderness. The black channel of the tear trough will take the longest to heal. The skin here is fragile, vascular. She has been told this many times and is familiar with the conformation. Paper thin, near to bursting.

The shadows of the bathroom blur the space between her and me. I withdraw my hand and find the switch for the bare bulb.

Fiat lux. Let there be light.

The mirror frames her face. And as I work the makeup brush around her upper and lower lids, I examine her the way I do a work of art. I shift angles, attentive. Holding that invisible taut rope between the seer and what is seen while I search for the right words to consider, to assimilate. To grasp.

Art, said Leonardo, lives from constraint and dies from freedom.

The girl in the mirror is a work of art. Unlike me, she will never find freedom.

I pack away the brushes. Twist my hair up with mismatched bobby pins. Close my eyes and mist the setting spray onto my face.

My hand again finds the switch.

Fiant tenebrae. Let there be darkness.

When I open my eyes, she is gone. I am here.

The streetlights flicker off as I step outside. Birds bustle in the plane trees, golden leaves drifting, late this year thanks to a warmer autumn. Airborne they appear weightless, but between my fingers they are thick, substantial, bigger than my hand. I collect twenty leaves, bright as suns, and stash them in my satchel, then gather twice as many smaller crimson leaves from the winged sumac crowding one of the row cottage's tangled gardens. The same number of burnished purple leaves strewn from next door's ornamental plum. I'll use them on my walk home to create the artwork. A tree skirt. Circling the base of the tree where the trunk meets the earth. Autumn leaf rings in yellow, red and purple for the towering sugar gum in North Adelaide's Warnpangga Park. It calms me, anchors me, to know I have this to look forward to.

I hoist my satchel onto my shoulder and remove the A4 envelope from inside it. Take a short laneway and turn right. At the end of the street there is a post box. My hand sweats against the envelope, the fresh ink of the address reversed on my palm. I could have emailed the application, but sending it by post gives me time to come to terms with whatever might come of it.

I push the thick envelope to the mailbox slit, trying to force it through. The metal clip holding the papers together catches and tears. My skin prickles, sweat beads rupturing the careful veil of makeup. I yank the envelope out and fan my face. There's a bigger post box near the gallery. A tidal wave of shame swells as I walk away, and I can hear her, the girl in the mirror.

Too fucking stupid to post a fucking letter.

*

At the Adelaide International Gallery's staff entrance, anxiety pain shoots through my chest. Day fifty-five at this job yet each one feels like the first. I go over the steps.

Five things I see —

Welcome sparrows wheeling, lilly pillies, threads of dew-speckled webs between deep-glossy-green leaves, the fruiting head of a dandelion, the frayed mat at the door.

Four things I feel —

The key pass in one hand, the envelope in the other, my satchel strap pulling on my shoulder, the open Velcro tab chafing at my hip.

Straightening up, I touch the key pass to the pad.

Three things I hear —

Traffic hum from North Terrace, the slap of sports shoes on pavement from early runners, a perfunctory click as the lock disengages.

Two things I smell —

The gallery has a neutral odour goal. Where hotels and boutiques strive for signature scents, museums and galleries prefer that smells don't violate the art-viewing experience. Sometimes it troubles me that they appear to have succeeded. I once knew little of the craving for a scent, of the brain's linking of smell, emotion and memory. Things thought lost can be found in scent. Like they'll never again be found in the footy shirts and shorts and school pants and sheets and greasy pillowcases and towels and socks and beanies I once washed, turning up my nose at their sweat and oil and grass and earth and scraped knees smells.

The first psychiatrist suggested pleasing scents. Did I have any old books from grandparents? Were there flowers from my childhood that could be planted, picked, vased? A scent from your earlier life, she'd said, breaking the very rule she'd set me to be specific, not vague. Because by *earlier life* she'd meant before the knock on my door. The knock from the hand whose fingernails sheened with emerald-green polish, which caused me to fix my attention upon whether this colour was appropriate for a police officer dispatched to deliver news that no mother should hear.

The hall lights blink on as I pass beneath them. A draft of cedar and wax when I open my office door. The cedar from a Japanese bath stool I had sent from Kyoto, and the wax from Tasmanian candles, wafting plant resin and honey.

One thing I taste —

A memory. Wild honey. Glistening and dripping from a fallen, cracked tree. We were on a short Queensland trip, on a rainforest walk. My then four-year-old son rushing ahead to explore, his hands coated with the honey lost from the hive, riddled with ants, but straight into his mouth. The delight as he offered me his fingers to lick. Our silent rapture as tiny native bees worked to rebuild their damaged hive. The taste of liquid blossoms and caramel spice on our tongues.

I place the torn envelope on the desk and pick up a printed image of the seventeeth-century embroidery in my care, one that will require all the skills I've acquired as a textile conservator. Almost four hundred years old, the piece had been found in a mouldering tube of a deceased estate shed and, despite its condition, I could see its rare and remarkable beauty. Our curator, Tris, had listened intently to my assessment and fought hard to acquire it for the gallery. The day it arrived she left me alone with the piece. Gave me time and space to unwrap and examine and relish it. To soak in the strange intimacy and awe a conservator feels in the presence of an historical relic.

I imagine its seventeenth-century embroiderer perched on a tapestry chair, her boned stays drawn tight under her bodice. The embroidery set in its slate frame atop trestles. The waft of chemise sleeves, lace flounces, with the deft arc of her hand as she stitches a background of silver metal thread in Elizabethan ground stitch. At the top, in crimped broadplate, a radiant gold sun. Threads that, in candelight, would have shimmered and glinted.

In the embroidery's centre, parts of two figures in delicate needlelace slips, now detached, have some fragments missing. But even in this state what remains prickles the back of my neck. A sense that every last button or bead or silk-shaded flower I'd worked on had trained me for this piece, catalogued as *Embracing Figures*. For there was no doubt in my mind, this was *The Visitation*. The tender meeting of cousins, Elisabeth and Mary, the Saint and the Virgin. Both pregnant.

I return the printed image to my desk and glance again at the envelope. I could tape it and post it right now. But this is not my routine. And my routines form a structure, and in the structure lies a pathway upon which I can always find my feet. I leave the envelope and take the stairs down to the exhibit space, to the ancient wooden statue that both captivates and haunts me.

In the quiet room the carved corpse lies prone. Rigor mortis fists, belly distended. A swollen tongue bulges from its mouth. Three carrion birds have begun their feast upon it. One black crow is perched on its chest, beak thrust forwards to pluck the fat worm of its tongue. A vulture looms at the feet, a piece of flesh in its beak. Another crow peers up at me as if sensing my agitation. Anticipating my revulsion, my recoiling from this sight of Death.

Death, Third of the Four Sights seen by Prince Siddartha.

I circle it, soft-shoed. Holding my breath. Wetness snaking from my armpits. I want to *see* this death. To register and anchor devastation in one dismantling epiphany. Hah! Death! I have captured you and you can no longer outwit me. The prince needed only one look for his revelation. His gaze, unlike mine, able to wholly fathom the sight. But I feel no reprieve. Before me, only art. Artefact. Hewn, painted, polished by Buddhist monks. Gleaming with devotion. A work in its wholeness. Not in pieces, like my son.

Heavy-heeled footsteps along the corridor. Tris's petite size is a mismatch with her gladiatorial stomp. I dab at my face with a sleeve cuff. Flap the armpit of my damp shirt. I am wearing navy. Like I do every day. The marvel of this colour to conceal.

I squat down near the wooden vulture at the statue's feet, so it will seem as if I am here to study the new graffito under its tail feathers. In the flood of recent high school visits, someone has drawn an elegant white arsehole on the bird. My early training was in wood and, with the objects conservator on leave, I must work out how to remove it without damaging the centuries-old carving. It's a clever graffito. A dilated anus drawn as Leonardo would have drawn it. As a five-petalled flower.

'Sirani's agent says they will send us *The Head*,' says Tris.

A flurry of specks before my eyes when I stand.

The Head is John the Baptist's, on a platter. Not the one removed by Herod after his seduction by Salome, but the *Study of Head (John the Baptist III)* carved by artist Caterina Sirani. A block of lime wood hacked and chopped and pierced and painstakingly painted, to arouse questions about power. About abuse. About why we turn away from the very things we should not. I've been trying to get it here since I started at the gallery.

Tris walks closer and I want to press my palm out to halt her in her steps.

'You bloody well pulled it off.'

She touches me on the arm and my fingers curl into their own rigor mortis clench. The piercing heat of her kindness like a nail through wood.

She can see I am uncomfortable, doesn't react. She is too self-assured, Tris. She is rare.

I fight back the urge to say I'm sorry. Recalling the repeated instructions from the third psychiatrist. You'll need to go cold turkey on apologising. You'll need to learn new associations for what it means to be touched. My urge to knock the oversized glasses off his unshaven face made me hot with shame. I didn't know myself without I'm sorry. The beginning of so many sentences for so long.

'When will they send it?' I ask, knowing Tris is accustomed to my professional diplomacy, my low-key reception of news, good or bad.

'Their current exhibition finishes in four weeks.' She is anxious.

If there's no issue with shipping or customs, there'll be just enough time for the carving to adjust to its new environment.

I can see Tris is amused by my lack of fluster.

The Head will feature in an exhibition about portrayals of power. The oily pallor of its face, the lifelike porcelain teeth set inside its gaping mouth, its gleaming onyx eyes. Its shock of black hair made brutal by nails hammered into its skull. All convey horrific sensitivity. With her startling, life-sized army of carved boat people, estranged people, marginalised people, Sirani's statues make us stop and stare and gulp, arrest us with their stark dignity.

But this is not the reason I find solace in her work. And not the real reason I want *The Head.*

'Any ideas for an exhibition title?' says Tris. She doesn't need my opinion, but I like that she asks.

'Only clichés and euphemisms,' I say, forcing a smile.

Then the moment happens. Her eyes meet mine, her gaze grazing the bruise, hidden by makeup. I flinch and step back from her accidental scrutiny, trip over the wooden vulture. A dull thud as the bird topples onto its back, stiff legs in the air.

'I'll write it up,' I say, mortified at the report that will now require a statement on any damage caused by my graceless stumble.

I bend over, fumble, as I check over the bird. It seems unharmed but my eyes cannot focus. I can hear the insults he'd have launched if he'd seen this happen. Flecks of spit fired from his mouth as he spoke them. But I can't unravel. Please no, not here. I bite at the inside of my cheek while I steady the vulture back on its feet.

Beside me I can see Tris trying to annul whatever she has done to disturb me. Her phone in her hand, thumbs working over the screen, then she pushes the device back into the side pocket of her oversized parrot-green dress, stitched with orange banksia and yellow wattle. The dress is one I might have worn, once.

'Come for staff drinks after work. We'll celebrate,' she says, dabbing conversational mortar over the crack in the silence. 'I'll email you the exhibition schedule.'

I feign distraction, still fiddling with the wooden vulture.

As she leaves, I wonder if I said goodbye. If she did. So many of these unfinished and fleeting moments pinned, stitched, patched together in a never-whole recollection.

I stifle the urge to call out and thank her. Not for the news of the centrepiece *Head* for the exhibition, but for being so unlike everyone else. For never asking me more about myself than I offer. For being interested but never prying. For needing nothing from me.

'What's the deal with the new girl?' I'd overheard one curator ask Tris. I'd held my breath. Not for what he'd asked but for what Tris might answer.

'Move on, Mike. Not every woman wants to suck your dick in the records room.'

Her answer had overloaded me. Firstly, I'd never heard her speak anything but clear and courteous English. Secondly, staff are sucking dick in the records room. And, thirdly, her comment revealed nothing of what Tris actually thought of me or what my *deal* was. This worry stuck for days. What opinion had she formed that precluded me from record room antics? Had she herself sucked Mike's dick?

Gallery staff are arriving and I am still kneeling at Death's feet, next to the vulture. I stand, brush the imaginary dust from the knees of my pants, walk from the exhibition spaces and cross the courtyard to the conservator's studio. The new microscope has at last been installed and I can examine the embroidery with breathtaking precision. The view through the lens not only shows every last stitch, but reveals hidden stories about how and why it was made. For a textile conservator, the first rule of the work is not to fix, but to understand what the maker intended. By the time I have studied every inch and made notes on each stitch and respective condition, the sky is dark and my head feels heavy, my stomach empty.

I walk back to my office and hear them all in the staffroom, spilling out into the hall. I accept the too-full glass of red pushed into my hand. When someone says drinks, I hear torture chamber, oubliette. A dark, suffocating room, inside which I will be interrogated and where the only means of escape is a trapdoor in the ceiling. Why leave Melbourne and a job with the NGV? What a dream! Why come to Adelaide? Married? Any children? It is always a woman who asks this last question first.

'No husband. No children,' is my reply, while the asker makes her silent assessment, ranks me in any number of categories of non-viable woman. But even this is preferable to telling the truth. So I become the good listener. But there's a penalty for this too, and that is getting stuck with the person who has saved their life story for this moment. Today, that person is Herb.

'I lost my Annie last month,' he says, tomato sauce from a party pie smudged on his tie.

'I'm sorry to hear it,' I say. 'How long were you married?'

'I never married,' says Herb, bristling at the suggestion. 'My cockatiel, she was a cracker!'

Loss is relative, I coach myself. To compare human griefs is a grave disrespect. But a part of me wants to set Herb straight. It's a bird. Not a human. Not a child.

My hand shakes. My fingers are losing their grip, joints crumpling like an old collapsible wooden toy. The glass slips. Wine down my front, emptied glass unbroken on the thick carpet tiles.

'Heard you removed an arsehole today,' Mike yells to me from across the room.

'And yet he's still here,' parries our receptionist, Denise, and the room swells with laughter.

It's too loud.

Herb prattles on while I dab at my shirt with a napkin.

'Had her for twenty-eight years,' he says. 'They live for up to thirty-five. A real beauty. Crest like sunshine.'

He can't see me shaking because he must tell his story of his bird growing old. And I want to deny him the strength of his sadness. But his cockatiel has outlived my son by ten years. Hundreds of weeks. Thousands of days. The two wolves inside me snarl at each other. One wants me to bite off Herb's face. The other wants me to hug him.

My eyes scan the room for the quickest exit. The route past those least likely to object.

'I loved hearing about Annie.' I squeeze Herb's arm as I leave, his shirt sleeve wafting mothballs. It's the smell of my childhood. Of my mother's cupboards and closets stacked with bolts of prized Italian linens and silks. Of the boxes under the bed stuffed with offcuts she dared not discard. When I was small, I'd squeeze in among them, my hands pressed to my ears while my father raged over luke-warm mashed potato, smashing plates against walls, stray shards slicing my bare feet when I later crept into the kitchen for a biscuit.

Then I'm crossing the footbridge over Karrawirra Parri. Then over the soft grass of Warnpangga Park. Kneeling at the giant sugar gum, pulling autumn leaves from my bag. Golden plane, crimson-winged sumac, purple ornamental plum. I circle them around the trunk's base, a bright skirt for this tree. An ephemeral artwork not meant to last. One to be blown away and scattered, disarticulated, dismembered. By wind or possums or snuffling dogs. To admire for a moment, and lose for a lifetime.

At home I sit by the light of my laptop, studying images of *The Head*. My stomach squeezes at the raw, bloodied fringe where the blade sliced the neck.

'It took me years, decades, to tackle it,' Caterina Sirani had replied during a video call to her European studio. 'I was struck by the Baptist's words to do violence to no man, neither accuse falsely. The parallels between his world overrun by Romans and other homelands struggling with invasion.'

Her voice betrayed pain, but also her undaunted creative spirit.

I asked how she achieved the colour of the flesh, in this piece showing death but yet somehow lit by the life that preceded it. 'I invented it!' Caterina said, roaring with laughter.

Her warm-heartedness, her largesse, her mind for invention, made me wish I was there in her studio as she picked up her laptop to show me around. Sketches in charcoal and gesso covered the walls, hammers and hatchets and chisels strewn across benches, chainsaws set onto wall mounts and hooks draped with oiled chain blades. The tools of her trade for shaping wood into people.

Sawdust coating every surface. Humans emerging from huge, half-carved logs.

When I asked where the idea, the imagining, came for the figures, she answered with conviction. 'These wooden figures came to me, like a rope to hold onto.'

How long has it been since I laughed like Caterina Sirani? Since I felt the coarse strength of a rope in my grasp?

When our call ended, I felt adrift. I tried to find a cheap one-way airfare. To visit her, to be in her presence, in the hope her vivid convictions might be contagious. But my credit card was declined. Nothing I had was in my own name, all accounts frozen or cancelled by the man I had fled.

Frozen, cancelled. Like the girl in the mirror.

I grow queasy and close the images of *The Head*. Open my file of images of John the Baptist's mother, Elisabeth. I scroll past Giotto di Bondone's fresco, the lithographs from the Spanish and German Books of Hours, Dürer's woodcut, several anonymous wall and panel paintings, the gilded walnut carving attributed to Heinrich of Constance. No images are of her alone, and all are of the same moment. The Visitation. The meeting of Elisabeth and her young cousin Mary, carrying their miracle babies.

I pause on an image of the painting by Mariotto Albertinelli, an oil on panel with life-sized dimensions. How did this painter capture such tenderness between women? What mother, what sister, what wife did he love? How would it feel to stand in the Uffizi Gallery in Florence before this Renaissance masterpiece? To take in the soaring and magnificent affection between these two women before the events that would take their sons. Their earlier lives. Their *before*.

My belly throbs like a second heart and I resist the instinct to rest my hand there. I know the joy of the pregnant women in these paintings. For Elisabeth especially, carrying her long-yearned-for child. I'd felt this with my first-born.

I scroll on through versions of The Visitation by Ghirlandaio, the Strüb brothers, Lievens, Maçip, looking for clues to the imagery in the embroidery. Clues to the delightful symbols, like the unicorn and peacock, that seem more pagan than Christian. Where stitches have broken or pieces have detached to reveal linen ground, I can see the faint remains of a drawn pattern. It seems clear to me it shows two arms embracing. The same motif in all of these paintings of Elisabeth and Mary.

The phone flashes, my mother. Again. My finger hovers over the screen. I let it go through to voicemail. Hit play on her messages.

Three 'call me backs'. At first curt, then demanding.

Then, 'He's worried about you, that's all.'

He's grasping at straws now, calling my mother.

I'd saved everything I could to hire a car to get out of Melbourne, to put away a year's rent in advance. All the secret machinations to secure a job. The clawing stress that any day he'd discover my plan. I'd expected to be hounded, cajoled, threatened. But I heard nothing. Until he showed up last week in Adelaide. Drunk, he cried at my door. Weak, I let him in.

'He understands you're complicated … he loves you.'

By complicated she means broken. And by loves she means tolerates. And while I recognise the fundamental flaws in her thinking, the knot of core shame in my guts tightens. This seeping, relentless shame that led me, dumb but not blind, to a man sure to remind me of how damaged I was. Who would confirm that everything would be different, better, if only I was.

I zoom in on the Albertinelli painting, to where Elisabeth clasps Mary's hand. I want to fall inside the story of these two women. To feel my hand held, like Elisabeth holds Mary's, so I might feel new strength.

'How many women get a proposal from a surgeon?' My mother's last message.

The girl in the mirror would say yes to this marriage. Would start every sentence with sorry. Would live with constraints. Would die from freedom. And if I keep listening, I will die with her.

2

Florence, 1497

The Ponte Vecchio is crowded, people jostling and shouting. Like us they are flocking to the Piazza della Signoria to see the tower of treasures the mad friar will burn in his Bonfire of Vanities.

My oversized shoes slip and trip over uneven stone pavement as I run to keep up with Zia Lucia, not really an aunt but a second cousin on my mother's side. She arrived early this morning with neither notice nor a hat, in a rare Florentine snowstorm. The tapestry bag slung over her shoulder blazes with wild crocus, the slender points of three paintbrushes thrust through one gaping end.

'Have they married you off yet?' asks Zia Lucia.

'I'm only nine,' I reply, two steps to her one, falling behind.

The workshops along the old bridge are a frenzy of industry, the sizzle of metalworkers forging tools, fishmongers crying their catch. A torrent of sewage spilling into the Arno. Butcher's offal in vat loads, tanner's dyes, the piss and stale beer used to soften their calf skins.

'*Presto! Presto!* Antonia!' calls Zia Lucia. I am falling behind. Without breaking stride, she throws back an arm, her hand beckoning me forwards.

I glance back to my mother, trailing behind us. She seems shrunken, ghostlike. Furrows shadow her thin-lipped mouth. The slack shape of her dress with more patches than seams. Not like Zia Lucia, marching ahead with no hat, her yellow-gold scarf streaming, a bright slant of sunshine through the unruly throng. I turn away from my mother and push through the crowd, grasp for Lucia's hand reaching for me, like Padre Renzo says San Pietro grasped for the hand of the Cristo.

'I know your father too well,' says Lucia. 'For him marriage is good business. No doubt he is plotting an early betrothal.'

'I'm not supposed to know,' I say, made bold by her boldness. I've heard snippets of conversation between my parents. I know there is a plan.

'Is he famous?' she asks.

'He paints,' I reply. I've heard that much at least.

'Painters carry the pox from *puttane*.' She halts and awaits my acknowledgement. I nod my understanding. I know about whores. 'You must check for chancres,' she says. 'On his *pisello*.'

I blush with shame at the thought of inspecting a man's privates.

Along Via Por Santa Maria the crowd thickens. Goldsmiths throw open their workshops, the *click clack* of shutters unlocking. Renewed hammering and sawing, the shaping of chalices and frontals for church altars. Men squeezing bellows to stoke up fires, others hunched over benches, tools angled and thrust for cutting, soldering and forging, enamelling and polishing.

On Via Vacchereccia the crowd is at standstill, but Lucia cuts her own path; nobody protests. I try to see Mamma, pushing a hand to my face against the mingling sweat and stink of the crowd, the grease and smoke, the fust of old cloaks. I press my face into Zia Lucia's cloak, inhaling its waft of white musk and pungent smell like pine needles and olive oil that I can taste in the back of my throat.

At the Piazza della Signoria, Mamma catches us up. The pinched fury in her face is loosened by disbelief as noblewomen arrive, their arms loaded with silks. Paintings wheeled in and dumped, some in gleaming gilt frames. Fine sculptures in all sizes. *Objects to tempt sin!* Savonarola preached in a fury.

'All to be burned?' I ask as a man tears the brocade cloak from his wife's shoulders, then tosses it into a cart wobbling under the weight of a huge bevelled mirror.

'*Dio mio!* What hell have we met?' says Lucia. 'They say Botticelli will cast in his sublime nudes. Can you imagine? Why not burn our own hearts lest they love too well!'

'*Che orrore!*' says my mother, appalled but transfixed.

'What horror indeed,' says Lucia.

We squeeze through to the front.

Eight *braccia* high, the tower soars before and above me, as tall as four men. Florentine nobles haul carts and cast in treasures. Playing cards, harps, lutes, zithers and books. Dulcimers, cosmetic cases, mirrors, perfumes and wigs – tiaras still attached – all manner of hair pieces.

'Marietta, hold onto your merkin!' Lucia says to my mother, her body swinging back with the sheer force of her laughter.

A heavy bell tolls and Savonarola's advocates preach to the masses. 'A New Jerusalem will dawn in Florence! Let the lavish Pope Alexander repent of his sins!'

An eruption of hissing and cheering. People beside me tap out the sign of the cross, some kissing at crucifixes carried like talismans.

'Savonarola will die at the hands of those who now praise him,' says Zia Lucia, her fierce gaze upon me. '*Capisci?*'

I nod, although I understand nothing.

'I cannot watch this ruin. Come, let us walk!' says Lucia, and we push out of the crowd.

The low grey sheet of the sky warns of a snow flurry. A chill sinks into my limbs.

'Babbo will expect us,' I say, growing uneasy because my father's fits of rage have grown more frequent and unpredictable since he opened the tavern. 'I promised him Signor Boncianni's *torte di mele*.'

'Your father demands apple tart in February?' says Zia Lucia. '*In bocca al lupo*.' Into the wolf's mouth. Our way of saying good luck.

'*Crepi*,' replies my mother. May the wolf die.

We take Via Porta Rossa past the soaring five storeys of the wool merchant, Davizzi, then Via de Tornabuoni. Cloth merchants and tailors are busy at work. Scents of camphor and smelling salts lace the air, from pomades strung up to keep moths from lush fabrics.

'Keep up, Marietta,' says Lucia, sensing my lagging mother's disquiet at walking a street often bustling with merchants' wives, dressed in silks trimmed with gold, their laced bodices pulled tight. 'Those who might frown at our dresses won't risk Savonarola's damnation by promenading in their finery.'

Lucia threads her arm through Mamma's, but my mother unlinks herself at once with the excuse that she must hold her cloak closed with both hands. Then Lucia clasps my hand in hers, and I do't resist.

'Do you love him, this painter?' asks Lucia, a clandestine tone.

'*Zitta!*' My mother casts me a glance sharp enough to slice onions. Then, to Lucia, 'Mind your business. Don't cause any trouble.'

I lower my gaze, unable to bear the enquiry.

'*Allora!* She loves another!' cries Lucia.

'The padre's young nephew is visiting,' says my mother. 'She thinks I am blind to her dizzy infatuation.'

I shrink at Mamma revealing what I thought I had hidden.

'Who is he, this nephew?' asks Lucia, hands set at her hips.

'His name is Eugenio,' my mother replies for me. 'And he couldn't care less.'

This strikes me, as her remarks often do, like a sharp rock to my breastbone.

'If we needed the world's Eugenios to care, we'd all die chaste as the Virgin.' Another burst of bright laughter. A trio of pigeons on a window ledge scatters.

A flurry of snowflakes drifts and lilts. Lucia throws open her arms and spins, flakes kissing her face, catching in her dark curls.

'Those who sing through the summer must dance in the winter,' cries Lucia. I shiver inside my thin cloak and she draws me to her, rubs my back with her hands, whispers into my ear. 'To appreciate the beauty of a snowflake, one must stand out in the cold.'

*

In the Piazza di Santa Maria Novella we admire the church's glorious façade. Once bare and plain, it now gleams with a myriad of green and white marble inlaid with intricate patterns in bold squares, rosettes and scrolls.

'Leon Battista Alberti, the master of order,' says Lucia, as if I should commit this to memory. 'See how the baseline equals the height?' She marks out the lines of the façade with her finger. 'And those spirals, they're a trick to distract from imbalance.' Even Mamma is enthralled.

The clouds peel back and sunlight strikes the façade, making us squint against the white marble, the sheen of fresh snow.

'What is white?' I ask, my mind lit with a peculiar spark.

'That's a silly question for a girl to ask,' says my mother.

'So if a boy asked, it would be clever?' asks Lucia.

'What use are such questions from anyone?' replies Mamma. 'Won't put food on the table.'

'It may well do so for an artist,' says Lucia. 'When it comes to painting, understanding white is essential. It primes the panel and carries the power to ignite or corrupt. It's the beginning that determines the end!'

Mamma huffs.

'You don't like that your daughter has a mind fit for thinking?' says Lucia. 'Doesn't get it from her father,' she adds, and nudges my mother.

And although my mother puts her handkerchief to her mouth, I can see the smile that broadens her face.

On the walk home, even Mamma looks refreshed, perhaps eased by the fact that Babbo will have left for the tavern. The three of us stroll arm in arm, squabbling about the best recipe for *cantucci*, the sweet, nutty biscuit eaten dipped in wine. *Bake them twice in a day! Bake it once but for longer and cool them quickly!*

Downstairs it is quiet. We climb the stairs to the kitchen, warm air rushing out when we open the door.

With his napkin tucked inside his shirt, a spoon in each fist, Babbo sits at the table. Waiting for the tart I'd promised to bring.

'Pigs could feed here,' he says, dragging a fist through the flour, the droop in his left eye proof he is already drunk.

My limbs stiffen, and I watch the folds in my mother's face deepen.

I step in front of my mother. '*Ci penso io.*' I'll see to it.

My father springs to his feet and throws down the wooden spoons. They split and scatter from table to floor.

'All a man wants is apple tart.' He picks up a chair and launches it at the wall. It splinters with a crack, one leg shooting back, so he takes it up again and throws it into the fire. I was long ago proud when others spoke about the strength of my father. How he had wrestled a boar, the souvenir of the struggle a ragged scar on his bicep.

Behind me, my mother shrinks back from the table. Lucia bends to her bag, pulls out a pot and pushes it into my hands.

'Babbo!' I speak loud and bold, not like I am feeling. 'You don't want your surprise?' I try to steady my hands as they hold out the pot.

My father turns to face me, a wine-sodden glaze to his eyes. He takes the pot from me as gently as he might take a sparrow.

'Is it jam?' He gouges at the waxed top and drives his finger inside, pushes it through his wet lips. 'God please me, it's honey.'

'Better,' says Lucia. 'It's Umbrian honey.'

'Of course!' he says, ignoring Lucia and looking at me as if solving some puzzle. 'You got me a good one, *mia pulcina*!'

My little chick. His nickname for me when I impressed him and which I've not heard since I brought home three duck eggs, enduring the ache in my heart as the hen batted her wings against me and squawked in distress,

'At least you can please me,' he says.

And my relief turns to shame, that every compliment to me is designed as an insult to my mother.

When he staggers off for the tavern, we tidy up and say nothing.

*

In Nonna's old room, I brush out Lucia's hair while she sketches with charcoal, sure-handed and fleet. Ash from the raging bonfire casts black flakes to the sky.

'A raven-haired Venus,' she says, holding up the image she's drawn of me with the brush in my hand. '*Bella, sì?*'

Every last detail is like gazing into a mirror. But all I can see is the unlovely truth sketched in my bitten-down nails.

'What is this?' I point to a mark at the bottom of the drawing. A small triangle, pointing downwards, a curling leaf centred over each side.

'My insignia,' says Lucia. 'Once I draw this mark, it is a promise to myself that I will not try to correct or change what I have drawn. An artist never knows when to stop fixing.'

A gust through the open window snuffs the candles, and ash from outside scatters across Nonna's old bedspread. Lucia leaps up and pulls closed the shutters. I throw myself on the bed to smother any embers that might catch.

'They will turn on the friar, Savonarola,' she says, tightening the latches. 'This is Florence! Loyalties shift like fish in a river.'

She lifts the chain from her neck, on its end a miniature flask in glass millefiori, then twists off the stopper. The room fills with the scent of sweetbriar flowers.

'Why worry about burning silks?' she says. 'In here we have roses.'

Fifteen moons later, a carriage arrives for Lucia. Swifts soar overhead in rippling black clouds. The summer sun angles high over Florence. And in the Piazza della Signoria, workers build a new pyre.

The carriage will take Lucia beyond the walls of Florence and the pyre will burn the accused heretic Savonarola's flesh to bone. I am told that Lucia is ill and that the friar will suffocate from the smoke before he feels any pain. Each I know is a lie.

In Nonna's old room, Lucia sits on the stool. I brush out her hair for the last time, while her deft hand sketches a woman cradling a fledgling bird. Its loose and soft feathers wrought in neat, precise detail.

She swivels to face me. 'You keep asking your questions,' she says, a furrow etched into the wide, smooth space between her eyebrows. 'What is white? Such enigma! Discoveries can only be made if you dare to ask questions.'

'I know you're not ill,' I say, being bold in the way I have learned from her. I've seen the growing roundness of her belly beneath her thin nightgown.

'Not ill, but maybe too old.' She slides a hand over her stomach. 'Too old for this.'

I am angered by the melancholy tone of her voice. More like my mother than Zia Lucia. 'Santa Elisabetta was an old crone when she gave birth to San Giovanni,' I say, calling on the well-told tale of the birth of Florence's patron. How his mother was old. How his father was ancient.

Lucia sweeps a hand around my face. '*Piccolo bambino*, meet your Zia Pulcina,' she says, taking my hand and pressing it to her belly.

I swell with pride at the thought of becoming an aunt. And we both squeal with delight at the strong kick to my palm.

'And don't blame your mother,' she says, taking the brush to my hair.

'For what?' I stiffen with a guilt I don't understand.

'For everything you will want to blame her for,' she replies, the room filling for the last time with the bright warmth of her laughter.

The horse hooves strike the pavement, Lucia is leaving. I wave hard and Mamma stands rigid, arms folded, hands fisted. Lucia doesn't look back.

'Zia Lucia says I will be an aunt to her baby,' I say, knowing I should remain silent and pretend not to know why she was leaving.

'You'll never be an aunt,' says my mother. 'You're barely a cousin.'

Cheers rise from the Piazza della Signoria. Babbo is there. He left the house sober, excited to invite the crowd to the tavern. For the first time in over a year, he will be open after sunset.

'Maybe open all night,' he announced, striding off.

Smouldering embers swirl skywards. The chants of the marching throng rise to a roar as Savonarola's charred bones are fished from the cinders and flung into the Arno. I long for Lucia, for the scent of sweetbriar and white musk and the pungent pine scent I now know as linseed, to quell the stink of burning flesh. For her eyes upon me, so unlike my mother's, bright as a river sunrise against the ash-blackened sky.

In the kitchen the next morning Mamma slaps at my fingers. 'Too much salt in the bread dough! Did you leave your sense under your pillow?'

Even when I do exactly the things I've done every morning since I can remember, I can do nothing right.

'Leave more fat on the hogget! Can't you peel the quinces without wasting the flesh?' She slaps again. 'Your hands are ham-fisted and your mind's off gathering wool. You belong on a farm, not in a kitchen.' She snatches the knife from my hand.

'Zia Lucia says I'm clever! I wish she was my mother!'

'Then go,' says Mamma, the knife aimed at the door.

I run from the kitchen, my shoes slipping on uneven pavement. Lucia is long gone, the city gates far behind her.

In the church of San Michele alle Trombe I hunker in prayer on the steps of the altar until the cold marble is scored into the caps of my knees.

'Why does she hate me?' I ask Our Lord and the Holy Virgin Mary.

Maybe Mamma already knows that as soon as I am able, I too will leave. Leave the smoke-stained walls of our kitchen, cooking smells soaked into mortar. Leave the cave of the tavern, every angle in shadow.

3

Ḥevron, 41 BCE

The announcement of my intended marriage to Zakhariya of the order of Aviya comes the same day as Yehuda quakes with the news of an unnerving betrothal. The last Hasmonean princess, Mariamne, has been promised to the governor, Herod. But my betrothal is not like hers, for I chose my husband long before he was chosen for me.

A storm is building over Ḥevron, a flicker of lightning. The white limestone hills are vivid in the overcast light. Imma glances upwards, her lips muttering a prayer; always frowning, my mother, when she invokes a blessing. The wooden tray in her hands is set with clay jugs of spiced wine and honeyed figs. When she crosses the open courtyard and enters the far room where the men are gathered, I steal down the stone stairs from our sleeping quarters and out through the stables. The goats bleat from the stalls, the cow moans and huffs. Imma will think it is the storm that disturbs them. One, now two fat drops hit the dust. A gritty scent from stone walls in the thickening air. The terraced vineyards want for rain and a few men, mattocks on shoulders, cast their hopeful gaze skywards. But this is a dry storm, all flash and grumble.

I pull my veil tight around my head, hitch my tunic to my knees and run up the slope to the ridge. When I reach the top, I throw open my arms to *sh'maya*, the heavens, the wind slapping my tunic hard against my body. I shiver with excitement at being here alone while the men sit around, scooping flatbread through *milut* and olive oil livened with sumac. Sipping wine and discussing my fate.

The wedding feast held in honour of me and Zakhariya won't be the lavish affair laid out for Princess Mariamne. For her, banquet tables will sag under amphorae of wine, raisin-stuffed fish and roast suckling calf, oiled skin bubbled and glistening. They say the royal Hasmonean line will be spared with this marriage, but Herod, so far, has shown his rule to spare none. My stomach churns at the thought of his great, dark shadow bearing down upon the princess, ancient generations dissolved by his sword. But I am eased by the fact that where my husband will only wait twelve moons to take me as his wife, Herod will wait longer. For his princess will not be of age for another three score moons. I pray that she will be protected from what her future husband will want to steal, long before he is entitled.

Sheet lightning flashes over the great trees of Ḥevron, terebinth and oak. Were these trees touched by Avraham? Cut by Sh'lomo? Did their leaves shiver with joy to hear the strum of David's harp? It thrills me to think so as they thrash back and forth, elastic on their great trunks. Carts and boats, the brute strength of timber used countless ways. But here it bends and sways low, branches almost brushing the earth. The yielding of wood demanded by a storm.

Imma says I shouldn't call such things a miracle. That this declaration undermines the mind of Ribon Alma, who created all things with great precision and purpose. But this impossible sight moves me in such a way that I can only express it so.

'More stubborn than an Egyptian,' Imma said when I'd confided to a once-trusted neighbour my secret voyages out into storms. 'Not a scrap of respect to spare me shame.'

Abba tried to calm Imma. 'She is curious, independent,' I overheard him saying. 'A little strong-minded.'

'And that mind will snap when it should bend,' she said, resolved.

Later that day Abba summoned me for a walk, while Imma muttered and huffed about stones that wouldn't grind wheat by themselves. He and I went alone. Up slopes, over hills, through terraces and groves until we reached a stand of trees whose bark sprouted clusters of cascading red fruit.

'The sycamore-fig is more at home in the southern coastal plain,' he said, plucking a leaf, crushing it so it leaked milky sap. 'Perhaps a pocket of warmth here, or groundwater, supports this rare grove.' He patted his hand on a thick trunk and picked a ripe fig, offered it to me. 'A thing out of place, Elisheva, is often a treasure.'

The sky flares blue-white. On a distant ridge a tree explodes, struck by lightning, and I pray with all my might for the hidden suppleness of trees. That I might find the grace to sway and twist and bow and flex, now that I will become a wife.

Imma prefers the lessons of water. Not wind and wood.

Once we'd travelled two days across the desert to the cliffs of Ein Gedi, my father insisting we visit an ailing uncle who'd crossed the desert to the Salt Sea in hope of a cure.

'See how water yields to the land?' Imma's slender finger had pointed towards the scalloped white fringes of the shore, where the salt crusts were thickest.

She would have me admire water as some great poem of strength and pliancy. But my attention was taken by the mountains on the other side of the Sea, reflected upside-down in the unruffled surface.

Now on the ridge, my hair lifts from my scalp with the charge in the air. Trees twisting and swaying like dancing maidens of Shiloh to pipes and timbrels.

Clouds of dandelion seeds spiral around me. The wild, bitter-leafed plant whose yellow flower carpets the earth in lush gold, sending workers into a frenzy as they work to remove it. To please Ribon Alma meant not letting herbs mix with the vines. If the season is warmer and drier than usual, the bright petals fold back in upon themselves overnight, like fingers twined into prayer, their sepals then peeling back and a fluffy seed head bursting through. I spin among the drifting seeds, their feathered ends catching in my hair.

'Like children's souls freed from one great soul,' my *savta*, my grandmother, once said.

'Not now but soon!' I call to those seeds, imagining the child-soul that might choose me.

I tried to tell my mother when the first angel came to me on the eve of the New Moon. She didn't answer, but handed me a torn tunic for mending. Passed a needle and thread with a look that suggested I'd imagined the messenger who had brushed a light-filled hand against my cheek, my skin rising to meet its touch, and told me without speaking that my marriage would be blessed.

'May I go to the hilltop?' I asked, angered by her doubt, and because outside the wind wailed and my request would unnerve her.

'And the goats will knead dough?' she replied. But in her mind were different words. I could hear them as clearly as what she had spoken.

This girl must learn her place.

So I told her with my mind as I threw down the tunic. *I'm a sycamore-fig that can grow in the mountains.*

She couldn't read thoughts as well as I, but I knew she'd felt my defiance and that was enough. As she left to fetch more grain from the storeroom for grinding, she turned to me, and I wondered for a moment if she might call me into her arms.

'Once you are betrothed, Abba will not tolerate your silly games.'

She placed both palms to the small of her back, easing the ache that has been there, I am told, since my birth. It is an action that feels like a complaint against my presence. More burden than gift. More woe than delight.

Daylight fades and the wind shifts direction. I look back towards the dim glow from clay lamps in our home. Soon I will be summoned to give my consent and accept the promise of the marriage to come. In six moons from now, they will write the *k'tubta*: the contract where my Zakhariya will promise me food and shelter and the satisfactions a husband owes to his wife, those that will ensure children.

I can feel my mother's thoughts turning to me and I know I must return. She won't call for me until the men are done, but that will be soon. I take off with the wind at my back.

At the east wall of our home, I climb the ladder I left to get back upstairs without being seen. Our maidservant Bayla will be up there, rolling out the sleeping mats. She shrieks, startled, as I squeeze in through the small window. Soon I'll no longer fit. I hold a finger to my lips and she nods her understanding. Summons me to the stool to dust dandelion seeds from my tunic and dirt from my feet.

Bayla is my age and, because Imma would forbid it, we have become secret friends.

'Has Imma called?' I ask.

'She left to fetch brushwood,' Bayla replies, now weaving my storm-harried hair into a smooth braid.

A knot of shame twists behind my navel. I was expected to help my mother with the gathering of wood.

I steal back downstairs, across the courtyard, and see my father in discussion with the man set to become my father-in-law. They sit bent into each other, fingers to chins, heads nodding consensus. A few more steps and I stop. Zakhariya stands behind his father, perhaps bored with the conversation or in some dream state of wilderness that he too might prefer. His expression remains composed and I wonder if he has seen me. But I move again and his eyes track me.

'Are you in love?' I asked my cousin Ada when I sat with her on the day of her betrothal.

'Dear silly cousin!' She tousled my hair and I slapped at her hand. 'Surely you know it is never about love.'

I was set to tell her that I'd been in love since the time I was eight. That I'd spied on my beloved as he worked the vines with his father in the vineyards. Zakhariya was already a man, bearded and muscled, working the mattock through soil between vines, rooting out stray sprouting seeds of mustard and rue. I hid.

Watching from behind a cascading caperbush that thrives in the cracks between terrace stones. Careful not to catch myself on tiny, hooked thorns paired at the base of each leaf. Sometimes I left carob water with horse mint, sometimes spiced wine, placed near their tools when their attentions were on picking fruit or hefting rubble and rocks to clear earth for more planting. He would wipe a forearm across his brow before drinking, scanning the terraces to see who might have left it.

I let him see me one day, moving out from where I was hidden. He raised a hand to wave. But when I went to run away, my veil snagged on the thorns, pulling it back from my head, and I didn't return to his vines for three moons because of my shame.

'I will marry you.' My whispered wish. But never for his ears.

'Marriage is not the important thing. It's everything that comes after,' Ada said as I sat in surly silence. 'Remember Idra?'

I am drawn from my sulk by the disquieting memory of Rivka's aunt, Idra, who did not bear a child and was cast out by her husband.

'As a wife, you must give your husband children,' she said. 'You must pray to be the mother you are expected to be, not like Idra.'

Zakhariya leans close to his father and speaks into his ear, his eyes still on me, then disappears from sight. I run across the courtyard and press myself against the shadowed wall near the storeroom. The wind is settling and in the last light, night insects begin their steady *thrip thrip*. Only this sound and the soft murmur of the men.

'*Sh'lama*, Elisheva.'

He's behind me.

It is not proper to meet like this and his boldness alarms and excites me.

'*Sh'lama*.' I turn and answer his greeting.

'It was always you,' he says. 'From the beginning.'

A distant rumble of thunder as the storm slides past.

He wants me to acknowledge that I understand him. That he is telling me I was his first choice.

I chose you first. I want to say it, but instead I think of the yielding, bending trees and do not.

A she-wolf cry close by prickles my skin. I've seen her vanish inside a small cave in the hills, swollen teats on her underbelly. Her high whistle and whine are a call to her cubs. I wait, like the wolf, for a reply. None comes.

Zakhariya reaches out his hand and I baulk.

'You have something,' he says, a finger pointed at my cheek.

I grope at my face. He points again, so close. My skin prickling, rising to meet his warmth like it did with the angel. But he won't touch me to take what he sees. I brush at my cheek and he stoops to collect whatever invisible thing has fallen. On the curve of his fingertip, a single dandelion seed.

He pinches it between his thumb and forefinger and offers it to me. I glance over my shoulder, panicked that the men might come seeking him. Or my mother, who is able to appear when I most dread it. His hand hangs in the space between us.

I take the seed in a whirl of embarrassment and think about releasing my thumb from my forefinger and blowing it away. But this thing, so small, ripples heat through my hand. Again the she-wolf cries out, a rising, melancholy note; a staccato of yelping replies.

'I'm unsure that Herod loves the princess,' I say, holding his gaze like my mother said a woman never should. But I want him to know I am not ignorant. That I have opinions.

He angles his head. 'I find it hard to believe you'd be unsure of anything, Elisheva of Aharon.'

An eruption of laughter from the men. Formalities are done. And already I feel the aching squeeze of the shift in Zakhariya's attention, no longer on me.

'*Sh'lama, ḥavivta,*' he says.

Then he is gone.

Ḥavivta. My chest swells and my thoughts wheel in giddy elation. He has called me *my darling.*

Not even when I'd run from Ḥevron's highest summit to be home before my mother had I felt such breathlessness. And now, without moving a step, I feel as if I've run the distance between here and the Tomb of Avraham and Sara. And the exhilaration his words have aroused in me make me feel I could run this distance once more.

I twirl the dandelion seed between my fingertips. Like children's souls blown from the one great soul. Some taking root, some passing on. Like my twin sisters, Babatha and Beruria, who lived for six days.

It flushes my skin, this inevitable fact. That twelve moons from now I will be led to the house of Zakhariya in a torchlit procession. That, once wed, we will delve into the secrecy of hidden skins and do the thing that brings a child into a woman's ripened womb.

I slide my back along the wall towards the door so I can hear them. Zakhariya's voice joins in with the lighter conversation now that business is done.

I press the seed to my forefinger and lift it to my lips. I blow. The tufted end ruffles, but sticks.

'Elisheva?' Imma is calling.

The scuffing of her fast feet across the courtyard, the muted slap of her sandals on stone steps as she climbs upstairs, where I should be.

'Sheva?' She calls me again.

I blow again at my finger. The tufted seed remains.

'Where is that girl?' I hear her ask Bayla.

'Has she not come?' Bayla replies, biding time for me while I flee through the front gate and re-enter through the stables, to make it seem like my mother has just missed me in the timing of our walks to and fro.

I press the seed inside the belt around my tunic. If it wills to stay, then let it.

After supper I retire early to my pallet. The humid evening air clings to my skin like damp linen. Outside the village, jackals keen in the foothills. The wild grass at rest, silver threads under moonlight. Within the village, the murmur of nighttime prayers.

And across all of this, drifting dandelion seeds will litter the earth. Some lost in the bushes, others wedged between stones or scattered on worn pathways and trampled unseen.

I pluck the dandelion seed from my belt. Tingling, unfamiliar feelings sweep through my body.

Let the other seeds fall where they will. Mine has found me.

Perhaps in our first year our child will arrive. Perhaps even a boy.

4

Florence, 1503

Angry tears blind me as I run along Via delle Oche and down Via San Michele. How many times have I fled from Mamma in fury? Her glare at my unacceptable presence. How is it that one glance can wither me? As if I am the undoing of the life she imagined.

Five years since Zia Lucia left and still I yearn to feel my hand inside hers as we walk through the streets. In my letters, I gush about the marble and bronze statues in niches on Orsanmichele, and how they'd marched naked felons through the piazza where, the day Lucia left, Savonarola burned to death. Even in her absence, I feel Lucia helps me imagine a place where I might better belong. A world outside the walls of Florence.

The streets bustle with pedlars and my awful shoes slip and clunk as I dodge milk carts and squeeze between street bakers jostling loaves. My chest heaves and my shoulders shiver, cold and yet burning with shame in my simple linen gamurra, my *mantle* left on the coat hook. Icy air blows down from the mountains, but it doesn't cool my right hand, still on fire with the desire to strike my mother's face.

The Torre della Pagliazza towers over its neighbouring church, San Michele alle Trombe, dedicated to Saint Michael, and named after the city trumpeters who once lived here. But there's no fanfare today as I rush across the piazza and push hard at the doors. They gasp and swing open, church-breath in my face, varnish and frankincense. A muddle of violets and jasmine trails in Signora Ottolini's shuffling gait to the altar.

I am ashamed to enter the church like this, hateful and seething. Panting and sweating. Every bit the shameless girl that my mother laments. I avoid looking up at the altar, the sacred symbol of the Cristos's tomb, and keep my eyes on my shoes.

'Time to cast off those childish slippers!' Babbo had said, displaying heeled shoes traded for wine with a tinker from Venice. 'Are you ungrateful?'

'*Mille grazie*, Babbo.' I received the shoes with the best smile I could muster.

The leather is tattered and resewn, scuff-tipped. Too wide, too long on my narrow feet. No doubt they've been found among a wealthy man's castoffs. 'They will last you,' my mother said. Like this old smock I am yet to grow into. I dab at my eyes with its moth-eaten cuffs, as I work through the storm of thoughts in my mind.

'Can I write to her?' I asked Mamma, after a season had passed and Lucia had not returned. My practised pages now free of left-handed smudges.

'I can't forbid writing,' was her reluctant reply.

Mamma can write Toscano and some Latin and read as well as any nun. Taught by her great-grandmother, who it is said visited hospitals and convents to teach young girls abandoned by parents whose desire was for sons.

Babbo is disdainful of things he considers bring in no money. 'Reading is for time-wasters,' he says. 'It's all up here.' A crooked finger tapping his temple. 'Everything I need to know, I remember. All I must say to another, I speak it to their face.'

He'll never admit to not being able to read.

I've written on the first of each month. And each month my mother has slipped the letter into her apron pocket. I've stopped asking about possible visits or Lucia's whereabouts, since it seems to cause Mamma anxiety.

'Where's your finished needlework?' Mamma asked me this morning, my apron already filthy with char from swept hearths and splashed by the brimming chamber pots I carried down to the river. I've been rising an hour earlier since, now I am tall enough, Babbo has me stacking the shelves in the tavern and I must complete my home chores before joining him at the Drago.

'Triple-stitched toes.' I handed her the stockings, worried by her stiff shoulders, the stoop in her posture over the bread dough. Then I passed her my latest letter for Lucia.

She put the stockings with Babbo's washed shirts and the letter on the bench near the dough board. 'Signor Belli is due his rent.' She untied a coin pouch from her waist and placed it on the table.

'*Sì*, Mamma,' I said, not moving. I couldn't leave until I saw the letter put inside her apron. 'Her baby will turn six years sometime this month. I wrote a poem.'

'And the rent is due now,' Mamma said, dumping chopped Certaldo onions into a steaming pot, her fingertips stained red from their skins.

'I'd like to be sure she gets it,' I said.

'So take it yourself.' Mamma reeled from the pot, her face flushed from the steam. 'Lucia, Lucia. Always *Lucia*. You prefer life with her? Then follow. I dare you.' She snatched up the letter from the table, held it out. 'Go on and take it!'

I took the letter from her and blinked back tears. She turned her back on me and yanked open the sideboard, rifled behind pots and pulled out a small oak barrel.

'While you're at it, take these.'

She knocked off the lid with the side of her hand and emptied out every letter I'd written. Neatly folded pages skidded over the worn wooden bench, tumbled and scattered, slid left and right on the floor. The bin clattered and rolled from side to side at our feet. I scrambled to collect them and the bin lest my father come stomping up and make hell for us both. The sound of Mamma's laboured breath above me as I dirtied my knees.

When I rose, she was doubled over like a snapped twig, her hands in the bread dough. I took her hands in mine, felt their trembling dampness. I thought she might faint. Instead, she slid her hands from mine, stiffened her body and squeezed her eyes shut as she spoke.

'She knows where you live. Has she sent you a letter?'

'She has a child. She is busy,' I replied, rattled and meek.

Mamma's eyes were dark stones at the bottom of a well. 'She doesn't want your silly letters. She doesn't care. She never will.'

'You don't know her like I do,' I yelled. 'You're jealous. You would have thrown any letters she's sent me into the fire.'

Burning with the rage and guilt in my heart, I ran for the church, before I could lift my hand to her cheek.

Inside the church of San Michele, I keep my shameful gaze on my ill-fitting shoes, muffle my sniffles with an oversized sleeve. I dip my hand in the font. Fingers to forehead, chest, left shoulder, right shoulder. Too much water and it drips from my brow down my nose.

Without looking, I know that the old widows Signora Ottolini and Signora Barolli will be knelt on the wide stone steps to the altar. Signora Ottolini on the third step, Signora Barolli on the first. Neither with wool padding under their knees, a suffering believed to purify their penance. The muted clack of their rosary strings; whispered Ave Marias.

While I calm myself, I trace the pattern of narrow bands of pietra-serena stone dividing the terracotta tiles. Signora Ottolini has dropped her handkerchief. I slide my feet across the tiles to avoid the clunk of my shoes, then reach down to collect it. Its lace edges are soft, a faint scent of clove. I fold it and look up.

And then I see the painting.

I clap one hand to my mouth, but the gasp has burst from my lips.

Signora Ottolini, hunched and kneeling, cranes her neck and squints my way, her top lip curled. I want to drop my eyes in apology, to demonstrate my respect for the quiet prayers I have disturbed, but the two women in the painting have my attention.

They are life-sized. Soaring above the altar in robes of lustrous verdigris and orpiment, greens and golds made luminous by the soft cast from high windows. My body surges with instant recognition. On the left the Virgin Maria, uncertain and pensive. On the right Santa Elisabetta, greeting her young cousin with a swell of affection. Sharing the news that they will both become mothers.

A sigh of awe leaks from my lips. Signora Ottolini hisses a *silenzio* my way. I wave the handkerchief and her hand pokes up inside a sleeve, retrieves nothing. She clucks her tongue in agitation, signals for me to hurry and bring it.

As I walk towards the altar steps, my awkward shoes do not matter. I keep my sights on Elisabetta and Maria, as if walking to join them. I can barely breathe for the tenderness in Elisabetta's expression. Its clemency. In every way the regard of a woman with profound love for her young companion. In every way the manner in which Lucia looked upon me. In every way that my mother does not.

And then I feel it, the lightness, the elation, the forgiveness rising without effort. It is neither Christ nor the Baptist that are the miracles before me, but this wordless conviction from Elisabetta to Maria. A testimony, a testament. *Ti vedo.* I see you.

'*Primavera*,' the nun, Sor Margherita, had said, a promise of the painting in spring. Commissioned by the Guild of Tailors, a grand altarpiece for San Michele alle Trombe, it had been a subject of gossip and speculation. But seasons passed and returned, and no painting arrived.

'I hear the artist spends more time groping trout,' a winking Luciano Manetti told my bristling mother.

I'd imagined the artist up to his knees in the river, grabbling for fish that slipped through his fingers. It seemed a strange pastime. 'Will the painting arrive soon?' I'd asked.

'If the artist stays sober,' replied Luciano.

And now here it hangs. As if it always was so.

I feel a swell of gratitude towards the unreliable artist, who had trouble staying sober and wasted time groping fish, but has, at last, managed to finish.

I pass the old lady her handkerchief and kneel down on the step behind her, my gaze on Santa Elisabetta.

A wheeze of exertion as Signora Ottolini rises, the muted thud of her knee on the stone as she genuflects towards the altar and loses her balance. Signora Barolli is snoring softly, her chin dropped to her chest, and Signora Ottolini shuffles over, gently wakes her. Arm in arm they cross the church floor to the exit, the short distance a voyage. They begin their gusto of gossip outside. The line between what is holy and what is everyday marked by church doors.

I wait for their chatter to fade, then I slip off my shoes and pad the steps to the altar. The sagristano will arrive soon with the clatter of keys, and I want to go closer to the painting. Inside my head, I hear my mother gasp her disgust. But without my shoes I can move quickly and, when the sagristano arrives, I can be back down the steps before he ambles through the sacristy door.

Above the altar, the painting is resplendent. This moment between the women, the bond that it captures, is alive and present before me. No longer a vague history droned from the pulpit. The two women lean close; the scent of their skins, the warmth of their breath, mingling in a silent exchange. So many prayers I have said to the Virgin Maria. For her strength and guidance. For her forgiveness. But now it is Santa Elisabetta whose expression of resolve conjures power. Her nose is almost tip to tip with the Virgin's, her gaze locked on to her apprehensive young cousin.

There are no haloes encircling their heads. As if the artist wanted to emphasise that these women were human. That their titles as Saint and Blessed Mother came long after their deaths. In this meeting they are Elisabetta and Maria. Maria is my age, a girl. Elisabetta is older than my mother. More the age of Lucia. Two living women who felt worry and fear, hunger and thirst. Who would have shed tears and shared secrets. Would have yearned. Would have bled.

In the shadows of their robes, Elisabetta's right hand clasps the left hand of Maria. I can feel my palm throbbing, as if it is my hand inside Elisabetta's.

How I ache to stand in the soft-slippered shoes of the Virgin, in the cast of Elisabetta's warmth.

'And so you approve?'

I pivot on my bare feet. The man who has spoken stands in the church. Dark wiry curls escape in every direction from under his cap. A faded *mantello* sits askew on his shoulders, his trunk hose twisted on his legs. Dangling from his hand are my shoes.

I look from my shameful bare feet to my shoes, and back again to my feet. I turn my mind from his question and try to place his face, but before any sense of recognition or answer finds me, he is walking towards me. I will myself to faint.

'*Sì o no?*' He fixes a terrible glare upon me.

I stammer my approval.

His expression softens. And he joins me in front of the painting, angling his head left and right. A wet dollop of paint on the side of his boot has left a red smear on the tiles.

'*Allora! Il bianco!* The white!' He frowns at the painting.

Besides vague clouds in the painted sky, the only white I see is the veil on Elisabetta's head.

He turns to face me and I am struck by the piercing blue of his eyes. But his face is confusing. The cupid plumpness of his lips and the high ball of his cheeks could be beautiful but, pieced together, it is a face not quite at ease.

'It lacks lustre!' he says, pushing a finger to the cleft in his chin.

He steps closer and throws his arm around my shoulder, reorients me to face the east wall of the church. Every detail of him demands my attention. His untidy dress. The ochre stain of his cuticles, more than one fingernail obscured with a muddy grey paste. The fine hair on his earlobes, the sour waft of sweat as he lifts his arm. He pulls a stained, ragged cloth from his doublet and rubs at his brow; the scent of linseed fills the air. The smell of Lucia that makes my heart leap.

He lifts his arm from my shoulder and points at one of the small arched windows set high in the wall. Its alabaster pane glows with morning sun and he opens his palm as if to capture its light.

'You see it? *Quel bianco?* That white?'

'*Sì*,' I reply, unsure I am seeing at all.

'The alabaster catches but filters the light so it glows.' He returns his attention to the painting. 'But how to create it? What nature does with ease, we strive for with toil.' He snaps from his reverie, a sudden fury arising. 'Leonardo says be subtle, Michelangelo says be bold! As if art is one or the other!' He scoffs and makes a noise in his throat so I think he might spit at our feet.

I want to recoil from the smell of his breath.

'What secrets do they share, Elisabetta and Maria?' He turns his wild gaze upon me. My shoes dangle from his hand as he speaks. '*Allora!* They spent three months together. For women, this much time in conversation is a lifetime's words for a man.' For the first time he laughs; it makes him look younger.

I'm entranced by his question, but remain silent.

'Signor Albertinelli!' It is Padre Renzo himself, not the sagristano, who bursts from the sacristy and onto the altar, a wad of keys clanking.

The man I now know is the painter Albertinelli drops my shoes to the floor. I slot my feet inside. They feel even more awkward now and I stumble before I've even taken a step.

The men embrace amid cheery backslapping.

'A triumph!' Padre Renzo gestures towards the painting. There is more thudding of backs, the percussive commotion of men greeting men. 'How goes your friend, the friar?'

'Fra Bartolomeo? Don't ask!' replies Signor Albertinelli. 'Still lost to the mad friar's ghost. Won't pick up a paintbrush. Sooner pick up a wife.'

'There are those who still believe the friar Savonarola preached the truth,' says the padre.

'If truth must destroy art,' says Albertinelli, 'then let me live in lies.'

I take the steps from the altar and across the church floor, the two men oblivious to the clunk of my heels. Their arms are still entwined as I splash my hand through the font water and hasten the sign of the cross.

'*Regazza! Scusami!*' The artist, Albertinelli, is calling me.

I push hard at the doors, morning light leaking through. Hurried footsteps as he strides towards me.

'Antonia!' Padre Renzo calls now. 'Forgive my distraction. *Giorno, giorno!* How is your mother? Your father? Business at the tavern? I haven't seen him since Easter.'

I turn to the men, the doors closing behind me with a cool, sharp puff.

'Next time you will tell me,' says the artist.

'My mother and father are well, thank you.' I ignore him and address Padre Renzo.

'Tell you what?' the padre asks Signor Albertinelli.

'What they say to each other, these women.' Albertinelli rolls his hand towards the painting and winks at the padre. 'They spent three months together before the Baptist was born. Can you imagine what secrets they shared?'

'One does wonder what our saints might have said to each other,' says the padre, but I can see that he does not wonder about this at all.

'Give my respects to your parents,' says the padre.

'*Sì*, Padre. *Grazie*.'

'Next time you will tell me their secrets,' insists Signor Albertinelli.

As the doors close behind me, I am satisfied in the knowledge that I will do no such thing.

The piazza bells are ringing and I feel dizzy, elated, already planning my return to sit with the painting. My thoughts rush and spill out beyond its frame, where the wildflowers at the women's feet become ancient hillsides with flourishing grapevines and olives. Farther and farther, I let my mind wander, along the winding switchbacks the Virgin Maria travelled with haste to her cousin, days walking a winding dirt path, uphill all the way; no doubt beleaguered by bandits. There was no time to send word, but did Santa Elisabetta sense her young cousin's arrival? Was her baby already kicking for joy in her womb? How the splendour of this painting, the swell of affection as the two women meet, renews my hope that I will once again embrace my Zia Lucia. That maybe she can sense my longing to see her. And if I am good to Mamma and keep Babbo happy, maybe an angel might visit me like it did the Virgin Maria. And direct me, like it did her, to Zia Lucia. And I will have an ally who believes I can have a life that is unlike my mother's.

5

Beit HaKerem, 38 BCE

The reed mats have been laid out on the flat roof of our summer house. Here we will catch the cool breezes that blow east from the Great Sea and funnel through Tawarei Yehuda, the mountains, to the valley of Beit HaKerem. Today the breeze also brings with it the trickling sound of the ancient Spring of the Vineyard that has watered our village for thousands of years and whose sweet water fills the jugs set at our meal. The slivers of dried fish I procured will be criticised as lavish, but I welcome anything that distracts Imma's focus from the topic of the grandchildren I have not produced.

We wash and sit circling the food: Imma to my right, my visiting aunt, Ahata d'Em Hanna, to my left. Bayla ascends the ladder, balancing the last of the dishes, then sets them on the mat as Zakhariya begins the blessings. First for the bread, then the wine. And we feast on gourd stew with lentils and chard and flavoured with coriander leaf and ground seeds of rue, artichoke spiced with cumin and hyssop, dried fish with fig paste and grape honey, dripping and sweet.

'You have your great-grandmother's hair,' says Ahata d'Em Hanna. She takes a pink cyclamen flower from its decorative place on the mat and tucks the stem through the long braid that peeps from under my veil. 'Others plaster their scalps with henna for hours for this colour.'

My hands twitch with the urge to reach for the barely visible bump under her tunic, I keep them in my lap. It was early in her last pregnancy that I spoke up about the young girl who came to me in my dreams. Who told me she was my cousin, yet to be born. 'Perhaps, Ahata d'Em Hanna,' I'd said, 'she will be born through you?'

When Hanna lost the child I was punished by Imma for my arrogance. But that night the girl returned to my dreams to console me, to promise me she would be born.

Reclining on a mat, Imma fidgets with unusual impatience and reaches for the flatbread. She peels a piece from the stack, works it between her fingers, tears it in two and takes a bite.

'How many times did you sift?' she asks, narrowing her eyes as she chews.

This throws me, as her veiled disapprovals always do. How many times did I sift? Four? Five? Three? I'd been intent on finding and extracting every last fleck of grit that can speckle our flour, to avoid an embarrassing crunch between Imma's teeth. I do not remember how many times it was put through the sieve.

Before I can answer, Imma wafts her hand in the air. 'No matter.' She places the uneaten bread in the bowl set before her. 'We have food. At least let us be grateful.'

Bayla returns again to the roof, with succulent honeyed dates, which Imma declines and I feel greedy savouring the one I have stuffed into my mouth. We all try to ignore the taut unrest that Imma imparts with her covert complaints.

'It is my hope that next visit Aharon will be well enough to join us,' says Zakhariya.

'The pain in his head never ceases,' says Imma, unsettled by my husband's mention of my father. 'Quick to lose his patience and manners. But let us speak of more interesting things.' She sips at her wine, rejects further offers of food.

A loud whistle from below and Zakhariya rises, dusting crumbs from his beard.

'Yirmiyahu's roof leaks and needs plaster. I promised to help. It is a pleasure to host you, Tsova and Hanna,' Zakhariya says to my mother and aunt, descending the ladder, a cautionary glance to remind me to be careful, patient, with my mother.

We sit in silence. My mother, Dodah Hanna, me. Bayla in waiting.

'Why not offer him Bayla?' Imma drops her question into our post-meal languor like a rock into a well. And now I understand Zakhariya's pained look as he departed.

'Let us finish our meal in peace, Tsova,' says Hanna.

'My daughter might as well learn there's no shame in taking a handmaiden,' says Imma. 'And if one is to be chosen, it should be Bayla.' My mother speaks as if our maidservant isn't present to hear her own name. As if the conversation is about the fig sap curdling cheese in my storeroom and not the subject of who will carry a child for my husband.

I bite down on my lip. I know it is too early to speak my own news that the signs have been clear, the north star above the chalice quarter moon as I prayed, the dreams of fleshy pomegranates blushing with ripeness. All the portents of fertility, of children, have flowed in a steady succession.

'Your maidservant wears a perfect braid today,' Imma says, not to compliment Bayla but to caution me.

She knows it was me who dressed my maidservant's hair, an oiled and gleaming braid with a silver hairpin at the side of her veil. The hairpin was a gift from Savta, my grandmother, who knew me better than my own mother seems to.

'A servant needs to know her place.' She holds out her goblet and Bayla moves to fill it, her hand shaking as she pours.

'Herod has landed at Ptolemais,' I say, offering information that men offer among men, trying to distract my mother from the subject she has set her mind to. 'His troops are pushing fast down the coast. Not stopping to sleep.'

The closing gap between the Romans and our Holy City is the least of her concerns, but the pace of the soldiers disturbs me.

Since Herod has been crowned king, there is no safe place for women when it comes to Roman soldiers. Sometimes it seems there is no safe place at all, wherever there are men. This is why I treasure the one real female friend I have, even though she is also my servant.

Imma sips loudly and sets her goblet aside. 'So has she carried?' she asks me, determined as a Roman soldier in her approach.

Bayla's eyes are downcast, hiding her terror at having to reveal the truth if my mother asks her directly. She is a poor liar and even a brief hesitation would cause Imma to turn up her nose. This is the corner into which women are pushed. Despised for what we have, despised for what we do not. And the thing that a woman has only once was taken early from Bayla.

He'd come for her on a dark moon in the parched end of Kayta. His bare feet soundless in the dust, weaving his way through the olive trees in the grove above her home. I secreted her jatamansi oil for the rope burns and cuts on her wrists that left scars. But there was no salve for shame. Even with the skin of her virginity intact, a woman's voice was not deemed as important as a man's, much less that of a girl already bled by a man. Only newly fourteen.

If I were my mother, Bayla would have been taken to the man's father and fifty shekels demanded, a marriage to her attacker thought to be better than no marriage at all. And the part of me still steeped in duty enquired discreetly about the donkey handler whose father came from Pinikiya. If he or his father or uncle spoke up, Bayla would be called for and we would have little say in the matter. How often I must now shake her story from my mind, how close by, but alone, my Bayla was on that hot night with no moon.

'I would never ask you to lie for me,' Bayla had told me, knowing the consequences for her if I was asked and told the truth. And for me if I was asked and lied.

She lost the baby in the first term, the blood clotted and dark, her sleeping mat burned in secret. The confusion of grief in her face, shocked to feel the loss of something she'd never wanted.

A stray bee circles the honeyed dates, Imma swats it away. Bayla, head down, offers more wine. Her shawl shifts back as she pours the jug, the faded scars still visible on the underside of her wrist.

'We don't need a handmaiden,' I say before I am ready, overwhelmed as I always am by the marks on my Bayla's body and unable to keep her as the subject of my mother's scrutiny.

Imma rolls her hands into neat fists on her knees.

'You must take charge, Sheva,' Imma says. 'Better you choose than Zakhariya chooses a less agreeable other.' She turns from me and addresses Ahata d'Em Hanna. 'How long before my daughter accepts that opinion is hard-earned, but duty is expected?'

Hanna is expected to show respect towards her elder sister's opinion.

'She's still young, there is time.' Her prudent reply.

'Ada is carrying again.' Imma returns her attention to me and I feel the twinge of envy high in my chest. 'Her eldest, Ittai, is already tall enough to load the donkeys.'

Imma drains her cup and Bayla moves to fill it again. Imma flaps her away. 'And you've heard about Helene? Already carrying!'

I fight the urge to glance Bayla's way and roll my eyes.

Helene's husband, Ishpah, is a drunk who vents his anger on his family. Young wives sometimes lose their babies at the hands of their drunken husbands and Helene will now live in terror that her baby's fate might be sealed by the fine skin of a grape.

'Tell Helene *mazala tava!*' The flat tone of my congratulations irritates Imma.

'She is saved from further shame, is the point,' Imma says. 'The women are talking to her again. She has been invited to Ittai's ceremony.'

Bayla sneezes and Imma glares. As if servants don't possess the usual needs like the rest of us, or shouldn't.

'Take the bowls,' I tell Bayla to relieve her.

She gathers and stacks our emptied clay vessels. My mother's fingers flex and curl on her knees. Only now, as Bayla leaves the roof, does Imma look directly at her, sizing up her hips. Satisfying herself that the maidservant could carry a child well.

'This is a subject for private conversation, Imma,' I say.

'She should know she would be chosen first to bring Zakhariya a child.'

'Who is choosing, Imma?'

'It is a wife's duty to direct her husband in the matters she knows best.' Her fists pulse on her knees. 'And a mother's duty to direct her daughter. I'm doing my part. But if you do not act, the Hand of Ribon Alma surely will.'

And it almost bursts from me. That I know with all my heart a child will come to me. That I have shared my visions with my husband, who drew me close and reassured me of his trust, of his patience.

'You're not the daughter I expected, Sheva.'

Her remark sends a small part of me reeling outwards from my soft centre, across the roof, spiralling downwards into the dust. I want to refute her, but the creeping shame that I am not the thing my mother wished for coils itself around my tongue and holds it fast.

'You can decide right now and be done with it, announce it before your eighteenth year,' Imma says. 'Return your name among the women.'

'Return my name?' I say.

Under my tunic, my skin becomes damp. Our people's names are sacred. You can only truly know another by their name.

'You must know they call you *Melḥa*,' says Imma.

Melḥa. Salt. The curse of fertile crops. And Ribon Alma's curse upon Lot's wife when she dared to disobey the command not to look back.

'I try to defend you, of course,' my mother says. 'I explain that you've always been different. But they have daughters now and don't want your hand upon them.'

'I'm not contagious,' I say, furious that the tremor in my voice betrays hurt.

'You're childless,' says Imma. 'You understand that is worse?'

She rises. And even though she has spoken with neither compassion nor concern for my feelings, how I wish she would take me into her arms and say my name as she knows it. But she walks past me to the ladder.

She starts to climb down, glances back. 'There are worse things, Elisheva, than being called *Melḥa*.'

There are worse things, always, for a woman.

Dodah Hanna and I remain on the roof.

'Shall we walk down to the spring?' she asks, and I make my excuses. Feeling shamed by Imma is already enough; I can't face the other women who will be gathered for water and gossip. Their unspoken judgments made clear, despite their tight lips.

Dodah Hanna gasps and presses her palms to her belly. I place my hands upon hers.

'I feel a daughter too,' she says, and it catches my breath, this secret she shares.

'Does she tell you her name?' I ask, bursting with the knowledge inside me.

Maryam.

She smiles but does not speak aloud. Neither do I. But I pray this daughter will be born soon, among so many sons.

'But not this one.' She rubs her hand over her belly. 'This child will be my fifth son.' She holds her fingers to her lips and I swell with joy at being taken into her trust. And when she leaves for Yerushalayim, I long for the warmth of her confidence, her favour.

'Mistress?'

Bayla calls me and I don't answer. I turn on my pallet and face the stone wall. I am usually glad to hear her voice, to welcome her in so we can mimic my mother or rub fragrant oil into each other's hair, sharing stories about the gentle goatherd who has given her a bracelet woven from flowers of chicory and purslane.

But I can't bear to see her, ashamed of the jealousy I feel. Not towards Zakhariya, but of what might change in our friendship, if she is the one chosen to lie with my husband.

'*B'tula d' shawshanata?*' Lily maiden, she calls me. For my love of these white flowers of the valley, their sleek, elegant petals. Even though I am no longer a maiden.

'*Shawsh'na?*'

'Leave me,' I say.

And without another word, she does. My beautiful Bayla, who is everything I am not. Who can do what my mother expects of a daughter.

6

Adelaide, Autumn 2018

'Where are you?' My mother has me on speaker, her voice distorted by the chug, chug, chug of the sewing machine. The clunk as she adjusts the foot.

'Central Market, buying fish,' I reply from the clinic waiting room. 'I'm about to be served.'

The doctor appears, calls my name, signals for me not to hurry.

'It … because …' My mother says something inaudible.

'I'll call you back, Mum,' I say. Then, so she can hear, 'Two fillets of King George whiting and —' I hang up.

The doctor pretends to ignore my charade.

I follow her into her consulting room. Mint-green walls and mid-century chairs upholstered in tapestry lilies create a parlour-like effect. Her perfume is too strong; tiny needles of irritation prick inside my nostrils. Behind her desk sits a ceramic rainbow, each coloured band painted with flowers. She looks over my file while I silently name them. Red protea, orange banksia, yellow impatiens.

'You're under no pressure to make a decision,' she says. 'However, if you need more time, we'll need a second practitioner to confirm the procedure.'

I'm aware of the legalities and how much easier this would have been in Victoria.

A gushing diffuser reeks lavender and I sneeze, trying not to rub at my eyes or scratch at my throat. She offers me a tissue box and I pluck one. I don't mention that I developed the same reaction with my first.

'It's the fragrance,' I say.

She angles her head, an indistinct expression. Adjusts her glasses with a fingertip.

'How are you feeling about your decision?' she asks.

Which decision? I want to ask her.

According to one shrink, twenty percent of the eight-hundred-thousand decisions the average human makes in a lifetime are regrettable. Which one shall we discuss?

She waits for my answer and I resist my need to explain. That yes, I am torn, conflicted to the point of screaming about why I am here.

'Would you like to speak to someone about your options?' She glances at the clock on the wall. Other women are waiting; she's already behind.

'I've made my decision,' I say, and while she taps at her keyboard I try to recall the name of the green leaves in the centre band of the rainbow. A tropical plant whose young leaves are shaped like a heart, but then split.

I press my hand to the ache in my chest. Pretend I need to cough.

Monstera! I mouth the small memory-victory.

Blue forget-me-nots. Indigo irises. Violets. Spring flowers I have embroidered in their thousands into sleeve cuffs and Dirndl skirts and dress hems and stoles, while my mother held her breath as she examined my work, picking out flaws until I mastered each stitch.

'We could do August eighth,' she says.

I know I look blank-faced, stupid. A throbbing welt on my throat where I've scratched at the perfume-caused itch.

'Any other date?' I ask, tears now streaming, nose dripping.

The clatter of keystrokes. 'None that won't need a second opinion. Shall I book in the eighth?'

My projectile vomit spatters her desk. A fleck on the right lens of her glasses. She is swift and professional. Glasses off, sterile wipes expunging my shame. Then, her hand in the centre of my back.

'You're okay,' she says, her hand circling as I sputter into a tissue.

'I would like to speak to someone,' I say.

She hands me a wet wipe.

'Your nervous system is in overload. It's all very normal.'

But is it normal, I will ask the *someone* appointed to me, that the one date I can book to terminate this pregnancy is the birth date of the son I have already lost?

I stand on the gravel footpath outside my mother's house. She will be in her kitchen at the laminex table, easing silk between the sewing machine foot and throat plate. Who could have imagined bolts of fabric sent from Florence's Casa dei Tessuti on Via de Pecori to Adelaide's Mile End? But indeed, they are in there. In the cupboards and wardrobes. In the pantry and the sideboard. Stacked on the patchwork bedspread of my childhood, for my mother to pattern and pin and sequin and stitch a gown for a dignitary's wife. Or a sports star's new girlfriend.

My earliest memories are of cotton spools as playthings. Pincushions and reels in my hands long before I could pass a thread through the eye of a needle. Tiny velvet buttons and Murano glass beads swallowed or spat out. Explorations of dressmaking scissors that sometimes left me in tears with a neatly sliced finger, but that taught me due diligence and then confidence in the tools that would lead me from executing simple patterns to restoring vintage embroidered dresses. To drafting patterns for designers like Jenny Kee and Linda Jackson. To designing and creating the curtains for New Parliament House because of my gift in blending threads to produce a photo-like image. New students in textiles call the technique silk shading, but I prefer the description 'painting with a needle'. At this art, I excel.

If my mother became disapproving and sullen, I knew how to win her over. I'd pick up a needle and thread and work over a dress in a fury, transforming plain hems with intricate rosettes and leaving bodices bursting with spring flowers. I could spend hours, days, on a piece, barely pausing to eat. Living for the moment when she would hold it out at arm's length, nod her approval and pass me the next.

The yellowing faux-lace curtains in her front window freeze time. She's never made curtains for her own house and so they do not seem fitting for Adelaide's finest couture seamstress. When I'd offered to make new ones, she'd scoffed at what she thought a frivolous venture. I picture her pulling them back, delighted to see me, beckoning me inside, her grandmother's pincushion cuff on her arm like a bracelet. The rose scent on her skin, filling each room. How I long for the days when to appease her was simple. A sleeve seamed and edged with turquoise peacock feathers and royal purple crocuses; a frontispiece embossed with gold Bayeux dragons.

I pull my phone from my handbag. I'll call first. Why can't the *someone* I talk to be my mother? Isn't that why I came back to Adelaide? Because she is my someone?

'Mmm-huh,' she says, and I know there will be pins in her mouth.

'How's the dress coming on?' I ask. I hear her exhale in frustration, for what seamstress wants to risk swallowing pins? 'I'll try and pop over later,' I say, watching her shadow move past the window.

She doesn't look out, could never imagine why I would be lingering outside her house. The lawn between her front door and where I stand like crossing a country.

On the footpath I snap slender twigs into pieces, set them into five-pointed stars and fill them with gumnuts. It seems right to make stars. Those distant glimmering suns, clearly in our sights. Never in our grasp.

The conservation studio is a cocoon. Filtered light, dustless and draughtless, designed in all ways to protect what it houses. Textiles in various states of repair that to my eye are rousing in their fragility. Some are mere ragged patches being stitched onto new supports or backings. Pieces clinging for life, ravaged by *agents of destruction*: the alarming technical term for the many enemies of a textile's wellbeing. High or low humidity, salts, acids, light, fire and insects. Even the change in temperature from where it was found to where it's kept. These fragments are held with care by the conservator, with hands free of lotions or oils or perfumes, undecorated fingers with no snagging jewellery. Bare and unencumbered, my fingers examine and clean and arrange, fleshing out shreds and tatters with the hope to regain a lost image. The skills of washing and stitching and matching are important, but the talent of the best is seeing the whole where there appear only parts. Taking that which is frail, frangible, scattered, and recreating completeness. A patient and determined vision for wholeness. When I am working, I fall into a world where what is spoiled is touched with reverence, with admiration. My focus not on what has failed, but of what has managed to remain.

I pull out the long drawer, take hold of the thick, acid-free cardboard with the fragile embroidery on it, lay it on the work table. Each time I peel back the protective tissue to reveal it, a part of me sighs with relief. Afraid that it might have been only a dream and the piece is in fact still rotting inside tubing, under seventeen dozen empty Emu Export Lager beer cans dated 1923, themselves worth a small fortune. It's the most exciting Australian find since Breaker Morant's bandoliers and Boer War bullet-pierced pendant were found at a tip.

The embroidery is stitched on a backdrop of silvery metal thread, its images wrought in silk floss and overspun silk. Some parts are in stunning metal threads including both fine and crinkled gold plate, and wrapped metal thread on cream and dark cores. On closer inspection, there are even tiny glass beads. As a post-Reformation work, it is common to find secular motifs of nature and, in the centre of the piece, I can just make out two figures, surrounded by trees, flowers, insects and animals. A long-tailed bird perches under a lily, with a hare, a leopard and a butterfly beneath. On the right is a peacock in near-perfect condition, its brilliant sky blue and gold giving a sense of how vibrant the entire piece once would have been. There are flowers that might be crocuses, and a unicorn being chased by a dog. The central figures themselves are flanked by an oak and a giant thistle, and what I would guess is a borage plant built up with tent stitch in metal thread, with complex wrapped-metal threads on the stem and overspun silk thread for the leaves. One sleeve of one figure remains in good shape, worked in coiled metal thread with cores of different colours, creating a dimensional and textured effect. But the hand on the end of the arm is missing. Above the figures are swirls of red and blue clouds, more like a Buddhist thangka painting than anything designed to please God.

It is an altogether disarmingly quirky scene. All that remains clear of the figures are parts of their outer robes. But this embroidery, abandoned and filthy, had with it a conservator's treasure. Inside the tube was a bag stuffed with detached pieces and threads. And I am determined to put it all back together.

In my world of bright whole visions, I manipulate thread with fine tweezers, align frayed edges, lay couching stitches to secure, then small supporting stitches at right angles, varying the placement so no discernible pattern will distract the eye. Each precious thread stitches the past to the present.

When I look at the clock, six hours have flown by, my eyes screaming for rest from their focused attention. I pack everything away and leave the corridors in darkness. A pale saffron sky over Adelaide Oval, the last of the sunset. Deep satisfaction as I turn into my street.

Old Mr Saler is pruning his roses. He waves a gloved hand from across the road. 'He left your mail on the doorstep,' he calls out, smiling. I freeze, sweat beading.

I urge my legs to move. My gate is ajar. Not how I left it. I halt on the footpath, looking around me. On my doormat is a neat pile of my mail. Beside it, a bunch of fresh flowers. I can hear the quick rasp of my breath. I close the gate behind me, walk up the brick path and pick up the letters. The first envelope has been neatly cut through at its top seam. I file through them, dropping some. They've all been opened. I fumble, dropping more. Pick them up. My nose is already reacting to the scent of the flowers. Stargazer lilies, viburnum and freesias. I'm allergic to all three.

My bin is out the front, but Mr Saler is still watching, still smiling. I wave back my thanks, let him feel complicit in some happy moment. I take the flowers through the house, now sneezing, eyes running, and straight out my back door, where I throw them over the fence into the alley.

Inside, I pace the kitchen. I want to be angry because it stifles the fear. I want to call him. Now, while I'm angry. My phone shakes in my hand. I finally press on his name, but when he picks up I crumble. The phone falls from my hand and I drop along with it. I cannot find tears, not at first. The self-loathing in these moments screams guilt and fault and failure. For fucking up those decisions that were once mine to make.

Make a new choice. The recurring bottom line across multiple shrinks and multiple sessions.

Make a new choice now.

'Like every stitch in textile conservation,' said the shrink who had brought in the embroidered nude of her lover and asked how she might improve on his hairline. 'Be as discerning with each choice as you are with each stitch.'

I won't call him back. I'll call Oxford. I should have heard by now about my residency application. I know how quickly their faculty works to acquire staff once new textiles are acquired. The outline said that those shortlisted would hear within four weeks.

I splash my face and apply lipstick, even though it's a phone call. It is 7.30 pm here, 11 am there.

'Doctor Reed from Adelaide International Gallery calling for Doctor Saadie,' I say to the bright plummy voice that answers.

Hold music, Handel's 'Arrival of the Queen of Sheba'. I close my eyes, take it in.

'Bad luck about the Ashes,' says Priscilla Saadie.

'For you,' I say.

She laughs. So do I, amused at how many conversations with English colleagues begin with cricket.

'Good to hear your voice, Priscilla,' I say, and now the tears come. I have learned how to manage this eruption on a phone call and I curve my mouth into a full smile. Let the tears follow the creases of my cheeks. A fake smile, says the science, still triggers feel-good endorphins.

'We were so sorry to hear you declined the position.'

I try to take in what she has said, uh-huhing and mmm-hming as she tells me they've taken on a post-doctoral student from the Queen Sirikit Museum of Textiles.

'Lucky find! She was considering the MET; we convinced her with pork pies and cider. But she's not you, of course!' Priscilla laughs again. How lovely, that laugh. Utterly innocent of the wrecking ball it propels. 'Anyway, as always I talk too much without asking what I can do for you?'

My cheeks ache with the science-fuelled smile, fixed in place by my desperate need to prevent any suspicion that I have no control over my life, over the man who opens my mail. Who leaves me flowers that poison. Who leaves marks on my face and convinces me that they are my fault. Who knows my passwords are a name and a birthdate I cannot change. Who has clearly intercepted an emailed job offer from Oxford University and declined on my behalf, because he knows I'm hopeless with emails and let them flood in and build up for weeks. And who keeps front of mind what I keep deep inside. That I will ruin the very things that I want.

Make a new choice.

He wouldn't have expected me to call them, to follow up. He'd expect me to back out. This thought triggers a flickering flame of victory within me, because I have acted in a way he did not expect.

'Sounds like she's a perfect fit,' I say to Priscilla.

'When will we see you over here?'

'When you win back the Ashes,' I tell her, but she makes me promise.

Make a new choice.

I know what I must do. And my tears cascade as I begin.

On my email account page I select *Change password* and type in my current password as it instructs. I click *Show password.* Hover the cursor over my son's name and birthdate, every letter and number, fragments of him I cling to. Jonathan08081997. A mantra. A spell. An invisible doorway, back to a past I can never return to.

Make a new choice.

Six therapists, three shrinks and countless mentors in books and in workshops. One point of consensus. Focus on the present. Over a textile, this concentration is natural. But how to maintain focus on this frayed, rotted hole in my centre?

Enter new password. My hands tremble over the keyboard. I type the new words. 2018ImStillYourMum!

4 am. I shower. Collect fallen leaves for my ephemeral artwork. The night security guard, Amir, is happy to see me. I hand him a bag with the Florentine biscuits I know he loves.

'Can't sleep again, Doctor?' His accent turns *sleep* into slip.

I can't sleep. But slip? I'm always slipping. No struts and no rope. A freefall only broken when I'm working on a textile.

The studio is a haven. I settle onto my stool. At four hundred years old, some of the embroidery's silver threads are greyed by patina. But at the top of the textile, the sun's gold thread gleams. The fingers that once held the needle were almost certainly a young girl's. Tasked to acquire three skills for marriage: to play an instrument, to learn a foreign language and to embroider.

As part of my learning, my mother and I made a trip together when I was eleven, to assess and buy fabrics in the old city of Florence. In the window of Casa dei Tessuti there was a mannequin swathed in an embroidered fabric so delicately sewn it looked like a photo. At the mannequin's feet was a silk-shaded banner. *Ogni donne e un universe.* Every woman is a universe.

As I work, I imagine the young embroiderer's deft fingers following the now-faded pattern drawn onto the linen. Most scholars argue that she would be thinking of the husband she would attract, the children she would bear. But a part of me wonders if women understood more deeply the benefit of the broad skills that could be developed by the arts they acquired. Problem solving for one, as they handled each stitch, in gracious pose plucked music from strings, or addressed foreign nobles in their native languages. If their husbands died early, which was common, these women were often left to manage the household and business. Perhaps this young embroiderer knew all too well the education she was gaining. That she was a universe all of her own in the making.

My fingers find the straining button on my pants, release it. I press my hand against the taut skin under my navel. I push myself back from the embroidery. The tears ~~fall fast, abundant~~. I keep my hand there, under my shirt, on my skin. This aching privilege of choice. Not all that it should be.

7

Florence, 1504

In the month before Lent, carnival spirit in Florence builds to frenzied excess. But in the church of San Michele, my knuckles are white with the pressure of prayer. My appeal is not directed to the heavens or to the holy place of the tabernacle; not to the crucifix sewn into the silks on the altar.

'Please help Mamma,' I beseech Santa Elisabetta, while the sotted world outside roars.

Marching parades crowd the streets as cheers erupt for the unruly god of wine, Bacchus, and men costumed as Eros dance the allemande and triple-time galliard. Young maidens, told by their fathers to stay well inside, peer down from their top-storey windows while masked carousers do their best to entice them into the street. Satyrs, nymphs and devils bang on drums and chant vulgar couplets. The revelling lower classes have their fill of all sins before the seasonal abstinence and restraint that will conclude in sober reverence with *Domenica di Pasqua*, the Sunday of Easter.

My mother is unfit for revelry but must work to keep up with the onslaught of tavern patrons. Her sickness each morning has shredded weight from her already small frame, but she carries on with her endless chores and says nothing. She's forgotten that I saw for myself the signs of a woman *incinta*. That I'd held back Lucia's hair when she retched into a pail. That we'd stopped using onions because the smell made her nauseous. When we now prepare food, only I slice the onions, and Mamma bunches her apron-skirt to her nose and exits the kitchen. And this morning I'd found the dried herbs. Silphium and tansy flowers, yellow like daisies; Italian catnip, its tell-tale purple flower; and the petite white heads of yarrow. Herbs to be crushed and boiled by women wishing to bring on their bleeding.

Babbo is oblivious. Too busy savouring the pride of his great tavern parties and the patrons they attract. 'Forget God's blessings,' he declares almost daily. 'Signor Michelangelo Buonarroti himself chooses my tavern. My wine.' As if that fact, above any, granted eternal absolution.

The truth is that Signor Buonarroti has visited the Drago only once, to meet with Signor Albertinelli. He'd stood, arms crossed like they were strapped to his chest, while Albertinelli complained about colours in art that failed to delight.

I'd been ordered by Babbo to keep their goblets full. Albertinelli's had been filled many times over.

'First learn to draw, then argue colour,' Signor Buonarroti said, refusing more wine as I refilled Albertinelli's cup.

'Hear how he insults me? He's too full with the adoration of others,' said Albertinelli, trying to lure me, once again, into conversation. 'See the snob from Ferrara? That's Ariosto Ludovico.' He indicated a man in fine dress. 'Serves Cardinal Ippolito d'Este, but thinks himself a poet. Joined us, uninvited, and recited grovelling rubbish! Impromptu!'

… and the one who looks
like he sculpts and colours
Michel, more than mortal,
divine Angel.

'All kneel!' cried Albertinelli to the crowd. 'Michel, the divine, graces us with his presence.'

'It's lovely,' I said, disregarding Albertinelli's mockery. 'Michel, divine Angel, I'll commit it to memory.'

Albertinelli again drained his cup. 'I'll dance for you later; you'll see I have other talents.' He kicked his feet out, left then right, in an unsteady galliard. Tried for the quick leap supposed to demonstrate a man's vigour and tripped, spilling wine. Michel's quick, strong hands caught the painter's flailing arms and stopped him from tumbling.

'I would excuse him as drunk, but he's no better sober,' said Michel. I liked him at once.

A gust of wind lifts my hair as the church doors swing open behind me. The shuffle of Signora Ottolini's slow procession from the door to the steps of the altar. She stops beside me, leans heavily on her stick. 'You are crazy for this painting, *no*?' She aims a crippled hand above the altar.

I stiffen and shrug.

She leans closer. 'You like them? The Jews?'

Her eyes glimmer as she asks me, and I am filled with unease. I'd heard Savonarola condemn Jews. Demanding these 'enemies of Christ' be expelled from the city. I didn't think of Santa Elisabetta or the Virgin Maria as Jews. Even though they'd lived in the Holy Land, I thought of them as women like me. I'm not sure if the old lady wants me to feel ignorant or intrigued.

'They despise them. Then worship them.' She clucks her tongue in disapproval. 'For those who still want Jews cast out, why not also this painting?'

She gets to her knees, pulls out her beads. Then she turns, stiff-necked, her voice in a whisper. 'Who is your favourite? Elisheva or Maryam?'

I can hear what she is saying but I don't understand.

'Elisheva.' She points to the woman on the right, whom I know as Elisabetta. 'Or Maryam?' She points to the Virgin. 'The names their mothers gave them at birth.' She smiles, a sparse eyebrow raised. 'I haven't heard my birth name uttered since I buried my mother.' Her bright, clever eyes darken, and she turns back to the altar.

Ellee-SHEV-ah. I repeat the name to myself while the signora thumbs beads to count out her prayers. Finally she is done and she rises. 'Which one do you pray to?' she asks me once she's on her feet.

'Elisheva,' I reply, and she smiles her approval.

'You wish to ask someone for help, best to use their right name.'

As she opens the doors, new cheers erupt from the festival crowds. I shift from kneeling to sitting, take out the bound parchment pages hidden beneath my cloak, then dig deep into my pockets for the charcoal stick left by Lucia. The same one she used to try and teach me to write neatly. Believing that nothing spoken held any real value until it was written.

'It's carnage!' Lucia had said, as my left hand with the charcoal dragged across the page, smudging the letters as I wrote. 'Try your other hand.'

I'd switched the charcoal to my right hand.

'*Dio mio!*' she'd said. 'A rooster could scratch neater letters.'

I'd wanted to impress her and tried not to look hurt by her frank assessment.

'I know a fine artist with *la mano del diavolo*,' she'd said, seeing my distress.

The hand of the devil. Lucia had winked to make fun of how my left-handedness was labelled.

'Can you keep a secret?' she'd asked me, and I'd nodded. 'Then close the door.'

From under Nonna's old bed Lucia pulled out the bag that carried her belongings. She withdrew a thin, square package wrapped in velvet and untied it with great care to reveal a small wooden board. She studied it, then turned it to show me.

The painting was in muted, earthy tones. A woman, eyes cast downwards, with an expression that might have been love or adoration towards a child in her unseen arms. Shadowy curls of hair fell loose and unbraided, but her face was touched with a wash of light.

'It is you!' I'd said, finally matching the soft arch in the eyebrows, the line of the nose, the wild curl of her hair. 'Who drew it?'

She tapped her finger to the artist's mark.

'Odra Noel?' I'd read it slowly, made curious by the unusual name.

'Take it,' she'd said, handing it to me. Then she took the polished tin mirror from the dresser and held it to her chest. 'Now read it again.'

I began to do as instructed.

'Not like that! Turn it towards me; read from the mirror,' she'd said.

Letters that had spelled nonsense now spelled a name.

OᗡЯAИOƎ⅃. Leonardo.

'Leonardo Bandini painted this?' I'd asked, and she'd laughed hard because Bandini was a tanner and left fingerprint-shaped stains on all that he touched.

'Keep it, and practise!' she said, taking back the painting but refusing the charcoal.

And I did. Teaching myself to write from right to left, back to front, so that I didn't ruin the page with my hand from the devil.

In the church, I poise the charcoal against the page. Try to imagine the letters that make out her name. Elisheva. Avehsile. Elisabetta. Attebasile. I write it both ways. Forwards and backwards. Then, I write out my prayer from its end to its beginning.

Elisheva. Please help her. Please help my mother.

I push the charcoal stick into my pocket and the pages inside my cloak. I promised to help at the tavern and Babbo will be waiting. I leave the church and hurry down Via Orsanmichele, Via Calimala, Via Por Santa Maria, towards the Ponte Vecchio

Hands on hips, my father stands waiting in the piazza midway along the old bridge as if needing to apprehend my escape. His face is lopsided with hangover.

'What's that you're hiding?' he asks.

My cloak has blown open in my haste and he can see my hand on the pages. I clutch them closer to my body. I don't have an answer I know will be safe. What would my father think of a girl who writes her own prayers? A girl who writes in strange languages, considered by some to be forbidden, with her hand of the devil?

'Give it to me.' He thrusts his hand inside my cloak, catching my small tender breast and pinching it as he wrenches the pages from me. He holds them at arm's length and flicks through the sheets, pretending to read when I know he cannot.

'What is all of this untidy writing?' he says, as if he could know what was tidy or not.

I'm too slow to answer and he turns on his heel and strides across the old bridge, holds my pages aloft over the stone parapet as if he will cast them down into the river.

'Please, Babbo, don't do it!' I run behind him.

'Speak or lose them,' he says.

And I feel the urge to challenge him to put them to fire, not water, if his goal is destruction.

'I'm taking notes on Signor Albertinelli's painting,' I say instead, not entirely a lie. 'His *Visitation* from San Michele. I don't want him to think my head is a cabbage.'

This is one of Babbo's favourite insults and I know it will catch his attention. He looks startled. His mind reaching back through wine-sodden memories to match the name and the painting I've mentioned.

'*Allora! La Visitazione.* I remember,' he says.

A lie, because he hasn't seen the painting and he'd rather be seen as a liar than a dunce.

'I want you to be proud of me, Babbo.'

He beams at the idea, mollified by my flattery. As is the way with Florentine men, their rage transforms to pride inside of a heartbeat.

'*Mia* Antonia. *Mia pulcina.* Sharp-witted like your father. If your head was a cabbage, you'd take after your mother.'

He gives me the pages and I feel a dizzy relief.

'The painter's work is superb, *sì?*'

'*Splendido!*' I reply, happy to find a topic on which we can truly agree.

'His use of chiaroscuro is better than Maestro Leonardo,' says Babbo. 'I heard it from Cardinal Soderini himself.' He points a finger to the heavens, an opinion of a bishop like word straight from God. But in truth my father had spoken with Gasparo Alberti, who had heard it from Andrea Pisano, whose job it was to clean the floor of the Duomo and who claimed he had heard Raffaello in conversation with the visiting cardinal.

'Hold out your hand,' says my father, his arm outstretched, fingers tight-fisted.

I hesitate, suspicious, then hold it out. He drops in a handful of silver into my palm.

'The tailor, Amadeo, is waiting,' he says, ignoring my shock. 'His granddaughter will help fit you a new dress. I need your mother here. *Allora!* Go straight there, come straight home. Your uncles are coming for business.'

Zio Lilo and Zio Renaldo weren't really uncles, but they helped Babbo with business and I would be expected to serve and impress them.

The coins glint in my palm. Enough money to fetch Mamma a year's worth of stockings, a pair for each day.

'Be dressed and ready before sunset,' he says, and I understand that he is also giving me the day off. '*Fretta, fretta!*' he says, hurrying me off. 'You want to appear ungrateful to your father?'

'Of course not, Babbo.' I kiss him on both cheeks.

'And make sure that miser tailor stitches gold thread, not silver, through the bodice, *capisci*?'

'*Sì*, Babbo,' I say, wondering how this silver could afford more than a single gold strand.

'Give them to me,' he says, holding out his hand.

I immediately offer him back the coins and he bats my hand away.

'The pages!' His fingers scrape the air, demanding my work. 'You'll ruin your new dress.' He shows me the black dust from my charcoal-pencilled words on the pads of his fingers.

Again I hesitate before him.

'What now? You don't trust your own father?'

'Of course, Babbo,' I say, handing over the pages.

'The patrons of the Drago can recite it out loud, learn a thing or two about art,' he says. When my face pales, he roars with laughter. '*Mia pulcina!*' He claps his hand to my shoulder and I feel his strength bear down on my bones. 'You forget your *babbo* knows how to jest.'

Before we moved to the city, my father knew how to make jokes that were amusing, not frightening. When we worked a small family vineyard a half-day's walk south of Florence, he would sing clever ditties about farmhands and milkmaids, and make others laugh with his flip observations. And I would upend the bucket and sit while Babbo chewed mastice and studied vine leaves for mildew and leafroll and told of his dreams to own a fine-wine bottega in Florence. The white Alberese stones set at the base of the vines would soak up the warmth of the sun, then, on cool nights, deliver this warmth back to the roots. At dusk, the reflected white light would cast a heavenly glow on the fruit. And we would marvel at bunches that seemed touched by God.

'Go, go!' he says, shooing me off to the tailor. 'Only an old dog arrives late. It's why I never see your mother before midday.'

He thinks he is funny. But I can't laugh with him now like I did in the vineyard.

When I return early, Mamma is waiting.

'Has it come?' I ask, both of us counting the days since her bleeding was due.

'The men are already here,' she replies, ignoring my question.

'But my new dress won't be delivered until later,' I say as she ushers me inside, smoothing my hair back from my face.

'What does it matter what you are wearing?' she says. 'They're already drunk.'

'Zio Lilo and Zio Renaldo?' I ask.

'And Zio Gerardo.'

'All three?' I ask. These men only joined forces to act on our family's behalf when a guarantee of one kind or another was needed.

My mother twists at her apron. 'He sent you out for the day so they could meet and discuss the terms,' she tells me as she might confess shameful sins: low voiced, reluctant.

The terms. The terms?

'Of the dowry, the engagement,' she says before I can ask.

Still, I don't quite understand how these words apply to me. But I can see that they must.

'Signor Albertinelli has proposed and your father has accepted.'

She spells it out for me and I stare at her lips, made thin by disclosure.

'I'm not yet sixteen. I'm not even bleeding.' My body shakes as I take in the news. 'And he's twice my age.'

'My parents signed papers when I was eleven,' says my mother. 'Signor Albertinelli is building acclaim. With Medici patronage, no less. And he has expressed interest in helping Babbo with the Drago.'

I can see her mouth moving, but the rage blocks my ears.

'If you make me do this, I will tell him,' I say. 'I will tell Babbo right now about your condition. That you've been to get herbs because you don't even want it.'

That was the threat I launched at my mother. Nothing like the consolation I had implored from Santa Elisabetta.

'Why didn't you stop it?' I ask her.

'How do you think I got this?' She pushes back the tunic from her shoulder to reveal a dark bruise.

The sight of the mark on her body fills me with despair. But also disgust. And I recall the haunting instruction from Lucia in our last moments together. *Don't blame your mother.*

'It's your fault,' I say, dismissing Lucia's counsel. 'I'll never be a coward like you are with Babbo.'

If I had known these were the last words my mother would hear from my lips, I might have bitten my tongue against my urge to insult her. I might have swallowed the hard knot of blame stuck in my throat. If I'd known she would not be there to help me into my wedding gown, I might have instead been grateful that day for the impatience she withheld: not barking orders, not scolding my every move, not tugging too tight as she helped fix my skirts. I might have been there when her bleeding did finally start. But then did not stop.

'More blood on the birthing bed than on the floor of Santa Maria del Fiore when the Pazzi stabbed Giuliano de' Medici,' my father had replied when, as a child, I'd asked if I would ever have a baby brother or sister.

We'd been working the vineyard, the vines heavy with fruit. Filling baskets with succulent bunches seemed to appease him, and he became more patient with my endless questions. But his answer hadn't made sense. Not like it would later.

I remembered Babbo's grim words when I found Mamma curled up like a cat in the kitchen, as I grabbed every cloth I could find to stem the red river that rushed from her body. It was then I knew that she'd not only taken herbs but had submitted herself to the copper spike, the *embruosphaktes*, the slayer of children. A decision she knew might take her life with the baby's.

For month after month, I stood rigid and numb, alone in our kitchen. Following ghost orders from my mother that played out in my head.

'Weak spirited,' I'd hear my father say, explaining his wife's death to his patrons. 'Not like my daughter.'

His spite a hard copper spike through my heart.

The belt of my wedding gown is a crimson silk weave laced with silver thread and trimmed with white pearls. Pearls for purity, chastity. It matches the pearl braids woven through my tightly pinned hair. Hair that has been combed, teased, braided and upswept around a thick round pad set on the back of my head. Never again will I wear the loose, free hair of an unmarried woman.

For all the suffocating layers of my gown, its ribbons, lace and metal thread, it is this belt that steals my breath. Because, once removed, it marks the line between worlds. In one world the pure young woman untouched by a man. In the other the new bride, a streak of blood on her sheets.

With me in his arms, Signor Albertinelli struggles up the stairs to the first-floor bedroom. He lays me on the bed, and pauses a moment to mop his brow.

'My father took me to the whorehouse to rid me of what he saw as the burden of my virginity.' He plumps the pillows behind me and sits down on the edge of the bed, catching his breath. 'I can't deny it gave me pleasure I had never imagined. But also regret. The moment of passion so fleeting. My mother, rest her soul, would have been mortified. So often tight-lipped, but more forthcoming as she grew ill. Cautioning me not to give away what could not be, in some way, returned, *capisci*?'

His piercing blue eyes are wild, inscrutable. And I know he is going to tell me that to take me, to devour me, will return something to him. My virtue to restore his own. And as he reaches for me, I prepare myself for what I have been warned might make me feel like I am being split through. I close my eyes.

But his hands touch my hair, not my body. And he plucks the pins one by one from my bun, letting it fall loose to my shoulders. Combs out my curls with his fingers.

'You are now my wife and must answer me with truth,' he says.

I nod, terrified, as he peels off his boots.

'*Allora!* When you are ready, you will tell me,' he says.

If he means what I think, I could cry with relief.

'Agreed?' he asks when I offer no answer.

I try to say thank you but the words barely sound.

He kisses my forehead and leaves the room.

Like a dunce I remain there, made rigid by disbelief, while he crashes around upstairs in the kitchen and returns with two hunks of bread slathered with what looks like boiled spinach and onion. In his other hand, a half-empty bottle of wine.

'You ate nothing at the dinner,' he says, handing me the brimming plate.

I realise I am famished and accept it with gratitude.

He sits beside me and drinks from the bottle.

'Your father will have a black eye in the morning,' he says, taking a long swig.

'I'm sorry for his behaviour,' I say. 'He's been drunk for three days.'

'The notary put him in his place,' he says, a hint of a grin. 'And, who knows, maybe Signora Ottolini will forgive and forget the piss on her shoes.'

We laugh so hard together I choke on the bread halfway down my throat, and he pats my back to dislodge it. We share wine and stories about his father, the gold beater; his mother, the one woman he had given his heart. And, later, he takes the chaise and I have the bed. And I begin to think of him as Mariotto, the man I have married. Wondering if we might make a life; a life different, at least, to the one I had known.

As I change into my nightdress and slip into bed, I notice feelings unlike any before. The down-stuffed mattress as it cradles my body. The heavy drape of the linen I draw up to my chin. The bedposts are sentinels and the walls of the room feel like a fortress. I know that I will sleep through the night without having to strain for the uninvited steps of a man intent on consummating his marriage. I try to find words for the way that I feel. Not happiness or excitement, or even relief. Never once had I felt like this under the roof of my family home. And I realise that for the first time in my life I feel safe.

8

Beit HaKerem, 37 BCE

The rippling hills soar into peaks and plunge into valleys. Tawarei Yehuda, the hills and mountains of our land referred to with honour, ancient and sprawling. It is Elul, the month of repentance. In the Holy City the blast of the shofar horn will echo each morning, calling for reflection. We sit, snacking on raisin cake and apple dipped in date honey, while my mother dominates conversation. My husband's cousin Avner has accompanied Imma on this visit from Ḥevron and, like us, politely endures her long-winded gossip.

'One who is loved is called "son of a goldsmith"; one who is despised "son of a potter". One who is neither loved nor hated is "son of a glassmaker".' She laughs as if she is joking, but her tone suggests she thinks of Avner as common. I remind myself that Elul is a time for mercy.

If he is offended, Avner does not show it. When his gaze rests, for only a moment, on me, it is to convey that he is at ease, that I should not worry. And the warmth of his understanding stays with me.

His lavish gifts are of glorious glass vessels. Not only bowls and goblets, but bracelets of twisted glass and necklaces strung with glass beads. Faceted and bright, the beads glimmer like gemstones. *Sh'erin* for our wrists and *ḥalit'ta* for our necks. And, more peculiar, *anak* for our donkey.

'A pendant for a beast?' says my husband. 'Leave that to the pagans.'

'He's hung jewels on his donkey as if it were a king.' Imma snorts her disapproval.

And indeed Avner's donkey, Hamor, wears an oversized medallion of twisted yellow and blue glass around his neck, and a string of yellow beads braided into his tail.

'What craftsmanship!' My husband, quite smitten, holds out his hand: a Tyrian-blue glass crescent, a slice of sky, in his palm. 'But for a donkey?'

'What man do you know who could carry loads like a donkey?' says Avner.

My husband chuckles, amused by the logic.

And so our old donkey, Luda, will wear her first pendant.

Avner excuses himself to tend to his own donkey and the air seems to shift as he leaves. I admire him, his composure, despite Imma's barbs.

Both he and my mother are unexpected in their visit, with him accompanying her as my father's health declines.

'Walks out the door and loses all sense of direction. I can't bear the hysterics.' It's all Imma offers on Abba's condition, preferring instead to needle at me. 'How frail you look,' she says, her eyes surveying my body. 'And yet flaccid.'

She takes my arm by the wrist and lifts it, waggling it so that the flesh above my elbow wobbles. 'See what happens when there are no babies to carry.'

I say nothing, although I want to blurt it all out there and then. Because with this full moon I am six days past my due bleeding.

'Not a word until seven days have passed,' warned Corinna, Zakhariya's maidservant since he entered the priesthood, who is known for her medicines to aid expectant mothers. 'A grandmother conjures a grandchild at any first sign and her loss doubles the moment she doesn't get what she wants. You think you've seen her worst?'

'*T'he*,' Imma says to my husband. As if an apology must be issued as long as no child appears. 'We would take her back, but what would we do with her? She has no brawn left to compete with my maids.' She laughs with an unsmiling mouth.

Avner rejoins us, so I don't make a fuss. I know that, once we have eaten, he'll reveal the special gift for my mother and I am hopeful it will divert her attention.

Avner and Zakhariya are distant cousins, but could pass as brothers. The shapes of their faces, the unrounded silver ends of their beards. Cheek tufted with fine silver hair. Their profiles matched by nose-bones knotted at the bridge, my husband's knocked out of place in a fall as a child. For Avner, I imagine something more daring. As they'd greeted each other, their shadows had drawn a matching outline on the wall of the courtyard. And I'd traced them round with my mind.

In a world where abundance of kin is valued, Zakhariya and I share the peculiar quality of being only children. And I am swept away with imagining a real-life brother for my husband. A brother-in-law for me. A man whose right to *y'bum* – to marry me if Zakhariya was to die before a child was born to us – would stir an uneasy but not disagreeable contemplation.

Avner's array of glassware is impressive, but the glass jewellery is dazzling. An Egyptian-style chest plate of conical beads in leaf greens, spaced by tiny facets of carnelian. A bracelet of slender cylinders, purple as mandrake flower. A necklace of yellow beads, the size of apricot pits, finished with a silver clasp. There are strings of ochre and red decorative beads for ankles and belts, as pleasing to the touch as the soft underbelly of a lamb. Zakhariya lifts a string of beads and remarks on their clarity, spinning them on their dyed thread so they glint like gems.

'We swoon over melted sand,' Zakhariya laughs, poring over a pendant etched with a cluster of grapes.

'They could be mistaken for jewels,' I say.

'I learned from the best,' says Avner.

'In Persia?' I ask.

'Ashur,' replies Avner.

'If only she'd shown as much interest in household duties,' says Imma. 'You remember?' She directs the question at Avner.

Avner sees my embarrassment at the memory of when I had crept into his Ḥevron workshop, hiding from my mother, asking more questions than a girl ever should. My mother screaming in the streets, fearing I'd been taken by bandits. I'd marvelled at two things that day. One, that Avner had not sent me home. And two, that my mother had not wished, as she often said, that bandits might relieve her of the burden that was her incorrigible daughter.

I study the beads of one of the necklaces, their colour like the washed blue of dawn. 'How do they make it?' I ask.

'The women of my village thread them,' Avner says. 'Much better than I could.'

'Not the threading,' I say. 'The glass.'

'You don't know it, the story?' asks my husband.

'Why would I ask if I knew?' I say, irritated by his pomp in front of his cousin.

'A mere accident,' continues Zakhariya, oblivious to my irritation. 'By Pinikaya sailors cooking on the beach. Such a story, eh, Avner? Tell the story, tell my wife.'

'A story indeed,' says Avner, doing as he is bid. 'The sailors had set up camp —'

'On a beach, near a river mouth,' my husband interrupts. 'Go on, tell it, Avner. Tell it just as it happened.'

'They set up camp on the shores —'

'And they tried to find stones to put their cooking pots upon,' Zakhariya interjects. He cannot control his excitement. 'But, no stones! Not one to be found. But the ship carried blocks of nitrum. So they used those instead.' My husband is bursting, taking over the story. 'Lit their fires, warmed their hands, placed their pots on top of the nitrum blocks and then – of course you can guess! – the nitrum heated and mixed with sand, making a river of glass beneath their feet.'

'A river of glass?' I ask, sceptical. 'From sailors cooking on the beach?'

Avner exhales and scrubs a hand at his head, not wanting to undermine my husband's conviction.

'Well told, Avner!' says Zakhariya, either unaware or ignoring my doubt at his version of the story.

Without wanting to, I leave it be. I am bold enough to ask questions where many wives would not dare. But I will not argue with my husband in public. I distract myself with admiring the pieces laid out on the rug. Admiring the colours and shapes of Avner's glass beads.

'Nothing I haven't seen,' says Imma, poking at some pieces.

Avner reaches into the sack by his side. Peels back the waxed linen to reveal a small vessel.

Imma stifles a gasp.

Where the other pieces are lit with sea greens and sky blues, yellows like thistle flowers, red like anemone blooms, this piece is pure black.

'Take it,' he says, discarding its wrapper, passing it to me.

Zakhariya wipes laughter-tears from his eyes, still enthralled by his own story. 'Can you imagine their faces, those sailors?'

I take the black glass. The shape is unusual, like nothing I've seen. Curvilinear, like an eye. Resolving into a softened point at each end. As if made to fit in my palm. It has an ebony sheen that winks and shimmers, as mesmerising as the eye of a desert snake under moonlight.

'My beautiful error,' says Avner.

'Because of its shape?' I ask, wondering at the value of a thing that doesn't seem built for any practical use.

'Because it is black,' he corrects me. 'It was meant to be blue.' He combs his fingers through the fuzzy ends of his beard, our attention fixed on the glass.

'Let me see it,' says Imma, trying to snatch it from my hand.

And for the first time in my life, I deny her, wrapping my fingers around it.

'Please go on, Avner,' I say.

'A noblewoman from Kafrisin sent me chunks of blue stone she claimed would make the brilliant sky-blue glass she desired for her perfume bottles. The grounds seemed blue enough, even as I fashioned the vessels, perhaps an odd tinge of purple, but when it had cooled, her sky blue had become night.'

'Without the gift of night, we cannot have each new day,' I say, offering it back.

He refuses to take it. 'It is every glassmaker's hope that his glass finds its way into appreciative hands.'

And while I feel it would be polite to insist on its return, I want this black glass. '*Hodaya*, Avner,' I thank him. 'I've never seen such a beautiful error.'

At the evening meal, Imma chews loudly and licks her fingers. She usually picks like a sparrow over her food, and I wonder what has brought on this appetite.

When we are done, Avner passes his gift to my mother. It is a glass turquoise pin for the mantle she wears over her tunic. She twirls it in her hand, its translucent green blue catches the light; a sharp spine of finely wrought silver is fused to a clasp at one end. It is only the length of a thumb, but each side is engraved with the same fruit that decorates the hem of the high priest's coat: pomegranates, three of them, in perfect miniature detail.

'Useful at least. Fix it on,' she says, and I move to attend her, but she holds it towards Bayla, who removes the plain bone that holds Imma's mantle to the shoulder of her tunic and replaces it with the sculpted glass pin.

'Too much cumin,' says Imma, pushing flatbread through her second bowl of lamb stew.

She wipes at her chin with a moist cloth, gulps some wine, then fills her mouth with figs soaked in carob juice, murmuring her pleasure as she chews. I've never seen her devour food this way. Not the food I prepare.

'I'm sorry,' she says, covering her full mouth with her hand. 'I was like this with you too. Ravenous in the first three moons of my term.'

She bursts salted caperberries between her teeth, sucks at their seedy insides, avoiding my eyes and pretending she doesn't know she has left me reeling.

'Why didn't you tell us you were carrying, Imma?' I ask. Falling for her trap like the credulous lamb I become in her presence.

'You were dazzled by Avner and his glass. How could I compete?'

'*Mazala tava!*' says Zakhariya, the first to recover from his shock and offer well wishes.

Bayla wary, awaits my instruction. My stomach is upside-down and the room seems to sway. Avner clears his throat in discomfort.

One thousand memories spill through my mind, of every bead she sewed neater than mine, every piece of flatbread rolled to perfection beside my clumsier versions, her balls of yard spun with strong, even threads.

Against Corinna's advice, I make my announcement.

'I am six days past bleeding.'

Imma looks first at Zakhariya, who nods.

'We are all blessed!' She bares her palms to the heavens to praise Ribon Alma. 'Our boys will be so close in age,' she says, keeping her thoughts from the possibility of a girl.

She cups my face in her hands, kisses my forehead.

'When shall I announce it?' asks my mother, at once making the news her own. But the part of me that yearns for my mother's approval cannot help but enjoy her excitement.

'We will wait until she is through the first three moons, Tsova,' replies Zakhariya.

'Better to be safe,' says Imma, nodding her agreement with my husband. 'After all, this is Elisheva.'

Avner is leaning against the wall of our courtyard. In his hand is a clay pipe with the smoke of died calamus rising from it, its sweet, pungent scent trailing on the brisk mountain breeze. The smoke from this leaf is known to make its inhaler dizzy and free with their mouth. He breathes deeply as the smoke coils to the stars. My body stirs with desire, then shame. I shake myself to my senses. Corinna has warned me that carrying gives a woman many feelings that are not her own.

I slip inside and take the black glass vessel from the shelf next to the clay pitchers. The soft cast of the worktable's clay lamp winks back from its glossy dark sheen. It is just as beautiful as it was in sunlight. Perhaps even more so.

Always, it seems, in our prayers a pursuit of white. Where are the prayers for the enfolding comfort of darkness?

Purge me with hyssop and I will be pure, wash me and I will be whiter than snow.

'But where could we find respite from the sun,' Savta had said, straightening the twisted belt of my tunic, 'if not for the presence of shadow?'

I touch the smooth coolness of the glass to my cheek.

A shadow shifts in the doorway.

Avner is beside me.

'*Ta'heh! Ta'heh!*' He apologises for startling me.

His body heat cloaks my skin. I step backwards, away from him, and stumble. The vessel slips from my grasp. But he is swift, his hands around the object in a flash. Close enough to catch it with one hand as it falls.

He offers me the object again and I open my palms. He places the vessel inside and closes my fingers around it. I want to snatch my hands away but, for a moment, I cannot. This man, so like my husband. But who is not. I pull back my hands.

'I could have made another,' he says. 'Perhaps made a few, but not many. I've tried to replicate the recipe without success. All my life I've managed to repeat my mistakes. But this one I cannot.' He laughs, fragrant smoke billowing sideways under the force of his breath.

'You must teach me how to work with the glass,' I say, being bold in the moment. Perhaps to spite my mother. Perhaps to impress him. Perhaps the smoke that I have breathed in from the pipe.

He sets the pipe on the table and folds his arms at his chest. Appears to consider my demand with neither amusement nor doubt.

'It's hard work,' he says. 'You will sweat, you will ache. You will suffer burns in distraction.'

Corinna warned me of the new feelings that might arise in my body in the first three moons of carrying. But my body burns in his presence. The glass in my hand is warm and slippery in my palm.

'*Sh'lama*, Avner.' I wish him goodnight.

'Of course. *Ta'heh*.' He apologises a third time.

He passes Bayla at the door. Her sixth sense for those who creep in the night has brought her to me.

He stops and turns again to me. 'If Zakhariya permits it, I will teach you.'

As my mother's body swells and ripens with a growing baby, mine does not. No bleeding, no miscarriage, nothing to tell me either way what is happening inside me. By the time my new brother, Tsadok, takes his name at *g'zura*, the ritual where a boy loses his foreskin and gains a name, I have been childless and bloodless for nine moons.

I both cherish and resent this new baby's squirming presence. His perfect maleness, his everything-my-parents-could-pray-for presence, his tiny fingers that clutch at my mother's breast, her adoration as he feeds. My visits home are reluctant, but it seems I am the only woman who can ease Tsadok's crying, and he reaches for me from Imma's arms, making her jealous. Any effort not to adore him myself is now futile.

When his first tooth appears, I try to teach him his name. He turns red with effort and blurts out, 'Tsad!' I clap and repeat it over and over, and the name sticks, much to Imma's objection.

On the evening that my brother takes his first steps, the wind shrieks and trees thrash and twist on their trunks. I too feel this fury. I take the dandelion seed, kept in a pouch under my pallet since the night of my betrothal, and go out, as I have not for many years, into the storm. I flick the seed from my fingertips and scream my despair into the wind. My prayers have not been answered. Perhaps not even heard.

When I greet Zakhariya later, he reaches his hand towards me, takes something between his finger and thumb; shows me, like he did so many moons ago, a dandelion seed plucked from my tunic.

'I don't want it,' I say, pushing his hand from me.

I lie alone on my pallet, holding aloft the black glass from Avner.

Does it fix its sight on me like a stalking snake under moonlight? Or is this an eye that sees this sorrow, and will not look away?

My arm drops to my side. Every part of me aches with the exhaustion of waiting, the fatigue of hoping. Of bearing the shame of being ignored by Ribon Alma, who seems to bless every woman but me.

I close my eyes and try to welcome darkness.

Where could I rest if not in shadow?

9

Florence, 1512

At our osteria, Il Pennello, there is no rest from the long hours of making food, serving it, cleaning up after patrons. Buoyed by the accolades for the food and wine during his time helping my father at the Drago, Mariotto, my ever-changeable husband, had been inspired to set up a hostelry for himself. Set amid Lorenzo de' Medici's famous taverns outside Porta San Gallo, patrons flock to his unpredictable but amiable hosting. And to be in company with many of the artists making their name in the city.

'When you serve food and wine, every man is your friend,' Mariotto said, by way of explanation. But we all knew the sharp tongues of Florentine critics had wounded his pride when it came to his painting.

'For goodness' sake, stop your pacing,' I say to my husband, who has not risen early, like me, but has not been to bed. 'Michel is right. You are a wretched *persona inquietissima*. More restless than a fly in a bottle.'

'Remember the ham hocks; the patrons devour them. Buy all you can carry,' Mariotto says. 'And go to the Piazza del Pesce for the fish. Not the market, *capisci?*'

'Seven years married and three years running your osteria, you think I don't know what I'm doing?' I say. 'How about you darn your own hose while I'm at the markets.'

'They need stitching?' Mariotto twists his neck to check for holes in the back of his hose, missing my point.

At the markets, I push my way through the dawn crowds who, like me, arrive early to barter for grain and meat and fish and wine. Trails of stewed eel and spit pork lace the air, some apprentices unable to resist a mouthful of the foods procured for their masters. As I fill my basket, I recognise my father's distinctive tenor, hollering to no one in particular.

'*Sono solo. Sono solo!*' I am alone. I am alone! His relentless lament.

I catch sight of him staggering to and fro under the soaring granite Column of Abundance, topped by Donatello's goddess of plenty. He wields a wine jug in one hand, the other scraping the air as he tries to find balance. He trips and slams one knee into the pavement, kneeling like a man pleading with his god for mercy.

'Go home, Franco!' yells Giovanni the Ortolano, his rickety cart topped with cabbages and onions and warm bread. He tosses a loaf and it skids across the stones. 'Go home, take a wash. Even the pigs are offended.'

'Babbo!' I call out as I hurry towards him. If he hears me, he doesn't show it. 'Babbo, here, take my arm.'

It is the anniversary of my mother's death, and my father's first years of callous indifference have resolved into an unexpected and prolonged grief that seems to worsen each year. His hair and beard have grown together like that of a man who has lived a lifetime in the mountains and stumbled, baffled and overwhelmed, into the city. The winter has been harsh and the wind bites at my cheeks until they sting, yet he wears only a grimy smock and torn hose.

I hook an arm through his to try to help him stand and the reek from his skin makes me retch.

'You left me too, *mia pulcina*,' he says, hoisting himself onto one foot, then the other, and leaning hard against me to stand.

'I told you, Babbo, Mariotto took me to Prato. He went to discuss a commission.'

'Prato? So he's painting again?' He throws back his head, tips the wine jug to his lips. The dregs pour over his face. He wipes at his mouth with a grimy sleeve.

'Did Isabella deliver fresh shirts and hose?' I ask. I have paid her extra to do so.

'*Quella puttana!* That slut!' replies Babbo, his instant anger making me feel short of breath. '*Finito.*'

'I'll get you fresh shirts, Babbo,' I say to quell him.

'*Mia pulcina,*' he says, his gummy eyes leaking. 'What have we come to?'

The cold wind whips through the small space between us.

'I hear the Lady Alfonsina has finally come into good fortune?' says my father, a fleeting sobriety.

It was a drunkard's most curious trait, of which Mariotto too was capable. Forgetting the most immediate and obvious things and then remembering in detail something nuanced and complicated. Of course, there was always an agenda to a drunken man's selective memory.

'*Sì*, Babbo,' I reply. 'The Lady Alfonsina has won back her money.'

Lady Alfonsina Orsini is Mariotto's key patron. She is also the widow of Piero de' Medici and daughter-in-law of Florence's beloved patron of the arts, Lorenzo the Magnificent. When Lorenzo's sons were banished from Florence, her dowry was seized. But it's said she'll now return victorious from Rome with it reinstated. And, likewise, Mariotto rushed to his lady patron, in the hope of restoring his own income and status on the back of her good fortune.

'*Allora* ...' Babbo waggles his finger back and forth. 'Your father chose well after all. A patron with Medici riches.'

And there it is. The mention of money.

'The Lady Alfonsina doesn't have the wealth of the family she married into,' I say.

'Balls!' says my father. 'A slut, like them all.' He kicks the loaf tossed to him by Giovanni.

I don't argue the point of my husband's imagined wealth with Babbo.

'Mariotto's student, Jacopo da Pontormo, is showing great promise.' I try to placate my father's distemper with good news. 'And has the added benefit of bringing gossip from Leonardo's workshop.'

'Is it true he inspects a man's arsehole in order to draw it?' Before I can answer he thrusts a hand to my belly. 'Married how many years? And no children?'

I recoil under the force of his touch. My instinct is to slap his hand from me but, in his state, I worry that he might hit back.

'Is the great artist a limp cock?' He grabs me and pulls me under his arm, the way he once did to my mother. Presses his wet lips to my cheek. 'So like her, you are. So much like your mother.'

It had been Signora Ottolini who'd taken me aside by the elbow one morning after church service. My father, still drunk to his hat, was making a rare appearance by my side.

'Men full with liquor and grief see their wives in their daughters.' She'd gripped my arm, even when I tried to politely retract it, until she could see that I'd heard. If not understood.

But I understand now. And decide not to take my father to his home but to ours. Isabella can bathe him and he can sleep off his stupor while I take care of lunch service downstairs at the osteria.

'Mariotto's latest wine is winning praises,' I say to persuade him.

'From Michelangelo or Pontormo?' he asks.

'Pontormo,' I reply.

My father is satisfied. 'Michelangelo couldn't tell good wine from horse piss.'

And as is the way with all hardened drinkers, my father suddenly finds his balance and sense of direction, and sets off for *Il Pennello*. His mind on the wine that awaits him and his ambition to get there as fast as he can.

*

'He needs to remarry,' Mariotto says, when my bathed father is snoring from the chaise.

I follow him up to his study, collecting flung clothes from balustrades and scrunched sketches scattered on the stairs.

'How about Isabella?' He is fussing about his jumbled desk, looking under drawings sketched with charcoal, opening and closing drawers.

'Isabella is already married,' I say, handing him a drawing from the floor near the fireplace: the head of a warhorse, contorted with pain.

'Not that one,' he says, batting it with an impatient hand. 'Buonarroti wants to see my cartoon for Benintendi's *storiette*.' He rifles through more papers on the sideboard under the window, sending them in all directions. 'Why doesn't the damned maid tidy in here?' He raises his voice, fumbling through the bundles stacked on a chair.

'Because you forbade her,' I reply, even though he's not listening.

'She's lost it!' He is pacing the room, cursing the maid for what he imagines she has done. He tugs on his hair and kicks over a jug crammed with brushes, left on the floor, then walks to his desk and begins the process again.

'Mariotto, *calmati*! You'll have Babbo reacting.'

He snatches his paint palette from the top of another pile and agitates a swab of blue paint with his finger, charging as he does from one task to another. 'Buonarroti needs to see this cartoon.'

'Buonarroti needs nothing!' says Michelangelo from where he stands in the doorway.

Mariotto throws open his arms. '*Ciao amico!*' he says, embracing Michelangelo, leaving a streak of sky blue on the back of his doublet.

'Welcome back, Michel,' I say, and he comes to embrace me.

Which, so I'm told, I should take as a grand compliment.

His musty smell is familiar. He is, as always, rumpled of feature and dress. I believe Mariotto when he tells me that when Michel is working a commission, he sleeps in his clothes. Even his boots. The work on the Chapel has seen him carry a perpetually harassed expression not wholly redeemed by his earnest brown eyes.

'I hear the pope's ceiling leaves all who see it struck dumb,' says Mariotto.

'All but the pope,' says Michel. 'He could choke on the eels he so likes to gorge and still find the air to bellow his complaints.'

Mariotto laughs with delight.

Michel's fiery rows with Pope Julius provide fine gossip in both Rome and in Florence.

'Lose the pope from your mind,' says Mariotto, leading Michel back downstairs. 'Aim to outlive him. Then you'll have the last word.'

A hurricane of mess is left in Mariotto's wake: paint and oil dripped and splotched, unfinished cartoons strewn on the floor. Among them a new sketch catches my eye. The Lady Alfonsina in profile with pleasing proportions that manage to bring out the best in her features. The squint of her eyes made more almond shaped, a delicate neckline to distract from shoulders that otherwise might appear hunched. I smooth out the discarded cartoons and neaten the sprawl of paint pots and wet brushes. It's only when I dismantle what I think is his reeking clothes from a filthy heap on his desk that I see his new experiment.

Under food-spattered nightshirts, soiled stockings and rags used for blotting, there are four jars packed into a crate. I lean closer and the smell hits me. The jars appear to be surrounded by rotting manure. I step back and cover my nose. The last time I found jars they were filled with honey and faeces, acquired after he'd been told by an apothecary this would ease his nagging sore throat.

This smell is different. Pungent but not putrid. Hands over my nose and mouth, I step even closer. Each jar is filled with liquid, vinegar from its smell. Suspended above the vinegar are slim grey metal plates. I know them to be lead, since I was the one sent to fetch them from the convent of Santa Caterina da Siena, where nuns' toil over medicines matches that of an artist's toil over pigment. Working with heavy pestles and mortars, grinding stones and seeds, heating elixirs, sifting and straining, to produce perfumes and potions.

A fine white powder coats the strips. I slide my finger across the surface, examine the residue that transfers to my fingertip. A granite pestle and mortar nearby overflows with this powder, a flint muller and marble slab scattered with amassettes to scrape the colour from the slab. Next to this is a palette with various splodges, from vivid white to a blanched grey. The gradation of colour is a work of art in itself, and evidence of Mariotto's obsessive attention to every measure that precedes the moment when his brush touches the canvas. If only all these painstaking steps could be known by those so ready to criticise a painter's work. Who deem the work of a painter to be base. Not like noble poets, who have no need to sully their shirtfronts to make their creations. But what would our churches and altars be without colour? Without the grinding labour of dust and stains that produces their glory?

I spy the cartoon he was seeking, stuffed at the back of the jars, fish it out and lay it where he might see it. Then return my attention to the experiments in white.

For all his haphazard ways, Mariotto's exacting eye towards pigment has taught me about the deeper nature of colour. What each shade should invoke. In his mind, a green is not green unless it captures some secret. A red not red unless it conjures some contrary sense of fervour and rancour. And how could a colour be named royal purple if one's hand doesn't move to one's heart before its radiance? As for white, this has become his obsession. A fixation with the colour able to present both transparency and transcendence. The colour that determines the beauty of all others. That, from the very beginning, determines the success of the work. Like I'd already learned from Lucia.

Per quei colori che desideri essere belli, prepara sempre un terreno bianco puro. 'For those colours you wish to be beautiful, always prepare a pure white ground,' I said, thinking it would impress my husband.

'I knew it long before Maestro Leonardo said it!' Mariotto is jealous of the older master, whose teachings are highly sought-after and esteemed.

I too felt disturbed, because I had believed these to have been wise words from Lucia.

Mariotto thuds back up the stairs.

'Sarto is here, vaunting about his atrium frescoes,' he says, begrudging Andrea del Sarto's broad-ranging talent.

Mariotto is shoeless, his unclipped toenails poking through holed and paint-spattered stockings.

'Will you not change?' I ask him, handing him the sketch he was seeking.

'My soul is as good as set,' he replies. 'No hope for me now.'

'Your clothes, you buffoon,' I say, finding affection and humour in my husband's hopeless self-awareness, his complete knowledge of his flaws with no apparent desire to change himself for the better.

'Will you join us?' he asks, touching a thumb to my cheekbone. 'Your father's awake, if not sober.'

It is uncommon in Florence to be invited to socialise with men. For that fact alone, I join my husband downstairs.

My father sits at ease with the artists around him. '*Mia pulcina*.' He opens his arms. 'Come, greet your *babbo*.'

I accept a kiss to each cheek and he holds me too long in his embrace.

'You look refreshed, Babbo.' I pull myself from him, resisting the urge to wipe away the dampness his lips left on my face.

'She refused to wash my balls,' he says of the maid, slapping his knee as if it was a joke we could both share.

'*Allora*, Franco,' says Mariotto. 'No such language in front of my wife.' He winks at my father to soften his comment. I am grateful to retreat to a chair by the hearth, where I take up my stitching.

The men are at ease with my presence and expect nothing from me. Later I will serve them marzolino cheese and olives, but they wouldn't fuss if I didn't. They'd tear up stale loaves, soak the crusts in cold broth, or to sop up the dregs of the wine.

Already Michel and Sarto are arguing. The same sticking point as always: Leonardo.

'He's a dreamer, not an artist,' says Michel. The bones of his face are as sharp as his opinions. He coughs hard. 'Thinks he can fly like a bird. What fool would try?'

'He hasn't hewn a man from marble,' says Mariotto, seeming to weigh up in his mind the fairness of Michel's claim.

Michel grunts in semi-satisfaction.

'They used his giant clay horse as target practice.' My father makes an unexpected contribution to the conversation.

'Well reported,' says Michel. 'Nothing more to be said.'

'How are things with the Chapel?' Sarto asks Michel.

Even I can see he has said it to goad him.

'Curse you, Sarto,' says Michel. 'For a sublime moment the Chapel was forgotten.'

'I doubt you could forget a single brushstroke you've made, let alone an entire ceiling,' says Sarto, draining his cup.

'And it will kill me,' says Michel. He scrubs his face with his hands, leaving his eyebrows mussed and wild.

'Why do you grieve?' asks my father, roused by Michel's angry despair. 'The pope says it is the greatest work yet to be painted. You are finished!'

'*Finished?*' Michel glares at my father, disregarding the compliment and hearing only one word. 'It will never be finished. And I will be damned to repaint that blasted ceiling in my mind for eternity.'

'All of us damned, one way or another,' says my father, swaying under the weight of this incurable fact within him. A mumble of agreement among the men.

'*Allora*, Antonia,' Michel addresses me, looking fearsome and doe-eyed all at once. 'How does Mariotto fare in his pursuit of the perfect white paint?'

'He can't find a brush in his study let alone a perfect colour.'

The men roar with laughter and pound their fists on the tables.

'She's a quick wit, this one,' says Sarto.

'Always too quick for me,' says my father. 'So much like her mother …'

I turn back to stitching the seam in Mariotto's worn doublet. Ignoring the continued laments by my father.

He sways on his chair. 'My dear Marietta —'

'You should give your wife charge over your pursuit of white paint, Albertinelli,' Michel interrupts Babbo, casting him a pitying glance. 'Unlike you, Albertinelli, she has the aptitude for endurance.'

Mariotto rubs at his chin, his eyes beginning to sag into the heavy content of a man well-wined. The men fall silent, the kind of silence that is said to occur when an angel falls from heaven. Punctuated by the sharp crack of my father's head on the tiles as he falls off his chair.

'I must leave tomorrow,' says Michel, setting my father back on the chaise.

'I am sorry to hear it,' I say.

'You want me to take him home?' he asks, a curt nod towards Babbo.

'He has no one else,' I reply, the confusion I feel towards my father rising up and tightening my throat.

'He is okay? Here with you?' Michel's tone is frank.

'He is my father,' I say.

'Still a man,' says Michel. 'A man who needs to remarry.'

It is an hour before dawn and, unable to sleep for Mariotto's snoring, I tiptoe upstairs to start the bread dough for those men who will expect food. Too drunk to get themselves home before curfew.

I see his shadow move in the corner. His smell sour in the darkness. He lunges. It happens quickly. He is forceful. My head smacks the stone wall, then he turns me and lays my arse bare. If I scream, the younger men will stir. Franciabigio or Pontormo, asleep on the floor of the loggia. But I think of their faces seeing this, my own father. And the crush of shame is already too much to bear. His fingers probe me and I'm trying to twist from his grip, to swing back my fists. Then I feel the hot stinging of my flesh as he pushes himself inside. Not in the place where babies are made.

'A man with no desire for a son but set on satisfying himself will take any hole,' Lucia had warned me.

'Marietta, Marietta.' He buries his face in the back of my neck.

The sickness of my mother's name being uttered.

And then it is over. My body throbbing, stinging. He pulls back and stumbles back across the kitchen, groaning and whimpering like a kicked dog. Chairs scraping across the floor and then tumbling, clattering, he careens down the stairs. He leaves the house, nobody waking. My prayer that they will not. As I breathe my ribs ache where he has gripped me.

I hide myself in Mariotto's study, under the desk. My face in my shaking hands, cowering with a shame that should not be mine.

Where can I put my mind that is not on this moment, this body?

'When one is painting, one does not think,' Raffaello said once.

'For me, to mix the paint, especially the white, is to make myself new,' Mariotto had replied.

I want to not think. I want to be new.

Back in the kitchen I boil a pot of water, add the last drops of costmary oil, a gift from Mariotto. Its mint and sage scents are known to calm and cleanse. I strip myself down and wash every part of my body; twisting the sodden cloth so warm water streams down my face, sluices my tears, purges my skin. Then I put right the furniture. Set the bread dough to rise. And, once that is done, I return to the study. It doesn't feel like my feet that walk down the stairs. I crawl under the Mariotto's desk and pull my knees to my chest, beseeching Elisheva to send me Zia Lucia, until morning light brightens Florence and the men stir from sleep.

I serve food and clear dishes, then excuse myself and return to the study. I cannot wield a paintbrush, but I've seen enough to know how to grind and mix paint. I will make myself new by creating a paint all artists will covet. A white so pure that painted wings of an angel will fly from the canvas. A white that, with a speck, will bestow divine light into the eyes of a saint. That will lift me out of this body. That will vanquish the shadows that crawl under my skin. A white to release me.

10

Beit HaKerem, 29 BCE

This lustrous black takes me under its wing like a phoenix. However this is not a bird that rises from ashes but from a crucible of molten sand and natron. I place the vessel of black glass, my best piece yet, back on the shelf. Then sit on my stool near the furnace and take up my blowpipe.

Every moment of this work, of flame and breath, of careful timing and the risk of loss, brings with it a bolt of joy as the lump of gather takes on form, becomes a vessel that, with steady cooling and prayers, I will soon hold in my hands.

I push the pipe inside the furnace, twist it into the melt to take a gather of glass. I withdraw the pipe, still twisting so the gather doesn't drip. Roll the gather across the flat slab in front of the furnace, to lengthen it and make it a uniform shape. A sharp inhale. I press my lips to the end of the pipe, a steady exhale, and the molten gather at its other end swells. I return the gather to the furnace, twisting it through the flames, and ready the large jacks on my thigh. The jacks are a single band of metal, forged and bent into a curve. Their pincers are tapered such that, when squeezed, they can grasp and press and pull the hot gather to shape it. But Avner also showed me how they can be placed on the upper leg, their dull-bladed edges used as a surface for rolling the pipe in the perpetual motion needed so that my hands don't suffer burns from the hot pipe, and so molten glass doesn't drip out of shape.

The workshop where I have mastered all Avner taught me is built above our home in Beit HaKerem. Easy to reach up through terraces from our courtyard, a switchback to its top. From up here, I can look down into our courtyard, and to the village. And behind me, up to the summit of the high mountain. The four small windows cut into the workshop's walls usher in enough breeze to stoke the fire and ventilate a room that would otherwise be stifling.

How can I dare say that this work too is sacred, like grinding grain or weaving or baking? This is *tsar.* The act of creating. Of transforming one thing into another with a simple breath. An act that might be called sinful should I express the elation it brings, how it makes my heart dance like the flickering fire that transforms grit into glass.

M'shuga'at. This is my name among some of the priests. A crazy woman. Their reasoning to explain a woman who doesn't appear to know her place.

Perhaps this is the name they will now call Princess Mariamne. Who will soon stand trial against her husband's accusations. I shake the grim thought from my mind and focus on my work. The scars on the tender underside of my wrist are enough to remind me that to lose concentration is to risk being burned by the hot metal tools.

'Calm yourself, *ḥavivta,*' Zakhariya said, as I recounted in shock the name I'd overheard.

'Making bread, spinning wool, bearing children. Every act serves a function for her husband, for her family,' I said. 'But if Ribon Alma creates daily for the joy of the work and we are made as our God, then why not I? Why must a woman with a mind of her own suffer insults?'

'I am too old to argue,' my husband said. 'Please! Be still.'

'What you mean is be quiet,' I said. 'Why don't you tell *them* to be quiet?'

He'd looked aged in that moment. Furrowed and defeated. And while I'd wanted to relent, to let him know that I was grateful for his tacit approval of my glasswork, for his calling Avner to teach me all that he knew, I could not pretend.

'Isn't it enough that I allow you to continue your work?' he asked.

'No,' I replied. 'It is not.'

The small furnace has been built with bricks fashioned into a dome, an arm's length in width, a height twice that, and smothered in mortar. Jujube wood and cedar brings the fire up to temperature, but it is olive wood and *gifta*, the highly sought olive pressings, that are best for the constant heat needed for glass. The firebox is small but efficient and the supply of wood is carried in by our friend Yirmiyahu, who lives at the edge of our village. His wife, Yiska, sometimes accompanies him and I always enjoy her kind, lighthearted company.

It takes five by five cubits of wood to burn at glowing temperature for three days. In the early days of my lessons, the heat was too much and I would reel from the workshop, dripping and breathless. But I have mastered another skill of this work. The calming of my body by slowing my breath. The rise and fall of my chest so slow, that the in-breath seems to blend with the out in one continuous prayer of existence. In this space, Ribon Alma feels close. Each precious moment of time holding its own discrete value, with its own unique sanctity. A sacred wisdom passed down to me by my grandmother. One I long to pass on myself.

So much of this work relies upon keeping the glass at the right heat, but the strength of the vessel is achieved only by a slow and steady cooling. An alcove has been hollowed in the top of the furnace, away from direct flame, where I place finished pieces to cool overnight.

The first vessel I made with any level of success was a goblet with a thick, uneven base and lopsided rim. It slouches on a shelf beside more elegant neighbours, to remind me how far my crafting has come. Now merchants from Cairo send for my pieces. Not only for my goblet's proportion and symmetry, but for my trademark rim: formed on one side by a slight, imperceptible depression, the perfect inverse shape of a drinking lip. I'm told that Marcus Antonius purchased one for his wife and queen, Cleopatra, from among the few pieces bought from me by merchants who trade at the ports and in the cities. Soon after, the queen's life was taken. Some say she was killed by a bite from an asp hidden in a basket. But there are those who claim she brewed poison and took her own life. I try not to wonder from what cup it was drunk.

I withdraw the pipe, blow again and the gather expands. One quick full-circle swing of the pipe to elongate the glass and it's now ready for shaping. I let my thoughts turn as I begin rolling the pipe across the jacks set on my thigh.

To think I might never have understood the ease a measured breath brings to each thought. When I am working the glass, forming its first shape with each exhale, everything that is hard to accept seems touched with a bearable clarity. Even the fate of Princess Mariamne.

Palgu-Yehuda'ei. She spat the name at her husband. Half-Jew. A title harmless enough when used to refer to the Petrans, whose ancestors converted to the faith of our people. Like many, Princess Mariamne's husband had a father who was an Edomite and who was a Yehuda'ei by conversion. And perhaps any other husband might have forgiven the name-calling. But Mariamne's husband was Herod, a man who found the thought of being half anything a torment, and who would not tolerate another who threatened his sense of power. Not even a wife.

As always, there is debate.

'Herod is a beast. She will be put to death.'

'He's a beast besotted. He will pardon his wife.'

'Pardon? He couldn't even spell it.'

'For her sake, pray he learns.'

I roll the pipe with one hand and wipe the sweat from my forehead before it drips into my eyes. Add a second blowpipe to the furnace to ready more glass for the base. This goblet is one of two for Ya'akov the Elder and his wife, Sara. I will mirror the twisting stems to show they are a pair when placed side by side.

'Pay close attention to the heat,' Avner had instructed me when he could see I was distracted by the steps, by the timing, the swift motions of pulling the pipe from the flames, to shaping the gather, then back to flames to keep it molten and liquid. 'Find your peace,' he'd say, the heat like a trap, all-consuming, smothering. 'Slow your breath. Slower. Find your pace with the heat and your peace with the flame.'

I push the glass against a pad of water-soaked leather, shaping and rounding in the protected palm of my hand. The idea so impressed Avner, he praised my husband for marrying a wife with a mind for invention. But I knew it was Avner's way of rebuking my detractors.

The radiant heat is fierce on my forearm; smoke hisses and billows and I blink hard against it. I squeeze the jacks on the end of the molten glass to draw out a narrow stem for the goblet. Hang this pipe on a hook. I take the second pipe with a small gather from the furnace, let a molten glob drop from it onto flat stone: this will form the base. I pull the wooden panel Avner made for me from the bucket of water beside me, using it to flatten the glob, then take the hung pipe and press the drawn stem to the centre of the base so they fuse together. A vessel begins to emerge. Then I use the jacks to perfect the shape of its base. I dip the jacks in the water and place two drops where the glass meets the pipe. The sudden cooling will create a small crack that allows me to detach the pipe from the goblet.

A dull throb in my temples warns I need water. A little salt in it helps; one of Avner's many pieces of advice. My thirst will have to wait. At this point timing is crucial.

With another pipe, I attach a small glob of molten glass to the base of the goblet so I can return it to the flame. Then I can shape the lip. Rounding out the opening, folding the edges to form a neat rim. Working against time before the vessel is too cool, a quick feather-light pressure to produce my near-invisible trademark dint on the rim. The finished vessel is tapped from the pipe, set in the alcove to cool. Always a rush of excitement at bringing a piece to fruition.

I stand and walk outside to drink long, straight from the jug. It's a relief to break from the heat and hunched posture in front of the furnace. The breeze has swung and now gusts from the west, cooling on my face. The trade winds bring their scent across the land from the coast of the Great Sea. A distance that takes a day to cross on foot whips across the skies in a morning. Such is the power of wind, of air. Of breath.

The Port of Azotus will be full with ships. Workers balancing their feet upon planks. Sacks of dyed wool hefted upon shoulders. Bolts of fabric hoisted and stacked. Maybe one day my pieces will be carried in the dark bowels of those ships to distant lands upon which I myself will never set foot. I feel a surge of both delight and shame at the thought. To want such a thing. To imagine my pieces as dandelion seeds, released and set free to settle in exotic empires and kingdoms.

When he agreed to my instruction by Avner, Zakhariya's condition was that it took place in Beit HaKerem, not Ḥevron. In the latter there were too many tongues casting too many judgments. I was uncomfortable at first with such an intimate arrangement. The workshop was small; he stood close to instruct and keep watch. But the urgent and ever-moving glasswork soon took all my attention. Every component demanded concentration and timing. And, oh! The elation of producing my first inexplicable pieces.

'Was your aim to make a rock hyrax?' Zakhariya asked, gravely inspecting one malformed glob.

And I had seen that it could be mistaken for the unclean rabbit that lives around the river banks of the Yarden. There are its ears, there's a snout, there the point of two tusk-like incisors.

'Throw it back in the fire,' I said, amusing Avner with my panic, as the rabbit glob was cast into the flames.

Back inside the workshop, I peer in at the piece that is cooling, no telltale signs of fine cracking. I tidy my tools and sweep the ash and dust and broken glass from the floor, then take my latest piece from the shelf.

Once I mastered my craft, Avner gifted me a small batch of the raw glass that made his beautiful error. The glass that entered the furnace as blue and emerged black. He has tried to create this colour again, but his lack of success means what is left is now rare. I turn the piece over in my hands, knowing Avner would admire its perfection. But I have added a new, secret element to his design. For this piece is hollow, with a tapered stopper fitted tight into its flared neck. I rubbed the neck smooth with a fine rasp, then flashed it again in high heat so the join disappeared. Inside there is room for a small piece of rolled linen or leather, upon which a prayer can be written.

I'm now ready to make the piece for which I've been practising. A gift for Tsad, for him to carry with him wherever he travels. So smitten is my little brother with onyx, the black volcanic glass found in the land of Havilah, that I'm told he carries a piece in a pouch at his waist. At first, Tsad's piece will look like Avner's. But hidden inside will be a prayer for his protection. Sealed in a way that you won't see its lid.

The thrill of my invention begins to dissolve. So often followed by overwhelming sorrow. For no matter what I can create with my hands, with my breath, my body has not created a child.

In Ḥevron, women stopped their show of polite smiles and forced greetings as we passed each other at the market. A protective grip on their children. The children of my cousins are now young men and women who have been betrothed, some married with children of their own. At first the sight of Aryeh, cousin Rivka's fifth boy, it hurt to breathe when she pushed her baby's head to her breast as if the sight of me would poison the child's unripe seed. At best, I am ignored. It is easier for me here in Beit HaKerem so, more and more, here I remain.

'Would you do it if I asked you?' I'd asked Bayla, overcome by a desperate pressure. Perhaps Imma was right and she was the one who should carry for my husband.

'I would have no choice,' she replied.

She did not appear the next morning to grind grain. The courtyard not raked. Water jugs still empty.

I know Bayla left for fear I might ask her in earnest. And once she left, I took refuge in my duties and my glasswork. I moved so quickly and completely into isolation that looking back on my life before seemed the life of another. Where once I would climb out my window and run to the hilltops in shrieking winds, I now close the shutters against the weather and whisper my prayers.

In Ḥevron, their name for me had been *Melḥa*. Salt. A substance that preserves but in which nothing grows. That would sooner poison than sprout a seed. But as I work, it strikes me as a glorious fact that salt is essential for these creations in glass. Avner taught me the exact amounts needed to lower the melt temperature. Without it, the furnace would run too hot. *Melḥa*. Salt. Here, the ingredient for fertile creations.

'*Ḥavivta?*' My husband announces himself with his term of endearment, *my darling*. He knows not to enter without calling. Any sudden draft or gust can change the temperature of the room and ruin a piece.

'You time it well,' I say, calling him inside. 'I must begin again.'

He joins me by the window and examines the piece for himself.

'*Paraḥta!*' he says, seeing as many forms in my ruined glass as he does cloud-shapes in the sky. Maybe I can see the vague shape of a bird.

He shuffles a moment, back and forth on the spot. And I know it has arrived. News of Princess Mariamne, what the judge has decided.

'He has condemned her,' he says.

He drags his fingers slowly through the ends of his beard. Despite the heat in the room, I bristle with chill.

Gamliel brought the report from Sart'ba, where Mariamne and her mother were kept hostage. He said that, as she entered the court, the princess's expression remained unmoved by the bullying crowd. Her own mother calling out insults, betraying her own daughter to save herself.

And so, by Herod's command, Princess Mariamne – his wife, and the mother of four of his children – will be sent to her death.

'She will hang,' says Zakhariya.

I feel my body weaken at the thought. The bird-shape falls from my grasp, smashes at my feet.

'The figs have ripened early,' Zakhariya says when he greets me in the courtyard at dusk.

I have seen as much in the valley, shocked that so many have dropped, their skins pocked by borers and honeyeaters, the rotten sides left untouched.

'The earth will grow rich because of what has fallen,' he says.

With his words, my exhaustion deepens. I excuse myself and retire early.

'I will come soon,' he says.

He arrives sooner than I expect. I am still brushing my hair, yet to braid it. His hand moves to my waist, his lips to my face. And my body rushes with the need for him. I kiss him hard and at first he pulls back, but I draw him to me. His lips and hands explore every soft, aching curve of my body.

'Where is your mind?' he whispers as we lie together afterwards.

I don't tell him that it's on the soft skin of Mariamne's neck.

He strokes my hair, his breath musky and sweet as sandalwood, traces his fingers across my cheek, then across my throat, and I flinch. I push away his hand and bring the linens up to my chin. Close my eyes to pray for the princess.

In the days after Princess Mariamne's hanging, Zakhariya visits me in the workshop. He knows I have not been sleeping. He brings grapes and a pile of flatbread with oil.

'You must eat, *ḥavivta*.'

I am bent over a piece that needs my attention, a commission for an Egyptian merchant. Zakhariya knows not to disrupt me. But he is lingering. Twisting on his heels and exhaling noisily.

'What else?' I ask, feeling impatient with his dawdling.

'Tsova wishes to visit.'

I stop rolling the pipe. The mere mention of my mother makes my hands unsteady.

'I've told them yes,' he says.

'Them?' The molten gather is falling out of shape, becoming lopsided, but I no longer care. Isn't this the true mark of a glassworker's grit? The letting go. The beginning again. The willingness to let one thing become another. I push the pipe into the fire and turn to face my husband. 'So she will bring my brother?'

I tremble with joy at the thought of seeing Tsad, who once bred such jealousy in me when Imma delivered her comparisons. His first words, four moons earlier than mine; his first steps, up and walking so quickly, not scuffing his knees in the dirt like I'm told I did until I was two; the sacred texts he could recite by age four.

'I requested it,' says my husband, and I rise from my work, grubby in my apron, to kiss his furry cheeks.

'What will you make today?' he asks, patting my back as if I were a child.

'I've finished Tsad's gift,' I reply.

'Remember your duty, *ḥavivta*,' he says, careful in his tone. 'Don't spoil your brother to punish your mother.'

And although he doesn't mean me to feel it, a coil of shame snakes up my throat. A flicker of jealousy that my brother will never know this relentless binding duty of a daughter to her mother. That no matter what, even when she is gone, the obligations to my mother, to her mother, to her mother before that, will live and breathe in every thought I ever conceive of myself.

'To ignore her will inflame things,' says my husband as he leaves. 'And please, *ḥavivta*, eat something.'

Pipe in hand, I gather the glass to its end. Warming it, turning it. I roll it back and forth on the slab near the mouth of the furnace. I will complete this commission so I can spend time with my brother. To walk and share stories and, away from Imma's prying eyes, to give him the piece I have made to protect him. A piece that he will carry to remind him that his elder sister loves him, to show off to his friends, who will remark on its beauty.

'What on earth is its use?' I could already hear Imma's doubt.

In her mind, a woman's time is for grinding and weaving and baking and cleaning and lamplighting and compounding medicines. And when she is not performing these duties, she should be tending her many children, her parents, her neighbours, her husband.

But she doesn't know that the glass holds my love and my prayers for my brother.

I set my mind to my task. To *tsar.* To this work that makes me *m'shuga'at* because it is not meant for the hands of a woman.

11
Florence, 1513

I take the heavy pestle into my hands, wipe it clean. Set it with my other tools. Mariotto's study is softened by moonlight. Like a sitter for a portrait painter, the moon is patient and still. I extinguish my lantern and go to the window, lift one of Mariotto's paintbrushes towards the moon, as if I might take its liquid glow onto the bristles. Even if I could, how would it perform on the panel or canvas? The colour might thrill when mixed on the palette but how will it dry? Will it crack on a flexible surface, like canvas? Will it lighten or darken? Will it erupt with reactions between pigment and temper? After centuries of experiments, there are still costly mistakes, making this work, for me, a mysterious meditation, a riddle. For how is it that the same ingredients, subject to the smallest variations, can produce entirely different results?

I once thought these quiet hours would be spent with a child at my breast. I tie the scarf around my face and, with a knife, split a lead cake into pieces, piling half in the mortar. Beginning again, the work of pigment grinding and paste making in search of a luminous white paint artists will covet.

It is no wonder Mariotto ends up bleary-eyed, red-nosed and coughing. His skin and clothes covered in the lead dust he grinds in a fury. After my first days at the pestle and mortar, the lining of my nose burned like fire as I breathed over my work. Within weeks, the skin on my forearms broke out in a rash of small blisters that itched like fleas and kept me awake. Along with masking my face, I now wear shirtsleeves and gloves.

As the crust builds on the lead strips suspended above jars of vinegar, I scrape it off and grind it, wash and rinse it three times, then press it into small pale cakes that I dry on the sill. It is a monotonous chore, but not nearly as demanding as producing the powders that I hope will make the white crisp and gleaming. Marble and eggshell. Cuttlefish bone and fine-grained alabaster. All must be pulverised, then ground to a texture that results in great depth and shine once the oil is added. It must also produce a paint that finishes well on the panel and does not dry too quickly.

Egg tempera offers luminosity and depth, but does not throw as much radiance as oil. It also dries quickly and so is more difficult to blend, a fact that once roused Mariotto to such furious impatience he stood back and pitched raw eggs at the panel.

As I test various ratios of powders to oils, some mixtures become stringy. Others must be put onto canvas quickly while the mixture is a workable texture. All the while I imagine the reactions of Mariotto and Michel, my goal to produce a result that will satisfy the least and most patient of artists.

'Maestro Cennino says the more it is ground the more perfect it will be,' Mariotto had said, the pestle gripped in his fist like a club in a battle. I'd been trying to get him to break from his grinding.

'At least cover your face,' I'd said, handing him a rag torn from an old apron.

'How can I see what I'm doing with my face covered?'

'Your nose and mouth, not your eyes,' I said, but he refused it, the bowl of powder he'd upended from mortar to palette billowing in small clouds that made him gasp and spit.

'*Vai via!*' Go away!' he said, snatching the rag from my hands and using it to blow his nose.

'You've lost your mind over this colour,' I said.

'I'll lose my mind with your nagging. Put your mind to something useful, like *anellini in brodo*.'

It wasn't like Mariotto to fall to such rudeness with me. Suggesting that my mind held only interest for making pasta in broth.

'Let me help with your quest for a white that every artist will want,' I said. 'I have some ideas that might yield *un bianco senza eguali*.'

'A white like no other?' He stood to attention, his eyes glassy with irritation. Scratched at his nose with the end of a spatula.

'Hold your breath while you grind,' he said, handing me the pestle. 'Damned powder makes my skin itch like the pox.'

He pulled on his cloak and kissed me on both cheeks. 'I will bring *Buccellato di Lucca*,' he said, knowing my delight at this sweet, rich in raisins and aniseed.

Far more likely indeed that he'd return in a week, breath like a corpse, no sweet in sight.

I add two drops of linseed oil to a small pile of ground lead, mix in a portion of powdered cristallo, the clear glass of the Venetians, use the palette knife to mix it a little, then take up the muller. Press hard so the oil takes the place of any air. As I push I feel damp warmth between my legs. My bleeding is more regular and reliable than the chiming of bells in the city, which sometimes sound for an event or announcement, but other times seem to ring for no reason at all.

It had been three years since my visit to the physician.

'How old?' he'd asked me, palpating my belly, fingers like winter.

'Twenty-one.'

'How long married?'

'Eight years.'

'And you understand which hole it goes in?'

Perhaps my shock at his question had been misinterpreted as ignorance.

'From where you bleed? Not shit?'

He pressed hard into my navel and I flinched. Then he pulled up my skirts, tugged down my britches and pushed his fingers inside me. My body tightened, retracted, against the force of him. He dug deeper inside me, making me wince, then pulled out his fingers and went to his desk.

I lay there, unsure of what to do, while he shuffled papers and rummaged through drawers in his desk.

'Have some pride. Dress yourself,' he said when he turned and I was as he had left me.

'My husband had an accident,' my voice stammered and I hated my own sudden frailty. 'On a horse, not long after we married. His *testicoli* ...' I'd wondered how to explain Mariotto's testicles, their small shrunken shape, dangling like apricots eaten out by ants.

'*Fica* ...' he said, under his breath but so I could hear it. The rudest remark that could be made to a lady. 'I presume you attend to your prayers and your penance?'

Did he think me a witch? Of course I prayed to Our Lord, of course I repented. But I also beseeched Elisheva. The gentle woman comforting the Virgin. Finding strength in the saint who keeps my memory of Lucia alive along with my dream for she and I to be reunited.

'As I thought,' said the physician, when I had no words to answer. 'Your condition is simply a curse you must bear.'

'A curse?'

'*Infertilità*,' he'd replied. 'The curse of the womb. Penance from God. Before you examine your husband's *testicoli*, I suggest you examine your conscience. Not every woman is chosen to carry God's children.'

I place a cover over the new paint mixture on Mariotto's desk and go to my room, take out the cheesecloth and gauze from my drawer and tie it with a kerchief between my legs. The blood is bright, like a glazing lake over *terra rossa*. As the wife of an artist, everything I turn my eye to now bears a relation to colour. And this colour means that if Mariotto does return tonight, I'll have reason to deter him. It's been six days since his promise to return with *Buccellato di Lucca*.

Often gossip would reach me that he'd been seen on Via delle Belle Donne spending our money on courtesans. But the only credible news came from the baker who claimed Signora Barolli's nephew saw him in Fiesole. His frequent visits to the hilltop town were to draw inspiration from the *sacre conversazioni*, the sacred conversations, of Fra Angelico, paintings where saints are depicted amidst ordinary life. Images that, Mariotto claimed, induced equal measures of respect and amusement. Even if he was seen there, it is futile to hope it is where he'd still be.

I push open the bedroom shutters and look out into the street, the familiar lurch of emotions between worry and anger.

I return to Mariotto's study and take a brush to my latest mixture of white, pushing it through the colour and then onto a board. Distracting myself from thoughts of my husband, of whose flesh he is touching, of how much wine he will drink before passing out in some dark, fetid alley.

'An-TON-yah!'

His voice wakes me. My head on the desk, my cheek plastered with paint.

'Annn-TON-yaaah!'

It is dawn. He is drunk.

'Antonia! My dear wife. Too smart for her husband.'

I go to the window, wiping paint from my face. He is below, in the street, one hand on his chest, the other waving his cap like a flag of surrender. He is dripping wet, wild hair pasted down over his face, a spreading puddle at his feet.

'*Sono un cane.* I am a dog,' he proclaims to a passing nonna, on her way to the market.

'Hush your voice and come inside,' I call back.

I run down the stairs to fetch him.

'You are soaked,' I say.

'The barber gave me a bath, I climbed in boots and all. I promised to pay him with a portrait. Once he stopped yelling.'

His breath reeks of wine but his skin smells like spikenard and clove. I pray that he will make good on his promise to the barber.

His forehead, newly healed after a drunken spat where he was hit with a poker, is open again and oozing.

'I am a dog,' he says again, as I help him up to the kitchen.

'Then sit like one,' I say.

He does as I say and lands heavily in the carver chair, a gift from his patron, the Lady Alfonsina. There is another bleed on his ear and a gash on the side of his neck. One dried, one weeping.

'Have you found it yet? The paint that will make us rich?' he asks, his words rolling together.

'Hush,' I tell him, drenching wool in vinegar to dab on his wounds.

'Witch's talons! You burn me.' He throws up his arms and knocks the jar from my hand. It smashes to the floor. He bends down to collect the pieces and topples off the chair, rolls onto his back, legs and arms in the air, howling like the hound he has claimed himself to be. Then he is laughing. Howling and laughing, and scratching himself like a dog lifts its paws to its gut.

I begin to laugh too at the comedy in our kitchen. The great Mariotto Albertinelli, a drunken lump on the floor.

He pushes himself onto all fours and wobbles there a moment.

'Where is your shoe?' I ask.

The stocking on his left foot is torn, his hairy toe pushing through. He grasps the edge of the table and drags himself back onto the chair, furiously scratching his head.

'You have itch-mites,' I say, fetching the bottle of myrtle berry and clary.

'Did I lose one or find one?' says Mariotto, lifting one foot then the other. 'I'm not sure this is my shoe.'

I see that it isn't. It's a buckled half-boot, too big for his foot. I think back to the day we first met, the Venetian shoes from my father too big on my feet. How grateful I am to now have shoes that fit me.

Mariotto hoists himself to standing and pulls off sodden clothes, tosses them onto the floor. His wobbling paunch hangs over his stockings. And then I see the extra lump at his groin. Like a well-risen biscuit stuffed down his hose.

'Are you hiding your supper?' I point.

'There it is!' he says, pushing his hands down his stockings.

He drops a velvet bag drawn in with twine into my palm. It is heavier than I expected.

'I don't excuse myself with it,' he says.

I loosen the twine and empty the contents.

The object sits neatly in my hand. The length of my palm and half as wide. It is coal black but not dull, polished like a jewel. I tap a fingernail at its surface.

'It's glass,' I say, running my fingers over the glossy, cool surface. It is curved to a point at each end, like the almond eyes of Etruscans that I have seen on tomb frescoes.

'Is it for perfume?' I ask, though each end appears sealed. Neither stoppered nor waxed.

'It is for admiring,' he replies. 'My mother would sit with it in her hand, twisting it in the light.'

My heart both soars and aches to hear him speak with such reverence, such sincerity, towards the mother he lost as a child.

'*Dio mio*, Mariotto,' I say. 'It's too precious. I can't accept it.'

'I lose the shoes from my own feet,' he says, his expression sombre with growing sobriety. 'It is safer with you.'

He searches my face in the way an artist will interrogate their subject. Seeking the way in. The angle, the point, from which everything else will be drawn.

'When she gave it to me, the glass was still warm from her touch,' he says softly. 'After she died, I'd leave it in the sun, the black soaking in the heat. Then I'd hold it while I slept, imagine that it was her warmth.'

I fold my fingers around the glass. Imagining the warm hands of Mariotto's mother, dead before he was five.

'There were two,' he says.

Always Mariotto to lose more than he gained. 'She liked that one best, so I give it to you. Take it over to the window, hold it to the light.'

I do as he says and a new world opens up in the palm of my hand. A glimmering myriad of tiny white flecks dance from the black.

I twist the glass so it flickers and glints in the pale morning light.

'My mother, she was not human,' says Mariotto. 'Not like the rest of us, dulled and wilted, dimmed by our own flaws. She was a woman of great, quiet depth. But every time she spoke, her words caught the light. Just like that glass.'

'Is your Santa Elisabetta inspired by your mother?' I ask. 'Is that why it is she and not the Virgin who stands in the centre of your painting?'

'This is why you are too good for me, *mia moglie*. My wife.' He takes me into his arms, kisses each cheek. 'Every day that you stay, I am luckier than the day before.'

He runs his fingers through my hair, front to back, then again. Ripples of release through my scalp, down my spine. All of me yearns to be touched. To be held and stroked. He turns me and brushes his lips down the back of my neck, his fingers massaging the small of my back. Then, his warm palms slide around to my belly, up to my breasts. From the brief conversations I have had with a few other women, it seems he is what would be called an unselfish lover.

I wonder if he touches all his women this way. At this thought, I feel a wave of angry reluctance, of not wanting to touch him, of not wanting the diseases that strike down bodies that pay no respect to a marriage. I pull out of his embrace

'You don't have to please me,' he whispers, coaxing me back, his lips kissing my shoulders, sliding the tips of his fingers inside my thighs, my skin shivering with delight. I want to lift my skirts and push his hand there, push his fingers inside me. Instead I grab his hand hard to stop it.

'It is my time of the month,' I say.

'Then you are more beautiful than any other time,' he says.

He twists his hand from mine and begins to undress me, taking each layer from my body as if unwrapping a gift. His tongue is at my nipples and his hands slide to the soft, aching space between my legs. Then his lips between my breasts, this place on my body that I would never know to be so tender had my husband not kissed me there. Working the folds of my sex as he kisses the soft cleft at the base of my neck. His fingers slide across the wetness, back and forth, his tongue a warm, wet brush, now at my navel. My hips rock with his thrusting fingers, my breath catching in the back of my throat. The damp warmth of his skin, everything like water, rippling and rolling; his fingers inside me, his thumb working the front of my sex, all of me flowing towards the endless great shudder.

He swaddles me with soft sheets and his nightgown, carries me to our bed and brushes out my hair. Presses new wool between my legs, for my bleeding. I want to fall into a sleep that will last for a year.

He sits a while on the edge of our bed; the weight of him beside me is soothing. Then, he leans close and I think it is to kiss me. Instead, he answers my question.

'Santa Elisabetta is at the centre because, although San Giovanni is the patron of Florence, Elisabetta is the mother. *La Madre.*' I feel his lips move on my ear. 'Without her, there is nothing. We have no patron. We have no city. We are not here. We do not live.'

In the morning, he is gone. I dress, pour boiling water over elderflower leaves, pat rosewater from the near-empty bottle to my face, and go to the study to continue my work.

Mio lavoro. My work. How alive I feel to take to my task. I slip on old gloves and tie the rag to cover my nose and mouth, the line between one world and the next now drawn. And I become something beyond the chores of my days. A woman creating a thing of her choosing.

I prise the lid from the box stacked with jars and manure. A powerful waft that, it is true, does carry the stink of old eggs, but with it a smell of grasses and fields and wet earth, scents that stir a vague childhood memory from a day in the countryside, Mamma picking wildflowers to make me a necklace. Inside each jar is a coiled lead plate, suspended above the vinegar from wooden batons. Excitement stirs as I examine the lead plates and select those upon whose surface the white powder is abundant. I scrape it off in flakes with soft, careful motions so that no small flecks of lead fall into the mix. Then, suspend the plate again above the vinegar and withdraw another. As the dish fills with what I will wash and dry, and grind into fine powder, I think of any number of ways my life could be worse.

'Don't be born a woman if you want your own way.'

It was Michel who'd announced that his former patron, Lorenzo de' Medici, had been furious with his sister Nannina's words, reading them out in a scornful tone while Michel sketched his portrait. When Michel relayed the contents of the letter to the men gathered in the loggia, it had caused great debate.

'How would a noblewoman know the life of another, who must sweat in the kitchen, then stomp piss for the merchant to whiten his wool?' Michel had said.

'A noblewoman wouldn't know her tit from a jelly,' said Franciabigio.

'Finery and jewels don't save a woman from her lot,' offered the more thoughtful Pontormo.

But Nannina de' Medici's malcontent is disheartening. This woman whose wedding saw five hundred guests sprawled across Via della Vigna Nuova, guzzling seventeen vats of wine and devouring sixty-three roast beasts, tearing their teeth through the best food in Florence. If Nannina was unhappy, what chance did any of us have?

I pile a small batch of the ground lead powder onto the slab and this time add walnut oil, taking my mind from Nannina to Lucia. Like Nannina, Lucia was brave enough to voice her discontents. And, even though my father had complained about her presence, her dress, her much-too-loud laughter, I realised it had never been to Lucia herself. Only behind her back. As if she could mute his opinions.

As I lean my weight into the muller and push it over the grinds, I push my thoughts of Lucia and Nannina into the rasping rhythm of stone against stone. Into the steady, firm pressure, sweeping the grind in a figure of eight. I'm so immersed in my work, I don't hear the latch on the door or Mariotto's light, sober steps up the stairs.

'What is it?' I say when he stops by my side. 'You look like the swine who has just met the butcher.'

'It is not good,' he replies, for once getting straight to the truth.

At the church, my husband emerges from the mortuary in which my father is laid.

'It's better you don't see,' he says, but I push past him. Sometimes what is imagined is more frightening than what is seen.

His skin is mushroom coloured and bloated. One side of his skull has been crushed, as if struck by an iron. His limbs are wrinkled and bleached. Pocks of flesh missing. No trace of the combative father of my childhood, whose fists swung with speed and precision. I'd seen him brawl with two men at once, not a scratch to his body. But his drinking had dulled the spark in his reflexes and at the same time heightened the delusion of whom he could take on. No doubt he'd picked another fight. One he had no chance of winning. Perhaps dead, perhaps not, he'd been trussed and discarded. Found by a fisherman netting tench in the Arno.

If only this turn of events could offer some sense of divine order. I'd long ago lost my once-beloved Babbo to every dark memory where he lurked as a beast. But here before him, I am still his *pulcina*. And his unholy death shreds my heart.

On the walk home, Mariotto holds me close to his side without filling the silence.

Don't be born as a woman if you want your way. Nannina de' Medici's words return to my thoughts.

'Is there any best way to be born?' I ask. Mariotto remains quiet.

My childhood dream had been to escape from my household. To free myself from the restraints of my mother and father, and vanish to wherever I imagined Lucia to be. Now, one by one, my family tethers have been cut. But I am not set free. Only adrift.

We arrive home and I take to my work. To scraping, to grinding, to mixing, to testing, to starting again. The muller, heavy on pigment, adding oil drop by drop, grinding again until my arms ache. Stripe after stripe of white across the panel. Angling the finish this way and that. While it dries, to distract me, I collect the glass vial; anchored by its soothing weight in my palm, this black that captures the light. So like Mariotto to gift me a small world of contrasts. The way its white sparks from within the black glass is what I am determined to capture.

I set down the vial and return to my grinding and mixing, chasing a colour as elusive as heaven, until the sheen of the moon disappears from the river.

12

Beit HaKerem, 29 BCE

A setting dawn moon sinks behind the mountains.

'I see them!' Corinna calls from the rooftop, and the composure, the self-possession I have practised for this moment vanishes. I am running to our gate as I once did when I was four and found a copper coin in the dust. I ran home to my father, my lungs heaving, bursting with the effort and pace of the sprint, and opened my fisted fingers to display my treasure. My father had chuckled, rolling the coin between his fingers before returning it to my palm. *Lucky*, he'd called me. But not as lucky as I feel now, for my brother, Tsad, is finally here.

He walks beside my mother up the steep hill to our home, his hand gripping the rein that leads the donkey. As I get closer, it is my mother who opens her arms to me. It confuses me, her display, distracting me from the embrace I long to give my brother. I do not deny her. She folds her arms around me; then her palms are on my shoulders as she holds me back at arm's length. Her face has more lines, but still carries its pleasing symmetry and soft angles. Perhaps there is a leniency in her eyes that I don't remember. Perhaps I see what I wish.

'Let me look at you,' she says, inspecting me. Assessing.

My thoughts return to the coin I'd once found in the dust. My mother had not shared my father's amusement. 'Are you a thief?' she had said. 'What if the owner is out looking for his coin and cannot find it?' I'd returned it, shamed and embarrassed, to the spot marked out by my grasping, thieving fingers only moments before.

Imma squeezes my shoulders and embraces me again. 'I don't recognise you,' she says, releasing me.

They already form a riddle, her words. I repeat them over and over in my mind, looking for the worst of what they might mean, looking for the best, rejecting both.

'*Sh'lama*, sister.'

The boy beside her speaks and now nothing matters but him. The boy with my father's eyes, whose head reaches my chest. Tall, I think, for an eight-year-old. When he offers me his hands, I pull him into my arms.

The heat in his child-body is fierce. He dashes away tears.

'Come, don't be silly,' says Imma.

Zakhariya joins us, scents of balsam, myrrh and cinnamon wafting from his oiled beard. '*Sh'lama* to you, mother-in-law, brother-in-law.'

'Abba will greet you now,' says Tsad.

'Abba?' I did not see my father arrive with them.

My little brother runs back to the tottering man, leaning heavily on a walking stick and muttering to himself.

Who is this stranger struggling towards us? Shuffling the earth like an ancient? As he draws near, I can see that spittle runs from his bottom lip down his beard.

'Of course, there are many changes you haven't been there for,' says Imma in the tone I best remember.

The strangeness of seeing Abba this way, shrunken and feeble, brings a sharp, throbbing pain to my chest and I place a hand there to ease it.

'Don't make a fuss,' Imma says through her teeth.

As he draws closer, Abba's mouth is moving, his jaw beating up and down as if a shiver of cold has set upon him.

'*Sh'lama*, Abba,' I say, kissing him on each cheek. 'How good it is to see you.'

'This is Elisheva, Abba,' Tsad says, introducing me to my own father.

Abba extends a shaking hand and I grasp its limp coldness. He looks at me as if I am a stranger.

'*Sh'lama*, father-in-law.' My husband greets my father and Abba wobbles, unbalanced, on his stick.

'Why didn't you send word of his worsening condition?' I say.

'Would you have brought a magic spell to cure it?' Imma replies.

'Beh, bah, bah.' Abba dribbles as he talks, glaring at me as if I should understand him, as if he is awaiting my reply.

'Don't upset yourself, Abba,' says Tsad. 'Come, we'll sit in the breeze.'

He takes my father's arm and guides him into our courtyard. We follow.

'He prefers to sit outside,' Tsad explains while Zakhariya calls for a chair to be brought and placed under the terebinth in the centre of our courtyard. And I see why he is so grown up, my little brother. Now the man of the house. Abba takes his seat and closes his eyes as the breeze riffles his beard, the fine strands of sweat-dampened hair across his balding head lifting like the crest of a bird.

'Bah, bah. Beh, beh,' he says, eyes closed.

'Yes, Abba, it is lovely,' says Tsad, agreeing with whatever he has understood Abba to say and wiping our father's face with a cloth brought by Corinna. 'He started to walk again last moon,' says Tsad, doing his best to sound optimistic.

'We shall continue our prayers for his health,' says Zakhariya, and it is the first time I see Imma falter in her resigned expression.

'Let's not fuss,' says Imma. 'We are just happy to be here.'

I want to take in the compliment, but I know Imma too well.

'I guess when you have time on your hands …' She leaves the thought incomplete, knowing I understand what she means.

'How long has he been like this?' I ask her.

'What does it matter?' she replies, lifting the cup offered by

Corinna to her lips, her hands shaking. 'Ignore me,' she says. 'I'm weary from travel.'

I wait for the rest of it. For the turn in what she says, after she says something that seems contrite.

'I'll tell you everything tomorrow,' she says, leaving me waiting for whatever will come next, something that I cannot prepare for or shield myself from. But nothing more is said. That night I do not sleep.

In the morning, Abba is snoring on the pallet I have had set up on the roof to catch the breeze. When I seek out Imma, Corinna points up the hill, to her striding up to my workshop. I catch her before she reaches the top.

'Afraid of what I might find?' she asks.

'I'm excited to show you,' I lie.

'Excitement is for children and men,' she says.

When we reach my workshop we are both panting and I realise, with satisfaction, she has tried to race me.

'He has a knack, that child, with his father,' Imma says, looking back down to our courtyard, where Tsad is sparring with some imaginary opponent, ducking and weaving, turning on his left heel and kicking out with his right. Abba clapping his hands, Tsad taking a bow. 'Reads a mind as easily as a scripture.'

'He's sedate for a boy,' I say, a flicker of jealousy at how my mother compliments my brother with such ease.

'He spends too much time with Abba,' she says. 'At his every beck and call.'

She pauses and pushes open the door to my workshop. Hot air wafts. Yirmiyahu has kept the firebox burning and ready, knowing I might want to show Imma how I work with the glass. Knowing me well.

Her face flushes in an instant and she retreats a step.

'Not a place for a woman,' she says, withdrawing her head and letting the door close behind her. She tsks and clucks and brushes her hands off as if soiled by the mere thought of entry.

'Let me show you my pieces, how I shape them,' I say, as if there will be an alchemy performed by her step inside the door. That my daydreams of more gentle and intimate conversations can take place within.

'Another time.' She turns away.

'They come from Suria for my pieces,' I say. 'Egypt, too.'

'Perhaps you could try your restless hands at pottery,' she says. 'So many good uses.'

Then her attention is back on my brother, now chasing down an escaped kid in the courtyard.

'I need you to take care of him for a while,' she says.

That's why she's come, to ask for my help. My ill father and a son are too much for her. My heart flares. To ask for help with my brother is as good as telling me I am capable.

'Of course!' I reply. 'I can take care of everything.' My mind races with all I can do. 'I can arrange a tutor. Several tutors. I know enough to at least guide a little. Abba taught me more than he admitted. Whatever Tsad should need, I can provide him. He can learn the sacred texts from Zakhariya; he's a most patient teacher.'

Imma is quiet, a weary exhale.

'How odd your thoughts are, Sheva,' she says. 'I don't mean Tsad. I mean your father.' She begins the walk back down the hill, knowing she has, once again, caught me off guard. 'What with Tsad growing up … And Rivka's children now too. So precocious, each of them. I treat them as I would my own grandchildren. I don't expect you to understand.'

As we descend, she recites more reasons as to why it is my duty to care for my father. Citing stories about my cousins and their many children: who are not her grandchildren, not really, but who need her because *one must make the best out of what one has.*

I walk behind her in silence.

In the courtyard, Abba is speaking to the sky.

'Bah, beh,' he says.

A look of disgust hardens the lines of Imma's face.

'He said "fig" two days ago,' says Tsad, determined to find a pattern in Abba's blathering.

A bird calls from the terebinth above us and Abba points upwards, his mouth flapping as if a whole stream of clever words should be issuing forth. Like they once did.

'See that strange bird?' he said one day, when it was just the two of us walking in Ḥevron to Avraham's Tomb. 'Could be a tern, or an oversized sparrow. I've seen nothing like it. Keep watching!' A finger pointed, then the bird batted its wings and took flight. 'There! See the colour under the wings? What colour did you see?'

'Black! Abba, I saw black,' I answered, clapping my hands with excitement.

'Good girl, well observed,' my father said, patting my back. 'Pitch black under white wings. Ribon Alma likes to delight.'

The sages say that our parents shape our minds from the day we are born. Perhaps this passing moment with my father shaped mine: gave me the eyes to spot a dark sliver of feather hidden within the pale down of a goose. To take interest in black when the world admires white.

Before dawn the donkeys are packed. Imma and Tsad will depart before it gets hot.

Abba is shuffling around the courtyard, heavy on his stick.

'He oiled his own beard this morning,' Tsad tells me. 'And then he put his nose to the bottle and said, "No galbanum."' My little brother's face is awash with joy. 'And I smelled the oil, and he was right!'

'And tomorrow it will be "there's two figs" while he points at a stone,' says Imma.

Tsad frowns at Imma in a way I would never dare.

'You look like your sister,' she says.

This time her insult has the opposite effect because I am delighted, in this way, to be compared to my brother.

'If he asks for bread, give him water,' says Imma, leaving last-minute instructions. 'When he clutches himself, he must use the privy. He remembers he must go, but not how or where.'

I want to find a private moment to give Tsad my gift, but my mother hovers around him.

'It is surprising how often he will say something funny or lovely,' says Tsad, leaving Imma to fuss about her baggage.

'I made this for you,' I say, taking my chance, holding out my hand with the glass vessel inside it.

'What is it?' says Imma, pushing past me. 'Let me see it.'

Tsad snatches it. Turns his back on my mother to view it in private.

'You'll show me later.' She huffs and returns to her packing.

'You know my love of black stones?' he says, and I nod. 'This is much better.' He closes his fingers around the glass vial and brings it to his lips, kisses it.

'Wherever you are, my prayers will be with you,' I say.

'Strap our bags to the donkey,' demands Imma. 'I want to rest in Beit Leḥem before noon.'

'She's harder to manage than Abba,' Tsad says, his voice lowered so our mother cannot hear him. A grin leaks through his serious expression. A glimpse of the boy he should be.

I offer my brother my hands, but he pushes them aside and embraces me instead.

'Talk to Abba as if he understands,' he says, and waits for my agreement. 'And always tell the truth. In case he does understand.'

He untethers the donkey, pauses. Imma beckons from the gate, hurrying him up.

'Come soon, brother,' I say.

'When you have a son, I'll come to visit my nephew,' he says, a wide grin.

I'm too shocked to reply. Eight years since I have bled, and I wonder if he is mocking me like Imma would with such a comment. But his expression seems excited, sincere.

'*Sh'lama*, sister,' he says, still grinning.

He pushes the black glass I made him into the pouch tied to his belt.

'Too hot, soon too hot,' says Abba, who has shuffled up beside me.

'Yes, Abba, the sun's heat will grow fierce,' I say.

'Too hot for the sparrows.' He dabs at his brow with an unsteady hand.

'Abba is safe here,' I say, as Tsad kisses Abba goodbye, trying to appear brave.

'Come, Tsad!' calls Imma. 'There's no good time to depart.'

'For once she is right,' I say to my brother, but I am unable to muster a smile. 'How about we both turn on three?'

He nods, and I brush the tears from his cheeks.

'One, two …' I link my arm through Abba's and force a smile to farewell him with cheer. '… three.'

My brother turns one way and Abba and I turn the other, walk our different directions. Corinna latches the gate.

In the morning, I guide Abba on a walk up the hill to my workshop. Zakhariya has set a chair under the old olive tree outside the door; the tree's gnarled girth would take three men to surround it.

'Beh, bah, beh,' he says, pointing out across the hills in the direction of the Port of Azotus.

'To Azotus and then the sea so blue, the earth that I would cross for you,' I say.

It's a fragment of verse I remember from my childhood, but I remember no more so I repeat what I've already said as I help him sit down.

'For, for, for,' says my father, straining. 'For you. For.'

'The air smells of the sea today, Abba,' I say. And I sit on the earth next to him. Wait until he dozes.

Inside the workshop the furnace is blazing and I am too hot. My skin leaks sweat and it drips from my forehead, burning and blurring my eyes. I am not breathing as I should. Not with ease, as is my practice. I drop the piece I am working on and rush outside, leaning over to catch my breath. Abba is sitting comfortably in the shade, the lines of worry in his face softened. His folded hands rest on his lap, the way he has sat in my memory every day of my childhood.

I wipe the saliva from his chin, his mouth working hard to try and speak. 'It's too hot for me today, Abba.'

'Too, too,' he stammers. 'Too hot for the sparrows.'

It's the phrase he seems to return to, and I wonder what pieces of his mind are stitching together to form the idea. What bonds of memory are then, just as quickly, broken.

'Are you hungry, Abba?' I ask.

'One fig,' he replies.

'Maybe two,' I say, helping him to stand, handing him his stick.

'Two, two. Two.' He points at the sky and I search for two clouds or two birds. Something in the form of two. There is nothing.

'Tsad, come back?' His inflection tells me it is a question and I feel the heat flare again in my belly, recalling Tsad's words of returning to meet his nephew.

'I hope so,' I say, remembering Tsad's first rule, to speak as if my father can understand.

'Bah, beh, come,' Abba says. 'Can't find it in here.' He pushes his hand against his head and moans. The strain on his face breaks my heart.

As we stroll, the slant of the sun casts long shadows.

Halfway down, Abba stops.

'A little farther, Abba,' I say, patting his hand that clutches my arm.

But he stands still as stone, his gaze fixed on my face. A flicker of recognition in his eyes makes me catch my breath, as if the thing that stole his mind has relented. A thieved coin, returned to its keeper.

'*Barta* Elisheva,' he says. *Barta*. My daughter. I can see his mouth working to express something his mind has latched on to.

'When, when? When Tsad come?' he asks, squeezing shut his eyes with the effort. The momentary sense that he is able to say what he means.

'He says he will return when he has a nephew to visit,' I say, remembering Tsad's second rule, to tell my father the truth.

'Yes, yes,' says my father in happy agreement. 'Tsad come back for my *barta*'s baby.'

Silver strands of his hair catch the sunlight.

II

Who'd be happy, let him be so:
Nothing's sure about tomorrow.

Lorenzo de' Medici

13

Adelaide, Autumn 2018

The gold thread in my hand catches light like a glistening fairytale hair. Leaning over the embroidery, my head is too heavy for my neck. The magnifying visor is too tight. I loosen the straps, bend again to my work. I am pushing too hard, anxious to finish the couched metal-purl coral in gold that surrounds a small fish, beneath the two figures, and move on to the grimy needlelace slips that fell out when the embroidery was unrolled. These fragile pieces must be cleaned without water and dried without shrinkage. And if my theory is right, while they might not yet prove these embracing figures are Elisabeth and Mary, they will confirm they are women, for I believe they are veils.

'I didn't mean to startle you,' says Tris, when I jump as she opens the door.

Her teardrop earrings lilt and twist as she speaks. They are woven with yellow silk threads pulled from tiny eyelets around the silver, like the warp of a loom, and echo the stamens of the lotus embroidered on her skirt. I try to listen to what she's saying, but in my mind I am rifling through the still-unpacked boxes lining my hallway. Where my bright silk blouses and embroidered skirts are tissue-wrapped and stored in acid-free boxes. My pretty clothes, from before he made it clear that I should only look pretty for him.

Tris has asked me a question and is awaiting my answer. I resist saying sorry. Sorry for not listening. Sorry for not replying.

Compared to the art of apology making, said the shrink I liked best, it takes significant practice to learn *not* to say sorry.

'My mind was lost to gold thread,' I say, pleased that I've avoided the 'S' word.

'Lost or found?' she says, leaning over the embroidery. 'Your stitch tension looks perfect.'

Staggering the end of each row to minimise straining the fabric is something I've always been good at achieving with the least possible stitches.

I pass her my visor so she can take a closer look. Her admiration of my work starts to make me feel awkward.

She removes the visor and picks up the print-out of the Albertinelli painting from my desk. 'I can see why you love this moment between two women.'

A flush of heat to my face. What can she see about the things that I love?

'Elisabeth's golden cloak is dazzling,' she says. 'As if the artist means for her, not the Virgin, to be most important.'

She is quiet, attention locked on the painting. Long enough for the colour to fade from my cheeks.

'Anyway, anyway …' She claps her dainty hands, a fairy batting its wings. 'It. Is. Here.'

I don't understand, so she makes it clear.

'From Caterina Sirani. John's head.'

It makes me flinch when she names it. It doesn't sound right. If anything, I want to correct her, at least use the name given to him by his mother. Yoḥanan. The name she would have spoken in her Aramaic tongue when she rejected the tradition that would have her name him after his grandfather. Yoḥanan. First and last son of Zakhariya and Elisheva.

I am silent while she gushes.

She wants to go there now. Right now, to unpack it from the crate in the storeroom, fragile stickers plastered all over. The 'S' word is unstoppable. Sorry, I can't. Sorry, I'm too busy. I have to clean all theses pieces. Sorry, not now. I'm so very sorry.

'I understand,' Tris says, her enthusiasm undiminished. This woman with unnerving power to take nothing personally. 'I'm halfway through writing the pitch for new donors. It'll be my reward when I'm done. Let me know when you're ready.'

The door has closed. She is gone. A gold thread in my hand.

I'm *not* ready.

I'm not *ready*.

I should have made that clear. Because she doesn't understand. This interminable mission, this threading, this stitching together of lost pieces. This world of fragments that I need to restore. To make something, anything, whole. If only for a moment. Like fallen leaves circled as tree skirts. Snapped twigs shaped into stars.

I drag my thoughts from the crate in the storeroom, from Caterina Sirani's work made with hammers and blades. Drop back into the world of the gold thread in my hand.

To make this gold for stitching and weaving, silver bullion was cast and drawn into a wire, then wrapped in beaten gold leaf and fired to bond. The resulting rods were then pulled into the finest of wires. These wires were then rolled to form tinsel, and spun around a silk core to make a gold thread. Often gold and silver metal threads can tarnish over time, even blacken, when conditions are poor. But the gold threads found stashed inside small bags are vibrant, thrilling against the pads of my fingers. To be immersed in the conservation of this work is to be steeped in the hidden worlds of the women who stitched it. And to flesh out the two figures who are its subject unleashes layer upon layer of story within story. When their imagined lives play out as I work, I feel safer to examine what I keep hidden.

I return to the embroidered coral. The trade in this thread once led to scandals and corruption, women thrown into jail for its spinning. If there's enough, I'll repair the outline of the woman's robe on the right. It will also strike through the gown of the woman on the left. I say 'woman', but of course it could be a king's cloak, a nobleman's stole. Until the veils are back in place, any number of colleagues might argue against me.

A last stitch. The coral is complete. I tear off my visor and rub where the straps buried into my scalp. I move away from the piece to gulp down some water. My dry eyes burn and sting as I blink. My tired mind spirals, full with this thread that delights, that pulls histories together. How complex and deceiving this history of gold thread, its glimmering beauty a winking eye at the past.

I try to clear my mind, so that when I turn back to view the embroidery I can see it anew. *Click.* Like a snapshot.

Click. In this brief, clear-minded moment, the memory finds me.

We are running through the airport, Jonathan and I. And I'm running through the checklist. Your passport? Your tickets? Got your phone? Is it charged? Call me from Singapore, okay? Did you pack your warm jacket?

His new camera bounces against his chest as he runs.

He's late. Always late. Scribbling homework at breakfast. Last-minute assignments. Mum, stop stressing! Always lacing his footy boots as we pulled up at the oval, his team huddled on field, siren ready.

Now he's late for his flight. We're the last to the gate. The hostesses greet him, he pats down his pockets. Can't find his boarding pass, even though it was just in his hand. His eyes scan the wide, white corridor behind us: there it is, on the floor. He drops his pack to retrieve it. Returns laughing.

When he broke the news he would be leaving straight after Year Twelve, I'd felt a strangling mixture of dread and pride. He'd won a cadetship with Benjamin Media UK: they'd loved his photo portfolio, they needed content creation.

'Once you complete a degree,' I'd said, pulling sheets and shirts from the line.

I'd been certain it was another Jonathan whim. That there'd be plenty more between now and when uni began. But when he picked up the clothes basket and followed me around, placing it back down to help fold fitted sheets, I'd known he was determined.

'The field's too competitive. I need to show I'm ambitious, be hands-on. Develop a profile,' he argued. 'A degree is useless. It's experience that matters.'

Back and forth, a whole week. Fuming. Slammed doors. Grunted answers to my questions.

Then one night, while I lay in bed and stared at the ceiling, he came into my room. Sat beside me, quiet and calm.

'Dad would have said yes.'

The digital beep as the hostess holds out her scanner. He hoists on his pack. It's unzipped at the side, a sweater sleeve dangling free. And I realised a part of me was relying on his disorganised nature, his easy-come-easy-go disposition. The fair chance that he'd miss his flight, change his mind. But it's happening. He really is leaving.

He grabs me and spins me around, lands me back down, hugs me in close. For a moment I feel reassured by the manliness, the strength, in his body.

Don't go. I stuffed the words down in my chest. How could I not let him follow his dream? Because it didn't *feel* right? It would never feel right.

'Your dad would be proud,' I'd said, resisting the urge to reach out and fix his half-tucked collar.

'Of you too, Mum,' he said, his soft, sincere gaze too young, too old, for this boy not yet eighteen.

He is the last passenger to board. Only him on the aerobridge. The aeroplane door like a painting's vanishing point. And I am holding my breath, holding a smile to my face, so that if he does turn around one last time his memory of me will be the mum who shared his excitement. I hold the expression in place until my cheeks ache.

He turns. His lit-up face, a portrait of possibility.

Then, he lifts his camera, deftly thumbs off the lens cap. It swings on its thread. He points the camera at me.

Click.

Camera down, he is laughing. He is gone.

He is gone.

I can't breath. I need to get out of this studio. I burst from the door. From the exit. Out the back way, down the side street.

I stop running when I reach the Lone Pine. Bend over to catch my breath. I've brought nothing with me. Not my satchel, not my phone, not even my keys. I lean on the tree and sobs wrack my body. Somewhere a dog is barking, a man whistling. There is a whining beside me.

'C'mon, Sassy. Here girl.'

A wet daub on my calf where her nose touched my skin. Now gone. She and her owner.

On busy North Terrace, nobody stops to ask why I'm doubled over, weeping, keening. So much of my grief has been lived out in private. But here and now, a public display. And yet I am still alone. Walkers and runners and mothers with prams glance and continue on. To them I am no one. Tears and sweat streaking my makeup. And, look, not even shoes.

Where are my shoes?

I straighten and press my back to the tree. My palms flat to the bark. It should be scoured and prickly, but I feel nothing. A cloud of tree martins stream across the sky on their way to nest in nearby Leigh Street. The light and noise of inner-city trees keep predatory falcons at bay. My palms start to register the rugged bark of this tree, seeded from the original Lone Pine on the Gallipoli Peninsula. I come to this tree because its mother has seen more death than me. With my spine pressed against it, I share in its pain.

The work day is ending. Pedestrians spill out of office buildings, traffic is honking. I wipe my face with my sleeve. Retrace my steps. Find my shoes kicked off on the footpath. I don't have my pass, so I enter the gallery through the door where visitors are now leaving. I don't look at anyone, not even Juni, our gentle giant at security, the day to Amir's night. I'm relieved that Maisie is on duty at the conservator's wing.

'I had an emergency,' I say. Not a lie. 'Left my bag in the room.'

Maisie has twins with cerebral palsy. Her husband left her when she was still in hospital after their birth. I've seen her wheeling the now-teenage boy and girl through the gallery. I'm yet to see her not smiling.

'Anytime, Doctor Reed,' she says, swiping her pass across the lock. 'If everyone brought their pass half as much as you, I'd be out of a job.'

'There's a clay-modelling class next week,' I say. 'Why don't you bring the twins? I'll set it up.'

The brief twitch in her lips as she smiles tells me what I already know about the shape of her days.

'You're a beautiful mum,' I say.

'They're beautiful children,' says Maisie.

In the studio, everything has been packed away. I have no memory of doing it. I sit on my stool and let the stillness, the rarefied air, settle around me. A swell of calm, of warmth, rises as my eyes scan the order that surrounds me. Drawers marked with codes, tools set into niches, jars labelled. Light meters and thermometers tucked into their pouches.

I hoist my bag onto my shoulder, set the dehumidifiers to *night*. The door latches behind me.

I stand in the hallway until the auto lights blink off. My breath high in my chest. Turn right and I'll reach the building's exit. Turn left and I will reach the room with the box. With *The Head*.

When nothing goes right, go left.

My late husband's advice.

As a photo-journalist, footsteps in which our son yearned to follow, he denied my accusations of him being a risk-taker. Insisting the correct term was *adventure proponent*. He went to Sri Lanka during its first cease-fire in five decades and strode into fields littered with mines; his desire to put Sri Lanka front page in the West outstripping his fear.

His love of photography seemed to benefit from his famous impatience.

'At least it's a quick one,' he'd joked about the cancer that had riddled his pancreas.

That same impatience made him deft and able to catch photos that others might miss. Like the fleeting appearance of a girl soldier in the stronghold of Elephant Pass. The troubling strain on her face; the machine gun slung over her shoulder, three-quarters her size. The sense of a war-hardened woman trapped in a child. The image won prizes. Every cent sent to orphanages in Jaffa. In his mind, never enough.

His repeated complaint of me was that I never listened to his advice. I'd ask for it, then ignore it or quarrel with his logic. But it never made him angry. Not like his illness made me.

When nothing goes right, go left.

We'd spent a whole day turning left in places we usually turned right, his drip stashed in the back next to our toddler son in his car seat. Ending up on Kaurna Meyunna country, at Second Valley Beach near the tip of Fleurieu Peninsula, our son enraptured by the beach stones struck through with quartz, clutching them like jewels, pressing them inside his pockets until the weight of them pulled his tiny shorts from his nappy.

In the gallery hallway, I turn left.

Unlike the cocoon of the conservator's studio, the storeroom has a cavernous, open-air quality. Each step echoes. The wooden crate is on the delivery table, the orange 'Fragile' stickers making it cartoonish. I circle the box, as I do the Buddhist statue of Death. It is set on a pallet; four screwed-in bolts hold each corner, straps crossing at the centre. Wrapped like a present.

Blood rushes to my eardrums as I rifle through my satchel for the curved-tip scissors left to me by my grandmother. The straps fall away. I yank open drawers and rummage for other tools, find a knife and work the screws out one by one. The effort distracts me from what will happen when I finish. I prise the lid up, hoist it off. Wafts of varnish and gesso.

I remove layers of padding, put on my gloves, and plunge my arms inside, finding a hard Styrofoam block. I lean in deeply and try to withdraw it. But it argues, squeaks, friction working against me. I angle the box, carefully taking the weight. It seems too big in my hands for the object I know is inside. I pull out more layers of padding from its sides. Set them on the table and lift off the lid. I expect another layer of foam blocks, but there's only cloth. Its shock-of-nails hair a tell-tale outline.

It. Is. Here.

The Head.

The Head of John the Baptist.

Of Elisheva's Yoḥanan.

I peel back the cloth.

I'm not ready.

But there it is.

Looking back at me with sad, haunting eyes.

No.

My voice cannot fill the vast space of the storeroom.

No no no no no.

I want to look away, but I can't. These dark eyes. They're not real. *Not* real. They are polished black onyx.

Only they're not. They're the eyes of my son. Isn't this what I thought I needed to see?

NO! I am screaming. My hands are trying to cover it back up, cloth catching on the nails struck into its skull.

Sobs rack my body.

Be careful, you hopeless bitch. Don't mark it! You'll stain it with tears.

I want to scream back at the voice in my head. *What the fuck does it matter? It's not a real human.*

I stumble backwards.

Away from the aching sorrow in those eyes. Eyes that betray a sad resignation. As if he had, in the moment of death, accepted his fate.

I stumble, knocking boxes. Cowering against the wall and screaming into my hands. Those beautiful, sad eyes, both strange and familiar.

Don't go! I finally scream the words stuffed down into my throat. Burning holes in my heart.

Where are the pieces of my son? Those that I stroked, that I kissed? That had lain in my lap? The witless, shameless, idiot self that was convinced I could confront all I had lost with a head made of wood seethes and rages against what is now clear. Pieces are lost. Unrecovered. Unrecoverable. *The Head* has arrived. But it is not a missing piece.

It is not my chance to begin a new whole.

The concrete cold from the storeroom floor has seeped into my spine. I drag myself to standing. Old pain, new tears. My life in a nutshell.

I can't go home yet. I need to walk.

I take North Terrace, King William, Hindley to Leigh Street. The roosting tree martins are raucous, their chatter like applause. Every branch in the Callery pear trees is crowded; their numbers maybe ten thousand. Soon they will depart and the dusk winter streets will be silent, but their sound well remembered. Like the soft sleeping breath I still hear from my son.

It's months since I've listened to the one message I'd saved. The background clamour and chitter of birds is like a sound-cloak of protection.

'... thanks, Mum ... I love you.'

Tacked on at the end of a long message asking me to find his dad's old zoom lens. Was it in Grandma's shed? Could I call her and ask?

Every week I'd sent him a postcard. Pictures of artworks he'd pointed at as a toddler, or paused on as a young adult accompanying me on NGV gallery rounds. On the back of the postcards, I wrote the same message. *I see you, Love Mum.* It was a private joke between us since he was a child. When he'd go quiet in his room I'd call from the kitchen, 'I see you, Jonathan Reed.' In the hope he would think I knew what he was up to. But the postcard message became something different, meant to show him the precious moments I'd seen when he wasn't aware.

Over time his emails and phone calls from London had grown sparser, as a big-city photographer's busy life began to take shape.

Then, one day an envelope had arrived in the post, addressed in his wonky, hurried handwriting. Inside the airmail envelope another, plain white one, unsealed. I presumed a return postcard to continue our joke. But inside, a photograph. The one he'd taken of me at the airport.

Click.

My face filled the frame. My mouth and eyes smiling. My gaze conveying every ounce of admiration, of trust, I'd felt for my son when I wasn't sidetracked by worry. The woman in the photograph held a bright, undaunted love in her gentle expression. So different to the girl who had begun to appear in my mirror.

It had been too much. I'd turned the photo face-down on the table. On the back, his message.

I see you, Love J.

I slide back the blue button fifteen seconds to listen again to his voice.

'… thanks, Mum … I love you.'

His voice saved. But still lost.

Why not a blue button to rewind my life?

The screen with his message vanishes. An incoming call interrupting the moment.

The mere sight of the name makes my hand tremble. I've heard nothing since he left opened mail on my doorstep. He might be standing on my front doormat right now, calling me to say so. Still that sense that he could be waiting around any corner.

Scott Harman. Scott Harman. Doctor Scott Harman is calling, so don't keep him waiting.

I pick up the call.

'There you are!' His charming voice. His assured voice. The tone he adopts when calming his patients.

Their illusions are flawless, one shrink remarked, of those able to lead a convincing double life.

Blood pounds in my head, in my chest. I ready myself to speak careful words. Until I think of the photo sent by my son. A woman so unlike the one I'd become. I summon her courage.

'Don't call me.'

I've said it. And the birds sound their applause.

'Speak up, I can't hear you,' he says, his tactic to pretend he can't hear when I dare defy him.

'Don't call me.' I repeat it. 'Don't come near me. Not at home. Not at work. My neighbours and colleagues all know who you are.'

The lie makes my chest near explode. I've said nothing to anyone. There is no one who knows. I hang up. My tongue feels engorged; it can't fit in my mouth. The trees are a blur of feathers and leaves, rustling and shaking, each bough a shamanic rattle casting out devils.

And now I am crossing the City Bridge, Karrawirra Parri's oily skin writhing below me on its way to the sea. Jolleys Boathouse upstream, diners laughing and toasting. How many of them see the charade of these steps I appear to be taking? A body in motion, its sights set upon freedom? For every step forward, two taken backwards. *Not this time*, I tell the girl in the mirror. Soon she won't need the concealer to hide what she isn't. Soon she and I will be the same woman. I can't leave her behind. I'm taking her with me.

14

Florence, 1513

In the church of San Michele, Elisabetta's golden cloak glows like sunset. Signora Ottolini swivels, stiff-necked, to face me.

'He is the son of a *battiloro*, a gold beater, your husband, *sì*?' she asks.

I nod my reply, words from Saint Paul's instruction about keeping silent in church are always front of mind when I kneel at the altar.

'Only one who knows gold could capture its lustre,' says the old lady. '*Allora!* See her expression? The Virgin's? So much worry in that young face.' She tsks her concern. 'But alabaster skin in the Judean desert? She'll look sixty years old at thirty! No wonder she worries.' She chuckles to herself, fingers working her rosary.

I hear the church doors open behind us. Signora Ottolini narrows her eyes towards whomever has entered.

'The prodigal nephew,' she says, raising an eyebrow.

But my thoughts are on Maryam's skin. I had seen on my father what sun does to skin, his cheeks leathered and scaly, the backs of his hands covered in blotches from working the vines as a boy. Why had Mariotto painted a Judean woman's skin with the sheen of a pearl? And did these women of Judea wear robes in verdigris and yellow-gold?

The man who has knelt beside me clears his throat. Loudly, like a man washing up for dinner. I glare at him for making such a noise. For interrupting my puzzling thoughts about the Virgin's pale skin.

I glance again and scowl.

He opens his hands in a gesture of innocence and points an accusing finger at Signora Ottolini and then at me. '"Let your women keep silence in the churches: for it is not permitted unto them to speak."' He repeats the verse that always sets me on edge.

When a visiting preacher quoted the passage from Saint Paul to the Corinthians, Lucia let out a plangent yawn. The crowded congregation stood shoulder to shoulder, and the appalled visiting padre scanned their faces, his double chin bubbling over his collar. To ensure that he found her, Lucia let out another great yawn.

The preacher had raised his voice to finish Paul's words. 'And if they will learn anything, let them ask their husbands at home: for it is a shame for women to speak in the church.' He glared at Lucia beside me.

'And what if the woman has a dunce for a husband?' cried Lucia, her scarf torn from her head.

'Be silent!' the priest ordered, but Lucia was not.

'How can I obey you?' she said. 'You are not my husband. Maybe you'd like to be? Or perhaps you'd like to make an honest woman of your mistress?'

'Cast out these devils!' The preacher raised his hands in the air.

'I'll cast them out myself,' said Lucia, waving her headscarf and exiting the church.

Lucia's outburst had not been the only surprise: my mother's composure had not flinched. In fact, in my memory I felt I'd seen a faint smile.

I have always found church conversations to be filled with tense contradiction. The very young and the very old tolerated for breaking the rule of expected quiet from women, children squealing out of boredom or the elderly speaking up because they were deaf and couldn't hear their own voices.

'Get to the point!' shouted Signora Baldovinetti, whose once nimble mind was known to be failing. 'My husband's pecker is as stiff as a biscuit.'

A ripple of chatter swept through the church. Yet the preacher continued, red-faced, leaving those less gracious among us to snigger into our handkerchiefs.

In church, conversations are abbreviations, fragmentations, where with a few quiet words meaning has to be captured. And more than once I was banished to my room upon returning home for being unable to hold my laughter at Lucia's concise observations.

'That dress begs a funeral.' Of Signora Novella Crocini, with more money than taste, whose flounce of black, rustling skirts, according to Lucia, could hide several Senese pigs from the knife.

'No tax on smiling.' Of Signora Ippolita Fonte, a newcomer from Venice with unrestrained scorn for her impious new city.

The man kneeling beside me moves closer. 'You don't recognise me, Signora Albertinelli?'

His question startles me, and I turn to see him smiling.

'Zio Renzo said I would likely find you here,' he says. 'I know it's rude to disturb you.'

He's referred to the padre as Zio, as uncle. And now I see it. The square line of his jaw, the almond curve of his pale umber eyes, the Cupid's bow of his lip. The boy from my childhood, Padre Renzo's nephew. Eugenio.

'You love it, this painting,' says Eugenio. 'You don't have to answer, I can see how you feel.'

I blush with discomfort, with anger, at his bold observations. Because my love for the painting exceeds most other loves, sometimes causing me to wonder if I could love my husband, if he wasn't its painter.

I want to move away from Eugenio, but this is my place. Second step, halfway along. Always here, my place in the church. With a direct view of the painting.

'There is a relic,' says Eugenio, 'of her son's finger, Giovanni Battista's, the finger he pointed at Herod.'

This is the subject of at least three of Padre Renzo's sermons in any given year. The indecent marriage of Herod Antipas, son of Herod the Great, to his brother's wife, Herodias. So many sins in that one act. San Giovanni, not afraid to aim his accusing finger at a king. It always hushes the congregation, husbands squirming in their seats as the padre expounds his views on the sanctity of marriage, lamenting that every imaginable sin of the flesh is alive and well here in Florence. Our individual and collective duties to stave off such vice.

'Zio Renzo pilgrimaged to see it,' says Eugenio.

'To the Holy City?' I ask.

'To an island in the Black Sea,' he replies. 'Took him months.'

'To see a finger?' I ask.

'A finger bone, really. A fragment at that,' he replies.

This conversation makes me uneasy in front of the painting. In front of Elisheva. I've grown to feel as if she is here, with me, in the church. An elder, a confidante. A flesh-and-bone woman who feels and shares my innermost contemplations. So this is like gossiping about somebody who can overhear it.

'The head is elsewhere,' he says, and I feel myself flinch, as if the mother-to-be of the painting might be hearing for the first time of her son's fate.

The hair rises on the back of my neck to imagine the blade that put his head on a platter.

'Your uncle would not approve of interrupting my prayers.' My face burns with offence.

Again, silence. Different to the last. The many faces of quiet within the walls of a church.

'I don't mean to offend you or your Elisabetta,' he says.

'Her name is Elisheva,' I say. 'Show some respect.'

'*Mi scusi*,' he whispers. I am sorry.

He rises from his knees and exits the church.

He is there when I open the church doors and step out into the piazza.

'Please forgive me. I speak before I think. Can we begin again?' he says. 'You always were gracious. And I imprudent.'

His beguiling half-smile is the one I wished every week would be directed at me. Out here in the light, his handsome features are lit by the sun. And I am again an eight-year-old girl with a crush.

'*Giorno*, Eugenio!' Signora Crivelli crosses the piazza and waves to Eugenio; her eldest son Benvenuto, bronze-skinned, cherub-lipped, grinning in his mother's wake.

Eugenio waves back and smiles: a courteous glance towards Signora Crivelli and a lingering gaze on her son. The young Benvenuto looks back once. Twice.

'I can see why Zio Renzo compares you to the marchesa,' says Eugenio.

But I am distracted by the dalliance that just took place between two men. And certain Eugenio has meant for me to see it. I hide my disappointment by turning my attention to the ragged scar on his forehead.

'You are intolerant. But in a dignified manner,' he explains. 'Like the Marchesa Isabella d'Este.'

'My husband admires her,' I say.

'He is one among many,' he says, his finger to the scar.

'I don't mean to stare,' I say.

'I was part of the mob that stormed the Signoria, demanding that the Council of the Night be called to account,' he says.

For a fleeting moment I want to be petty. To tell him I already took his first hint that he doesn't bed women. The Council was a group of men who hunted down other men who preferred the world's Benvenutos. Whose brutal punishments often held no account.

'My uncle came to our home and begged me not to join in, in case I was jailed. Or worse.'

'So he knows?' I ask, unsure of how to be clear.

'About what he calls my *persistent bachelorism*?' he replies. 'I am certain.'

'He's unlike most priests,' I say.

'He's unlike anyone.' Eugenio laughs. 'And the opposite of my father. Hard to believe they were brothers.' He muses on the thought for a while.

'My uncle told me you lost both your parents,' he says. 'I am sorry to hear it. Do you have other family in Florence?'

And the tear in my heart, never quite healed, opens a little.

'My mother was an only child and my father's family only small, just him and one sister, one brother. Both died in the plagues.' I answer things the wrong way around, making excuses for my lack of family, my lack of connection. 'My father had no extended family.'

'Forgive me for saying, but maybe having less family spares you particular griefs?' he says, grinning.

The ever-present ache of loss spreads through my chest.

'*Allora!* A family tree needs its branches!' he says, now earnest. 'What of that woman who once came to the church with you and your mother? The one who put that old priest in his place?'

And I could kiss him for taking my mind to Lucia.

'A second cousin on my mother's side. More like an aunt. To me, she was Zia Lucia.' I feel a lightness flood my chest to mention her name.

'*Allora!* She's family worth having,' says Eugenio, pushing his hands to his hips and, for a moment, looking every bit the strapping man his father probably wished him to be. His face all angles and shadows, an expression that would have an artist reaching for his charcoal.

'She left,' I say. 'Many years ago now.' The lightness in my chest dims, fades.

'You never asked where she went?'

'Who would I ask?' I reply. 'She was not popular.'

'Unpopular people are the most interesting,' he says.

'I wanted to find her,' I say.

'But your parents forbade it?' His finger works the scar on his forehead.

'She was unlike any woman,' I reply.

'And therefore a threat. My father whipped me until I bled when, as a child, I asked why I couldn't live with my nonna. His own mother! She was eccentric, outspoken. The only person who could render him red-faced and speechless. My father called her "*Un cane in Chiesa*". A dog in a church.'

We are quiet together, our histories meeting, touching at frayed edges. The clatter of vendors pulling carts across the piazza.

'I am certain my father was terrified of Zia Lucia,' I say. 'Freehearted. Bursting with colour. Came to visit us, paintbrushes and all, on the day Savonarola tried to burn every artwork in Florence.'

'Spurned by a lover and destined to make the world pay,' says Eugenio, rolling his eyes.

'Not Lucia,' I say. 'She'd sooner spit in the face of rejection.'

'Not your Zia, the friar,' he says. 'He fell in love and she didn't want him. That's why he joined a friary, to reject all women because he couldn't have one.'

'How do you know the things you do?' I am enamoured with what Eugenio tells me about spurned friars and saints' finger bones buried on islands.

'I was born a man. I'm allowed to ask questions.'

'But only those that didn't upset your father?'

His mouth smiles, but his eyes are forlorn.

'We were in the small field my father worked. I was five. Two sheep were rutting. I was captivated by the act, baffled. I stood studying the scene, one sheep scrambling to get up on the rear of another. I was unable to make sense of it. My father kneeled down beside me and spoke plainly, as if he was teaching me the types of cloud that would bring rain. "When you take a whore you must take her like this, from behind." He pointed to the ram mounting the ewe. "In the hole between the cheeks. From where she shits. You understand?" I was terrified that if I didn't understand I'd be beaten. I did at least know the difference between the holes in a woman, but I had no idea what I'd put in either of them and why I would want to. "You won't get her with child. But you will drop the weight from your ballsacks and feel better for it." It was the only time he touched me in any way that didn't draw tears or blood. A light cuff to my chin.'

My skin becomes greasy as Eugenio tells his story. My body erupting with memories my mind doesn't want. These feelings rise often and I bully them down. Deep, deeper. But in Eugenio's presence I cannot suppress them, and they rise now, pushing back, punching their way to the surface.

'Let's walk,' I say, hooking my arm though his.

We wander the streets. Past rowdy taverns down narrow alleys, high-storeyed homes squeezed together, blocking out sunlight.

'I wish I'd had a brother like you,' I say as we make the final turn and arrive back at San Michele.

'My grandmother told me that once you share a secret, you're family,' he says, plainly eager for me to share something with him.

But I am not ready to share. Not the most secret thing that happened in the darkness of my kitchen. It occurs to me that the most terrifying thing in the world would be for Eugenio to read me like he read my love for the painting.

'I hear her voice inside my head,' I say, deciding to share a different secret.

'Zia Lucia's?' he asks.

'Elisheva's,' I reply.

'Does she inspire the performance of outrageous deeds?'

I laugh, shake my head.

'Disappointing,' he says. 'I'm in need of ideas.'

'It's more a sense of her as a woman,' I reply. 'As a real person who might walk out of the painting and take my hand in hers. Like she does to the Virgin.'

His expression takes on a vague hint of suspicion. 'You will tell me when you are ready,' he says.

'What Elisheva says?' I ask.

'Your *real* secret,' he replies.

I wonder if my cheeks look as flushed as they feel.

'You didn't finish your story of the Baptist's finger on the island,' I say, changing the subject.

He falls quiet, as if he made it all up.

'Do you lie?' I ask.

'All my life,' he says, grinning. 'But not about this.' He taps out the sign of the cross on his body. 'As God is my witness.'

'Then tell me everything about the finger bone,' I say.

'Why hear it from me when you can talk to his mother?' he teases.

The piazza bells chime and Eugenio becomes distracted.

'Did my Zio Renzo know your Zia Lucia?' he asks.

His question makes my belly flutter. 'As you know, she came to church now and then, so he knew her by name.'

'A name is enough. We Florentines imbibe gossip like the air we breathe. Sucked into our lungs when we open our mouths.'

I'd asked Padre Renzo. Once.

'Don't chase after butterflies. You will upset your father,' he said.

It was more than enough to deter me. Not upsetting my father had been the daily goal of my childhood.

'I'm sorry again, Signora Albertinelli,' says Eugenio. 'For my insensitivity in the church.'

'We've shared secrets, we are friends,' I say. 'And please, to an old friend, it's Antonia.'

'Do you think she ever lost faith, your Elisheva?' he asks. 'Even Florentine women would think themselves closer to death than motherhood had they not birthed before their twentieth year.'

I have not considered this question and it makes me feel uneasy.

'I guess a saint cannot lose faith,' he answers himself.

'She was a woman long before she was a saint,' I say, defensive, because I am now twenty-five and have not borne a child.

'I'll make some enquiries about your Zia,' says Eugenio, striding away. 'This is Florence,' he calls out as he crosses the piazza, kissing his palms and offering them to the sky. 'Everyone needs family to drive them bat-crazy.'

15

Yerushalayim, 20 BCE

Abba's behaviour is testing my patience. I try to remember that he is doing his best. We ascend the last ridge of our journey across the Mountains of Yehuda, and the pilgrims shout and whoop as the Holy City, Yerushalayim, comes into view across the Valley of Hinnom. The stone city walls are set high on precipitous cliffs above deep ravines, smoke spiralling skywards from the braziers set before the entry to the Holy of Holies.

'Go, go. Go!' says my father. He tries to push in.

'We must wait our turn, Abba,' I say, weary with both him and the long and rowdy line of pilgrims carrying livestock and birds to present at the altar.

His language has much improved moon by moon, but his mind still struggles through cycles of fixation or despair. In periods of fixation he becomes wilful, aggressive. I pray he calms down and does not make a scene at the Gate.

As we wind down the well-worn path into the depths of the valley, I wonder what the Holy Temple will look like when Herod's ambitious plans come to fruition.

He claims he will restore the magnificence of Solomon's Temple, lengthening the Temple Mount's walls in the north, west and south. Pilgrims travelling on our path will one day be struck with awe at the sight of the new Temple at sunrise. *Amamei*, too, stunned into silence. After days and even moons on the road, regardless of race or religion, few will see the magnificent gleaming structure and be untouched.

But for now, the new Temple is still only a promise from Herod. Some say the dream of a madman. One who is working to win our trust and conjure excitement by recruiting ten thousand men and rafts of machinery as proof of his intention to deliver his vision. He has even begun to quarry the stone. Colossal blocks for walls to support the plaza that will make a vast flat top of Mount Moriah. Upon this will sit our Temple. Our Holy of Holies. A new temple for Yerushalayim. A renewed heart for Yehuda.

It is Herod's quarrying of stone that has captured Abba's attention. As usual, his unruly mind wavers between despair and obsession; in the latter state determined to unravel some mystery that has formed in his thinking or achieve an explicit deed that has sprung to mind. This journey to Yerushalayim is no different. He seems unaware of our purpose, to visit and pray at the Temple, and is instead driven by his latest curiosity: that stone can be cut by water.

When Herod first declared he would rebuild the Temple destroyed by the Babylonians, he trained one thousand priests to perform the labours on the inner sanctum. Since it is forbidden for an Amam to enter the Temple, this was his solution. Always, it seems, a clever plan from Herod. Word travelled fast, scraps of gossip becoming extravagant rumours, and Abba was captivated by the quarrying process relayed to him by Yiska's son.

'They cut into raw stone, then hammer down logs. Tight and hard into the chiselled outline of where the stone will be cut. Then they pour in the water. The wood swells and *crack!* splits the rock. It's true, I saw it for myself!'

Abba became obsessed. This he had to see.

At the lowest point of the valley, beside the south city gate, Cousin Oshaya is waiting and he greets us with joy. He brings two lambs and a bird as our temple offerings.

'Hanna and Y'hoyakim left only an hour ago,' he says, embracing us both. 'They're leaving Yerushalayim to visit Y'hoyakim's sick mother.'

'I'm sad to hear she is unwell,' I say, my heart squeezing to have missed them.

'They waited as long as they could. Little Maryam wanted to see you, begged them to stay longer.'

Little Maryam. The little girl of my dreams for so long. The sister of my heart whom I wished was my blood.

'A bright spark, that child,' says Oshaya. 'Doesn't say much, but played my lyre like an angel. Hanna said she won't leave the house without her bone flute or frame drum. A four-year-old girl already with a mind of her own.' His cheeks flush as he laughs.

Abba starts his gibberish. I'm not sure if it's deliberate, to gain our attention. I whisper an urgent prayer for patience, feeling myself frown like my mother.

Oshaya ushers us towards the Pool of Siloam, where we will immerse our bodies to be cleansed for the Temple. Again there is a line, to pay the tax for entry, and Abba moans and shuffles like a kid goat straining against its first tether.

'It's like having a child,' Imma had said. 'And you might as well know something of it.'

Each time I must calm my father during a tantrum or clean his tunic and mantle when his bowels empty without control, I do my best to forget Imma's spite and instead recall the countless hours he took to teach me my letters. To repeat for me the names of birds and trees and seasons and prayers until I knew them by heart.

With the disappearance of memories and words from Abba's mind, it seems that the boundaries forever dividing people from people have, likewise, vanished. He cannot discern who is Roman, who is Jewish, who is P'rishay, who is Tsadukay, who is Amam.

'Can't find it, can't find it. Can't find it in here.' Abba raps at his head with fisted knuckles, both of us distraught with what he knows he has lost, unable to find the words to express how he feels.

'It's okay, Abba,' I say. 'Oshaya will go with you to the makva.'

His expression transforms to immediate joy. 'Yes, yes. To the water!'

Then my father spies the water where he will perform his ritual cleanse, and it knits together some broken connection in his mind. He takes Oshaya's arm and hurries towards the water, launching into conversation like some miracle of Ribon Alma has unlocked his tongue. I know it will not last.

After bathing, we ascend the thick stones steps to the Temple. The clamour of vendors and haggling, lambs bleating, the urgent warble of doves. In the Court of the Amamei on the summit, priests teach huddled groups, and people swarm and drift through the grounds in states of sombre ritual or rapture. Around us is the heady mixed scent of burnt offerings and incense.

Abba again finds his mind in the security of the sacred. I am glad for the relief of being left to myself. I drop back, and quietly begin my own prayers. This is our Temple; in our Holy City. Here, and now, time dissolves into reverence.

On the way through the Upper City to Oshaya's home, Abba hurries ahead. Leading the way and telling me the sights. An etched pattern of time past, unearthed like a treasure.

'That's the home of Yitzhak the Short One. A small man but a big voice. Don't start an argument with him: you'll lose and the whole city will know it.'

'I learned that truth the hard way,' Oshaya agrees.

'And there!' Abba points, his expression as I remember as a child, lucid, engaged. 'That's Marinus the Sandalmaker's home. Finest shoes you will find.'

I let myself fall behind, feeling weary. Letting Oshaya walk and talk with my father. Taking respite while he is happy.

We reach the narrow street that leads to Oshaya's small stone house, and I hear my name called. Called again and again. The slap of fast feet upon cobbles. I turn to see a girl running towards me, beaming, a front tooth missing. I kneel down to greet her and she throws herself into my arms.

'I told my *imma* you'd be here,' says Maryam.

She twines her arms around my neck and kisses my cheeks, pecks light as a sparrow.

'You took your first steps the last time I saw you,' I say. 'Now you could outrun an ibex.'

She giggles, delighted. 'My *abba* says my feet arrive before I do.'

Hanna catches us up. 'She was bereft not to see you,' she says, cheerful despite the demands of her young daughter.

I stand to greet my aunt and Maryam clutches my hand.

My uncle, Y'hoyakim, joins us, and I am touched by his concession to acquiesce and turn back from their long journey to visit his mother.

'Six sons, now a daughter. How can her mother and I tell her no?' he says, and Maryam grins her gappy smile.

'We can't stay,' says Hanna.

'For a meal, at least?' says Oshaya.

'I'll play my drum for you,' says Maryam. 'I wrote a song to go with it.'

Over the meal we share stories and Abba stammers a little, savouring fig cakes until he falls asleep, a sticky piece in each hand. Maryam plays her drum, then plucks out plainsong on Oshaya's lyre; it rings in my chest long after she is finished. We applaud and she snuggles onto my lap, falls asleep in my arms. And when stars pierce the black sky, they depart.

I embrace them in turn. Y'hoyakim, Hanna, and Maryam last.

'Will you visit Beit HaKerem again soon?' I ask, and she nods with excitement.

'I like the sweet taste of the spring water,' she says, her grey-green eyes offering more than what she is saying.

'As sweet as your music,' I tell her. And hope my voice doesn't betray what I feel.

A quickening of my breath, a heat through my chest. In my ears the trickling sound of the ancient Spring of the Vineyard. Perhaps even King Sh'lomo stooped, cupped his hands and drank. Its abundance is the finest to flow down from the mountains, with a passage through limestone that leaves a tingling sweetness in our mouths. The Spring became the place where women gather. To draw water, to drink. To exchange gossip and stories. To first meet a potential betrothal. Women and water. A natural accord, it seems, since time began. But with each moon that passes I am welcomed less and less at the Spring. Omens and portents do not favour a childless woman in her third decade of marriage.

Before dawn Abba is pacing.

Half asleep on my pallet, I try to ignore him.

'Time, time,' he says.

It isn't yet dawn and my skin prickles with irritation at the sound of the stress-whimper from the back of his throat. I pull myself to sitting, then rise slowly, while he paces and rubs hard at his forehead, leaving a red mark.

When I move his hand away from his face and his fingers take up scratching his arm.

'Don't hurt yourself, Abba.'

'Like your mother, like your mother,' he says, raising his voice.

'Be quiet,' I say. 'Your cousin is sleeping.'

'Beh, bah. Bah. Two, two. Beh, eh, eh.' The gushing staccato of his gibberish, as if the sounds have built up in the time he's not been uttering them.

'Sit a moment, Abba,' I say, leading him to a chair. 'We will leave soon.'

I pray he won't launch into a tantrum. I hand him a coin I keep for these moments. He seems to find comfort in turning it over and through his fingers, a trick I admired as a child.

The coin rolls back and forth over his knuckles. Calming his mind.

'You understood everything,' he says. 'A baby, but so clever.'

He's told this story many times. How when I was born I understood everything he said. That perhaps I didn't forget all that I should have when the angel of birth placed its finger to my lips and told me *hush*. Leaving the dint in my top lip, the mark of its duty to ensure I forgot all the secrets I'd been told in the cave of the womb.

'She screamed,' Abba says. 'Twenty-seven hours. And then you.' I knew that part too. Told time and time again by Imma of the misery of my birth. Twenty-seven hours. His favourite number to express 'many', in this case, might well have been true.

'Tsad, so different,' he says, a new story that shocks me. 'Slid, slid! Out from your mother like the pit from a date.'

'How would you know if you weren't there?' I say, feeling piqued at his memory of Tsad's ease into this world. 'Men don't attend births, so how could you know?'

His face crumples in confusion, knowing that I am correct, yet unsure of why he would know at all.

'It's time, it's time. The stone now, the stone!' Abba says, following behind me while I tidy our room.

'Let's wash and eat, then we'll visit the quarry,' I say.

'Stone cut by water!' Abba brightens, shifting his focus. 'But how? If water can cut stone, how do we not lose our limbs in the makva.' He stares at his hands as if having them still attached after bathing is a miracle. 'My second, my second ...' He is struggling with a word that must be close to his recall. He squeezes his eyes shut, his hands fisted and shaking.

'Don't upset yourself, Abba.'

'Second-favourite day!' He is elated. The pressure of his thinking reveals the words he is seeking. 'Stone cut by water. My second-favourite day! My second. My second.'

And I am relieved, thrilled, that he has found the right words that I don't want to risk confusing him again. So even though I suspect it was the birth of my brother, I don't ask what was his first.

Outside, the Holy City still bustles with pilgrims and travellers who have heard about Herod's grand plans, and Abba insists on greeting each passerby, including the livestock.

'*Sh'lama*, dear donkey. Did your ancestor carry King Sh'lomo?'

'*Sh'lama*, fine gentleman!' he says to a Roman procurator, whose *toga praetexta* with red-purple edging shows his high status. 'What splendid garments,' says Abba. 'Did you buy them in Egypt? Fine clothes. Fine, fine. Is your robe whitened with piss?'

An anxious group of consuls hurry to the procurator's side, their specially whitened garments bright in the overcast light. A colour that, as Abba said but Savta first told me, is made white by a mixture to which urine is added.

'Move on, old man,' one commands, another lifting his hand to cuff my father, who cowers and whimpers. 'Watch your lip.'

'Watch your lip, watch your lip,' Abba stammers, reduced in a second.

How many ways have I found to explain his condition? How many apologies to those to whom I would rather not speak? Once respectful and pious, solemn and eloquent, how strange it is to have a father whose actions can be so offensive. Most often his strange greetings are met with puzzlement, but there are times when a jealous husband or official reacts with anger, one magistrate pushing him to the ground in frustration when Abba insisted they had met once on the road to Damascus.

I apologise to the consuls and move Abba on.

As soon as we are on our way, he seems to forget the incident and grows impatient again. Clutching my arm and leading me through winding streets, seeming to know exactly the way. *Hurry hurry.* He mutters as he strides, his limping gait moving fast.

'Aharon!' A broad-shouldered man, his beard streaked with silver, steps into our pathway, and Abba stops in his tracks.

'Asher, my dear Asher. My friend.' My father turns to me, lucid and bright. 'Elisheva, here is Asher. So long! Too long! Our grandfathers, best friends.'

'*Sh'lama*, old friend.' Asher's voice quakes at the emotion of this unexpected meeting. 'Will you sit a while?' He motions towards a clutch of small stools and table set next to a doorway, curls an arm around my father to lead him. 'You are limping, old friend. Did you fall off a donkey?' A roaring laugh rumbles from his belly.

'Nothing, nothing,' says my father. 'Nothing at all.'

I am overcome with how, here in the Holy City's streets, my father has slipped back inside his old skin. I sit as they chat, enjoying Abba's relaxed disposition. Then my attention is captured by a wafting smell I know well, the scents of char and silica and wax. The smell of a glass workshop.

Asher and Abba are deep in conversation and so I wander up the street, past the stalls and storefronts, following the scent. From the street, I peer inside the workshop. A man and his younger apprentice sweat over flames, molten glass swelling from blowpipes.

'Your father tells me you do glasswork.' Asher and Abba are beside me.

'Clever girl, clever, girl,' says Abba, beaming, and I can't help but feel pleased. 'Twenty-seven hours,' he continues, now a grim tone.

And now I am cringing, expecting to endure, yet again, the story of my difficult birth.

Asher doesn't follow what is being said, casting me a curious glance. I shrug, too tired to explain yet again my father's behaviour.

'Twenty-seven hours,' repeats Abba. 'Then Elisheva arrives.' He takes my hands in his. Pats them, squeezes them. 'My first favourite day.'

'Here is Pappos,' says Asher.

But I am struck silent by what my father has said. I stand dazed in this moment. Our hands clasped together.

'You are my *barta*, my daughter.' Abba is now weeping.

'And you are my *abba*.' I pull him to me and hold him, feel the tremor in his body, the muted whimper that arises when he is overwrought.

'Come see Pappos's work,' says Asher, made uncomfortable by my father's emotion. 'He's a talent and he'll tell you.' Asher's laugh rumbles again as he ushers us inside the workshop.

The men greet each other. Right hands on right shoulders, cheeks pressed to cheeks. Glass vessels of all colours, sizes and shapes are stacked on sagging shelves lining the walls. Goblets and jugs, plates and amphorae, slender perfume flasks and translucent kohl tubes. Handcrafted metal tools hang neatly from hooks. Metal tools and pipes, shears and wooden paddles. Imperfect vessels are piled in one corner, to be crushed and reused. I circle the room and relish the familiar heat and vigour of production, Asher explaining my shared interest in glasswork.

'The woman?' I hear Pappos ask.

Shutting out the men's talk, I study the vessels, noting Pappos's clever style with two colours, so difficult to achieve in uniform bands. I pick up a rippled cobalt and aquamarine vase.

'What ingredient gives this colour?' I turn to enquire.

Pappos and Asher are stooped over a crate stacked with glass pitchers. I scan the small workshop. I can't see my father.

'Where's Abba?' I ask.

They look at me blankly.

So well had I learned to ignore the judgments of those right beside me, I'd closed down to the talk and did not notice my father had slipped from inside.

'He's not well, he can't manage alone!' I run into the street, calling for him.

I push past those strolling, Asher behind me, a crowd swelling up ahead. I reach the edge of the rabble, calling for Abba. There is yelling and jostling. I begin shouting for him, groping my way through the mash of people, trying to catch sight of my father. Children are crying, a scuffle around us escalating.

'Kill the Roman pigs.'

'Slay the zealots.'

A roar of men with tempers flaring.

And the throng erupts in a frenzy of shoving, of heaving. Of the sound of blows, women screaming.

Then the crowd breaks open, people scattering as quickly as they gathered. But not Abba. His body is lying still and wide-eyed on the street, in the path of a blade not meant for him. A slash through his throat like a Passover lamb.

I can hear the sound of my own voice wailing. Feel the splitting of skin as my knees hit the stone pavement. My hands on Abba's chest, praying for the rise and fall of his breath. I am screaming for help.

Asher and Pappos shout instructions to help gather up my father. And though I saw him as frail, a wisp of what he once was, it takes four men to lift him. Blinded by tears, I follow the body of my father back to our cousin's. Where I will grieve and not eat. Where I will seethe and not sleep. Where I will beseech an answer of Ribon Alma. Where I will come to no answers. Where I will gather up the rubble of our last conversation. Clumsily piece it together with my unclean hands, the warmth of my father's body still on my skin, the stain of his blood in the creases of my knuckles. And when I wash myself clean I will wonder if it would be easier not to know what I learned on my Abba's second favourite day. That I was the cause of his first.

I leave the Holy City in a caravan that will return west without my father, to our village, past the unending line of arriving pilgrims. Many look tired, their garments filthy from travel. What of those who do not have the shekel to admit them to the waters for purging?

Purge me with hyssop and I will be pure, wash me and I will be whiter than snow.

The prayer Oshaya spoke as he dipped a hyssop branch in water and sprinkled it upon those of us who touched my father's dead body. It haunts me as I walk. For how do I purge this rage that burns in my skin? Where is the potent hyssop that can purify the memory of my father's limp body, of his bright leaking blood turning dark in the dust?

16

Florence, 1514

The white paint on the palette sheens like shot silk. A brightness that shifts with the light, creating an illusion of depth. The texture grabs the brush, not too stiff, not too soft, and I can work the volume with ease across the scrap of wood panel. My skin prickles as if something terrifying, not exhilarating, has appeared before me. How is it that elation can feel so much like dread? I place the brush aside and take the panel to the window. Blow at it, impatient for it to dry. A rush of gooseflesh, a hard pulse at every soft place as it catches the light.

The white is like Florence the day Lucia arrived. Like a fine dusting of snow, both lucent and vivid. I take the chunk of stone from the pocket of my apron, the secret ingredient for what I have created. A secret that was hiding in plain sight.

A memory of my father brought me to it, him and me in the vineyards. And glinting inside the dark memory was Alberese stone.

From the riverbed of the Arno to the hills around Prato, Alberese was found all over Tuscany. But I saw it first in the small vineyard of my father's family. The white chunks piled at the base of the vines, which reflected the sun to the plants, storing and feeding them warmth and light in the winter.

'It hurts my eyes,' I'd said to my father one afternoon, the sun at its zenith, the white stone blazing.

'Don't blink,' he had said. Demonstrated by keeping his eyes wide. 'You must toughen up your eyes so they can bear the light.'

I had tried to copy him, my sun-stung eyes leaking, tears bathing my cheeks.

'Don't blink, don't turn away,' he'd insisted. 'How else will you greet your Maker and his fury of light?'

I recall him in his death bloat, his once familiar features distorted. The scar on his bicep; the cold, heavy smell of faeces and stinking flesh. His eyeballs fixed in a clouded stare. Had there been light in the fate he had earned?

Downstairs Mariotto is talking to a visitor. I'm not really listening, until he raises his voice.

'You come here, to my house, and demand what is not yours until the due date?' says my husband.

And for two reasons I know the other person is Raffaello Santi da Urbino. First, since borrowing fifty gold florins, Mariotto has been avoiding Raffaello for weeks, finding any chance to grumble about his fellow artist's ongoing requests to be repaid sooner than they had agreed. And second, because I cannot hear the reply of the other man. Raffaello is the only man that I know who never raises his voice to be heard.

'You have popes throwing money at you and you come here to complain about a mere twenty florins. *Mi insulti!*' says Mariotto.

I strain to hear the other side of the conversation, but the reply is inaudible.

'Fifty, you say? It was never fifty. Maybe thirty. Thirty-five at most,' says Mariotto.

A pause that indicates Raffaello is speaking.

'We are all in need of materials,' argues my husband. 'I owe you. Others owe me. Here, I have lead powder for your palette. Take some, take it all. Mine's the best you will find. Ground and rinsed many times over.'

He is speaking of my batches, because Mariotto himself barely rinses the grounds.

A door slams.

'You leave with no kind words, Santi?' Mariotto yells. 'Too good for us now that the pope pays your wages?' He stomps up to the kitchen, clattering pans.

My husband has filled half the kitchen with jars of his concoctions, still set on producing his own perfect white, and I know he has made this a competition between us. Often spending more hours grinding than painting. Refusing to cover his mouth, coughing and spluttering. The more he works with the powder, the more irritable he becomes. His wrists have developed strange blue lines. His ankles too.

'I can't shit!' he will yell from the pot. 'God help me! My bowels are so full they will burst through my navel.'

The physician prescribed him a purgative boiled with onions that made his stomach swell and gurgle, and dried the spit from his mouth.

'My own shit will poison me,' he complained to Michel.

'Such is the scourge of humanity,' said Michel.

'I shit on your contempt,' said Mariotto.

'You couldn't shit for a florin,' said Michel.

Pots and pans crash in the kitchen and Mariotto, in argument with someone no longer there, mutters as he throws what I presume are his usual six eggs into a pan.

Another knock at the front door.

'I'll answer,' I call up to Mariotto.

I place the wood panel painted with my white on the desk and push the chunk of Alberese back inside my apron. If I decide to share what I have produced with the stone, I will make them earn the details.

'I have news,' Eugenio says, flush-faced and smiling.

'News of what?' Mariotto appears in the doorway, a hunk of bread in one hand, a cup of wine in the other.

'Your eggs are burning,' I say. 'How can you not smell it?'

'*Santa Madre!*' says Mariotto, stomping back up to the kitchen. 'My blocked nose couldn't smell a pig's gizzards!'

'He looks like he needs a few drops of theriac,' says Eugenio, when Mariotto is out of earshot. A viper flesh and opium tincture, made by apothecaries to ward off the plague.

'And this is a good day,' I say, weary of the furor that is Mariotto.

'I crossed paths with Raffaello,' he says.

'Who hasn't this morning?' I say.

And I wonder how well Eugenio knows the famously amorous Raffaello, letting my expression show what I am thinking.

'I won't answer,' he says.

'I'm not asking,' I reply, relishing Eugenio's self-conscious reaction. Rare as it is for me to catch him off guard.

'*Allora!* Your news,' I say. 'Tell me all.'

'There's a log in the sacristy my uncle has kept for decades. Births, death and marriages for all his parish.'

'Padre Renzo's private log?' I am mortified. 'It wouldn't be decent.'

'Being decent will not help us,' says Eugenio.

My stomach churns as if it were my very own hands that turned the pages. 'How could you pry?'

'There was a young man chasing my company. I was looking for details.'

'You're a criminal for looking,' I say.

'According to most, I am a criminal anyway.'

Mariotto reappears in the doorway, picking at his teeth with the sharp tip of a knife. 'You think you're the only man in Florence who takes pleasure between the cheeks of an arse?'

'Your sweet words rival Dante's,' says Eugenio, unfazed by Mariotto's crass banter.

Mariotto makes his way across the room, his eye catching the wood panel I placed on the desk. 'What's this?' He points with the blade.

'See for yourself,' I reply, handing him the panel.

'*Dio mio!*' Mariotto snatches it and moves nearer the window, into more light.

I push a finger to my mouth to warn Eugenio not to speak any further about sacristy logbooks. Mariotto's loose lips would get us all into trouble.

'On God's bones!' Mariotto says. 'This is your white?' He shifts the panel close to his eyes, then to arm's length. Shifting angles. 'Crisp and bright, but not stark.' He sucks at his teeth. The same noise he makes when deliberating over details like how the poise of a hand should rest in a lap. 'But how?' he asks. Almost too softly for me to hear it.

'You won't guess,' I reply.

'My wife knows how to goad me,' he says to Eugenio. 'So now I must prove you misjudge my guile.' He examines the panel, paces the room. 'Crushed pearl?'

'How could I afford it?' I ask.

'So something more common,' Mariotto says, thumbing his chin.

'Crushed eggshell?' guesses Eugenio.

'*Imbecille*,' says Mariotto. 'To an eye trained to see it, eggshell makes it too grey. This is a white like God's nightgown.'

'Give us a clue,' says Eugenio, holding out his hand towards Mariotto to ask for a closer look.

Mariotto refuses, keeps the panel tight in his grip. 'If you guess it first, you can share in the riches that flood in when we sell it,' he says, forever making bets he has no intention of keeping.

'Then my guess is marble.'

'Buffoon!' says Mariotto, his wild eyebrows peaking. 'Marble dust is too dry for this shine.'

'And marble must be quarried and transported,' I say.

'So your recipe includes something found close to home?' says Mariotto, latching on to my hint.

'Is it dug from the earth?' says Eugenio, getting caught up in the game.

'You think pigments are found in the clouds?' Mariotto glares. 'Of course from the earth.'

'From earth and under the water,' I reply.

'In the Arno?' asks Eugenio.

'Allora!' says Mariotto, confounded.

'And in the hills and in vineyards.' My own excitement is growing.

'In the vineyards of your father?' asks Mariotto, and I urge him to make a guess.

'But it can't be? So simple!' He studies the panel in his hand, a grim doubt sweeping over his face.

'I dare you to guess it,' I say.

'Alberese?' says Mariotto, and I applaud him.

He's hardly guessed on his own, but is chuffed to have spoken the answer.

'What a game,' says Mariotto. *'Brava!* Good work!'

'But the stone is only part of the answer,' I say with excitement. 'The temper too is important.'

At this revelation, Mariotto begins to look sullen. As if he should have been told that there were more things to predict.

'Olio di noci?' asks Eugenio, and Mariotto glares at him, not happy to be outguessed by a man with no talent for art.

Even I am surprised that he has come to this answer.

'It says here on the bottle,' says Eugenio, pointing to the brown jar on the desk. 'Oil of walnuts.'

'He's cocksure, your friend,' Mariotto says, sniffing at the oil in the jar. 'What a strange combination,' he muses. A moment of stillness.

'Not only walnut, but a margin of linseed,' I say. Sun-warmed is better.

'Now my wife thinks she's an apothecary,' says Mariotto.

'The muller and slab are essential.' I take the heavy glass muller, acquired by selling a pair of earrings, and show him the surface. 'Both surfaces must be scored with grit. It makes a better texture because it captures the ground, pushes out all the air.'

Mariotto says nothing, hands me the panel.

'The brew of the vinegar, too, is important,' I persist. 'And using new oil slows the drying. But washing the grinds, Mariotto, that's part of the secret! After grinding with vinegar, of course. Eugenio, here look, at first it turns black!' I show him a slab where I've been grinding. I know I am gushing, trying to share all I have discovered, reciting the steps all out of order. 'Washing and grinding, many times over! Only then can you achieve the brightest of whites.'

Both men observe me. No particular awe in their expressions. Perhaps the mention of so much washing has cost me their attention.

'Albertinelli? Are you up there?' A voice calls from the piazza below and Mariotto peers out the window.

'Pig misery! It's Santi again,' he says. 'Tell him I'm in Rome.'

'When only moments ago he saw you were right here in Florence?' I say. 'What is it that so galls you about Raffaello Santi?'

'It's not for the money,' Raffaello calls from the street.

'You're a demon, Santi. Do you lie?' Mariotto calls down.

'Alfonso returned. He brought news of Baccio, from Rome,' answers Raffaello.

Mariotto stomps back down the steps, cursing under his breath.

'Cocksure is right,' says Eugenio, pulling a folded parchment from inside his doublet now that Mariotto has left. He opens it to reveal black, curling script written in Padre Renzo's hand.

'You stole the page from the logbook?' I ask.

'She was taken in by the nuns of Santa Maria,' he replies, undaunted by my accusation.

'In Fiesole? So close by?' I am struck still. Cannot breathe. She was so close by all this time.

'See for yourself.'

I take the parchment and read it. Trace the slope and pitch of the writing with my finger.

'But there's more.' He takes another folded leaf from his pocket and smooths it out across the desk. 'There is a child. A girl. It doesn't list any name.'

In a moment I am back in Nonna's old room, the warm swell of Lucia's belly under my palm. The sharp kick of the moving child that saw her sent from our home. Unmarried. Disgraced.

'Are you certain of this?' Mariotto bellows as the men come in from the street.

'Let's come back to this later,' I say to Eugenio. 'If I don't go down to my husband, there might be a fist fight.'

In the loggia, Mariotto's hands are flapping as he speaks, even temperate Raffaello seems flustered.

'*Buongiorno*, Signora Albertinelli. Forgive my intrusion.'

'Not at all, Raffaello. You are always welcome.'

'Not with this news!' says Mariotto. 'Curse him! He comes here uninvited. First to tell me to pay up his money when my patrons won't pay me, and now he comes back to tell me my dear Baccio is ill.'

'*Mal aria*, it seems,' says Raffaello, quick to offer me details where Mariotto is incapable. 'There are others with it, those who live by the river.'

'I must go to him,' says Mariotto.

'Will you inform the Medici?' I ask, as his work on their commission is overdue. Mariotto's ventures, even nearby to Fiesole, often stretched into weeks.

'Let the Medici sell their arses!' says Mariotto. 'Raffaello, forgive me. You and I, we have our differences, but we both love Baccio, *sì?* Can you bear it if I join you? Back to Rome?'

'For the sake of our friend,' says Raffaello, hat in hand, hand to heart, to demonstrate his good humour.

'And that is why Baccio loves you,' says Mariotto. 'Just because I do not have it, I still recognise good grace.'

'I leave tomorrow. First light,' says Raffaello.

And I worry for a moment that after this news of Baccio, despite good intentions, Mariotto may visit the ale houses all night and not return.

'Come for me,' says Mariotto. 'I will be ready.'

'Will you stay for a meal?' I ask Raffaello.

'I cannot offer you eggs; they are ruined,' says Mariotto. An earnest lament over something trivial.

'My fiancée is here and expects me.' Raffaello casts a side-glance towards Eugenio, who has joined us.

'You proposed to Maria?' I clap my hands together.

'He won't marry,' says Mariotto, momentary courtesies done with.

I glare at him.

'Mah!' said Mariotto. 'A woman can't bear a lie and then burns me to cinders for telling the truth.'

'We didn't meet.' Eugenio raises a palm to greet Raffaello.

The artist's elegant composure, for a brief moment, falters.

'*Sempre un piacere*, Signora Antonia. Always a pleasure,' says Raffaello, taking my hand to his lips. He lingers in the kiss.

'I am a jealous man, Santi,' Mariotto says. 'Remember your manners.' But he hasn't seen that, while his lips are pressed to my hand, Raffaello's sights are set on Eugenio.

'Your husband's work on *La Visitazione* rivals the frate's,' says Raffaello as I see him to the door. And I know this comparison to Fra Bartolomeo is not meant so much as a compliment to Mariotto but to reassure me of his respect for my husband's work.

'I was young when I lost my mother,' he says, pausing at the door. 'His Elisabetta brings something of her back to me.'

I cannot respond lest tears follow my words. For me too, Elisabetta brings me something of Lucia.

'Don't tell him I said so.' Raffaello pushes his cap onto his beautiful hair. '*Domani*.'

'*Sì*,' I reply. Tomorrow.

I follow Mariotto into the bedroom.

'Before you leave, I want to talk of my paint,' I say.

'You should put your smart mind to medicine,' he says, with a sudden change in temperament. 'Wasting time on the filth of mixing paint for miserable artists.'

'I want to test it, then sell it,' I say. 'We can pay back Raffaello.'

'I must take the baptism cartoon to Baccio,' he says, appearing to lose interest in what I have to say. The panel with my white is pushed aside with a pile of other scraps.

'It's a delight for mixing with other colours. See here? See the hue?' I pick up a panel I'd striped with tinted red and blue paint.

'You saw for yourself its merit.' I persevere, desperate to recapture his attention, to gain his agreement. 'I'd like to give it to some artists to try for themselves.'

I follow at his heels as he scours the disorder for a cartoon that he might well have drawn onto paper, but equally might still be only an idea in his head.

'Mariotto, look here. The lustre is perfect for a cheekbone, for the pout of a lip. The twinkle in an eye.'

This seems to capture his interest, and he turns to cast his eye across the panel in my hand, taking it from me for a moment and then returning it.

'I don't have time for this now,' he says, scattering more piles, looking without looking properly. Finding one slipper, putting it on. Then searching for the other, forgetting he sought a cartoon for Baccio. 'That damned maid has hidden my slipper.'

'I was thinking of offering it to Pontormo. To try it.'

'No!' Mariotto slams his fist on the desk, brushes scattering.

'Why?' I ask, afraid but not willing to back down.

'The business of paint is done by *vendecolori!* Colour men, not colour women. *Dio mio*, woman! You're like an artist who can't see the horns on his angel. Your white is okay, but nothing special. There's no spectacle. It doesn't rise off the page. It doesn't dance.'

'It's not a bear brought in to perform for the Medici,' I say. 'What do you mean, it doesn't dance?'

He turns his back on me.

'Pack my bags so I am ready,' he says, leaving the room.

'You're an impossible dog,' I yell after him, not caring about my dignity in front of Eugenio.

'Better a living dog than a dead lion,' he calls back, the front door slamming behind him.

Eugenio lifts his shoulders, sighs, lets them drop.

'When he goes, so do I,' I say.

'You'll go with him to Rome?' asks Eugenio.

'With you to Fiesole,' I reply. 'To the convent, your address for Lucia.'

In the study I survey the room and its mess. How well it conveys my husband's impetuous nature. If only we could secure an unfaltering income, then he could paint without pressure or the obligatory fawning he detests. And I could sleep without worry of commissions he might lose because of whom he offends.

My mind was made up. By morning the study would be in order, with my own defined work space. My bags would be packed and my work ready to show the person who would appreciate it most. Why give it to Mariotto or Pontormo or Michel, or any number of men known to me through my husband, when it could be Lucia who first dips in her brush? She will know the best way to help sell my paint.

'*Allora!* Did you discover the secret of white?' she will ask me.

'Open the jar!' I will reply. 'You will see for yourself!'

It's a morning's walk to Fiesole and the air is laced with wild iris and pine, so unlike the coal fire and sewer stink of the city.

'What if nobody will tell me anything?' I say. 'What if Lucia was able to keep all her secrets?'

'One morning, my father whipped me to bleeding for tripping and spilling a fresh bucket of milk,' says Eugenio. 'Then ordered me to confession to repent my clumsiness and for causing his anger. He dragged me, pants still bloodied, to the house of the *prete*, who marched me into a back room where he took urgent confessions. As I knelt behind the confessional partition, I caught sight of something shiny, under the edge of the rug. While the priest, eyes closed, recited his confessional prayers, I reached down to snatch it.'

'A coin?' I ask.

'A newly minted florin, slipped from some penitent's pocket.'

'So you bought your forgiveness?'

'I did no such thing. I tucked it into my boot, where it rubbed and cut into my heel as we walked the three miles home. I hid it in a tin box in the milk shed. But how proud I was of that blister and the secret it stood for. After my father died, I retrieved the coin and bought my first book. Printed letters, *Mundus Novus*, by

Amerigo Vespucci. I spent the rest of the money on a tutor in Latin, so I could read it.'

'And the point of your story is to distract me from my worries?' I ask.

'I still have a small scar on my heel.' Eugenio seems lost in his reverie. 'The point is,' he says, 'all secrets leave traces.'

17

Beit HaKerem, 7 BCE

My body is a map of time. These faded scars on my hands and wrists are traces of my journey with glass. Burns and cuts from moments when my attention wandered.

'As your skill grows, so too must your attention,' Avner warned me. And right he was, since these marks tell a story not of inexperience but of growing confidence. A loss of the reverent focus that a novice shows towards her work.

This deep scar, here, on the jutting bone of my left wrist, is from the jacks. I've learned that a glassblower is more likely to be burned by her metal tools than molten glass, by the fierce heat they soak up as they coax the gather into shape.

A glassmaker can also be cut. When a vessel cools too quickly it can shatter. The slivers and shards sharper than any honed blade. The gash on my thumb is still healing from cleaning up an exploded pitcher.

As I roll the molten gather over the slab, I see my work as a prayer. I feel its fluid sanctity. Others disagree. Disdainful, sceptical, at a work that does not produce a vessel for a function, like a goblet or a plate. But if a thing is produced with the limbs and fingers Ribon Alma has made, why can't a thing of beauty be a thing of God?

My wrists flare and ache as I twist the pipe. They will limber up. I have been working long days and am inconsistent with my stretches. But I am mesmerised by the miracle of Avner's black glass.

As I touch it, this blackness, I feel I can touch the darkness within me. The part of me that cannot speak its grief, that spilled itself into the dust beside my father. But also the part of me that waited. Moon after moon. Season after season. Aviva, Kayta, Akh'n'shuta, Sitwa. That for so long was unwilling to surrender what the angel told me. Of the certainty I felt about becoming a mother.

This black is not simply an absence of light. Not like shadows in the crevices of the mountains, untouched by sunlight. Nor like the suffocating obscurity of a cave without a lamp. This black is a silent sea under a moonless, star-struck sky. Something within its depths ever moving. A colour with the grace to keep, and bear, a secret.

Many years ago, on the road from Yerushalayim to Yeriḥo through the mountainous desert of Yehuda, I first saw the Salt Sea from the heights above the land between the tribes of Yehudah and Binyamin. The pale cliffs of Moav to the east, stark and soaring.

'Not what it seems,' our donkey handler, Nadbai, had said, when I asked about the white rock walls that lined our path.

He pulled out a small axe from the saddlebags of his beast and drove it into the rock, chipping away a hunk, revealing a rock seam blacker than night.

'Incense, sealant, mortar and glue,' he said. 'They even use it as a pigment to decorate pots.'

Asphaltos. The viscous black liquid that exudes from seeps in the Salt Sea's floor, rising to float and cool on the surface. Used to seal boats and line baskets, or as glue for woodwork. Or melted by potters to make ink so that clever hands can paint patterns on pottery jugs.

I'd stood at the top of the cliffs, where the land sheers and drops to the giant inland sea in which nothing can sink. Great buoyant lumps, lolling on ripples made by sailors hurrying to claim it. A black that made things strong, safe. A black that made things whole.

I dip the jacks in water and press a dripping end to the neck of the piece; two deft taps on the pipe for a clean break, and I set it to cool.

My black is not useful, not like asphaltos. A fleeting shame disturbs my sense of accomplishment. Disturbs my own sense of wholeness, that comes from this work.

Zakhariya is calling for me long before he reaches the workshop. From my door I see him turning the last switchback, wisps of silver hair wild around his head.

'Three hundred have been put to death,' he says, out of breath and barely able to relay it. 'And the soldier, too. Tero.'

'The one who gave Herod counsel?' I asked. A skin shiver lifts the hairs on my arms as I recall his words: *Has your understanding gone and left your soul empty? Will you kill the accomplished sons of your queen and leave yourself with the stupid son?*

'That counsel has now been deemed a crime,' says my husband.

We were alarmed, fearful, smug, to know a subject had spoken this way to his king. But all of us waited to see, if it was true, what would become of Tero, the soldier who challenged Herod's intention to put to trial his own princely sons. If Alexander and Aristobulus were sentenced for treason, Tero declared, it might bring the King to ruin.

'All will be stoned,' says Zakhariya.

'Why all Tero's soldiers and not just Tero?' I ask.

'He claimed the whole army and its officers despise Herod's actions,' he replies. The gossips, so far, had not revealed this important detail.

But rumours are spreading that Herod grows ill. That he is racked with palsy and itching skin that he rubs raw in crazed fits. That worms crawl from his privy parts. That his unpredictable actions grow ever more violent. And now three hundred soldiers and their leader will be put to death in one morning.

'Those who have ridden from Kesari will tell what they saw,' says Zakhariya. 'Will you come to hear them?'

I turn to lift my shawl from the hook on the wall.

'You've cut yourself again, *ḥavivta*!' he says.

Many times I've been sliced without knowing until I see the blood. The exploded slivers are so fine that they often cut without any immediate pain.

'You've sat on glass,' says Zakhariya.

It worries me to think I have sat on a shard and not noticed, no matter how small. He twirls his finger to indicate I should check the back of my tunic. A cherry-red stain, large as my palm. I am aware of the sticky warmth between my legs. And we realise it together. Me with joy, my husband with embarrassment. My bleeding has returned.

He folds his arms across his chest as I cry my gratitude and praises.

'*Ḥavivta*.' His tenderness is palpable. But I know he is willing me not to get my hopes up, as I have done so many times.

'If we are blessed, would you open your heart to it?' I ask.

'Why would Ribon Alma grant an old man a young child?'

It is such a strange thing to say, I almost laugh. What man of Yehuda, at any age, would not welcome a child? Would not pray for more sons?

'When he is of age to join me, what if I cannot walk to the Temple by his side?'

'We would walk together,' I say.

The distant sound of raised voices drifts up to the workshop. My husband is distracted by the world outside that awaits him.

'I will change and join you,' I say.

I know I am not meant to go, now that I am bleeding. But my life has grown so accustomed to not participating in the rituals of *nedda*, I am tempted to ignore it. And my husband knows me too well, knows that to demand I remain will only make more certain that I will not. He unfolds his arms. Folds them again.

'What now?' I say. 'If you must say something, please set about it.'

'She is here too,' he says. ' Yiska brought word.'

A knot tightens in my belly. I know who *she* is. I can feel her. My mother. Whom I've not seen since she made a great show of lamenting the journey her husband took without proper attention to his condition. Never once looking at me while she spoke, never once directly accusing me. While those who comforted her silently cursed the barren daughter unable to, at least, take care of her own father.

'And Tsad?' I ask.

'She is alone,' my husband replies. ' Yiska thinks she's come looking for him.'

'He's disappeared again?' I ask, feeling sick at the thought.

'I know nothing else,' he says. 'But let's both remember our patience. For our own sake, if not hers.'

I gather a log from the stack and walk to my furnace, push it inside to stoke up the fire.

He leaves without me.

But I cannot work. I hang up the pipe, descend the hill to the house and change my tunic. Rinse my bloodstained garment of its new mark. As I pull on fresh clothing, my thoughts shift from my mother to the menace that is King Herod. I wonder how it might look, many moons from now, that our people would enter a temple built by his depraved hand.

Has any city seen more lives than Yerushalayim? Before Dahveed, it was built up and torn down, blood in its dust long before vineyards and groves. What stories the waters of Gihon Spring could whisper. And now the Romans infiltrate our lives, and Herod erects massive structures that he thinks will echo his name for eternity. His quest for immortality in stones and mortar has raised temples at Kesari, Shomron and Pamias. Theatres and fortresses and a harbour. It takes a madman to ignore what history screams in his ear. That everything, each of us and all we create, is perilled to vanish.

I want to go to the village. But all that was steeped within me as a young woman rises up to object. While I bleed, anything I touch is deemed impure. Anyone I touch, the same. After such long cessation in my apparent impurities, I feel indignant at these restrictions. But, still, I remain in our home. Sitting in Abba's old chair under the terebinth. When Zakhariya returns, I listen as he relays details in an usually long-winded manner.

'Herod's brutality has crossed a line,' he says.

'The line was crossed when he murdered his wife,' I say.

'His paranoia will be his undoing,' says Zakhariya.

'His paranoia makes him a hero in Rome,' I say. 'I hear … by each drop our blood.'

Voices outside our home. Zakhariya breaks from his story. An ache begins in the centre of my chest, becoming a throb that pulses with my heartbeat. For all the disservice I feel she has done me, I can't help but yearn to reunite with my mother.

I run to the gate, throw it wide open. I feel the air escape from her in a rush of surprise when I embrace her, but I hold her close, tight. Pouring everything I want her to know from my chest into hers. I feel her try to draw away, but I do not let her go.

It is she who cries first. Then her arms tighten around me, and I bury my face against soft, jasmine-scented skin and whisper the regret of our time apart. Of all I should have known to say, to understand.

She pushes away. 'Between women,' she says, 'nothing is lost.' Her fingers grip my arms, as if she wants her words to sink beneath my skin. 'We are so connected to each other, so rootbound, that sometimes the only way to breathe, to grow, is to be apart.'

It is something Savta might have said. Not my mother. I let her words linger, taking them in.

'What of Tsad?' I ask.

Her expression collapses. 'He returns with fresh wounds. Tells me nothing. But I found four blades, in a box hidden under straw in the stables.'

I hold her and hush her, even though I too ache with fear for my brother. Fearing that he might meet a fate like the bold soldier Tero.

'Stay with us for the night, Imma,' I say. 'Please rest before you depart.'

'Yiska heard he was seen in Beit Leḥem. I will stay, but tomorrow I must see for myself. Then return to Ḥevron, to be there when he comes home …' And already, I feel her absence.

'You wouldn't worry if you knew how it aged you,' I say, a clumsy joke intended to lighten the moment.

She looks like she's been slapped. My mother and all her vanities, more concerned with appearances than anyone I know. But then her mouth is wide open and we are laughing together.

I wake in the early hours. A she-wolf is calling to her mate. In a pack the two alphas, male and female, will breed. The others must serve the offspring as their own. How does Ribon Alma hand-direct the flow of births between men and women? How is it decided which couples will breed? Which will serve?

The blood has flowed heavily overnight and there is a pressure in my womb that makes me curl my knees to my chest. Since it is my bleeding time, I have left my husband to our bed and taken the pallet with my mother. I toss and turn beside her, unable to ease the pain.

Imma rises and returns with warmed oil of galbanum, hyssop and cedar. She rubs first at the small of my back, her hands warm and firm against my skin, then, carefully, slowly, around my navel. Easing the cramps from my body. Helping me back to sleep.

By morning the deep, twisting pains have eased and the blood that was clotted and dark is red and bright as the flesh of a pomegranate.

'Tell Tsad I look forward to greeting him,' I say, as my mother prepares to leave.

I can't help but admire the elegance with which she takes her seat on the donkey. The skin of her face and hands glistening and clear like warmed honey. A feat in the sun and dust of Yehuda.

'Your stew needs more coriander,' she says, flicking the reins. The beast snorts.

It is a remark that once would have stung.

'Some henna will hide those grey hairs,' I reply, and we share a smile.

'Wait!' She orders the handler to halt the beast, then summons me. 'Your cousin Ada invites you to her celebration,' she says, wiping at the sweat already beading on her forehead. 'Finally, a daughter.'

'Ada bore an eighth child?'

'Of course. As easily as her first,' she says, in her assertive Imma way that can make even a man feel like a dunce for asking a question. She cups a hand to her mouth as if to share a secret, but doesn't quiet her voice. 'Seven boys and she prayed, "All these men and no one to help me? Bring me a daughter or I shall see the world to come before the new moon."'

Imma is amused by the recollection, and a suspicion and uneasiness arise inside me, waiting for the words that she might speak to unravel me. A statement of my own deficiencies. But no harsh words follow.

'She will be happy to see you,' says Imma.

It is the closest she will come to a compliment. It is enough.

My bleeding arrives with each dark moon, a sky bright with stars to mark my time. After seven days I push the cloth inside me to show that bleeding has ended and I am no longer *nedda*. No longer forbidden for my husband to touch. At first Zakhariya seems shy and reluctant, but soon he becomes the man I remember from our first years of marriage, and I relish the heave of his breath in my ear.

'Sometimes you must look behind you for what you are chasing,' Savta had once told me when I ran to her in tears. The sunbird chick I nursed had grown strong and flown from my handmade wool and grass nest.

'Ribon Alma's wish. Not yours,' Savta had told me when the bird did not return.

After sulking all morning while I processed her wisdom, I later announced, 'When I have a son, I will know how to let him go.'

'Then tear the world apart to find him,' said Savta, a sadness in her expression that silenced my boasting.

We sat in the shade and she attached a small floccule of fleece to her spindle draped it across her left hand. Her right hand spinning the distaff, then shifting to pinch and twist, pulling downwards with perfect tension as fleece became woollen yarn. And I fell asleep watching her steady, sure rhythm.

I lie in Zakhariya's arms, enveloped by the sweet scent of his skin. When his sleep sounds deepen, I roll over and face the small window in our room. The shutters have been closed by our diligent manservant, Bohan. When Corinna passed into Alma d'Atei, the world to come, her second cousin, this humble man, travelled across lands to knock at our door. Willing to do his best to take Corinna's place. We'd already taken on two young men for the groves and the stables, and I would have politely declined, but clutching his hand was a child who gazed up at me as if she knew that I could not refuse her, not like I first did my now-beloved young brother. And so Bohan and his daughter, Thalia, became part of our household.

I move quietly from our pallet and push open the shutters. A breeze through my unbraided hair. A half-moon is making its way towards the sky's zenith. The earlier warm air has cooled, telling me the wind has changed and blows from the mountains.

'A child blown in with mountain air is restless on earth.' This was Yiska's way of explaining to herself why her son vanished for days. He was born during midwinter, when the north wind was strongest, and he grew into a solemn, unsettled young man. With factions of zealots and protestors increasing, every mother worried for her son. 'But how do I keep him home, keep him safe?'

'Don't be fooled,' I wanted to tell her. 'We are keepers of nothing.'

I wonder if Thalia was blown in on this same restless air.

'In Florentia before the Romans, the old women said that their great-grandmothers didn't labour all day,' Thalia told me once, as I was preparing food for Zakhariya. 'And, Matrona-Imma, often the men would bring them their food.'

Matrona-Imma. Aunt-Mother The nuances of her Etruscan culture using our language to adopt me into her life as both aunt and mother.

'I want my husband to cook for me,' she said, brushing her floured hands across her face, leaving streaks. 'Venison and rosemary, baked in the ground.'

Thalia. The girl whose furor of thoughts could stir up a wind in her wake. Whose Etruscan descent made many suspicious. Who turned every small task into a great urgent mission. In whom it pained me to instil the art of discretion. In this art, and only this, she was a poor student.

Often I'd find her gazing at the sky, studying some line of bird flight, muttering to herself as she observed the pattern and movement. When I told her about the sunbird I'd held in my hand as a girl, my conflicted desire for it to fly free and for it to remain, she grew quiet and still.

'Matrona-Imma, you of all people should know a bird is born for the heavens.'

I study the bright night sky, the stars set eternally apart from one another. If a star could make a wish, would it yearn to be closer to the next? Does each star even know of the bright presence of its distant neighbour? One flickering star seems to grow bigger. My vision blurs and my head spins, and I wonder if I am waking or sleeping. I turn and look towards our pallet. The rumpled bedclothes next to my husband. And when I again look to the heavens, the star grows brighter, streaming its light towards me. My skin prickling, rising to meet it. The touch of a familiar light-filled hand to my cheek.

My hands move to my womb, and the light floods through them.

Ribon Alma's wish. Not yours. This is what we are taught.

But where is God's mercy, when it comes to my wishes?

Ribon Alma's wish. Not yours.

If these are the words I must remember, must I forget my own heart?

18

Fiesole, 1515

'My heart will explode from my chest,' I say, panting. The steep, narrow road from Florence to Fiesole is not the comfortable afternoon's walk Eugenio promised. I stop at an open area and collapse onto the grass. 'I've taken ten thousand steps. My boots are worn through.'

'But we're so close,' says Eugenio, indicating a sharp switchback in the road, where the incline is even steeper.

'Closer to hell than to the top,' I say.

'If hell has this view, then give me damnation.' He flumps down beside me and opens his bag, pulls out two goblets and a flask.

'You've carried a wine flask the whole way?' I ask.

'An adventurer must always have his supplies.'

He pours, hands one goblet to me. Each sip tastes like cherries, and I feel my cheeks blush like the sunset.

As I catch my breath, I gaze north across the bluish-green rolling hills; then south to where the Arnolfo, its high fortress top like a castle, juts skywards. Through the treetops, the Duomo, its cupola catching the light.

'There's a whole view of the city from the top,' says Eugenio. And while I do not doubt it, right now I care little.

'We'll visit the convent of Santa Maria first thing tomorrow,' he says, perhaps sensing that I need reassurance that we will fulfil the point of our journey.

'Do you think Lucia's life was miserable in a convent?' I ask.

'For a woman with intellect or skill, and you claim she had both, a convent may well have been a good fit. The Santa Maria nuns, like many, are ambitious in business, wheeling and dealing like merchants. And now they boast the best girls boarding school in Florence.'

I let his answer placate me. Sip again at my wine and take in the view. Being outside the city walls invokes a sense of release, of adventure.

'Will you think me vulgar if I take off my boots?' I ask, wanting to feel my feet on the hillside, in this soft grass.

'Not me, but maybe others.' He gestures towards a stately older man and a finely dressed young woman, their servant tethering two handsome steeds.

I hold out my emptied goblet. Eugenio raises an eyebrow, lifts his clutched flask, splashes in more.

'Will you join us for wine?' I call to the couple, surprising Eugenio, the wine lifting my spirits.

The man seems reluctant, but the young woman ushers him over. Eugenio wipes out his goblet, fills it, and offers it to him.

'I'm Vittoria Colonna. This is my father, Fabrizio,' says the woman.

Fabrizio Colonna's name is well known as a papal alliance general; I can see now in his face a man weary from war. If it weren't for the wine I might faint from embarrassment at being sprawled out on the grass.

'Are you here for the reception at Villa Medici?' asks Vittoria. 'I hear Pope Leo himself will make an appearance. He is never one to turn down a party.'

'How could we miss it!' says Eugenio, before I can answer the truth. 'Signora Albertinelli's husband could not make it. He's with his companion Fra Bartolomeo, in Rome.'

'A friend of the frate?' Signor Fabrizio takes sudden interest. 'He's agreed to paint a portrait of my daughter, but she can't sit still for a sweet minute. Except to write her poems. If we are lucky, she will recite some.'

I cringe to see Fabrizio scrutising our dress.

'Did you walk from Florence?' he asks, as if trying to excuse our understated attire.

'A charming jaunt,' says Vittoria.

'Except for the bandits!' says Eugenio. 'Every bag stolen. Including our fine garments.'

I am stunned by his lie, and cast him a stern glance.

'Those mongrel-dog thieves grow worse every year,' says Fabrizio, sucking hard through his teeth. 'Should be tossed down a well.'

'Calm yourself, my dear father. We are here for a party,' says Vittoria, and I know all too well her desire to appease him. Then to me, 'I have a gown in violet brocade that will suit your complexion much better than mine.'

And, as is the manner across Italy to honour connections, my marriage to Mariotto Albertinelli and therefore acquaintance to the respected Fra Bartolomeo, sees us mounting their horses and riding the last steep ascent to Villa Medici.

At the gate, Signor Fabrizio announces his name and servants rush to unhitch saddle bags, offer refreshments and take the horses to feed. While the men are whisked away for refreshments, Vittoria and I are led through a columned foyer and grand loggia to the guestrooms set aside for her and her father. She hangs out her garments in embroidered silk and cut velvet, then takes an elegant teardrop-shaped toilet flask in green glass from her bag and splashes her face with a water that smells powdery and sweet, like violets and irises. She pours some into my cupped hands and I inhale its scent and enjoy the refreshment. Then she helps me change into the dress she has offered.

We stroll arm in arm, my skirts swishing with each step, the gown's small train fluttering behind me, out through another grand foyer and onto the open-air upper terrace.

I could swoon and gasp and laugh with delight, all of which would make me appear common. Instead, I remain attentive while

Vittoria expounds on the villa, trying to commit this spectacular sight to memory because, as Eugenio promised, there's a whole view of Florence.

The late-afternoon light shrouds the Duomo in pink; the golden-copper ball on the top becomes its own burning sun. Wine in glass goblets is offered. I accept it. Vittoria's voice is melodic, her trilling laughter endearing.

Unlike other Medici villas that stand at a working farm's centre, this magnificent residence, cut into a steep, stony hillside, exudes the atmosphere for which it was intended. As a place to host artists, philosophers and men of letters. Every square pietra serena-stone window and broad loggia boasts views. Hedges of laurel and myrtle release their sharp, lemony-sweet smell. And on the terrace below us blossoming lemon and orange trees waft citrus and honey. Terracotta vases brimming with lavender, marjoram, mint and basil are set between even larger vases overflowing with wild red and white roses.

The music and wine and food flow fast and abundant, and Eugenio drags me up to dance the galliard on the marble tiled verandah. Then we all perform the ridda: forming a circle, the baritone voice of Tommaso Vitolini singing the plainsong.

'That's Cavaliere Pietro Bembo – he's a poet and loves Tuscan language,' says Vittoria. 'Over there is William Grocyn, a scholar from England. And that handsome woman with the silk scarf stitched with gold, that's Cassandra Fedele, once a pupil of Poliziano. I hear that soon she's sailing for Crete! A vivacious speaker, but an exceptional poet. Confronted the Venetian senate on higher education for women.'

'What happened?' I ask, curious as to why I've not heard of this woman's fine talents.

'She married,' replies Vittoria, and perhaps it is the wine that makes us laugh until we are bent over, unable to breathe.

Eugenio arrives with prosecco and grappa. And Vittoria recites her poetry with fervour.

... we were led to believe that we were not worthy of ourselves.
We couldn't love ourselves.
So we felt alone.

Together Eugenio and I are the rarest of couples. Those happy in each other's company. And I enjoy the delicate pressure of Eugenio's warm hand on my arm, on my back.

I describe in detail to Signor Fabrizio my husband's painting in San Michele alle Trombe. The way the women from the Holy Land have captured my heart.

'It's as if Elisabetta and Maria are my dear Antonia's best friends,' says Eugenio.

'Elisheva and Maryam,' I correct him, explaining to our hosts their Aramaic names. 'And if it wasn't for those women, I'd be lonelier than Adam.'

'*Salute!*'

We refill our goblets and cheer. Then grow serious over topics of family and Rome, and raucous over politics, and dissolve into laughter at Eugenio's impression of Pope Leo, pulling his hat down to his eyebrows and puffing out his cheeks, shrugging his shoulders to shorten his neck. Then filling both hands with *spongato*, the cake filled with honey, spices and dried fruit, and cramming every last morsel into his mouth.

We dance until I feel my feet will burst from my shoes.

Soon Signor Fabrizio grows weary and bids us farewell. 'We were invited to stay but I must visit my cousin.'

'Keep the dress,' says Vittoria. 'It was made for your figure. And please, make use of our rooms. Your travel garments are hung in the closet.'

Eugenio can't quite suppress his amusement, for my *travel garments* are some of the best clothes I possess.

Eugenio and I stroll through the lower terrace, a space made splendid by the pope's great-uncle Giovanni de' Medici's passion for botany. His exchanges in bulbs and exotic plants with European lords have created a garden of unfamiliar plants, but also of pomegranate and golden iris. The intoxicatingly sweet, mingling scents of blossom and roses.

Sated by food and good company, I slip into my nightdress and fall onto the huge walnut bed, made up in softened flax, silks and cotton.

'Let's stay here forever,' I say, propping my head on plump feather pillows encased in silk slips.

Eugenio pulls off his doublet and shirts and flops down beside me. His hair frames his cheeks in soft chestnut curls.

'Signor Fabrizio's room is next door,' I say.

'It's twice as big,' he says. 'It's yours. You deserve it.'

He rests the back of his hand on his brow.

Often a beautiful boy will become an ordinary man, but this isn't so with Eugenio. He is more lovely than Raffaello in the shape of his face, the glow of his unblemished skin over a barely haired chest. So accustomed am I to the wobbling paunch that is Mariotto, I can't help but gape at the ridges that ripple from his chest to his navel. The sight prompts an urge to run my fingers across them, to find out how they feel.

'Do you think the nuns will be helpful tomorrow?' I ask to distract myself from the thought.

'See how the roof spins.' Eugenio draws circles in the air with an unsteady hand.

'Stop clowning and answer.'

'One step, then another,' he says softly, turning onto his side to face me. His finger touches the cleft of my top lip. '*Chi va piano va sano e lontano*. She who goes slowly, goes far.'

And I am back in the church of San Michele, a girl of nine years, my single prayer being that Padre Renzo's young nephew might glance my way.

'Even in your travel garments, you are the most beautiful woman in any room.' He traces the line of my cheek with the back of his hand. Moving closer, his cheek against mine. And I know if he kisses me, I will not resist.

He pulls me to him, the softness of his lips at the base of my throat, the hot pressure of his hand in the small of my back. He peels off my nightdress, and I think to draw back. But then his hand is between my legs; his lips, his tongue, gliding around my breasts, across my nipples. Everywhere his lips fall becomes warmth and light. He pushes open my legs and kisses his way down to the crest of my sex, his lips at the swollen folds of flesh between my legs. I draw him back up, his hardness in my hands, and I pull him into me. His lips on my neck, then my cheeks, then my mouth. Every hair on my body rising to meet him, to take him, to swallow his loveliness inside me and pretend it is forever. He waits for me, sliding his hand down to rub between my legs as he thrusts until my body soars and explodes. Then, I am floating like a dandelion seed through the breeze, spiralling down slowly, landing beside him. Drifting to sleep, cloaked by the smell of his skin.

'Get dressed,' says Eugenio, stirring me from a sleep I am unwilling to draw from. 'I've spoken to the abbess: we can visit, but only for the next hour.'

He hands me a goblet of bright orange liquid. 'Citron and rose,' he says. I throw the lot down.

Yesterday's mild air has passed and an autumn chill has returned.

'I'm sorry for my behaviour last night,' says Eugenio as we walk to the convent.

'Tell Papa Leone,' I say. 'Your impression was not sympathetic.'

He reaches for my arm and stops me. And I wonder if he could be so dull so as not to realise that I understand what his apology is for.

'I don't want to mislead you,' he says.

'Then walk behind me,' I say, taking off at a clip.

After a while, running footsteps catch me up.

'But, you know, I am not husband material,' he says.

'And I am already married.'

It is me who laughs first. And then he.

I link my arm through his. '*Quel che é fatto é fatto.* What's done is done. Let's blame the wine that tasted like cherries.'

'The women learn everything from philosophy to tapestry,' says the abbess, indicating rooms where young women sit at looms or desks, reciting after their teachers. She is explaining the income, how the education in arts and philosophy will provide a new acumen in women. But all I can think of is the painting on her reception-room wall and how it snatched my attention.

'I was appointed two years ago,' she says as we return to the room in which we were greeted. 'Your Zia Lucia left before I arrived. For Rome, so I'm told. Maybe to Tor de' Specchi. They accept older women seeking kinship but not complete seclusion.' The tone of her voice suggests scorn at the idea of convent life without cloisters, but her expression is impassive. 'Or maybe San Cosimato.'

It's all she can, or is willing, to tell me before my concentration again wanders as she reiterates her explication on the primary aim of the nuns, despite their business transactions: to pray for our *sublime republic.*

Eugenio nudges me and I know my distraction is ungracious.

She turns to see what has my attention, tells me what I already know of the painting behind her. 'Santa Elisabetta and the Virgin Maria, *La Visitazione*.'

Maria on the left in blue and red, Elisabetta to her right, a cloak of radiant yellow-gold. The two women are flanked by two others, perhaps a chaperone and handmaid, and while these figures aren't quite as refined as the Saint and the Virgin, there is no doubt they were painted by the same hand as the painting in San Michele alle Trombe, and that hand is my husband's.

'It was here before I was,' says the abbess.

'May I take a closer look?' I don't wait for her consent. It was not unusual for a master to allow his apprentice to help with a painting; the style of the woman's face behind the Virgin suggests Bugiardini.

As I step closer, I look for Mariotto's mark, a cross with two interlaced rings. If he'd forgotten to sign it, it would be nothing new.

'He's taken her face out of the Virgin's shadow,' I say, beckoning Eugenio to the painting, indicating the clarity of the Saint's face. And any frustration or ill will I ever felt towards my husband is banished by this new light he's cast on my Elisheva.

'What's this?' asks Eugenio, a finger pointed at a mark scratched into the dress hem of the woman behind Elisheva.

It's not Mariotto's. I lean closer. It's not Bugiardini. It's a small triangle, pointing downwards, a curling leaf centred over each side. I step back as if slapped.

Outside it is spitting rain as we walk back to collect our belongings. Eugenio presses me about my agitation.

'It's Lucia's insignia, on the painting,' I say. 'She's copied his painting.'

'Mimicry is flattery,' says Eugenio.

'Only that Lucia wasn't the type to flatter, least of all men,' I say.

But this isn't what bothers me most. It is the fact that I now know she has been back in Florence. And clearly spent time in the church of my family, to see the painting she has set about copying. There would have been more than one viewing; I know all too well how artists study their subjects. There might have been several visits. Or dozens. And yet she never made contact.

The rain falls in cold, heavy drops.

Eugenio throws an arm around my shoulders.

'Why not leave your Lucia to wherever she is?'

I push his arm from around me, startled by his suggestion.

'Sometimes, as children, we make too much of the people who pass through our lives. They seem grand and beautiful in the context of our world, but really they're just like every other human. Preposterous and vain.'

'Speak for yourself,' I say. 'Lucia is the only woman I know who doesn't grovel or flatter to gain approval. She would know what to do, who to speak to, to make a success of my paint. And were you too blind to notice that it's me in the painting, the girl, on the right, at the back?'

'There's a resemblance,' he says, reluctant to admit it. 'But, if she gave half a damn, she would show up on your doorstep. She moved to Fiesole, Antonia. Half a morning's trip into Florence. And downhill all the way. It's over. She's gone, like the Etruscans who once built all these fortress walls and then vanished. Remember what you can of her, be grateful, but move on. You're no longer some silly girl blinded by the memory of a woman more colourful than your own wretched mother.'

My hand strikes his face with full force. He reels back, draws his hand to his cheek. And I realise what I have dealt him. A blow not meant for him. But a fury that has burned deep in the palm of my hand since the day my mother emptied six years of letters on the floor of our kitchen.

The downpour flattens Eugenio's hair and brings a forsaken shadow to his expression. He turns from me and walks away, the splosh of puddles underfoot.

The magic of Fiesole is over. I yearn to be home.

After rain, when the cloud is still low, the hard edges of Florence are softened like Leonardo's sfumato. Smoky lines transforming from shadow to a light that appears as if cast through white silk, so that it falls about the city in a cloud-tinted mist. In Mariotto's study I hold the black glass vial up to the milky light – the shape of the vessel like a hole in the sky. Black against white. Rival colours that here do not argue but appear to rest, one nested inside the other, making a doorway between worlds.

Again and again, I return to the vial. Holding it to every light to study its peculiar black, so different to any other I have seen. Shaking it, tapping it, as hard as I dare. Turning it over in my hand. Guessing at it like a wrapped gift.

From his bed, Mariotto is groaning. Thrashing about in sleep-fits provoked by the medicine. Weeks now, and no real recovery, since he was brought home in a litter with broken ribs and a punctured lung. That lung has now developed infection. And the rain hasn't helped, the air oppressive and damp.

'Jousting in La Quercia.' It had sounded like the punch line to a joke. Delivered by the scruffy boy accompanying two men, who ferried my husband up to his bed. 'At the festival, Signora Albertinelli. He fell from his horse.' The boy held out his hand for payment for delivering these details.

'You can take bread from the kitchen,' I said.

'*Via, via!*' Mariotto shooed them away. 'Don't pay them any extra,' he shouted. 'They've robbed me already!'

It took days for Mariotto to relay the whole story. His work on the frescoes in Viterbo, his dash to Rome to call on Baccio, struck down with the water disease borne on the Tiber. And then news of the festival in La Quercia. Unable, as he is, to resist a celebration and its sports. But Mariotto is not built for horse riding, let alone jousting.

'You can hold a brush, but you can't wield a lance,' Michel said on one brief visit to Mariotto's bedside.

'And you can wield a chisel, but you can't hold a decent conversation,' Mariotto wheezed.

I miss the bustle of the loggia, the debates between artists. And without Eugenio here, Fiesole and Villa Medici feel like a dream.

Upon our return, Eugenio learned his mother had taken a fall.

'Promise you'll be careful,' I pleaded when he left for Vergato. For since the French took Milan, citizens were unpredictable with their anger. Enraged with Pope Leo, with the Medici. 'There are those looking for any reason to enact their dissent.'

'If you mean not to attract attention with improper behaviour,' he said, 'you'll be pleased to know Vergato lacks for excitement. More likely I'll be in the woods, hunting for truffles.'

'And don't worry your mother with gossip,' I said.

'I shall be prudent.' His hand to his chest.

'More chance Papa Leone remains silent about the German monk, Luther,' I said.

'I can, at least, agree to be careful,' he said.

'Good enough,' I said. '*Patti chiari, amici cari.*'

Clear agreements, good friends.

But there's been no word from Eugenio. And with Mariotto in and out of delirium, days and weeks come and go and I feel like I don't have a friend in the world.

I sit on the bed beside Mariotto. He winces.

'Maybe you'll let me wash your hair?' I say, smoothing back the wild, matted mess from his face.

'Tomorrow,' he says, a barely audible rasp.

'I can't keep turning the visitors away. The padre, Michel, Pontormo. Even Raffaello came by.'

'Only Baccio,' he says, cracking open his eyelids. 'To hell with the others.'

I take his hand to my lap and stroke it. Such beautiful hands. And, for once, clean of paint.

'Help me up,' he says.

'*Calmati!* Mariotto, the physician says more bedrest.'

'An old dog doesn't grow used to the collar,' he says, trying to push himself to sitting, gasping in agony.

'Please, Mariotto, you're making too much effort.'

'Let me speak,' he says, nursing his ribs. 'Whatever should happen, there's a box I gave Baccio. If it ever comes to it, tell him to bring it.'

'Give the box to me yourself. What's inside? Your manners?'

He waves me away and slides back down into bed.

'And tomorrow, when I rise up like Lazarus, we must talk,' he says. 'I have made a business arrangement with a merchant from Genova.'

'A commission?' I ask.

'*Allora! Domani,*' he says. Tomorrow.

I take the paring knife from the nightstand and trim his nails. Rub almond oil into his fingers, the back of his hands, his forearms, massaging each limb until he is snoring, puffing out air like a hound by the fire.

Then I slip from his room, needing to take rest myself. I lie my head on my pillow and consider how I might break my news to Eugenio.

The drummer wakes me. The *rat-a-tat* of drumsticks. But not the usual sound of a tamburo's stick on vellum. Sleep-muddled, I struggle to make sense of the noise, a tinny sound like fingers thrumming metal.

I pull my nightgown around me, and halfway to the window I realise it is rain. Fat drops drench the piazza, rushing already in small veining rivulets, curling their way around pavement. But another sound too. The hollow clang of metal, where it should simply be the patter of raindrops on roof tiles.

'Mariotto?' I tap on the door to his room.

No answer. I push it open. His bed is rumpled and empty. The rain grows heavier and the sound becomes louder.

'Mariotto?' I call out again.

He's not in the kitchen, the table spattered with egg. The loggia is littered with discarded drawings, wineglass rings on many, a trail of spilled food on the floor leading out to the verandah.

'Mariotto?' He doesn't answer. On the verandah, I see why.

He is face-down on the tiles. A plate cracked in two, one half shattered near his left hand. In his other hand is the lid of the *conserva mezana,* the large cooking pot used by our maid to make broth. The raindrops beat out their sound on its large copper top.

I kneel by his side, sobs issuing from me in great shuddering waves. I roll him onto his back, then stand and try to grasp his wet, slippery skin. Try to drag him out of the rain by the wrists, by the ankles. I finally get him indoors and collapse by his side.

'You great dog of a man,' I say through my tears, my face pressed into his chest, my arms unable to raise him from his place on the floor. 'What on earth were you doing in the rain with the lid of the *mezana*?'

'He was a man of strange habits,' says Baccio, patting my arm like a grandfather might, hesitant to leave me alone.

The funeral guests have departed after almost two days of mourning. Many would have stayed on had I not explained that my grief was exhausting. Of course, it isn't only my grief that draws on my reserves. And I'd wondered, as Michel bid me farewell, if his shrewd eye might not have guessed at the truth of my condition. For there is now no doubt in my mind. I am pregnant.

Those who knew us well, or even a little, knew of Mariotto's appetites for pleasure and will have little trouble believing that our marital life continued as normal despite his malady. And while few questions will be asked, if any, about the legitimacy of my pregnancy, I intend to tell Eugenio. Not because he is my baby's father but because, more than ever, I need his friendship.

'People always compared us, your husband and me,' says Baccio. 'The priest and the varlet. The angel and devil. But in so many ways, he was my better half.'

I understand what he means. For Mariotto's friendship, more than our marriage, had served me. I wonder if I might tell Baccio my news. My jaw twitches with indecision.

'Mariotto said I must ask you for something,' I say instead. 'A box of some sort?'

I feel myself begin to quaver as I speak, as if the mention of something left behind somehow makes my husband's death more real, more final.

'A box, you say?' Baccio's fingers tap his leg as he thinks.

My heart is already sinking. So like Mariotto to make a false promise.

'Not to worry,' I say. 'He wasn't in his right mind for some time.'

'*Allora!* I remember it now. *Sì*, a box. Balsam wood, so he said. Light enough to be so.'

'What's in it?' I ask.

'I can't say he ever mentioned,' he replies. 'When I return to Rome, I'll have it sent.'

'When you can,' I say, part of me wishing that Baccio wasn't a man of such scruples so he could tell me, or at least hint, what the box might contain. Any other might have looked and known what was inside. Or lied and kept the box for himself.

I open the front door and we both squint into the overcast sky.

'A shame really, the timing,' he says, stepping outside, scrubbing a hand across his bald head. 'With his paint recipe sold, Mariotto might have bought back his family's vineyard. Laid some old ghosts to rest.'

My mind trails behind Baccio's words. A mistake on his behalf. He, of course, meant to say *with a painting sold.*

'Ingenious, the idea.' He is animated. 'Simple and feasible, like most brilliant ideas. You agree?'

I am certain that I have misheard. Or that, soon enough, Baccio will correct himself. Make clear that the sale was a painting. And I will see that my fears have been manufactured. That, between pregnancy and grief, I am overreacting.

'Who would have thought? Alberese stone?'

I stare at Baccio's mouth as if it has summoned the devil. I can't quite find my voice to ask what he means.

'Most people, perhaps even some artists, don't understand that the one question to answer before any brush touches the board is the one Albertinelli always asked: what white?' His expression lights up with fond recollection. 'It is *white* that determines how colours will tint and mix, how they will feel under the brush or spatula, and how opaque paint layers will be. Who would have thought this white could be made from stones common as gravel?'

I steady myself as the clouds blow over the piazza and rain patters again on the steps where we stand.

'*Allora*, you are tired. I must leave you.' The friar's hand touches my shoulder, his face close to mine. His breath not as sweet as it should be. 'Forgive me, I always seem to pick up my conversation on the verge of departing.' His forced smile brings a strain to his doleful expression. 'The point being, your husband's paint has great commercial value.'

I want to tell him. To come right out and say it. The recipe was mine and not Mariotto's to take. Not Mariotto's to sell. But I am gripped by the thought that Baccio might narrow his eyes and wonder at my claim. He is a friar. But still a man, and loyalties between men are jealously held. To depart on any terms that might injure our shared grief seems more unbearable than knowing the truth by myself.

'Who bought the recipe? For the paint?' I stammer over the question.

'He didn't say, I didn't ask,' he replies. 'I've no head for business affairs and Rome is brimming with merchants.'

'Sold in Rome, to a Genovese?' I ask.

'*Sì, sì.* In Rome. I remember because he went to arrange it on his last visit.'

Baccio seems pleased to offer me confirmation of this fact.

'Will you visit soon?' I ask, pushing back anger, blinking back tears. After wishing Baccio would stay longer, I now wish him gone.

'My commissions in Rome will keep me a while,' he replies.

'I shall miss you, Baccio,' I say, sensing that his return to Florence is unlikely. At least for a while.

'*Dio ti benedica*,' he says, offering me God's blessing: one hand to my forehead, the other drawing a cross in the air. 'Above all, keep your faith.'

'Under one condition,' I say. 'That you keep your brush in your hand. And never again abandon your art.'

He is startled, seems to reel for a moment in the wake of my insistence. Appears flustered as I kiss both his cheeks.

'And I will send the box,' he says.

'*Quando puoi*. When you can,' I say, uncertain now of wanting it at all.

I close the door behind him, resisting the urge to pound my fists upon it to loose the furious shock from my body. My marriage bed did not enjoy the fidelity owed to a wife, but my friendship with Mariotto, in many ways, meant more. My mind explodes and divides. One half seeking reasons to explain and excuse. The other wanting to raise that dog from the dead to lance him myself.

19

Beit HaKerem, 7 BCE

The latter rains of Aviva have come early, streaking the craggy valley in rippling grey veins. People rejoice in the streets, with no concern that their garments will be soaked. As I hurry up the hill to my workshop, the rain drenches me, and I pray that it will bless me too. That it will wash me of what is not clean. Of what I have already done once and what I will do again now.

For the last seven days, with trembling hands, I have collected my own urine. Closed my mind to the crudeness of it, the imagined gasps of disgust from my mother at doing a thing so unholy. Each day, I have poured it over the barley seeds I set into moist wool. I'm not the only one to break the rules of cleanliness to perform the test brought to us from the Egyptians. My longing to know if I am carrying burns stronger than my obedience and I've summoned the resolve of the girl I once was. The one unafraid to run up to lightning-struck hilltops during a storm.

If the seeds sprout in the first week, then I will know my body is rich with minerals. Minerals to feed a baby growing within me.

The high peak above our valley has vanished into a raincloud, as if it were a figment of my imagination. But when the skies clear, the slopes and parched terraces will be tufted with small nettle and prickly burnet and yellow flowers on blessed thistles will burst open like tiny suns.

As I take the final switchback I've taken countless times before, my legs feel heavy, slower to move. But even this fact sweeps joy through my body. Heavy limbs are a first sign, I've heard mothers complain. As I open the door, my stomach twists with the suspense of what I might find. Of what I might not.

I kneel down and reach my hand into the back of the niche where I stack my raw glass, slide out the tray set with wool and seeds. My heart slaps at my chest and inside my ears as I pull back the cloth.

The tray is littered with green shoots. Other seeds, not yet sprouted, show cracking in their seed coats. I try to count how many, but my excitement is too much. I close my eyes and try to catch my breath. Then, in case what I saw has disappeared like a mountain in a rainstorm, I open them. Tiny green tongues still poke out.

I push the tray back into its hiding place. I will need to calm myself before I greet my husband. It is not customary to reveal a possible pregnancy until after the first three moons, to avoid tempting fates or spirits that might be carried in on prideful boasting. And demons are always waiting. Ever ready to coax and beguile an anxious mother-to-be.

How I long to run to the hilltop and shout it to the valley below. Let the rain sluice over me in great cold sheets. Press my hands into the tautness beneath my navel. Open my mouth to drink in the fertile tears from the sky.

Zakhariya is due to return from the Holy City where, in his white breeches, tunic, turban and woven sash in hyacinth blue, Tyrian purple and kermes scarlet, he will sprinkle the incense upon always-burning coals in the Temple. A finely ground mix in equal parts stacte, onycha, galbanum and frankincense, salted and pure. Presenting the prayers of the people along with his own, while the smoke coiled and curled.

I pace the courtyard while Bohan observes with puzzlement my unusual restlessness, unable to distract myself with the glass or the sewing or the grinding of grain. While I long to share my news, I must not get ahead of myself. Losses happened, even well into a pregnancy. Even after the birth. A woman with five children may have birthed ten.

Then, a babble of rowdy men's voices outside our gate. I rush to open it, expecting to greet my husband.

A tall man, flanked by two others, stands in the street. All three men are scruffy and unwashed.

'*Sh'lama*, sister.' Tsad opens his arms and I shriek with joy.

'You didn't send word, my brother,' I say, throwing myself into his arms. Then step back to try and take him all in. He is three hands taller than me and it makes me feel I am the younger sibling. The thick curl of his hair, on his head and his chin. His wide-set stance. How much he looks like our father.

He embraces me again, a hard tension in his body. 'You never age, my sister.'

His deep voice is like Sava's, our grandfather, who according to Savta made other men sound like sparrows.

'This is Ḥarsom and Binyamin.'

The men flanking my brother look as strong as him but are shorter by at least a hand. Old scars line their faces and arms, and the one called Binyamin has a tourniquet tied at his bicep, fresh blood seeping through.

'Leave us now. I'll come for you,' my brother says to the men.

Ḥarsom and Binyamin stride away, falling into a deep and serious conversation.

'Do you visit to bring news of Imma?' I ask.

His half-smile reappears, enquiring, expectant.

'What?' I say, becoming self-conscious, wondering what is out of place with my veil or my tunic. Touching my hands to check there are no crumbs on my face, craning my head to check for spilled food.

'You don't remember my promise?' asks Tsad.

I flush with embarrassment. How could I go a day without recalling his promise? How could I have lived at all without his certitude in my heart?

'So?' he says.

But I cannot answer. I am overcome with his timing. With the truth of things. The truth I have no right to tell until I tell my husband. I push my hands to my mouth, try to cover the smile that has burst to my lips. But I can't hide the flush that burns in my cheeks.

'I knew it!' he says, whispering blessings. 'What does the old man say?' he adds, meaning my husband.

But still I refuse to deny or confirm what he believes.

'He doesn't know yet?' says Tsad. 'So my dream was right.' He slaps his thigh, satisfied.

'You have dreams that bring forecasts?' I ask.

'Don't tell Imma,' he replies, looking for the first time like the boy I remember. Serious, and worried about Imma's approval. 'But I am right, yes?'

'Zakhariya was called to the Temple,' I say, evading an answer. 'He is due to return.'

'Then let my congratulations be for the glass, at which I hear you excel.' He embraces me again, with the warmed, salty scent of a man.

'The master returns!' Bohan calls from the roof.

'Will you tell him your news?' Tsad asks, expectant.

'Will you tell me where you have been?' I challenge.

'Let's greet your husband,' he says, now his turn to not answer.

My husband, head down, is striding towards us. Waving an impatient arm at the men by his side as if to drive them away.

'Call to him, let him know it's you,' I say, breaking into a new worry that Zakhariya's agitation might be at seeing an unfamiliar man by my side. 'And don't call him "old man".'

'*Sh'lama*, brother-in-law,' Tsad calls, lifting his arm to wave.

But Zakhariya ignores him, keeping his eyes on the path he is stomping along. There are four priests walking with him, voices raised in debate. I can see the distress on my husband's face. The group are arguing between themselves and my husband gestures wildly back, his cheeks red with frustration. He reaches me and stops, opens his mouth to speak. No sound comes forth. He closes his mouth, squeezes shut his eyes and opens his mouth again. Balls his hands into fists and shakes them at the sky.

'He can't speak,' says the priest Avishai, and each man looks as puzzled as the next. 'Something happened in the Temple, but he will not tell us what.'

'How can he tell without speaking?' says the younger priest, Avshalom.

'He can write it,' says Avishai, presenting a wax tablet and a stylus that my husband snatches and pitches into the dust.

'He must rest, he is exhausted,' I say, trying to direct attention away from the hysteria the group has brought with them.

Zakhariya opens his mouth and tries to speak. A strange rasp issues from his throat.

'He must tell us what he saw,' says Avishai, collecting his tablet and stylus, dusting them off.

'I am Tsadok of Aharon,' says Tsad, taking charge. '*Sh'lama* to you and may peace be on your families. My brother-in-law clearly needs to rest. I will watch over him tonight and visit with news.'

Muttering their distaste, the priests leave us in peace.

Tsad loops his strong arm around my husband and leads him to the chair, still in place, from when Abba would sit in the breeze. Zakhariya sits down and buries his face in his hands.

'You must calm yourself,' Tsad tells him. 'I have seen men suffer great shock and fall silent for many moons. When you are ready, you will speak. Take your time. We will wait.'

Zakhariya lifts his head and again tries to speak. Both Tsad and I concentrate on his lips, trying to make out what words he is saying.

'Speak slowly,' I say. 'When you speak quickly, we can't read your lips.'

Zakhariya throws his hands in the air, tears streaking his face, his beard made wet by frustration.

Tsad snaps a twig from the terebinth, strips it of berries and leaves. 'Write it,' he says, handing the home-made stylus to Zakhariya. He drags his hand through the dust at our feet to make a blank slate.

Zakhariya leans forwards and scratches the dust. *Great light. Inside Temple.* He lifts his hands and describes a circle as wide as he can spread his arms.

'A vision?' asks Tsad.

Furious nodding, hands shielding his eyes as Zakhariya mimes being blinded by the glare of a light. More scratching of letters.

'With rays like the sun from its body and head?' asks Tsad.

Zakhariya's face lights up. Mouthing a word we understand. 'Yes.'

He swipes the dust clear again and writes: *A voice.*

'A voice spoke to him,' explains Tsad. 'It was the same in my dream.'

Did not listen. Did not believe.

'Believe what?' I ask.

Then my husband takes my hands, his face creased with remorse. And my heart slaps again at my chest. Without him having to speak, I know what he's been told. The thing he does not believe.

Zakhariya asks me with his eyes.

'Yes. Yes! It is true,' I cry out. 'We have been blessed.'

He kneels before me with his lips to my belly. All three of us huddled together, Tsad's strong arms cradling us both.

'Please be joyful,' I plead, trying to take my husband's hands from his face, as he cowers with regret.

Once more he leans to the dust, this time writes with his finger. *Punished.* He circles the word. Once. Twice. Shakes his head in dismay.

'Perhaps Ribon Alma wishes you to remain silent about this,' says Tsad, and Zakhariya shoots him an irritated glance.

'You are well into your years and, for a first child, so is my sister,' Tsad persists, undaunted. 'There should be no gossip to tarnish this news.'

At this, Zakhariya's expression becomes more optimistic.

'You are an honest man,' says Tsad. 'Too honest for me.' He laughs. 'If you were asked by the priests, you would not be able to lie. This way you need say nothing. Explain nothing. Until they tire of their questions.'

I hadn't thought about gossip. I'd thought about nothing other than my own exhilaration and my hope for the same in my husband.

'But he can write and nod and shake his head,' I say.

'He *can*, but he doesn't have to,' says Tsad, satisfied with his own argument. 'He has been called to silent prayer. It's hardly a lie.'

My husband seems sceptical but calmed.

'When does the child come?' asks Tsad.

'In the bridge between the seasons of Aviva and Kayta,' I reply.

'Can you hold proud until then, old man?' asks Tsad.

Zakhariya nods.

'Your devotion will grant you good favour,' says Tsad.

My husband bends once more to write in the dust. *Ta'heh.*

'There's no time for sorry,' I say, throwing my arms around his neck and holding him close. 'Our baby is coming.'

Zakhariya, exhausted, retires early to bed, and Tsad and I climb the stairs to the roof. The clouds peel away and soon the night sky blinks, bright with stars.

I sit cross-legged on my woven rug and Tsad reclines on his back, his hands behind his head.

'Will you ever tell me?' I ask.

'How I knew you were carrying?' he replies. 'I told you, I dreamed it.'

'You know that's not what I mean,' I say. I mean where he went when he disappeared and moons passed before his return.

He lies silent as the sky. 'You have enough on your mind,' he says after a while.

'Is it not better that I know where you go, rather than having to imagine the worst?' I say.

'How bad can the worst thoughts be inside the head of a woman?' he says.

'I imagine you gutted and headless with the hobnailed boot of a Roman soldier grinding your gizzards into the dust.'

'Only if we get caught,' he says, a tender smile, like our father.

'I'm not like Imma,' I say. 'I'm not afraid of the truth.'

'You're right on both counts,' Tsad says through a yawn.

'I know you're only agreeing to quiet me.'

'Then you know me well,' he says, almost a whisper.

'I have my own secrets,' I say. 'Dreams that tell me things.'

But my brother is snoring.

When I wake before dawn, Zakhariya is not beside me. I find him outside. Seated on Abba's chair, eyes closed, fingertips pressed together and pushed to his chin.

'*Sh'lama, ḥaviv*, my dear husband,' I say, kissing his forehead.

He shakes his head and lifts his hands in a mock surrender. Mouths recognisable words. *Sh'lama, ḥavivta.*

Tsad strides into the courtyard, his two companions beside him. 'We must leave, my sister,' he says.

'But I haven't shown you my workshop.' I cannot hide my disappointment. Or my worry.

'Is that where you keep your secrets?' he asks, winking at me so that I blush in front of his friends. 'Always remember, I can hear in my sleep.'

'Where is it you go?' I ask, even though it is bold of me.

Tsad clears his throat. His two friends exchange glances.

'At any rate, you won't have room for us all here,' he says, avoiding the question.

'I have room for all three of you,' I say.

'But not four,' Tsad replies.

'Your cousin Maryam will visit,' says Binyamin.

'We rested in Natsrat. She and Yosef are well,' says Tsad. 'She is planning to visit.'

A thrill sweeps through my body. 'Maryam is coming!' I say to Zakhariya, who does his best to look happy.

The last time I saw Maryam was one of grave sorrow. Ahata d'Em Hanna and her eighth child had died during birthing. Maryam refused to discuss it. Preferring to beat softly on the frame-drum always in her hand, her lips moving with inaudible words. The tiny silver discs set around the circular frame making a tingling, glittering sound. She was barely six years.

My mother had chastised her, and tried to cajole and then goad her into conversation, disquieted by the tinkling thrum of the drum. And I regretted not hushing my mother, when I could see that Maryam was trying to make sense of what had happened. The soothing percussion helping her put all her thoughts in order.

Maryam studied me with her blue-grey eyes. 'Will you be our mother?' she asked me, a small wrinkle forming on her unblemished young forehead.

'Don't be silly, child!' Imma interrupted. 'Your father will remarry.'

And Maryam drummed louder, the silver discs rattling her anguish.

My chest aches now, as it did then, with regret. How did I not take her into my arms, even if I could not agree to her wish.

'How sure are you that she will come?' I ask, wanting to be buoyed by Tsad's news.

'Sure enough,' Tsad reassures me. 'She loves you as a sister.'

'And when will you return?' I ask, emotion gripping my throat.

'When you least expect it,' replies Tsad, bending down to his bag and reaching inside. He takes the glass vial I made him between his finger and thumb, lifting it to the light to admire it.

'How it's not broken astounds me,' says Binyamin.

'Not until I break,' says Tsad.

And I flinch at the thought. 'Don't even speak it.'

'*Sh'lama*, my dear sister,' says Tsad, pushing the vial into the pouch tied at his waist. He takes my hands in his, his smile making him look like our mother. Imma rarely smiled, but when she did, so my father claimed, it could light a candle without a flame.

I'll expect you for the naming, I want to tell him. To be bold and defy any spirits who are listening for the careless and premature words of a woman in the early days of her pregnancy. 'Return soon,' I say instead.

'*Sh'lama,* old man,' Tsad says, embracing my husband. Then, leaning close so only we two can hear him, 'Don't worry about your voice. It's your legs you'll need, to chase after your son.'

Maryam does not arrive.

My bouts of sickness grow worse and I lose every meal. I take to resting with my legs propped up by straw pillows, too afraid to move for the bile that will rise in my throat.

'The sickness is good,' I once heard my mother reassure Rivka. 'Good grace purges you. The child will be blessed.'

'I know it is early, but I want to tell Imma,' I say to Zakhariya as we both lie awake in the darkest hour of the night.

He reaches for me, clasps my hand. A new language growing between us. One squeeze for yes, two for no.

Two squeezes. He exhales long and slow.

By the end of the season of Sitwa, the sickness has waned. At first, I feel relief. But then I am overcome by new worries. The sense that feeling normal is, in fact, not normal at all. I wake from fitful sleep in a panic, clutching my belly, thinking that the mound of my growing child has vanished. Soon, the joy of my pregnancy gives way to a persistent unease.

Then comes my first dream of the mountain.

20

Florence, 1516

Eugenio's chest barely rises with each faint, shallow breath. For weeks he has lain in his unquiet world between worlds. Not dead, but somewhere in a purgatory, breathing but not living. Physicians peeling back his eyelids, peering into his black pupils as if trying to see the hills through a duststorm. The room is made dim by closed shades, and he appears more like a charcoal sketch. All outline and shadow.

They came for him on the Night of the Witch. Beat him and dumped him in Via di Camaldoli. And like the old witch, *La Befana*, who leaves sweets for good children but coal for the bad, they shoved great lumps of coal inside my Eugenio's mouth. As if under a hex, he'd been left in a sleep spell.

San Michele's eldest parishioner, Ferdinando Bracciano, had taken to the pulpit to lead prayers for the padre's nephew.

Let us be content with our sorrow. For where sorrow stands, love has passed once before.

We all prayed for answers. But when answers came, we then questioned our prayers.

I place my hand on his chest.

'Are you off exploring like your hero Vespucci?' I whisper to Eugenio.

A faint wheeze in his exhale.

I put my lips to his ear. 'It's time to come home.'

That night we had walked through the celebration-filled streets, discussing our plan to leave for Rome the next day, as he had promised, to search for Lucia. Fluttering silks and banners strung to honour the Magi, but also gory effigies of the witch hung from awnings. Children screaming and laughing, relishing the enchantment but also terrified of the coal they might find, later, inside their stockings.

'We can marry quickly, nothing too lavish,' Eugenio had said, when I told him about our baby; looking stung when I laughed.

'Rid yourself of the worry,' I'd said. 'We were born to be friends.'

Tailors in candlelight sewed in a fury of thread from rooms above shops displaying their finest. Sparkling buttons and shimmering taffeta, noblewomen at windows trying clothes on for size. We took the road from the Piazza della Parte Guelfa to the mercato, where furriers, more glorified than tailors, stitched under lamplight the outfits expected before dawn. The pageantry of the *la Cavalcata dei Magi* to follow the next day would draw all of Florence into the streets. Men in their finest, sleeves studded with jewels, courting their women festooned in silks. Golden brocades gleaming, corset bones pinching.

We laughed about the festival's two faces. A day that begins with witches and ends with wise men. And we contemplated the fancy of Florentines to swing from one extreme to another. To celebrate and parade and cast judgments and throw compliments. To cry poor, then splurge. To sin and repent.

'I'll bring you food in the morning,' Eugenio said, farewelling me at my door.

'Don't go out chasing boys,' I said.

'Who's saying I have to chase them?' he replied.

I blew him a kiss, as he crossed the piazza, smiling at the echo of his soft laughter. Wondering if our baby would have that same laugh.

*

After sitting all morning by Eugenio's side, I visit the painting on my way home. There are fewer and fewer visitors coming to pay their respects for my husband's passing. And as the weeks pass towards spring, and the house grows ever quieter, my mind turns again to Lucia. To the places in Rome the abbess said she might be.

I have already imagined how we will reunite, the water gushing behind us as we embrace at Trastevere's famous fountain. Her hand on my belly as mine was on hers so many years earlier. A meeting of women, like Elisheva and Maryam at the Spring of the Vineyard. But day after day, Eugenio remains in his sleep.

If I stay here in Florence, I can be with him until the end. But soon I will no longer be able to hide my pregnancy. And it will be harder to travel. And, once the baby arrives, what more to do but to remain here in Florence?

On my way to visit Eugenio, I stop by San Michele, going over in my mind the meeting of the women in the painting. Maryam, like me, early in her pregnancy. Yet she took the dangerous journey, surely six days on foot, to greet her cousin. My journey will be only two. I can bring Lucia back to Florence; she will have her own room. And she will know what to do with the paint I've created. She'll know how to handle the men who come almost daily to demand repayment of debts unsettled by Mariotto.

I've sold all that I can, including the small gold cross, my mother's only pendant. But the repayments have prompted others to come for their money. Even Raffaello, apologetic as always, called the matter to jury, where I signed a writ to promise reimbursement. But I can only pay in pieces. Denari by denari. And every month I fall further behind. I try to stave off resentment as Raffaello's growing status and papal appointment seem to imply he's not short of money. I've tried to keep the osteria open, but I can't afford staff. I'm barely keeping up with the cycle of work.

Each day I kneel in the church, my hands clasped in prayer, my brow pressed to my knuckles. I try to focus on my petition to Our Lord and the Holy Virgin Mary. But then my mind drifts. What might have happened if Mariotto had helped me test my white paint? To perfect it? What different life could I have made by its success?

When I arrive home there is a boy on my doorstep. His velvet doublet tells me his family has money.

'*Giorno*, Signora Albertinelli. I bring this from Fra Bartolomeo, who sends with it fond wishes.'

'Are you Giulio, Baccio's new assistant?' I ask, accepting the small box from his hands.

'I am Goffredo di Marco son of Ludovico, Signora,' he says. 'I prefer Fredo.' He gropes inside a bag and offers me a small silk pouch. '*La chiave*,' he says. The key.

'You came from Rome?' I ask, ushering Fredo inside, fetching my purse to pay for the delivery.

'Montevarchi. Fra Bartolomeo sends his apologies for the delay. He has been painting for Pope Leo.' The boy's eyes light up with the importance of having such connections.

'Tell me of the frate's painting,' I say, missing the fuss and surprise of Mariotto at work. Of the din of the artists who once gathered in our home.

'A painting of Christ presented in the Temple. The influence of Perugino is clear. Bartolomeo is a master of balance.'

I am amused by the sincerity of this young boy's insightful opinion.

'Do you wish to be a painter yourself, Fredo?'

'My father says I will be a merchant.'

'Merchants live well,' I say.

'Commerce is predictable. Art is an adventure.' His eloquent passion, like Michel's, is curtly expressed but infectious.

'Your father is a friend of the frate?' I ask.

'He ordered a small commission for my sister. She's two years younger than me,' he replies. 'Father spoils her.'

I offer the boy coins. Ashamed of how few I have to give.

'Use it for brushes and paint,' I say.

He is uncertain, anxious. 'My father would not approve.'

I am relieved. I need the money myself.

'Do you travel alone, Fredo?' I ask.

'My father has brought fabric from Rome for the Duke of Urbino. I'm here with him and my uncle. They hope I'll learn the trade.'

'And then you return to Montevarchi?'

'The day after tomorrow. And back to Rome the day after that.'

'Then, Fredo, please tell your father the widow of Mariotto Albertinelli and long-time friend of Fra Bartolomeo requests a visit. I have something important I must ask you to deliver to Rome.'

Fredo seems unconvinced, clearly made nervous at the prospect of making any request of his father.

'And tell him Signora Albertinelli sends her regards to the Duke of Urbino's mother. The Lady Alfonsina was a great admirer of my husband and a loyal patron.'

This seems to appease him. He will have news to deliver to his father containing important connections. 'After sunset I will bring him,' says Fredo, bowing. An excessive but sweet gesture.

The box brought by Fredo is light in my hands. I carry it up the stairs to the study and set it on Mariotto's desk. Place the pouch with the key beside it. I hesitate, wanting both to tear it open and at the same time to linger in this moment where anything is possible. I shake the key from its pouch and fumble with the padlock. Trying the key one way and then the other until it clicks open.

The box is full of torn sketches and scrawled notes stating promises to pay debts. As if shredded in a fit of rage then, in a surge of remorse, gathered up. I sift through each one, try to piece them together. I gather more from inside the box, my frustration growing, none of them matching.

I grab the box from the desk and pitch it across the room. The pieces flutter and scatter like oversized snowflakes. I kneel among the fragments and weep, then let my fists pound at the floor.

'You leave me nothing but debts, lies and riddles, Mariotto Albertinelli!' I scream with such force that, if the spirits did hear the living, my husband would hear me. Defying the scriptures preached from the pulpit not to liaise with demons, not to raise up the dead, I challenge him to arise from his stupor of death and to be present here in this room where I created the recipe for white paint that he sold as his own.

But no spirits come. No shifting spectre of Mariotto, his hair finally tamed, his stockings clean and not twisted, his shirtfront made stainless by the hand of his Maker. Once I am calmed, I gather the pieces one by one. Collect the box from its upturned place by the wall. As I lift it, the thick velvet bottom slips out onto the floor. And, with it, a sketch.

It is small but clear. Elisabetta and Maria, flanked by two other women. Not the image from the church. The one from the Santa Maria convent. And, at the base of the sketch, the artist's mark is Lucia's.

Lucia left many sketches behind. Some for me, some for Mamma. Some that we found in a box in Nonna's old cupboard. Perhaps after Mamma's death, my father had found them, shown them to Mariotto on one of their many wine-sodden binges. To make fun of a woman who thought she was an artist and tried to copy his work.

'Everything that damned Raffaello does, he gets from me,' Michel raged to my husband. 'He's not an artist, he's a thief.'

'The smallest distance is between two artists and one idea,' Mariotto said. 'We must all learn to live with this suffocating truth.'

I set the sketch back inside the box, close the box, lock the lid. I will hold back my anger with a new determination. To find out the truth. For if I love this image, and it is from the mind of Lucia then, even more than before, she deserves my admiration.

At sunset they arrive. Fredo's father, tall and broad-shouldered; his uncle, squat and bleary-eyed. I conceal my fatigue with the liveliest welcome I can muster.

'I am Ludovico di Marco, and this is my wife's brother, Alessio di Giorgio.'

I serve wine and offer freshly baked twists of bread filled with cinnamon, dates and raisins, Once they are seated, I come straight to the point.

'Signor Ludovico. I know you must be busy during your brief visit to Florence, so I will not keep you.'

'Goffredo tells me you have a delivery for Fra Bartolomeo,' says Ludovico. 'The frate is a friend and I will gladly see to it.'

I pause, setting myself to speak to this man with the confidence to which he will be accustomed in his buying and selling.

'I have lost my parents and my husband, and now my dearest friend lies in a sleep from which no one can wake him,' I say matter-of-factly.

The men are impassive, but Ludovico leans forwards in his chair, twisting the oversized emerald ring on his finger. '*Continua*.'

'I am expecting a child and am quite short of family. There is a cousin on my mother's side residing in Rome. More an aunt to me when I was a child.'

Ludovico flicks his gaze across the skirts covering my belly.

'I lost my husband the first month of my pregnancy,' I say, to challenge his obvious suspicion.

His cheeks colour.

'If you would help me, I will reward you for your efforts,' I say, rushing over this part, though I try to remain calm.

'I understand your position,' says the merchant, sitting back and crossing his legs. 'You wish me to take a letter of enquiry?'

'I wish you to take me,' I say, watching to see if the businessman flinches.

He glances at Alessio, who grimaces and squirms in his chair. 'There are only two horses,' he says. 'And, more so, you must be able to ride.'

'I am quite capable of riding. If you and Signor di Giorgio would share.'

'And my son?' he says. 'You expect him to walk?'

'Why not let Fredo stay here in Florence?' I say. 'I'll see to it that he has lessons with some of my late husband's best colleagues and students.'

I can't tell if Fredo's expression is one of dread or disbelief.

'It's an impertinent suggestion,' says Ludovico. 'My son's interest in art is merely a fancy.'

'I've lived with artists too long not to understand what I see in your son, Signor Ludovico,' I say. 'Of all fathers, a merchant should know that his son will inherit the impulse to cut his own path. Under the tuition of a master, he can at least claim to have been taught well. Would you prefer to have him try out his art under your supervision? Or to awaken one day and find he has run away with the humanists to follow his heart?'

'What does a boy's heart know?' says Ludovico, and Alessio sniggers.

'You were a boy once; perhaps you can tell me?' I reply, standing my ground. 'Here in Florence a fancy can become an eminent career.'

'What names do you have?' he asks.

'Pontormo, Franciabigio,' I reply. 'Maybe Innocenzo da Imola or Bugiardini.' I can see he is impressed. 'And Michelangelo visits often.' I cast my best lure. 'Always with an opinion. Not for the meek-spirited, but for those who wish to learn. And he will not withhold judgment. He is one of Florence's finest masters of art, but he has no skill for tact.'

The merchant taps his foot as he thinks.

'And what of riding in your condition?' asks Alessio.

'I'm pregnant, not crippled,' I say. 'I'll ride back after one week, two weeks at most. Fredo can return to Rome on my horse with a report from his teachers. If they say there's no talent, you'll be done with the subject.'

'We shall collect you in two days,' says Ludovico, rising from his chair.

'There will be no room for trunks stuffed with perfumes and dresses,' says Alessio, grumbling.

'Unless you wish to wear them, Signor di Giorgio,' I reply, 'I shall leave them behind.'

Upstairs, I throw a few scant belongings into a bag. I will enjoy Alessio's expression at seeing how little I've brought. I place the box in my bag.

At Eugenio's bedside I kiss his forehead and cheeks.

'Your Vespucci would be proud,' I say. 'I'm taking an adventure.'

21

Beit HaKerem, 6 BCE

The high mountain rumbles and shakes. The earth of Yehuda is rolling, rippling, like a great sea. A thunderous crack. It explodes and splits open, rocks fired to the sky, great billowing dust clouds cloaking the landscape. I am coughing, choking. Dust in my eyes, filling my mouth. I pull my child to my chest. He is sobbing, loud and confused. Feeling my terror. I must hurry, but the only path before me leads to the mountain. Under my feet the ground shivers, and behind me the earth is collapsing; great slabs of stone shear off and plummet into darkness. I run with my child, spitting dust. And when I try to call out for help, I suck dust into my lungs. Then, to my face, a familiar touch. A blinding light.

I wake in a sweat, gasping for air, my mouth gritty and dry. I push myself to sitting and gulp water straight from the pitcher, always set near my pallet. Water spills down my front but it does not quench me, my lips sting as if sunburnt. I push my hand to my belly, where my navel is throbbing. Compared to others in their sixth moon of a first pregnancy, my belly seems huge. It's hard to believe it will continue to swell. Already my breasts leak tiny drops of rich milk.

'This didn't happen with you,' my mother said, when her pregnancy with Tsad brought early milk and unslakable thirst. 'It must be a boy.' And her face held a joy that I'd felt shame to resent.

I am alone on my pallet. The nights have been unusually hot, and Zakhariya has been sleeping on the roof. Still I call for him, reach for him inside the sodden and twisted linens. I leave my pallet and throw my shawl around my body.

In the courtyard, night noises calm me. The *chir chir* of crickets, the rustle of the small birds that nest in the terebinth. I search the sky for the stars that tell me how long until dawn. The great star in the north flickers like firelight. I lick again at my lips, taut with thirst. How I long for a sip of Beit HaKerem's spring water.

The walk to the spring is downhill, but steep to return, and my belly is bigger than most who carry their first child. Zakhariya is sure to object. He is snoring from the roof and, although I could slip out, I return to my pallet. But I cannot sleep. I rise again and dress. I must go. No matter the hour. No matter that I will walk alone. The half-moon will provide enough light for the path. And at this hour no soul should be out. No women, at least.

I am tolerated but not welcomed by the women who gather at the spring. At first shunned for not carrying and now viewed with suspicion that I am pregnant at an age where many are nursing the children of their children. Mothers and grandmothers hurrying girls to drink before I touch the water.

The young women's words are cruellest. They are, otherwise, women I might know as friends.

Her husband was struck dumb because he could not believe a rotted bough would bear fruit.

Then let us all be struck dumb. Who among us could believe it?

I couldn't hold it against them, so desperate are we all for the approval of our elders.

The path down to the spring is soft grey under moonlight. It's a relief to walk like this, my legs so often numb. Where other women complain of the shifts in their bodies as their unborn babies grow bigger, I relish each change as confirmation of the motherhood that awaits me.

As I approach, I hear the familiar trickle, the steady flow of spring water growing louder. My child kicks within me.

'You hear it too?' I ask, touching my hand to my belly.

I halt in my tracks and quiet my mind. For a *mal'akh,* an angel, might be instructing my baby. A sacred moment of *kol haTorah kulah*, where every wisdom and self-knowledge can be imparted, teachings the child will forget upon birth and must hope to regain. The angel touching the newborn's mouth to say *shhh.* The mark of imposed silence left behind in the cleft on the baby's top lip.

My baby stops kicking, and as I walk on, I see somebody already there, bent to the water. I draw back into the shadows. Perhaps a young shepherd who has crept down from the foothills? I peer out and the figure pushes their hands into the water. A soft woman's voice singing. Then, as if feeling my presence, she turns. Water spills from her hands.

'*Sh'lama*?' she calls.

The slanting light of the half-moon reveals her face.

I step from the shadows and call out her name. And before I can greet her, Maryam is rushing towards me and her arms are around me. A swell of warmth explodes in my breast. The child inside me kicks hard, again and again, as if its heart, too, somersaults with delight.

She kisses me on both cheeks, then again. Touches her cool hands to my face. Spring water bathing my cheeks. I press my lips to each of her cheeks, my hand to her face. Then her hands are on my belly, a wild heat that makes my child kick.

'Already a strong one!' says Maryam.

I kiss her cheeks again, unable to speak for my tears.

The spring trickles behind us, a rippling backdrop of joy.

'Where is Yosef?' I ask, finding my voice.

'The animals were slow; he's not far behind.'

The young girl I knew is now a grown woman, her watchful eyes filled with a doubt that makes my heart spill over with the desire to protect her.

'Did the angel come to you too?' she asks. 'Did you know I would come? To see for myself your news of a child?'

And I recall the urgency to leave my home without company, to quench my thirst at the spring, to rinse the dream-dust from my mouth. The blinding light that awoke me.

Then, I feel it, within her. I know at once, without her having to say, that she too is carrying.

'You have arrived here with child?' I ask.

She is small and light in my arms, as if a spry gust might lift her skywards.

'I feel it is too early. I'm not ready,' says Maryam.

'Too early? Too late?' I say. 'Who are we to know when our children may come?'

I again take her cool hand in mine, clasping it even tighter. Willing that my strength might become hers. That the reassurance in my heart flows into hers. Through my chest, down my arms and from my hand through hers. A breeze stirs around us, swirling the veils on our heads, and I think of the women who will gather here later, their judgments blown away by our faith in ourselves, in each other.

'Let us be happy and grateful, like our matriarch Leah,' I say. 'And may generations to follow remember that mothers of all ages are sacred and blessed.'

She keeps one hand on my belly and my child kicks again, and I see first her delight, then her understanding. That my child will arrive before hers and therefore have a friend in the world.

We return to the spring, each cupping our palms for the other to drink. Sharing prayers for our unborn children, prayers for their children and children to come. Hand in hand, we sit together until the pale light of dawn swallows the stars.

As we climb the path home, I strain with the effort. She crooks her elbow and I thread my arm through it. I tell her about Zakhariya and the loss of his voice. My glasswork. My time spent alone. She shares with me that her brother, Y'hoyakim the Younger, has at times disappeared with men carrying knives under their cloaks. And that Yosef has chased others away that have come seeking them moons later.

'Yosef must return to Natsrat in three days,' says Maryam. 'He says the apprentice mason is willing but hoof-handed.'

'Your husband's stonework is as prized as his woodwork,' I say. 'He needs to be fussy.'

She looks at me again in that unnervingly clear manner, and I am certain I hear her speak, but she hasn't opened her mouth.

I will stay until he is born.

Did she speak it? I am not sure.

'That's my workshop,' I say, pointing to the small hut above our home.

'Your mother says your glass is like holding the night sky in your palm.'

'She doesn't say so to me.' I sound stiff where I want to sound witty and light.

'I was frightened of her as a child,' says Maryam.

'I think she wished I was more frightened of her.' I laugh, thinking of the time I stomped my foot to insist on playing in the mud in the rain and was told that if I preferred to play like a boy, that I should stand in that muck until the rain stopped. It lasted most of the morning, but I stood without moving. Then lay filthy and shivering on my pallet, too stubborn to clean and dry myself off.

'I think you both chose each other for good reason,' she says.

Her comment takes me off guard. 'Zakhariya would say that it is Ribon Alma who wholly chooses,' I say, unsettled.

'But since we are part of that whole, and part of Ribon Alma, it stands to reason we are part of the choosing,' says Maryam, at ease but determined in her point. 'My thoughts, anyway.'

'Do you share your thoughts with Yosef?' I ask, wondering how he might respond to her ideas. Most men are not as patient as my husband.

In the mind of most men, a woman's role is to bear and raise children. Preferably sons. Men who can continue the family's landholdings and work the land as a woman cannot. Or so it is believed. It takes a woman half a morning to grind grain into flour. Then her afternoon is filled with spinning wool into yarn, feeding children and livestock, cleaning. Attending to her parents, her husband, the neighbour who is ill and in need of a tonic or the boy who is injured and requires an ointment. To keep a household running is the work of a woman. Keeping the roots of a family fertile and alive.

'Not the rudder of a ship but the wind that shifts the sails,' Savta said. 'That's us women. Often invisible. But strong like the wind. And most men, if asked for the truth, would say that when it comes to the household they sail to conditions.' I didn't understand what she meant until many years later.

Morning birdsong drifts from the hilltops. Maryam closes her eyes, taking it in.

'The season will be dry but the day your son is born, there will be rain,' she says.

My heart quickens. *My son* will be born. Will I have a son?

When she takes my hands in hers, a dampness breaks out on my skin. She keeps her eyes fixed on mine, then glances over my shoulder. Maybe expecting my husband to interrupt us before she is finished.

'Have you dreamed it?' she asks, a troubling gravity in the tone of her voice.

There's a pressure, an urgency, to her question that tightens my chest and my temples. I feel panic rising, wanting to deny that I know what she means. Wanting to shut down every sense that sounds an alarm.

My husband waves from the rooftop and I beckon him down, even though I secretly wish him, in this moment, anywhere but here. Soon he will be the centre of attention. His need to be understood, the time-consuming task of others learning how to read him, will mean my cousin and I might not resume our private conversation for days.

'Have you dreamed it?' she asks again, determined in her question, Zakhariya almost upon us.

I don't need to reply; she can already sense it.

'Then later,' she says. 'We will speak of the mountain.'

*

My workshop becomes our private sanctuary. Maryam never seems to tire of watching me work, attending to me as I craft each glass vessel, as if it has always been this way. Sometimes I look up to see her observing me, an expression of such kindness that my heart leaps and my baby kicks. Other times, she places her stool in the slanted light from the window and sits to spin wool. Stopping to circle the room, tapping softly on the frame-drum she's carried since she was a child. On hand to wipe my brow, to refill my water jug with spring water. I wonder if it is having company that distracts me, makes me feel the heat more than usual, because it is more difficult to pay attention to my breath. Or perhaps it is because I know that the moment will soon arrive. A quiet moment in our conversation. A pause, pregnant as my belly, that will mean all other subjects have been exhausted. That it is time to begin the conversation for which I know my young cousin has come.

'Don't misjudge the small talk,' my mother lectured me when I turned up my nose at the nattering of women, the gossips, the speculations. 'This is how a woman finds her place among women.'

And such has been the case with Maryam and me. Circling in on where we stand with each other as we speak about weaving and sewing and husbands and shared family memories. Working our way to the most intimate space between any two women, where each knows that what is shared will forever become either a treasure or a weapon in the hands of the other.

'You're too hot,' she says, her hand upon my forehead.

She sets a moistened cloth on the back of my neck, a goblet of nectar she pressed from pomegranate seeds to my lips, as I turn the glowing gather through the flames, withdraw it and blow gently, the end swelling. Then place it back into the heat to keep the temperature constant.

'We are accustomed to it now,' I say, meaning the baby and me. 'He kicks like a donkey when I need fresh air.'

I hold out my hand and she passes me the jacks to shape the glass. She knows I must be quiet as I work the glass, easing the gather so the sides are smooth, gaining symmetry. This piece will be a gift for her to take home to Natsrat, a chalice.

I drop the jacks into the bucket of water beside me and return the vessel to the flames. Take it back out, blow again on the pipe.

'It's a terrifying splendour,' she says. Flames licking, tools hissing as they drop into the water.

I draw the wooden mould from the water and cup the gather to form the globe that will become the bowl of the chalice.

'Have you dreamed it again? Since I arrived?' she asks.

I cannot take my focus from the glass or it will cool too quickly and I will lose this piece.

Each night of her stay I have dreamed of the mountain. Stone splitting, rocks fired into the sky. The earth shuddering, collapsing. My child clutching my breast. Only one path to follow, and it leads to the mountain. Me running towards it. Dust and grit in my mouth.

Maryam stands and walks to the small window. I know her attention will be on the high peak above us, the soft arc of its summit drenched in sunlight.

'The other pipe,' I say, and she hurries to draw the second pipe I have in the flames with the smaller gather that I'll use as its base.

'I write, sometimes, in secret,' she says. 'Yosef doesn't know.' She looks at me, childlike. 'He can't write. I don't want to offend him.'

'Do you write the sacred texts?' I ask.

'I like to write songs,' she replies. 'He watches over me so carefully, I have little time alone now. But I try to write before he returns. Or before my chaperone arrives. Or my cousin Yona, who fills the time between the other two.'

'Sounds like a task,' I say.

'The carrying is a task,' says Maryam, pressing her fingers to her temples.

I found the first moons of pregnancy the most difficult, and I can see Maryam is feeling the same dragging sense of fatigue.

'You will feel better after the next moon,' I say. 'Your body will be accustomed to sharing.'

'I don't mean carrying the baby,' she says, an edge of impatience. 'The dreams, the visions. The pictures that move inside my head when people speak. Pictures that show me what will come.'

She holds my gaze with defiance. Daring me to ask for more details. I look away.

'Even you refuse me,' she says, her voice breaking with grief.

And here I am, once again, before the little girl who asked me to be her mother. From whom I turned away. I can't do so again.

I set down my work and meet Maryam's gaze. Her eyes fill with tears of relief at my tacit consent. Then, in her face, myriad shifting expressions. As if she is sorting through every thought she's conceived in her life. I recall a great-uncle whose face would shift through the most dazzling smiles, frowns and wonder, changing from moment to moment as he recounted his stories or listened to ours, his head pitched the smallest degree forwards or sideways, to lend his ear better to what was being told. What a joy it had been to be listened to the way he had listened.

'How can I carry all this around inside my head?' asks Maryam, pressing a palm to her forehead, the skin of her cheeks stained red by frustration. 'People say they want to know the truth, but only if that truth doesn't threaten what they believe. Truth is a real, living thing. It is conceived and wants to be born. And it will find a way. Like rains form a river in the middle of the desert, truth travels. It yearns to find a pathway. And, like water, it will.'

My child begins to wriggle and kick inside me, and Maryam doesn't take her gaze from mine. Her expression shifts, transforms before me, like my great-uncle's, as if she is following the inner terrain of my thoughts.

Let me tell you what I know.

A great pressure fills my head. A tingling flush through my skin. The same sense of thrill I once felt as a girl who danced in the storms. I can hear Maryam's thoughts as if she is speaking aloud. I want to resist. But the pressure grows and spreads from my head down my neck, through my shoulders, floods down my spine. My chest burns hot, inflating like the molten glass on my pipe. I give in to it, I let it all in. A torrent of vivid images, as if I am both asleep and awake. Both heavy as stone and light as the plumes that carry a drifting dandelion seed.

I see us both. Perhaps older, perhaps old. Tearing our clothes, grieving for our sons. Wave after wave of pulsing energy washes through my body. Iron nails driven through flesh, a whetted sword lifted high and swung hard.

'Enough,' I say.

Stillness.

She is beside me, weeping. Her head in my lap, hot under my palms. And I understand the weight that bears down upon her.

'The curse of clear eyes,' Savta called it. For those who might carry the gift of foresight. But these women, once hailed as revered prophetesses, are no longer encouraged to share what they see. Wisdom was not the domain of a woman.

We remain this way: her head upon my lap, my hands upon her head. The heat of our skins mingling. A sombre clarity arising that, even when what is clear is difficult, brings a strange calm.

'If we both outlive our sons, whatever is the point of any of it?' asks Maryam quietly.

I muster all my strength to share what my heart knows. 'That our sons will be born.'

Maryam sits back, her wet eyes creasing and narrowing around the thoughts in her head. I brush tears from her face.

'Sometimes I see only in fragments,' she says. 'But in every fragment I see the mountain. And the dust. Great clouds of dust. Swallowing the sky.'

I shiver when she says this. The smell of the dust in my nostrils. The gritty taste as I breathe. A madness of grief that closes my throat.

'They will come for our sons,' I say, and she does not deny it.

'When you see the dust rise,' she says, 'do as you dream and run for the mountain.'

*

The birth is fast. The first month of Kayta but already hot, our bodies damp with effort, as Yoḥanan slides into the world big and wet and loud. Maryam's hands are there to catch him and bring him to my breast. And, as my baby first suckles, a sheet of rain sweeps through our valley.

'Let him feel it,' I say, urging Maryam to take Yoḥanan outside, his skin new and untouched by the world, to feel the miracle of rain. So unlikely it is for water to fall from the sky at this time of year, wetting the earth, cleansing the air.

She takes my wriggling child and returns him to me quiet and rain-kissed. Droplets coating his face. I whisper to him to remember this rain, this water that blesses.

If that was the last moment of real joy in my life, it would have been enough. Yoḥanan in my arms, his father whooping in celebration, his voice returned but still unable to speak coherent words for his weeping. The strange, guttural sob of a man, humbled by fatherhood.

My new family life begun in a tumult of sweet-smelling rainstorm. For now, refreshing our parched earth. For now, settling the dust.

III

A half truth is a whole lie.

Jewish proverb

22

Adelaide, Autumn 2018

The imminent thrill of completion unsteadies my hand. The delicate profiles of the two embroidered figures have cleaned up to reveal one face as a maiden's, the other with stitched wrinkles suggesting an elder. Each tiny loop of their needlelace veils is in perfect condition and, stitched back in place to me, provide proof of my conviction that this is The Visitation. Elisabeth and Mary. Elisabetta and Maria. Elisheva and Maryam.

The women's restitched cloaks follow the contours of their bodies. The elder woman's curving around her swollen belly, to me indicating her second trimester. The maiden's cloak falls close to her body, her chest out of proportion to her slenderness, the swelling breasts of an early pregnancy.

I press my hand to the sharp, stabbing pain behind my navel. The expansion of my body to hold what's growing inside. It was like this with Jonathan, but not as persistent. Being bent over my work doesn't help, so I stand and it settles. When I called the clinic to cancel my August eighth procedure, the doctor called me straight back. Did I need legal counsel for future custody issues? She could offer me names. Not now, I reassured her. Not yet. I needed time to be an expectant mother, before the complications of legal arrangements. But I feel clear on what I must do. And every day that I am strong in all my new choices, I learn to see as a victory.

The studio phone bleeps. Tris returning my call.

'Can you come down before your meeting?' I ask. 'I have something to show you.'

'I can be there in an hour,' she says.

An hour's all I need.

'Are you okay?' she asks.

I wonder if she's mistaken the frisson in my voice for disquiet. 'I really am,' I reply, surprising myself with this fact. 'Do you feel meeting-ready?'

'Not ready, but prepared,' she replies.

I know how she feels.

Since her announcement last week of potential new donors to fund a growing textile collection and ongoing conservation, I've been determined to finish the piece in time for this morning's big meeting. I want Tris to have the thrill of presenting the 'before' and 'after' comparisons and I've been working from first light to midnight to make sure she has them.

The desk behind me is littered with print-outs showing different versions of The Visitation. I want Tris to see how the embroidery reflects it. They are a small selection of images from the hundreds across centuries that have been painted in oils and sketched in charcoal and pencil, statues fired in porcelain and engraved into silver. Those I have collated are those that touch me most deeply. Piero de' Medici's for the way the women clasp hands. Philippe de Champaigne for the way they are pressed face to face. The intertwining figures in sunset orange, flamingo pink and chartreuse in Jacopo Pontormo's fresco. The frescoes in the Church of the Visitation in Ein Kerem, Israel. The modern Eisbacher: Maryam and Elisheva lit up with wide smiles. Elisheva's head thrown back laughing, her eyes to the heavens. Why isn't this, their shared joy, painted more often?

And the work that always catches my breath, by Mariotto Albertinelli. Elisheva's reassurance of Maryam conveying a power of eldership in which her young cousin could take refuge.

How many times have I studied this image in the hope of some wise clarity from their stories? What would they really have to tell me of loss? Of grief? Of forgiveness? In their own words, in their own time? Not through the writings of men who came so long after. In return, what could I really teach them from my time? Would they have hoped, prayed, that for women and mothers and children more would have changed for the better?

I sit back, take a breath. The last piece to set in place is like a missing piece in a jigsaw. It is Elisheva's left hand, the one touching Maryam's arm. How perfect to complete this work with the flesh of her hand. The thread had to be an exact match with the other parts of her skin and the order from England had taken almost two weeks to arrive. Her fingers are slender and require my full attention. To rush at the end is often tempting and can lead to painstaking corrections. I must finish the same way I began. A methodical, calm focus on each single stitch.

I thread silk floss and with tiny diagonal stitches, as few as possible, I set Elisheva's hand back in place. While I work, my mind turns again to her scant biblical mentions that fail to do justice to the breadth of her life, and to what would have dominated her every waking moment after she married. The desire for a child. The expectation that she would bear one. Bear many. The sense of failure as year after year no children appeared. The onerous fact that only once God approved it would she carry. When it seemed that God could have ended her anguish much sooner.

The last stitch. It is done.

Here they are, the two women. Touching, embracing, sharing their news. Lit up in glimmering gold and glittering silver. Surrounded by flowers and caterpillars and animals of charm. Overseen by an eternally bright sun.

I hear my slow, satisfied exhale.

There's no fanfare of trumpets.

No standing ovation.

Silence.

Like the silence of bread baking in an ancient clay oven after the chattering industry of women, grinding grain for hour upon hour, picking out grit caught in the grains, sifting and refining to the perfect milled finish.

The silence of paint as it dries on the canvas, a Renaissance artist already in the tavern lamenting its imperfections.

I collect the image of the Albertinelli from my desk, hold it next to the embroidery. One in paint, one in thread. Created centuries apart. But the essence, the intimacy, has travelled through time. The sun in the needlework pays an unwitting respect to Elisheva's cloak in the painting, a burst of yellow-gold warmth.

I've searched for more on Albertinelli, trying to find his muse for the tenderness he portrayed. Countless searches before I found any details. The artist had married a young woman, Antonia Ugolini, whose father owned a tavern named *Il Drago*, The Dragon, near the Ponte Vecchio. The thrill of this find kept me searching all night. Finally, a scrap more. A writ in Latin containing her name. I'd sent it to Priscilla for translation and felt troubled to discover that, after Albertinelli's death at forty-one, the writ summoned Antonia to account for his debts. Raphael himself took her to a judge to extract payment. From hopes of finding a love story, my thoughts wheeled into darkness. Did Antonia manage to pay back her creditors? What shame did she suffer if she did not have means? From all accounts Mariotto Albertinelli was fond of the good life, but was he fond of the twenty-seven-year-old wife he left to settle his scores?

I hear Tris's footsteps. I twist open the vertical blinds and the studio fills with soft southerly light. A tap on my door. I call her inside.

She is wearing purple and red. Eyes smoky. Pastel lips. It suits her, but I can see she is anxious.

'Stop there!' I say. And she halts in her tracks.

I hold up the first photograph I took of the embroidery. 'Before,' I say, letting her take it in. I can see her eagerness, so I beckon her to the table. The embroidery laid out, glimmering in soft light.

'After,' she whispers.

She shifts her gaze back and forth from the enlarged photo I've printed of the fretted, frayed piece when it arrived here, to the piece on my worktable.

'I can't do justice explaining how you made this magic happen.'

'More luck than magic,' I say. Quietly thankful for whomever kept the detached fragments with the embroidery, before it was pushed into a tube and abandoned among beer cans.

'I need you in the meeting,' says Tris. And I am moved by the vulnerability I see in her eyes.

And where I am accustomed to panic that swallows me whole, that spits me out in shivering, jellied pieces, it feels unnaturally natural to accept her invitation.

In the boardroom, water jugs are filled: half with still, half with sparkling. Biscuits and cake set onto trays. A silver platter of fresh scones, crystal cruets with jam and thick cream.

'You'll be brilliant,' I tell Tris. 'You already are, without trying.'

But her attention is elsewhere.

Voices chatter in the hallway, growing closer, and we turn to greet the arrivals. Tris steps forward, hand extended.

Above my right eyebrow there's a thick, ragged scar. Ten tiny white scar-holes where the needle pierced skin. It came from a car accident I'd had while at uni, the other car trying to beat a red light. As I slammed on the brakes there was a hiss in my ears. As if something was whispering. *Stop. While you can.* I could not stop. My head smacked against the driver's-side window on impact.

I can hear the hiss now.

'This is Doctor Scott Harman,' says Tris.

Impact.

'Please, call me Scott.'

All noises are muted except for his name, the hiss in my ears.

His hand is outstretched with all its familiar markings: the signet ring from his father, the dark hair on the back of his hand, the peep of his Breitling watch from his cuff.

His hand hangs in the air. I don't reach to shake it. I am embarrassing Tris, making everyone uncomfortable. *Because that's what you do.* I hear his voice in my head. *You fuck it up. You fail. That's what you're best at. Fucking and failing.*

'Not for me,' he answers the secretary offering coffee.

His smug composure is too busy drinking in my stunned silence.

'Doctor Harman has a passion for textiles,' Tris says. I can feel her trying to size up this moment.

'I thought my reputation might have preceded me,' he says, winking at Tris. But really he is calling me out for my lie on the phone.

You've told nobody anything is what's being made clear. All the old motions of dumb, silent obeyance whir in my body as he pulls out a chair and directs me.

'Please, take a seat.'

But I hear what he means. *Sit. Like a dog.*

I want to steady myself against the table but I can't move my arms. I want to run and not stop, but he's blocking the doorway. I lose control of my body. Piss streams down my legs. Cramps slice my belly. But still I stand without moving. Without speaking. A storm of shame rages, turns my brain to mush.

'Please,' he repeats, offering the chair.

Sit and wait for the morsel tossed to your paws.

Sit down and shut up. Sit down. Sit, you dumb cunt.

Tris's hand on my arm. The only part I can feel of my body. Whatever she is saying is drowned out by the noise in my head.

But her warm hand on my skin anchors something inside me.

'Get out.' The quietest of words from my lips.

'Excuse me?' he says, his mock surprise is persuasive. But he is challenging me to repeat what I've said.

'Get. Out.' I raise my voice. I am calm, like it's somebody else speaking. But there's his sly grin, the one that enjoys watching me unravel. The rage in me surges. 'Get out of my life!'

I am heaving and panting and hot with the effort. Sharp, stabbing pains flare in my stomach. But with Tris's touch burning through me I charge over to him, shove him with both of my hands to his chest, and he stumbles.

But now I am unhooked from Tris and I flounder. Wet down my legs. Now that I've pushed him aside there's a straight line through the door, a door between worlds.

I run. I run. Always this running. Even when I am still.

Tris is calling my name. Following me out the staff door, down the university paths, over the footbridge. I'm sprinting and sobbing. The blue-ribbon schoolgirl from every sports day. Because if you can run, then you are safe. And I will myself to beat her because the last thing I need is to see how I've failed her. Her glazed look of disappointment that will haunt me forever.

But I can't run anymore. My stomach slashed through with cramps. I stop near the footbridge and she pants beside me, unable to talk while she catches her breath.

When she does speak, it is gently.

She doesn't say *how could you embarrass me with that appalling behaviour?* Says nothing like *your outburst cost me more than you could imagine, you silly bitch, worthless cunt who might as well use her hole as a drainpipe.*

'I will fix this,' she says. Her chest rises and falls, teardrop earrings swinging. 'Tell me what I can do. I'll drop the deal in a second.'

I am confused by her sincerity. What does she owe me? Why take my side without explanation?

'Who is he? Did he hurt you?'

And I almost surrender. Almost fall into her strength, into her warmth, to soak in her safe touch. But I must shut people down. I must shut people out. I must do whatever it takes to keep the shameful secrets inside me.

'Mind your own business,' I say, backing off. 'I need nothing from you.'

Cramps flare through my belly, my shoulders. It's hard to stand straight, harder to walk.

'I think you're bleeding,' says Tris, coming towards me. Her eyes are frightened. Not the eyes that I know to be hers.

I hold out my flat palms to keep her away, my cramps now like contractions.

'Call an ambulance!' she shouts to passersby, reaching for me, tucking her arms under mine.

'I've got you,' she says, as I let myself be held, nausea sweeping, thighs leaking my warmth.

I can't run anymore. Can't resist. My legs buckle beneath me.

She cradles me against her. Paramedics are running towards us.

The hospital bed is narrow, the mattress rustles like cellophane. The doctor is explaining complications of miscarriage. Haemorrhage. Infection. Laceration. Scarring. Depression.

'Let her rest,' says Tris.

The doctor is miffed, but leaves us alone.

And I want to say sorry.

But she says it for me. 'I'm so sorry,' she says, her warm hand inside mine.

Those words I once used to begin every weak sentence, now a spell-breaking poem. Perhaps hearing it, not having to say it, is enough. Or at least a beginning.

Then, inside me, an unravelling. Thread loosening, unspooling. Pieces detaching. Every frail stitch, sewn to keep me together, near to bursting.

I feel them, words releasing. I can't stop their escape. And then it comes, all of it. Although she hasn't asked.

You should have seen them together. Him and his dad. By sixteen, when Jonathan walked into a room, I'd look up from my stitching and catch my breath. The exact image of his father. In photos of Paul at that age, you could barely tell them apart.

He wasn't meant to be on that train at that time in that city. He was never on time. But that day he'd been early. It was luck, they said, that there were not more people aboard. How I'd trembled with rage at their version of luck. The bomb took four lives. And for the life seated closest, it left nothing intact. Save for a camera bag left in the toilets. Always losing things, mislaying things. It drove me mad. And I drove him mad by complaining. And always late. But not that day.

Not. That. Day.

And my heart wants to explode and leave nothing intact.

But all I can feel is my hand being held.

Tris holding my hand. Holding me together while I fall apart.

23
Florence, 1516

I wake sodden and shivering with fever, grasping my belly. Am I in Rome? Back in Florence? The effort of moving a limb is like hefting a slab of stone. My hands find it. This small mound of my flesh, taut and hot. I wonder if I am dreaming or if I can feel it, my child, throbbing like a second heart beneath my palms.

I let my arm drop from my belly back to the bed. I try to open my eyes, crusted and hazy. I don't know where I am. I roll onto my right side and fumble my hand across my nightstand. My fingers find the glass vial I keep by my bed. This is my bedroom. I am in Florence.

A creak of floorboards. The room swims in a blur. The bed shifts with weight, a hand on my brow. And while I was certain that I woke in my room, home in Florence, and not in the many fever-dreams of the last days, now I am unsure. Because of his voice.

'*Sei tu, morte?*' My dry lips crack and sting as I speak. *Is that you, Death?*

I try to focus my eyes. Try to reach my hand for him, this unwanted visitor, to push him back from myself. From my child. His voice in my ear.

'*Sono io,*' says the voice. '*Sono io.*' It is me.

'*Vai via lasciami, morte!*' Get lost, Death!

'*Dormi. Dormi,*' says the voice. Sleep. Sleep.

Again, I slip into fever.

*

The chills come and go as if the angel of death comes to brush its wings across my body, to see if I will stir. I can feel my limbs lifted to wipe me down, sips of water poured into my mouth. How many days pass I cannot tell. But one morning I can move without struggling: the sweats have subsided. I think about the familiar voice in my ear that lulled me to sleep. If Death has come calling, I have not answered. Nor has my baby. Tears slide from my eyes at the thought, but I have no will to cry.

Soon I can sit up and take a thin broth. When I am able to rise from my bed long enough to wash my own face, it is a small victory.

'The *mal 'aria* in Rome causes illness. It's the filth of the river,' the physician tells Fredo, pressing his fingers deep into my belly. 'But who knows the effect? If she delivers an *imbecille* it will be no surprise.'

It is clear he is unimpressed that I journeyed so far in the early stages of my pregnancy. I am too weak to care. I hear the chink of coins from the merchant's son into the hand of the physician.

'He's ill-mannered, but one of the best,' says Fredo, whose recent shift into adolescence makes his voice wobble. His father is pleased with reports from Sarto and Michel, that his son has talent for fresco and has given permission for him to stay longer.

I lift my hand to let him know it doesn't matter what has been said.

The door closes and I hear him taking the stairs down to the kitchen. I feel myself drifting.

A gentle tap at the door; it squeaks open. I don't try to respond, but I open my eyes, not so heavy this morning.

He stands in the doorway, leaning hard on the stick in his shaking left hand. I am already crying, reaching for him, expecting him to wash away in some shifting dreamscape. But he limps slowly towards me. I can smell bread baking downstairs. If this was a dream, could I still smell the bread? With great effort I push myself to sitting, opening my arms to him. He is warm against me, not like a dream. I bury my face in his neck. Feel his ribs at my chest. A hardness, a frailness, a greyness about him. But still him. My Eugenio. Awake from his sleep.

'Where did you go?' I ask through my tears.

He lifts a shoulder as if to say *what does it matter?* '*Sono qui*,' he replies, his speech slow and awkward. *I am here.*

I embrace him even more tightly and take in the smell of his skin, my body heaving with the grief I have refused to allow. When I can bear to release him, I sit back and take my hands to his hollow cheeks, my fingers through his long hair. I can see half his face does not move like the other. And he lifts a kerchief to blot the spittle that leaks from the side of his mouth.

'*Il bambino?*' he asks with slow, laboured speech.

'*Tutto bene*,' I reply, taking his hand to my belly.

'But Rome?' He shakes his head slowly, looking pained. It is clear he, too, does not approve of my journey.

'I have so much to tell you,' I say, summoning optimism and trying not to look alarmed as he struggles to coordinate his body and mind.

'Lucia?' The single word with its question comes out in extra syllables, quavering and indistinct.

A sense of deflation almost overwhelms me. I'd visited the places the abbess suggested in Rome. And quite a few more. Neither their books nor their memories held any clue. Not a trace. Not even a suggestion for where to look next.

'Not Lucia,' I say. 'But something else, quite unexpected. I found the name of a woman, Bianca di Biagio di Bindo. Plain as you like in black ink on white paper. I'm certain I've found a distant relative of Mariotto's. Di Biagio was his father's name. You understand what this could mean?'

Eugenio's expression is doubtful.

'I have an address on Via Santa Margherita, here in Florence. Can you imagine her face to discover she might be related to a painter of Florence who once worked for the Medici? We must visit! Please don't deny me.'

'Soon,' he says, trying to bring his handkerchief to his mouth to blot his lips.

'Not soon enough,' I say, pushing my head back to his chest to hear for myself the aliveness inside him.

He stays by my side. Sometimes I wake and watch him sleep in the chair placed next to my bed. When fatigue comes again I do my best to remain awake, terrified that I might emerge from a sleep and find the chair empty.

He practises his walking back and forth across the bedroom while I tell my stories through tears. I tell him about the sketch that came in the box. About the pig, Alessio, who resented having to take me to Rome. About Fredo and his talent for fresco. About Baccio's apprentice, Giulio, who was my patient guide in Rome. About the home for unmarried mothers and the widower, Alberto Cabibe, who started the place with his wife. About the leather-bound book with the names of women and children, and the name of Bianca. That perhaps he was right all along and I should let Zia Lucia fade into the past and vanish, since it seems clear that's what she wanted.

'Bianca,' he says, the effort of three syllables too much for us both.

I press myself inside his arms, against his thin body, making him promise to never again leave my side. He covers his face with a trembling hand and silently weeps. Both of us falling asleep with exhaustion.

Once the physician reports I can venture out for a walk, I announce to Eugenio we will head the next morning to Via Santa Margherita. To see the woman, Bianca, whom I pray is Mariotto's relative. A branch for my new family tree.

My heart swells with emotion when I open the door to see Eugenio in his finery. Fitted Perpignan hose, a tailored brocade *farsetto* cut close to his now smaller chest, a blue velvet doublet, and over this a fine black wool *mantle*, pleated to fill out his frame.

On his beautiful curls, a black velvet *berretto*. To dress and groom himself like this will have taken all morning. Even leaning hard on his stick, he cuts a fine figure.

'You don't approve?' I ask when he frowns.

I've changed from my cornflower-blue gown back into my plain shift and apron. I tried my masticot-yellow gown with beaded sleeves. Took it off, put it on. Settled on a frock, once my mother's, that I felt looked proper.

'*Di chermisi*,' he says, waving an unsteady hand to shoo me upstairs to change into the fine red velvet gown I had made when Mariotto sold a painting to a merchant in Venice.

'But I don't have a cloak or hat to match it,' I say, in truth feeling the dress is excessive.

'*Sbrigati!*' he says, telling me to hurry, leaning his weight against the wall so he can point his stick to emphasise his impatience.

'*Irascibile*,' I say, heading up to my room to change.

'But not deaf,' says Eugenio, less slowly than usual.

My *chermisi* skirts swish under my cloak as I walk; they took almost eighteen *braccia* of fabric dyed with a red powder brought in from the East. The one pair of shoes Eugenio approves, chopine, slip back and forth on my feet with each step. I am grateful for how slowly Eugenio moves. At his usual pace I could never keep up in these wedged heels.

As I walk Via Santa Margherita, my stomach churns in the way it would if I was meeting a lover. And although I have been certain that myriad unforeseen obstacles will hinder my progress to the house of Bianca di Biagio di Bindo, sooner than I am ready I stand at her door.

A woman with a tight bun that pulls at the skin on her temples answers my knock. Spoon in hand, spattered apron: she is clearly a cook. But even her overdress is made of brocade and fine linen, and I feel a rush of relief for Eugenio's good taste that saw me change into this dress. If the cook wears such fine clothes, Bianca's are certain to be finer.

From somewhere inside comes the piercing squawk of a bird.

'If you're seeking *il padrone di casa*, we don't expect him before the Feast of the Baptist,' the cook says.

'Forgive me for arriving unannounced,' I say, already tongue-tied with what I rehearsed.

The woman looks me over, top to toe, toe to top.

'Bianca,' Eugenio interrupts, his need to articulate slowly, carefully, making him sound derisive. *Bee-ANH-kah*. As if talking to someone hard of hearing. Or stupid. She taps out her impatience with the wooden spoon to her palm.

'We are friends of the family,' I say.

The woman appears unmoved, and I expect the door to be thrown shut. Instead, a great bird, wings splayed in dazzling green and turquoise, flies towards us screeching, landing its sharp claws onto the woman's ample shoulder.

'Malachite!' A younger woman appears in the hallway, shimmering embroidered violet-red skirts lifted to reveal dainty bare feet as she walks. Silver brocade drapes from the hems of each sleeve. A figure so dreamlike in its vivid colour and poise it is as if she has walked out of a painting. 'Rascal bird!' she says, nuzzling her face in the bird's emerald feathers, taking it from the woman's shoulder and onto her forearm. 'Are you bothering Monna Catalina?'

The bird gabbles objections while Monna Catalina, tight-lipped, swipes a round dropping from her shoulder and leaves us without hiding her displeasure.

'You are here for Marcello?' the young woman asks. Her pale skin is framed by a tangle of black curls; her eyes are bright as blue glass.

'Bianca?' I ask this woman, who could less be Mariotto's distant cousin and more his younger sister.

'I am she,' replies Bianca, stroking her bird. Its eyes closed and now purring like a satisfied kitten.

'Bianca di Biagio di Bindo?' I can think of nothing else to say.

'Until last year,' she replies, smiling. 'Now it's Fratelli.'

'*Sì, sì*,' squawks the bird, bobbing up and down in a frenzy.

'We have come … I have come …' I stammer over my words.

Eugenio pokes at the back of my leg with his stick.

'I went to Alberto's place in Rome, the hostel, and saw your name in his register.' I try to explain, but my thoughts are a mess. 'We thought, myself and Eugenio here, he came with me, you see, that you might be related to Mariotto di Biagio di Bindo Albertinelli.'

'Does he owe you money?' asks Bianca, her delicate brow spoiled by a wrinkle. The bird flaps its wings.

'No, *no*! Not at all,' I reply, and Eugenio groans with impatience. 'Mariotto was my husband. An only child. He lost touch with his family and once spoke of relatives. And, well, now he is gone, I have no family of my own …' My voice trails off while Bianca, like Signora Catalina, looks me up and down. Seems to study my clothes without obvious disapproval. Casting a glance at Eugenio beside me, wiping spittle from his mouth. I imagine, with shame, what a peculiar pair we must seem.

'Take the biscuit,' says the bird, spreading its wings to full width. Their undersides are vivid blue, unlike the top of the wings, which are green as the stone after which it is named.

'Malachite, shut your beak! Mind your business!' says Bianca.

'*Sì*, *sì*, mind your business,' the bird screeches without heed, batting its wings hard, the air rushing as it lifts from her arm and takes flight down the hallway.

'Ignore the bird,' she says, as if excusing a drunk uncle. 'He's being punished today for eating Cook Catalina's bread dough.' She brushes a green feather from her shoulder. 'Mariotto was my father.'

The feather sails back and forth to the floor in a time that takes a moment. In a time that takes forever.

Lucia once told me there are two kinds of truth. The one that you know and the one that you tell. I'd been seated cross-legged before her on Nonna's old cot, rapt by the serious and grown-up conversation.

'The trick,' she said, drinking the tavern's best wine straight from the flask, 'is in knowing what *must* be told.'

She sat back and examined me, and I tried to look as if I understood.

'*Allora, exempli!* Where is the truth in a painting?' she asked. 'Is it in the mind's eye of the artist, her first vision of an image?'

I remained silent. Did not blink, did not dare breathe.

'Or in the final picture, bright and bold, on the panel?'

She offered me the flask. I hesitated and then reached for it, and she snatched it away. '*Allora!* You see? I offer you the flask but I'm not offering you wine. What is the truth?'

She took another swig.

'Where? Oh where is truth? Is it in the bristles of the artist's brush? Or the paint on her palette?' She threw her arms in the air, the wine sloshing out of the flask. Then she leaned into me so I could smell her. Linseed, roses and wine. '*Dov'è la verità?*' Her voice asking me like she was sharing a secret. Where is the truth?

My mind raced with answers, but for fear of her ridicule I dared not share any.

'So many artists think truth can be captured in white,' she continued. 'So bright and so clean. Not blemished or sullied. A white halo. An angel. A beam from the Almighty. Such lies!'

'What colour is truth?' I asked, caught up in the moment.

Lucia threw back her head and the room filled with her laughter.

'That,' she replied, wiping wine from her lips, 'depends on the light.'

On Bianca's front doorstep, the light is too harsh. Too clear and bright. A blinding spotlight upon the woman who says she is my late husband's daughter. I stand rigid, a fleeting reel of memories whirring. Mariotto disappearing for days. My worst thoughts were brothels or the beds of rich patrons. Not a child. A daughter. I am losing my breath, the bones of my corset crushing my ribs.

'You are quite pale,' says Bianca. 'Please come in and sit down. I did not mean to shock you.'

But I cannot move and I am unable to speak. Eugenio's hand is on my back. I try to whisper my apology, that I must leave. That I should not have come without notice. But if I opened my mouth, would I speak or scream?

'Let me offer you a drink,' says Bianca, extending her hand.

It is rude but I refuse it. My attention is now caught on the shape of her face.

And there it is. I see it. In the strong, rounded shape of her jaw. The sleek symmetry of her nose, a soft-lipped, wide mouth. Bianca told me Mariotto was her father. But now I see the more important truth. The one that is known but not told.

Lucia, pushing through the crowd, her yellow-gold scarf a bright slant of sunshine, her uncovered black curls, the reach of her hand beckoning me as I run to keep up.

'Have they married you off yet?' Lucia, asking me.

'Mind your business,' my mother, snapping. 'Don't cause any trouble.'

Trouble? What trouble had she worried that Lucia might cause?

Mamma had known the two truths of Lucia. And I now know it too, right here, before my eyes, in the fierce beauty of Bianca. I can see it, like Nonna would say, clear as the pearls in a virgin wife's headpiece. Not only was my husband Bianca's father. Her mother was my Zia Lucia.

My dress is too tight. My shoes are too high. How I want to run from her, to flee to the safety of San Michele alle Trombe. To catch my breath, quell my rage. I try to stand tall. 'Did you know he was married?'

Eugenio objects to my question by grasping my arm. I shake off his hand.

'I was a child. How could I know anything?' says Bianca, but her tone is offhanded. And at this something pent-up and strangled bursts forth.

'You lie,' I say, and her eyes widen. 'Like your mother and your father.'

I turn on Eugenio. 'Did you know this? Did you keep it from me?' I ignore the sadness in his eyes that I would accuse him.

He tries to object but his slack mouth stammers. He reaches for me again, an unsteady hand, but I shrug him away.

'You're both pig-licking liars. You can both go to hell.'

I run from Via Santa Margherita towards the church of San Michele. Casting off my shoes so they don't slow me down.

24

Beit HaKerem, 5 BCE

High on the terraced slopes above our village, I slip off my sandals. It calms me to feel the earth under my feet. Crouching low, I gather a fistful of mountain sage. It's a lush patch that, to my shame, I've kept secret. I discovered it on one of my many walks to sooth a restless Yoḥanan, who whimpers and points up here until I bring him, revelling in the adventure of a space so much bigger than our courtyard to crawl and explore. But, in truth, I love these moments alone with my son.

He crawls fast, then comes to a halt and sits himself by a globe thistle, a long trail of saliva hanging from his pink lip to his pudgy knee. Spellbound by a clicking insect perched on the purple orb of its flower, its front legs pawing the air as if trying to balance.

'Dat?' he asks, barely breathing with his effort of concentration.

'Grasshopper,' I reply, gathering leaves quickly while his attention is fixed.

When I glance back a third time to check on him, because my son is so quiet, I see it. The dust.

I rise slowly from my knees so as not to startle Yoḥanan, stuff the sage inside the pouch tied to my waist and scoop him up from the ground. He squeals with dissatisfaction as the insect springs into the air and is lost inside the bush. In the distant valley below, a dust cloud billows, bleeding upwards into the sky.

'What's that?' I say, directing his ever-keen attention to a speckled butterfly alighting a leaf and circling overhead.

'Dat?' he asks, ignoring me and pointing at the dust cloud that is coiling, spreading.

Trouble, I think. And his eyes fix upon me, as if he hears my thoughts.

'Dat?' he asks again. Creasing his face around the new sight.

'Dust,' I reply.

'Dutt,' says Yoḥanan.

I tighten the string on the pouch holding the sage. Ya'akov the Elder and Sara will come. Our home will be filled with the warmth and scent of shared food.

'Dat?' Yoḥanan asks again.

'Dust,' I repeat.

'Dat!' He is insistent. Impatient that I am not answering his question, which is no longer about the dust but something else that has caught his eye. Soldiers on horses, hooves thrashing the earth.

I pull Yoḥanan close to me and crouch low behind the small outcrop of limestone that shields my secret batch of wild herbs from the harshest hours of sun. He presses his head to my chest and falls silent.

Here is a child who wails over the smallest inconveniences. At the confiscation of a fistful of goat spoor he has decided to lick, or at being extracted from the henhouse after discovering that he only need draw himself to standing against the gate and push the latch to gain entry. I feel a troubling foreboding that he knows not to protest.

I peer around the rock. Below us, the soldiers are now clear. Those leading the charge are hunkered low on their horses to maintain their speed. I can see their helmets, the metal glinting under the sharp angle of the sun as their horses pound the road through the valley and up to Beit HaKerem.

'Why do they come?' I ask aloud. Only the wind answers, whistling up a whirligig that my child scrubs from his eyes without a murmur. I don't need to ask who has sent them.

Herod's feverish suspicions means no-one is safe. Since the execution of his wife his manic fits grow more frequent. Unrepentant yet haunted by her death at his hand, he has begun a building frenzy. Monuments, cities, towns, ports. As if vast accomplishment might subdue his guilty grief. But his paranoia is unbridled. A morning rumour can launch an order for an afternoon execution.

My breath grows shallow as I wonder what hot-winded whisper has provoked one of Herod's devastating reactions. What man or woman in our village has become the focus of his vengeance? I scan the road through the valley into the village, up the steep path to our home. Where are you, my husband? The sun is almost at zenith and Zakhariya should be meeting with villagers who require special guidance. Husbands whose sons are too weak to work. Young men who have trouble attracting a wife. Women whose husbands visit their mothers and do not return. Inheritance issues, squabbling between brothers. Flagging negotiations during a young couple's year of betrothal. Helping these people is where my husband should be.

When you see the dust.

I push back at the memory that wants to rise up.

Yoḥanan's head pulses against my heaving chest.

A dust cloud this size means at least fifty horses. I strain my eyes to try and count them. Some of their helmets are crested with red feathers, others are not. In a lineup of Roman soldiers, their uniforms were often motley or ill-fitting. I recall the sight of a young soldier, sparse whiskers sprouting on his chin, weighted down as he walked wearing chain mail that clearly once belonged to his father or uncle. The *lorica*, metallic fish-like scales, hanging down past his knees, the arm guards falling beyond the reach of his fingers. If he needed to flee or shoot an arrow, he would be too clumsy, too slow. Caught or shot before the bowstring was drawn. I felt a surge of compassion as he loped awkwardly in his too-large leather *caligae* boots. The nails in his soles studding the earth.

We'd crossed paths in a narrow street near the Holy City's old market. Me striding in a huff far ahead of my mother, him lagging behind a group of drunk Roman soldiers, mourning the murder of Yulius Kaisar, their caesar.

'*Sh'lama*,' I said. Because I'd been young too and still naïve in my belief that simple courtesy could build bridges.

'Jew-whore, die.'

The menace in his voice, not yet fully broken into a man's, left me baffled. 'Why do you hate us?'

At first he looked shocked that I'd asked such a question.

'You hated us first,' he replied.

It was the type of riposte I'd heard when children argued. *Don't hit your sister. She hit me first.* And this soldier was young. For him, perhaps his answer felt true. So much of our history had been built on who provoked whom. Centuries of actions and reactions like beads strung upon the same tight thread, until we forgot who threw the first insult. Or if an insult was even thrown. Like our grandmothers, Maryam's and mine. Two women who stopped speaking and so were never spoken of in the same room. In the same sentence.

When you see the dust. Her voice again. Maryam's. Breaking through my thoughts.

'My husband, where are you?' I ask it aloud and Yoḥanan whimpers.

I stroke his head. Its ruffle of auburn hair is streaked with strands of bright red, not seen in our family since a great-great-uncle on my mother's side. And Yoḥanan, too, displays signs of his past uncle's infamous short temper. I kiss his head, hush him.

I search for details among the soldiers, strain to make out the haze-smudged shape of their faces. Hoping they are too young, like so many are, to wield a sword, to shoot an arrow.

The mounted soldiers charge into the village and I stand up from my hiding place. I cry out. 'No!'

One horse begins rearing, perhaps not yet fully trained to withstand the fever of a charge, the blinding flash of raised swords, the shouting of men. It rears again and again and throws off its rider, who squirms in the dust. Another horse gallops over him, no doubt crushing his bones.

'Zakhariya!'

But he won't hear my call. I clamber across rubble, down the slopes to our village. To my home, to my beloved. Slipping, tripping, skinning my knees, getting back to my feet. Clutching my child, who now screams at my breast.

And still the dust spreads, kicked up from pounding hooves, enshrouding our village like a cast spell. Already the wailing of women, the shouting of men. I hear myself groaning too, a low whining that I cannot stop issuing from my throat. I want to look away and watch my step, but I cannot tear my eyes from my village, from my people. As if closing my eyes to it would be closing my heart to all those below. My husband, my neighbours, my friends for whom I climbed here to pick bush sage for our supper. The leaves are bigger and sweeter than ordinary sage. I will steam the leaves. I will fill them with minced lamb and herbs. Sara and Ya'akov the Elder come to share food.

I trip. My knee splits against a rock. Yoḥanan's face is red, sweating with his outburst. People below run in all directions, making a dash for their lives into the crags and caves of Beit HaKerem's rolling hillsides. But the soldiers are too fast. I see them throw a rope around one woman fleeing; I'm too far to see whom, but not too far to see them tear the child from her arms. A blade catching the sun as it swings.

I stumble and scramble, try to get up. To go to my people. But then two soldiers see me.

They will come for our sons, I had said, with the hope I was wrong. But the answer had been clear in Maryam's face.

Yes. They will come.

My child screams, fever pitch. And I cannot keep from my mind my young cousin's instruction.

When you see the dust, run for the mountain.

Against everything that pulls me down to the village and my husband, to the defence of my neighbours, I turn back to the slopes, tugged there by the weight of Maryam's words in my ears. Towards the high peak's summit. Away from the dust.

I scramble and slip back over the rubble. I kicked off my sandals to feel the earth under my feet while I collected leaves and sang to myself and my son. My unshod feet are now slashed by the stones. Still I run on, my child screaming at my breast. His fingers gripped tight to my tunic.

I stumble across the rocky spur to a trickle of water seeping from the side of the slope, a rockpool in my path. The heavy rains two moons ago have done more damage than good, digging up newly planted crops and flooding the low-lying parts of the valley, but the hidden remains of the downpour are welcome and cool as I wade in, soothing my bleeding feet. I scoop some to my lips, to my son's, and keep climbing, exiting the pool where the rock widens and noon sun lights the gorge in a single bright shaft. Before me the gorge narrows again, a funnel of damp air cool on my face. Yoḥanan becomes quieter, sniffling, hiccoughing, spent from his outburst. Dragging on his breath like a child does after a tantrum.

'See the sparkles,' I say.

Moss and lichen glimmer with dew. I can hear my own panting. Another breeze gusts through, cool against my head. My bare head! I raise a hand to feel only the braid in my hair. My veil is gone. I twist this way and that. Where did I lose it? Did it flutter away? Was it caught on a twig? Flapping and slapping like a flag in the wind?

'*Aliquid inveni!*'

A young man's strident voice. I strain to hear more. My knowledge of Latin is not enough to understand the words, but his urgency needs no translation. He is calling to another. Perhaps waving my veil. Perhaps coming my way. The narrow gorge is a whisper of echoes. I feel the urge to turn back, to search for my scarf before they find it, if they haven't already.

'*Perge! Perge! Porro indage!*' Another older man's voice. Hard-edged and gravelly.

'*Pergam, dux!*' He is closer, the young man. '*Domine ilicet.*' His voice quakes with its recent breaking, some high notes squeaking through as he speaks.

But now silence. No sense of their proximity. No footfall or clambering over rocks towards us. The men sounded near and now there is no sound at all. I stop and strain to hear something, anything. Only the thud of my pulse in my ears. I push my forefinger to my lips to show my child it is quiet time. He pushes a finger to his own mouth.

'Good boy,' I whisper, and in a burst of excitement he claps his hands together.

It shouldn't sound so loud, his tiny hands, but the sudden clap sends two swallows skywards. I grab both his hands in mine. I know I am squeezing them too hard and my eyes are fierce. He is startled, bottom lip quivering, and while I am overcome with the desire to reassure him, I must make it clear that the game is silence.

Inside the gorge, my child becomes calmer, reaching his hand to my face, as he has done since he was born. He pushes his fingers to my lips and I whistle the two short flute-like notes of the hoopoe, as is our game. He grins, knowing he should not laugh. I whistle again.

The coolness seeps from the rocks and cloaks our bodies in a fine mist. The sheer walls of the gorge feel like a fortress.

'Dutt!' Yoḥanan tests his new word against the echo of the rocks.

I push a finger gently to his lips and hold it there, shaking my head.

'*Dutt.*' Softer now.

I smile my approval.

The gorge walls have tapered and are almost touching my shoulders, and in two steps we will once again be in water. A dead end beyond a shimmering pool. I move closer and peer into the surface. I push my foot in and cannot feel the bottom. I push it in further, but it is up to my knee and still I feel no earth beneath my feet. Even if we can get across it, there is nowhere to go.

Seams of quartz sparkle through the creamy-red stone. The *chit chit chit* of some tiny bird that has found refuge. A chorus of them now and Yoḥanan is delighted, in his element as always when surrounded by nature. I take the chance to put him down at the edge of the pool for a moment, the crook of my arm aching from his weight. So large for a child of his age. His head alone is bigger than any baby's I've ever seen. Zakhariya and I laughed about him having to grow into it before he will be able to balance on his tiny legs.

The chitter of birds again, and he points his finger at the sheer slope of the wall, searching in earnest for the source of the sounds.

'Dat?' he asks, pointing a chubby finger high.

'Bird,' I reply softly.

'Beh.'

My father's only word for so long. How I ache to recall the frustration and anguish he felt. The effort he made to convey what was in his head with a meaningless word.

'Beh.' Yoḥanan tries the word again.

'Bird,' I repeat, and then again, slower. 'Bah-erd'.

I hear a scuffle echo behind me. Rocks clatter under my feet as I stumble around the edge of the pool, searching for a place to hide that I know I won't find. Praying that the mountain opens up and swallows us both. How far away are they now? I can't tell. I hear a man hock and spit. Yoḥanan looks up at me, presses his grubby finger to his lips. I nod and do the same.

I take him back into my arms, wriggle one foot to plant it in the earth and, with the other, test the water again. The pool takes my leg up to my knee. I venture further, to my hip. My toes touch a silty floor.

Heavy footsteps now. The clatter of tumbling rocks as somebody clambers over them. The grunt and pant of the effort.

'*Angustius est.*' The older soldier's voice. '*Minas! Perge! Perge! Porro indage!*'

'*Quam sedulissime ago.*' The young solider, Minas, answers.

'*Sedulius age!*' growls the older.

Yoḥanan is wide-eyed and silent in my arms. A swallow soars out of its nest and its hatchlings chitter and cheep at the promise of food.

'*Audio aliquid*,' the young soldier calls.

Audio. He hears. I understand the word. You don't hear anything, I think. You hear only birds.

'You be found!' The older soldier. Speaking these words poorly in my language. He catcalls and it echoes, making my skin shiver.

I glance back to check the width of the gorge. A tight fit for a grown man in armour, but the young soldier might squeeze through.

'*Video aliquid*,' yells the younger, the sharp clang of his sword thrashing rock.

Video. Another word I understand. He sees.

'*Te aucupabor!*' His scream echoes. Birds screech and dart skywards.

I don't know what he says. But I know he is coming. I am left with no choice.

I grip Yoḥanan to my chest, wade into the pool and suck in a great gulp of air. Squeeze my child's nostrils between my fingers, and plunge beneath the water.

25

Florence, 1516

I open my eyes from below the surface, the shifting blur of the bathwater above me. The city of Florence honours the patron of immersion in water, Giovanni Battista. Water to cleanse, water to bless. When children are born they are baptised, sometimes within hours, to save their souls from Limbo should they perish too soon. To be baptised banishes inborn sin and triumphs over past evils. The child is made perfect and new. No misdeeds of the mother, no sins of the father.

The water breaches the sides of the wooden tub and slops on the floor as I rise and sink again. Why is it that another's lies and sins have made me a fool, with a shame that sticks like mud to a hog. I hold my breath under the water. The water has turned cold but I do not yet feel cleansed.

Mind your business. The squawk of Bianca's bird is still shrill in my ears.

'Mind your business,' Mamma cautioned Lucia. The wildness in her face when I reported to Lucia the fragment I had overheard about my future betrothal; that he was a painter.

'She'll be of age when he's mellowed and ready to marry,' I overheard my father say.

'A mellowed painter? In Florence?' scoffed Mamma.

Mind your business. Don't cause any trouble.

The bold arch of Lucia's eyebrow to hear of a painter; my mother's stern warning for her to not interfere.

The expression on my mother's face as she drove the lid off the flour bin, my letters to Lucia scattering across flagstones. A sadness, a burden of knowledge, in her eyes that I hadn't understood then. The cloying fug of our kitchen, the rage burning high in my chest. Mamma's fisted hands, not waving as Lucia left in the carriage. A final silent warning for her not to return. Not with the baby she now carried, by the man they wished me to marry.

I burst through the surface, panting. Scrub my skin with castile and clove oil again and again. Tears mixing with bathwater and the scum of the past.

My hair is still wet, my gamurra thrown over damp skin, as I knock once again at Bianca's front door. When she opens it, she is smiling. I can't speak for crying. I'm not sure what answer will be harder to bear. If my Lucia is still alive and I must see her. Or if she is gone and I will never see her again.

'Will you come in?' she says.

I shake my head and stammer an apology. Then blurt out the question.

'She passed away in Rome,' replies Bianca.

'I'm sorry,' I say.

'Two years before Babbo.'

She waits to see how I react at the word she has used for my husband. Babbo.

'*Allora!* Come inside. Perhaps we've made an elephant out of a fly.' She links her arm through mine. 'Let's share a drink. *In vino veritas.*' In wine there is truth.

In Bianca's sitting room, the truth is green. Lush fabrics in turquoise and verdigris hang at the windows. Armchairs whose legs are carved with trailing vine leaves, seats covered in emerald silks and furnished with forest-green velvet cushions trimmed with leaf-green tassels. Silk and wool rugs embroidered with more vines and oak leaves cover the floors. On a perch near the window Malachite preens, the shafts of light making jewels of his feathers.

Bianca offers me a plate of biscuits. I take one but don't eat. She takes one for herself.

'She wasn't herself for a long time before her death,' she says. 'Irritable, unpredictable. Not eating. Headaches that would see her laid up for days. She complained that her hands and feet were numb and always cold, but I was more concerned for how swollen they were. Walking from one room to another left her wheezing and breathless. We sought out the best physicians ...' She tries to smile through her tears and I feel ashamed for wanting her to relay any details.

'"Painters colic" they said, insisting she should stop painting and start praying. You can imagine her reaction.'

She nibbles on the biscuit, puts it back on the tray.

'I can't keep anything down,' she says. 'I'm two moons along, says the physician. Marcello will turn purple.'

I am not sure if this means Marcello will be happy.

'I'm twenty-four weeks,' I say.

'*Che splendido!*' She claps her hands. 'Perhaps a birth on the feast day!' She taps out the sign of the cross to pray for such luck as to be born on the feast of Florence's revered San Giovanni Battista, ideally a coveted boy. 'I don't know where to start,' she says. 'You must want to know everything.'

Of that I am uncertain. If I do want to know everything, it depends what everything is. 'I don't mean to press you,' I say.

Bianca rises to fill the petite green cup set down on a table beside me. The smell of the wine turns my stomach. It was the first sign of my pregnancy, this sudden distaste.

'It's porcelain from China.' She returns to her chair and raises her cup to sip at the wine. 'My husband is a collector. He'd be furious if he knew I used it.' She twirls the cup and drinks. '*Mi se*. Mee-sir. It means mysterious colour. I think all colours are mysterious, not only green,' she says.

I am beginning to feel an onset of chills, rarer since my recovery from the bad air in Rome. But the coldness begins in my chest and spreads to my limbs, where it becomes hot and spreads again, back towards my centre. I fan my face with my hands. Malachite squawks as if sensing unrest.

'All this news, it must be a shock.' She unlatches the window shutter and beckons me over to take in some fresh air.

Malachite lifts off his perch and collects the *mi se* cup I've not touched in his beak, wine splashing to the floor.

'Rascal bird!' Bianca stomps her foot and holds out her palm. 'Drop it now!'

The bird does as he's told. Flaps his giant wings towards her, alights on her shoulder and places the cup in his mistress's hand. She nuzzles him, rewarding his obedience with her uneaten biscuit.

'He finds rare objects and sells them,' she says, twisting the *mi se* in her hand to the light. 'My husband, not the bird.'

'Take the biscuit,' gabbles Malachite.

'I have a piece he might like to see,' I say. 'A glass vial in black. It doesn't sound much but, well, it's hard to describe.'

'*Allora!* Say no more.' She returns the bird to his perch, sets the cup aside and opens a small cupboard. She cradles something in her palm. 'Like this?'

At first I think it is my piece. A glossy black vial of glass, the same curvilinear shape. But then I notice it is smaller, sitting more neatly inside her palm. And it doesn't appear to sparkle like mine. Mariotto said there were two and I presumed one had been lost. Again I feel dizzy, a swinging sense of anger and despair. I stare at the vial in her palm. Her hand so like Mariotto's. His beautiful hands, rounded fingertips, soft knuckles. The hands of a nobleman, not a painter.

'From Mariotto?' I ask, rankling with jealousy, feeling guilt at this fact. Part of me wanting to proclaim that my piece is more special than the one in her hand. That it was his mother's favourite. That it sparkled.

'He brought it to me the day after she died,' says Bianca. 'Staggered in, stewed as a Medici goose. "One for the daughter I could not give my wife. One for the wife who deserves more than I am." I didn't think much of it at the time. I mean, what does it do? It doesn't sit properly on a shelf, I can't put anything in it. I was more selfish then. I know that's hard to believe.' She is awkward for a moment, quickly recovers. 'He didn't sleep, just kept drinking,' she goes on. 'Then one morning I found him outside on the step. Head hung between his knees. "My wife knows I did not go out for *Buccellato di Lucca*."'

We fall silent, torn fragments of our lives stitching together. I am grateful for her sharing and feel obliged to do likewise.

'I tried to find her in Fiesole,' I say. 'And Rome.'

'Whether it's better you didn't, I can't say.' She yawns.

I can't tell if she's tired or bored.

'Marcello says the technique is not modern.' She returns her attention to the black glass. 'That he's seen something quite similar among the wares of a merchant from Rhodes, who'd travelled from Egypt.' At this her eyes seem to cloud with fleeting suspicion. 'But Babbo told me it came from his mother. Said she died when he was a child.'

At last, a story from Mariotto that appears to be true.

'I should call her Nonna,' she says. 'But she's more of a ghost than my father. Does that make me sound heartless?' She waves a dismissive hand through the air before I can offer a response. 'I'm not. Truly. But sometimes I feel so angry. At him. At both of them. It's childish, but I can't bear to look at his paintings.'

'Not even the one in San Michele alle Trombe? *La Visitazione?*' I ask.

Bianca's pretty face tightens into sharp angles. 'That damned painting,' she says. 'They fought over it, you know. Whose idea it was. How it should look. But I saw her original cartoons for myself. *Dio mio!* Always a point of contention between them. But I was there when they painted the one that hangs in Santa Maria. Please tell me you saw it.'

'They?' I ask, conflicted.

'I was six when they finished it,' says Bianca. 'Babbo painted the two figures in the front, she painted those in the background. She would always paint me if there was any girl to be put in her pictures.' She pouts. 'But I could see the young woman in the background was not me. I was always a little jealous of the *la pulcina* in Florence on whom she said it was modelled.'

I feel myself wobble, my legs giving way. Stepping, falling backwards as if shoved in the chest. And then Bianca is beside me. Taking my weight in her arms. Malachite squawking. *Roll the bread dough. Mind your business.*

Mia pulcina. My little chick. My father's greasy lips at my ear.

The green of the room becomes grey. And the memory steals me from my place beside Bianca. My hand clasping a jar of Umbrian honey, my father's finger piercing the wax. The sweet scent of honey, the stink of old cooking. Lucia behind me, linseed and roses. So many scents, so real in my senses. His stale, panting breath so strong in my nostrils.

I double over and retch.

The bird squawks. I put my hands to my ears, but I can't block out the screech of the bird. Nor the sound of my father's groaning. The rasp of desire from the back of his throat. His hot, stinking breath on my neck. Wave after wave of memory rising out of my body and onto green leaves of Bianca's tapestry rug.

I wake in a different room, one as yellow as the last room was green. A velvet chaise beneath me, soft on my skin. The child of my husband smoothing my brow. I try to sit up.

'My physician is on his way here,' says Bianca.

'It was a memory that upset me. I'll recover in a moment,' I reply, soothed by the glow of gold that saturates the room.

'My mother would detest all this colour.' Bianca laughs, pushing a plump, sun-gold pillow under my head. 'She liked herself to be the most dazzling thing in any room.'

I understand why Bianca has created a colour-soaked world. Every surface, every fabric, every trimming, every stitch. All of it as close as she can come to being, again, in a room with Lucia.

I wrap my hands around myself; another onset of chills.

Bianca lifts an yellow-gold shawl draped over the back of the chaise and wraps it around me, soft and warm on my skin. 'Keep it,' she says. 'It was her favourite.'

I breathe in its smell.

'I've missed her forever,' I say.

And her hand is inside mine. Her palm soft as Mariotto's, warm as Lucia's. Hand in hand, like Elisabetta and Maria. Like Elisheva and Maryam. The chord their tender meeting struck in my chest. How I yearned to share in a moment like they did. With my mother. With Lucia. With Elisheva herself if I could have made it happen. If I could have dreamed so hard that, like Eugenio's long sleep, it might have swallowed me into a whole other world.

'Do you hate me?' she asks.

The question takes me off guard. I push myself to sitting, shaking my head.

'I didn't know he was married, I swear it.' She casts her hands through the sign of the cross. 'Not until later.'

'I wouldn't hate you if you had known,' I say, my words feeling pinched.

'It had finished between them,' she says. 'And almost three years since his last visit. My mother had rejected all communication. You know how she was, once her mind was set. She erased him as if he never existed. Changed her name. Introduced herself as Clementia Sforzosa.' She pauses, and I can see she is thinking over what she might say next. 'She forbade me to have contact.'

'And you complied?' I ask.

'Of course not,' replies Bianca. 'I am my mother's daughter.'

'And your father's,' I say.

'Alas not an obedient bone in my body,' she says. 'I came to the funeral. San Michele packed tight. I stood out on the steps. More people than I'd imagined.'

'Why didn't you come to me then?' My belly tightens.

'I intended to,' she says. 'But, once I arrived at the church, I was overcome with guilt. I had promised her, my mother.'

I understand it, this guilt. This sense of loyalty to a mother, fastened like a burr to the hem of an apron.

'But it was mostly your grief that stopped me making a scene,' she says. 'I am my mother's daughter, but not to such an extent that I would steal that time from you. To grieve, I mean. I'd lost my mother by then. I knew how it felt.'

'So you recognised me when I came to your door?' I ask.

'Now do you hate me?' she asks, pouting like a child.

I shake my head but say nothing.

'She regretted it. The affair. "More pain than childbirth and no gift at the end!" she'd say of my father.'

'He was inconstant,' I agree.

'Every memory of them carries an argument. Then that *white*! Coughing and spluttering after hours grinding lead dust. Mixing up paint. Both determined to find that perfect, elusive colour they imagined existed. They were working together, but always competing. "*Our* white" when together, "*my* white" when apart. He brought in buckets of rock he was sure would be its success. In the end, it all came to nothing. Damned white paint.' She tsks in disgust. 'I told them.' She raises her voice to relay it. 'Blue is where the money is!'

She is nattering, griping, and I want to cover my ears to shut out her prim exposition. But her voice grows more distant as a new darkness enfolds me.

I have every reason to feel betrayed by the Zia Lucia who bore a child by my husband. The Lucia I adored and in whom I saw every last quality of the ideal woman. Someone entirely her own person, with no heed for the opinion of others. Who could love without restraint. Who could look upon me like Elisheva did upon Maryam. But as I imagine Mariotto and Lucia grinding pigment together, humiliation smoulders, my eyes welling with the tears of a more wounding betrayal. Of them working together using my ideas while I worked alone.

'I'm certain it's what made her ill,' says Bianca, ignoring or not seeing my torment. 'That dust made her irritable, her eyes cloudy. Thin blue lines began to appear on her skin.'

'On Mariotto's too,' I say, remembering the darkening blue of his gums. Michel's quip that Mariotto was drinking his paint.

Bianca walks towards the painting above the fireplace. An ultramarine blue knight slaying a dragon, made more blue by its contrast with the gold in the room. She traces her finger along the curl of the biggest blue oak leaf. Rests it on an acorn. 'Merchants built manors off this blue,' she says, tapping the painting. 'Why waste time on white? It's not even a colour.'

The artists argued likewise against Mariotto's obsession with white. They urged him to shift his distraction from paint and back to painting, shaking their heads as he sneezed and blustered, eyes swollen and reddened, after grinding lead powder all day.

'Without white there is no moon,' he declaimed. 'No stars in our night sky, no flour for our bread, no lilies for our vases. No clouds, no mists, no sudden snowstorms, no mountains of marble.' The latter directed to Michel, his *David* newly completed. 'White is where a painter begins and where his brush ends, on the gleam of an eye: a touch of white on that black pupil is what brings the portrait to life. Without white there is no art!'

'And no virgins,' Pontormo said, to which all the men but Michel erupted in cheering.

'My husband has explained it but I never quite remember,' says Bianca, her mind not on white but on blue. She lifts her finger from the acorn. 'They quarry rocks in the mountains and crush them to dust that is made into dough. Dough from a rock? How unexpected.' Her delight is infectious. 'Then more water is added to draw out the colour. It makes bright blue liquid. I imagine it like a great magical lake. My husband says I think like a child. As if imagination is an unsophisticated pursuit.' She pauses to pout. 'Anyway, the blue liquid is placed in the sun until it dries back into powder.' She sets her hands on her hips, satisfied with what she has reported. 'What vanity! A whole process that swallows its own tail. Why not use the rock dust they had at the start?'

I could tell her the answer, but I leave it.

She throws back her head and laughs. I can't help but laugh with her, she sounds so much like her mother.

'*Vieni!* Come!' she says, threading her arm through mine.

We take another flight of stairs up to a landing, a door either side.

'Lucrezia Borgia would have a covetous fit,' says Bianca, her hand on the doorknob.

Lucrezia Borgia is the daughter of the late Pope Alexander VI, and her reputation for finery equals that of her scandals. That Bianca might have something to make a woman of such power and wealth envious makes my heart thud with anticipation. She pushes open the door.

Inside, cascading black silk draperies ripple, oily and shining, like the skin of a grass snake. They billow in the breeze against brilliant white walls. In the centre stands a bed, half the size of the room, carved in black walnut and draped with white silks embroidered with roses in black silken thread. And, above us, a small glass cupola where light floods in, emphasising the drama of black against white.

'Sick with envy, she'd be,' says Bianca. 'The curtains and bed silks are *morello di grana*. They cost more than seven of Lucrezia's gowns. I bartered with my husband when he took a mistress.'

Lucrezia Borgia brought black out of the domain of mourning and clergymen's dress and into high fashion, commissioning silks and velvets that stunned with their lavish audacity. So long had black been the colour of gloom that her velvet gowns were met with a mixture of awe and confusion. Feared for their powers of seduction. Once a colour connected with devils and doom, on Lucrezia, black became a symbol of wealth and desire.

'Damn the mistress.' Malachite flies through the door and settles on a tall bedpost, bobbing up and down, batting his great wings.

'Rascal bird,' says Bianca. 'Who knows where he learns it?'

She walks to the bed and strokes the bird, who purrs like a kitten. 'He taught himself that sound,' she says. 'Confuses our cat.' She scratches the bird under its throat and his eyes, half closed, flicker with pleasure.

'The room is inspired by my father's gift,' she says, opening her hand. The black glass vial, so like mine, in her palm. 'My way of saying sorry for being ungrateful.'

'Take the biscuit.' Malachite clacks his large beak against the glass in her hand.

She snaps her fingers closed around it. 'Rascal bird.' She nudges the bird away. 'You'll get a biscuit when you behave.'

The bird drops its head in a sulk.

She reopens her fingers. 'Who knew black could shine like a jewel?'

I take it from her palm and hold it up to the light that streams down from the roof. Perhaps now I will see it glimmer like mine. I twist it this way and that. But it doesn't, it is a truly pure black. In some ways more stunning.

'I want to know what's inside, but my husband says I'll ruin it. "Can't have your wine cask full and your wife drunk," he says. Go on, shake it!'

I put the object to my ear and shake it. I hear nothing.

'You must shake it hard,' she says, impatient with my caution.

I do so. A dull rattle.

'*Allora!* You must bring yours to my husband; he's sure to know everything about it.' Bianca claps her hands with excitement. 'He says if this one's not from Egypt or the Levant it is certainly from a glassmaker who learned the art there. Although the black is unusual. But he says we may never know what treasures lay buried, things that might cause us to question all that we know.'

I turn the vial over in my hands, hold it up once more to the cupola's light. And it all happens too fast.

Perhaps Bianca screeches first, or the bird swoops then she screeches, but before she or I can do anything to save it, Malachite snatches the vial and flies out the window.

'Drop it now, rascal bird!' she orders, leaning half out the window, her palm outstretched.

'Please be careful,' I say, gripping her skirts.

Malachite circles the rooftops while Bianca whistles and pleads, offering bribes, making threats.

'Marcello warned me I should clip his wings,' she says. 'But what is a bird if he can't use his wings? "Clip off your tongue," I said. "Let's see how you argue your deals and pleasure your mistress."' The bird wheels above us, flying higher and higher. 'Drop it now, rascal bird!' She is outraged at not getting her way, reaching out her hand, palm to the sky. '*Fai come dico!*' Do as I say!

And the rascal bird does indeed do as she says.

We both watch the vial fall. Plummeting like a sparrow felled by a slingshot. Out of the heavens and down to the street.

26

Beit HaKerem, 5 BCE

A heavy drop into the water above us. From under the surface, I blink and try to focus. Did a rock shear off and plummet? I listen for the soldiers, but hear only the rushing of bubbles. I expected the world beneath the surface to be clouded, dark, but it seems the sun has lost its way and shines upwards from the centre of the earth. I blink again and see that the light streams through an opening in the rock. I pull myself along the pool's rocky floor towards it, kicking my legs, flailing. As a woman of the hills, I've had little chance or desire to learn to swim. My lungs scream for breath. But I know this feeling, this pressure, from years spent inside the heat of the workshop, where the body begs for relief. So I do as Avner taught me and replace my distress with calm, with focus, so my body can endure.

I grope for the rim of the hole, its edges jagged like teeth. I pull Yoḥanan against me and try to angle us through. It's not big enough. Not for us both. My son's eyes are wide and frightened, but he does not struggle against me or my hard pinch on his nostrils.

Panic racks my body and my lungs squeeze harder. I try the gap again. We cannot pass through together. I meet his eyes with mine and hope they tell him to be brave, then I push him through with all the force I can muster. I follow. Push my head through and catch it on a jutting rock, a shot of pain flaring through my skull. I ignore it and push my shoulders, my hips through. Rock edges bite at me. I can see the wriggling body of my child, falling back down through the water, his small body in spasms. I flail behind him and push him upwards, thrashing my legs.

A moment, an age. We burst through the surface. His body is limp in my arms. The tips of my toes touch the rocks beneath me. I push through the water and my feet find a sandy embankment. But the water is still up to my chest and I can't quite find my balance.

My eyes scan the rock face but I can see no place to rest, so I take my child and pump his body against my own. Once, twice, scrambling on tip toes, keeping his head above water. I thrust his body into mine until my ribs ache.

'Come back to me. Come back.' My voice echoes and bounces around the rock. One thousand voices calling back.

A fountain of water spurts from his mouth, and he blinks and coughs and struggles for breath. I hold him above the surface, lean him over and shake him, then pump my hand against the back of his chest. The water drains from his mouth and nose and he spits and whimpers. I hold him close, kissing his head and telling him how good he has been. How well he has played our new game.

The rock walls surrounding me scrape the sky, narrowing at their far top, forming a rim, From below it seems I am inside a hollow mountain, its top sliced off to let in the sunlight.

'*Video aquam*.' The young soldier's voice from the other side. '*Sanguis in aqua est!*'

I cannot make sense of what he said. But I realise that while we are separated from him by a wall of rock, both his side and mine are open to the sky. The sound is echoing, travelling, finding its way between our parallel worlds.

Yoḥanan's eyes search mine and I push my finger to my lips, make my eyes fierce so he knows not to defy me.

'*Sanguis ubique in aqua!*' The soldier is excited by whatever it is he can see.

I work my mind over these words, willing comprehension. *Sanguis*. Blood. I touch my hand to the throbbing spot on my skull, my fingers covered in blood. I hoist Yoḥanan high with one arm and wade towards the wall of rock. There is a firmer embankment underfoot, but the water is now up to my chin. I circle the pool searching for an outcrop, a place to rest. My limbs tremble with exhaustion and I clutch my child tighter.

A splash from the other side. I imagine the young soldier's lean body swimming easily below the surface, finding his way through the underwater hole in the rock to this side. Another splash. But too light to be the weight of a body.

Above me the rock walls soar, almost touching, but leaving an opening, almost circular, where the sun streams through. It is so bright I squint against it. My eyes sting and run with tears. The stone around me seems to swell and shimmer, rock softening into a blur of rippling colour. I am out of air, out of energy. I blink and blink again against the glare of the light. Trying to discern somewhere to hide.

'*Altum est.*' The young soldier sounds baffled. The plunk of a rock into water. I know he is standing at the edge of the pool where I stood moments earlier. Another plunk. A larger rock into water. He is testing its depth.

I scan the rock walls again, circle after circle, my body twisting in the water. Unable, unwilling, to accept these stone walls for what I know they are. A cage. A trap. Thinking I will drown my child with my own hands before letting him die at the sword of Herod. Terrified at what I am thinking. At what this has come to.

'*Festina!*' The voice of the older soldier is impatient. '*Tolle gladium.*'

Gladium. This I know. Sword.

I push through the water, following the rock wall yet again, running my fingertips across the stone, searching for a place to grip, to rest. But the walls rise from the water with no place to hide. My arms burn with the growing weight of my child. A sack of flour. A slab of stone. We could slide under the water and be done.

A flash of light. A quartz seam in the rock wall catching the light. An explosive upsurge of water. The sound of a body plunging in. The young soldier has dived in. He will see the light from below. He will find his way here.

I make for the sparkling seam in the rock face, gulping mouthfuls when the floor drops away. A slight shift in the sun's angle strikes a bright jagged line through the stone. It runs up the length of the rock face but, as I reach it, I can see it is darker on one side. I grasp at the darkness and my hand hits a ledge.

I pull myself close and see a narrow opening, an opening not visible from the centre of the pool where we emerged. I push Yoḥanan inside and hoist myself onto the narrow ledge at its opening. I hear the outward breath of the soldier as he bursts through the surface, gasps and splutters, and I slide myself inside the rock, scratching the skin of my arms, my legs, as I squeeze through.

My foot is caught. I hear the soldier panting, sucking in air. I change the angle of my foot, set it loose and drag myself into a small cavern, damp rock walls on all sides. I scramble with Yoḥanan, push myself as far from the narrow opening as I can, the cavern floor gritty and cold. There is only enough room to sit, so I coil myself around my son, my hand on his mouth.

A sharp clang. Silence. Then another. His sword striking the rock. I hear him breathing hard, treading water with his sword weighing him down. But Roman soldiers are trained to swim in their armour, helmet on head, gladius in hand. To march in their armour, league after league, without rest.

'*Ubi es, cunne?*' he screams.

Cunne. The profanity spoken towards a woman, never far from any Roman's lips. I pull my child closer, try to cover his ears. As if hearing these insults is the worst thing that could happen.

The young soldier strikes his sword against rock. I hear him making his way around the wall. Closer and closer, an echoing clang as he swims with his sword and hits the wall as he goes. I hear him splash by us. The flail of his arms slapping water. He is panting and I pray exhaustion takes him. Sends him with his sword to the bottom of this pool. In my arms, my child's body pulses like a trapped bird.

'*Propera, asine!*' The elder's from the other side of the rock pool yells its abuse.

'*Verpe*,' the boy says under his breath, comparing his superior's head to his groin. All these insults I knew.

'*Cinaede*,' roars the older soldier.

I hear the younger swimming back our way. He pauses to rest. I can hear the rasp of his breath.

'*Evaserunt*,' he calls back.

'*Evaserunt? Quomodo?*' The elder soldier's rage explodes in a litany of fast words that I cannot make out. The boy is calling back, not matching the tirade. Perhaps objecting. Perhaps begging. It is a discord of bawling.

More clattering stones. The elder's harangue is growing harder to hear, perhaps swallowed by the gorge as he makes his way out. There is a splashing of water as the boy swims, not out of the cave but to somewhere near by. The scrape of rock scrambling, dislodged rocks lobbing into the pool below. Puffing, exertion. He is scaling the wall. Climbing out on some footholds he must believe we have followed. I hear him slipping but still climbing. The sound of the older soldier's voice now from above. The two of them shouting like rivals, not comrades.

I do not dare move, but gently, not completely, I loosen the hand I have held on my son's mouth.

'Clever boy,' I whisper, and kiss his warm head, his hair soft on my lips. I sit and I rock him, my tears silent as sunlight. And when I hear his sleep sounds, his short, measured breaths, I let my eyes close. Darkness in the cave now, but behind my closed eyes, so much light. The light of the quartz seam as it glimmered in the rock face. I surrender to sleep. Leave the world of what is seen. For now, my fervent prayer, not to be seen. Not to see.

I don't see the swallow flit back and forth, building her nest with pellets fashioned from mud. I don't see the water spider emerge in a bubble and scurry into her dew-speckled web. I don't see the fight break out above us. The older soldier cursing the younger for a wild chase on the strength of a torn veil. The violent shove from the elder to the young soldier's chest, sending him tumbling, his elbows scuffed on the rocks. I don't see the bullied young soldier charge for his elder, swiping his sword across the man's weathered cheek. A deep slash, bone exposed. I don't see the fury of the man transform into hatred. A single, deft strike. A blade through the young soldier's juvenile chest. His body left in the dust they rode in on.

I don't see the incensed soldier in the village, nose bent sideways from battle, tear the first child from the arms of his mother. I don't see the flex in his muscle as he sets his mark in the soft sternum of the baby boy and bears down his blade.

And I don't see my husband look up at the mountain to which he knows I have fled. Calling out to Ribon Alma to watch over us both. His body spread across Yiska's and her one-week-old boy, the blotched marks of childbirth still on his scalp. The soldier's mouth open and screaming for my husband to stand down. To depose himself of his futile protection and let King Herod's work be done. Roman spittle pasting my husband's face, his cheeks and forehead. The soldier's final impatience, tearing my husband from Yiska's cowering frame and piercing man and child in two swift stabs. Snatching Yiska's scarf from her head to wipe the spatter of blood from his face. Pitching it into the dirt at her feet.

I see none of this. Only a light behind my closed lids. A beckoning dancing light, forged into stone. Bright as a lightning streak that shreds the night sky.

I awaken with a start. Silence. Soft dripping of water. Yoḥanan in my arms, breathing against me. Droplets of mist on my face, my skin. My child stirs, his small hands reaching for my breast. I bring him in to feed. His fingers then find my lips and I whistle the call of the hoopoe, as is our game, so he relaxes and feeds long. Tiny diamonds of water sparkle from the points of his lashes.

The swallow darts past us to her nest high up the rock wall. My eyes have adjusted and I can see her fine work. Tiny mud pebbles, layer upon layer, to cradle her eggs.

'Bird,' says Yoḥanan, pulling his lips from my breast.

He has mastered his new word and I pull him towards me and kiss his face.

'Bird,' he says, his chubby finger pointing. And I kiss him again. Bird. Kiss. Back and forth it goes until we both are laughing.

He pushes himself to standing against the cavern wall. I manoeuvre myself in the cramped space into a half-seated, half-crouched position, leaning over to peek out from the crevice into which we have crawled. The water is still. I cannot tell what time it is. I fret to think we must leave the way we came in, wondering if the soldiers will be out there, taking pot shots at ground birds with sharp stones, playing out the boredom of waiting to kill. But Herod's soldiers are as notorious for their poor concentration as for their menace. More likely to have rushed to the village and carried out their orders, wanting to return quickly to gather their payment, to return to their drinking.

'Shall we play in the water again?' I ask Yoḥanan, who is reaching, straining towards the bird in her nest. Propping himself up to the wall, he shuffle-walks towards me and falls into my arms.

I squeeze myself out first, then reach for him. We wade through the pool to the underwater hole in the rock. Pinching his nostrils, I dive under the water. Him first, then me. I break the surface and press my finger to his lips. Listening for them, the soldiers. Only the chittering of birds. We follow the gorge the way we came in, the stones clawing at my tender feet. As the gorge opens up, a rush of desert air greets me, already drying our wet bodies. I descend unsteadily, clambering across rubble. And then I am back in the place where my wild sage grows, hidden. My sandals set neatly where I have left them.

Below me, Beit HaKerem. The Spring of the Vineyard. I lick at my lips and realise I am thirsty. All that time in the pool but not a thought to drink. The hot wind gusts, and if there is sound below, I cannot hear it.

I pick my way back down through the terraces, glancing down at our village. The silver-green of olive leaves and the twist of bare vineyards. Around this, the rolling land as I have always known it. All of it familiar, but yet all of it strange. The feeling unsettles me and Yoḥanan whimpers. His fingers clutch tight to my tunic.

I see my veil flapping ahead of me, caught on the sharp hooked thorns of a caperbush. I hurry to pull it free; there's only half of it, ragged threads hanging. I lean over the terrace wall in search of the other half. Instead I see the body of the boy soldier. So much younger than I imagined. His reedy limbs look out of place, in his armour. Forgive me, I beg Him. For walking on. For leaving the body behind me. For not looking back.

A lone figure is making its way up towards us. I squint to see who it is. He looks up and I can see it is Ya'akov the Younger, Sara and Ya'akov the Elder's first child. I quicken my pace and stumble, and Yoḥanan grizzles louder in my hold. Ya'akov's pace quickens too and we meet, his small frame heaving under shuddering sobs. He scrubs his hands across his face, wiping tears, more tears falling.

I shift Yoḥanan to one arm and draw Ya'akov close with the other.

'They tore Avdi'el from her arms and stuck him through,' says Ya'akov the Younger.

Sickness lurches at my centre. Yoḥanan's fingers grip the skin at the base of my neck.

'Who else?' I ask. I am curt because I know that to make him get to the point will relieve him of the great responsibility of delivering this news.

'All boys under twenty-four moons.'

Yoḥanan is now crying, clawing at my skin, and I grasp his fingers, too tight.

'Your mother?' I ask, dreading the answer.

'She sent me to find you,' he replies. 'To tell you about Zakhariya.' He tries to be the man his father urged him to be and tell me straight about this man he, like so many, loves like a father. 'Bohan took it from the street. Zakhariya's body.'

I can hear what he tells me, but I can't take it in.

'Ab-ba!' squeals Yoḥanan, hearing the familiarity of his father's name, pointing his finger towards the village. I let my gaze follow my child's finger, although I know I will not see him. I will not see my husband rushing to greet me.

'And Thalia?' I ask.

'With her father,' replies Ya'akov.

'Ab-ba?' Yoḥanan says again, looking for my confirmation that this is who we are headed back to see. Heading back to our village. To our home. To our family.

Ya'akov is sobbing again and I draw him back under my arm. 'Say no more,' I tell him. For his sake and my own.

'Bird,' says Yoḥanan through his tears, his face pressed into my shoulder. As if the new magic word has old magic that might make everything different. Better.

'They are gathering the bodies,' says Ya'akov.

'With bodies we can have burials and with burials we can see our people to Alma d'Ateh,' I say.

'What if the soldiers return?' he says, shivering with new terror.

I have no good answer to offer.

I let him lead me back down to the village, my hand cradling my son's head to my chest. In my tired arms, the weight of his body is like a great stone from the Temple.

As we draw close, I see four men crowded around a woman collapsed to her knees. The woman is screaming, refusing their help. Pulled close to her chest is a small, bloodied bundle. When she stands and runs from the men, I see it is Yiska.

27

Florence, 1517

What mother endured the loss that led to the words inscribed on this linen? The slender strip of cloth has a coarse texture between the pads of my fingers. It is a plain, muted weave and flecked with incongruities at which a Florentine tailor might scoff. More like the linen worked by the nuns, seen as inferior to the wool and silk controlled by the guilds. As my baby feeds at my breast, I pull him in closer. This cloth that fell, rolled and sealed, from Bianca's smashed vial, reveals words as clear as the day they were written. But since the birth of my son they've provoked more haunting questions.

עבדיאל בר יעקב קשישא ושרה

I speak the words softly, as Messer Abrama Uzziel da Camerino instructed when he came to translate them. A *khk* sound from the back of my palate, unlike the roll of Tuscani.

Avdi'el bar Ya'akov K'shisha w'Sara.

A physician first and foremost, and in matters of health Marcello's trusted advisor, Messer Abrama has had the benefit of one of Pope Leo's more noble encouragements: education. Leo's desire for the exotic ensures that those who wish to learn things foreign in our world – foreign arts, foreign histories, foreign languages – have access to those who can teach them. If, of course, they have the money to pay for the privilege. Messer Abrama became a scholar of language.

Abdiel, son of Jacob the Elder and Sarah.

'It is a funerary dedication, I am certain,' he said, casting his eye back and forth across the cloth, his lips moving, an indistinct murmur. 'This snapped branch signifies the death of a baby, a boy, his parents in mourning.'

'My wife thought it a curse,' said Marcello, a hoarse chuckle.

'If only she could hear how beautiful it sounds,' I said. 'Too beautiful for a lament.'

'Some scholars say Old Aramaic was the language of Christ,' said Messer Abrama.

'Not Hebrew?' I asked.

'Aramaic was the common tongue at the time. For most of the Holy Land, at least. Thanks to the Assyrian Empire.'

'Please repeat what it says, but slower,' I requested.

עבדיאל בר יעקב קשישא ושרה

The language of Christ. That alone should thrill me. But what caught my breath was the fact that, if Christ spoke such words, then surely so too did his cousin San Giovanni. And if our Patron Saint spoke this ancient language, then so too did his mother, Florence's beloved Santa Elisabetta. My Elisheva.

'What is Aramaic for Giovanni?' I asked Messer Abrama.

'Yoḥanan,' he replied. 'Keep in mind, as in our own country, even languages from neighbouring states have their own nuance. Some similar. But not exactly the same.'

Aramaic names. Abdiel. Jacob. Sarah. Elisheva. Maryam. Yoḥanan.

Lucio fusses and I shift him to my other breast. His small hands grip my feeding gown; they are strong for their size, even at six moons. He pulls back from my breast and watches me with pale umber eyes. A golden-earth colour, autumn vine leaves kissed by sunset. Or like the yellow citrine I have seen among Marcello's quarry of raw ingredients, bright among the lapis and malachite and cinnabar, chunks and lumps of rock and quartz crystal, brought in to sell to the apothecaries who make artists' paint. My son looks up at me and I feel like a treasure. A glinting crystal spied in the earth.

'What is this word?' I'd asked Messer Abrama, pushing a finger underneath three letters.

בר

Bar. A soft edge to the sound as he spoke it. Like an exhale.

'Here, it means "son of". But it can mean, simply, "son",' he said.

Bar. I repeat the word that speaks of another woman's son.

'The cloth is likely from flax. A staple of the Levant,' Messer Abrama said. 'Like wool, it was woven by women.'

It was then that the linen on which the words are written had burst to life between my fingers and thumb. Not dull and plain and crude like Bianca had claimed, fearing it a curse, but a texture of industry and creativity. Something made by hands that belonged to female bodies. Warm bodies of women whose mouths might have chattered like the seamstresses in the workshops along della Condotta. Who gossiped and laughed and stitched and listened. Who shared complaints about husbands and proud stories of children.

I set my son in his crib, in the warm kitchen. Eugenio will arrive before dawn to watch over him, calling me up from the osteria downstairs when it's again time for his feed. This cherished sliver of time alone with my son, between cleaning up after patrons and rising to prepare food all over again, is the day's gift.

My cracked, calloused fingers sting as I scrub pots, grind and peel, pound and press, doing the work of staff I cannot afford to pay. But as I work, I keep my thoughts on my son so the work is a prayer. For his health, for his success. For all he can be that I never will.

Moons and feast days and festivals arrive, pass and arrive again all too soon. I become curt with the patrons who dine at the osteria. Disgusted by their insatiable appetite and thirst, no longer interested in their trite debates and discussions. My sleep is short, interrupted. My patience worn thin by Lucio's teething and Eugenio's slow-footed pace. Unwilling to feel any tenderness lest it rob me of the rage I feel is my right. I don't see that I am becoming my mother.

*

Plates stacked on each arm, I ferry them into the kitchen. The young girl, Bernadetta, washes dishes like she has a whole week to finish one bowl.

'Too slow! Hurry up! If you want to be paid.'

A table of drunken men shout for their ham hocks. From upstairs I can hear Lucio screaming. I dish out thick rabbit stew with torn loaf and serve it to patrons, and when I return with the ham hocks, one of the men has pulled down his stockings. He pisses onto the flagstones.

'Enough! Get out!' I whip him with the dishcloth until he staggers out the door. I pitch a hock after him. He's too drunk to notice it glance off his head.

Back inside, the men have calmed down. I run up the stairs to check on my son.

Cradled in Eugenio's arms, Lucio is quiet, smiling like one of God's cherubs.

'How did you calm him?' I ask, flopping onto the chaise.

Eugenio reaches down and prises something from Lucio's grip. My son screams, his face red and enraged until Eugenio returns it. I rise from the chaise, intrigued by the charm that can stop my son howling.

Then I see what he has.

'You can't give him that!' I snatch Mariotto's glass vial from the hands of my son. He screams at being deprived of his treasure.

The men downstairs begin chanting for sugared donuts. *Portare le ciambelle! Portare le ciambelle!* Other hungry patrons awaiting more stew. Lucio's face turning red, turning purple, I hand him the glass. He stops crying. Hiccoughs. Hands sticky with tears and snot grip the vial.

'You're to blame if he breaks it,' I say, a finger pointed at Eugenio.

'But he is quiet now, *sì*?' he says, a shrug of surrender.

I cannot argue. And downstairs drunk, hungry men are shouting for donuts.

*

It's almost midnight, another day finished. In Mariotto's study, wind hassles the shutters. I sit in the old armchair, one hand resting on my sleeping son's head; with the other I gently remove the glass vial from his hand.

I hold it up, twist it back and forth so it catches the candlelight. Tap it with my nail, shake it close to my ear. I follow the barely visible join near one end, its been cleverly hidden. Did my vial, like Bianca's, hold the grief of a father, a mother, with the memory of their son?

Avdi'el bar Ya'akov K'shisha w'Sara.

Abdiel. Son of Jacob the Elder and Sarah.

A handful of words from which to conjure real lives. To unravel the riddle, this story of Abdiel. The son who died before both of his parents.

My vial is larger than Bianca's, perhaps only by half a *quattrino*. And hers did not have these flecks of white that wink from the black. I lift it to my ear again and shake it. Not really a sound. Maybe a shift in the weight of something inside. So slight it could be my imagination. I tap the vial lightly on the edge of the desk. I've asked Marcello to enquire with the glass artisans in Venice, to find out if my vial can be somehow broken open but fused back together.

'You can't whistle and drink,' Nonna would have said of my desire to both keep the vial but also know what's inside.

This piece once held in the hands of my husband's mother, that may have been held in the hands of a mother long before hers, now warm in my own hand. Catching light, catching shadow. Under each light it is different.

Like a struck flint, a new thought sparks. I sit up with a start, causing my Lucio to stir. I calm myself down, then bundle him and nudge Eugenio awake, tucking my son in beside him in Mariotto's old room. 'I must visit Marcello.'

'The glass?' he asks, holding out a shaking hand, knowing that it will be needed if Lucio wakes and I haven't returned.

'I'll be back before he wakes.'

Eugenio groans, drops his hand.

'*Te lo prometto.*' I kiss them both. I promise.

Marcello is still in his doublet and hose when he answers the door. He is wine-mellowed and at ease with my late call.

'Who can I ask about how this was made?' I say, opening my palm to reveal the black glass.

He takes it from me with strong, careful hands that have held all manner of treasures.

'Good luck asking the Venetians,' he says, holding the vial by each end between his finger and thumb, drawing his lens from his pocket. 'Their secrets are as guarded as the Vatican treasury. At least as it was under Julius.'

'Surely you know a trader, a merchant, somebody who can help me?' I say.

He drops his lens back into his doublet pocket. 'There's a trader, in the Mugello. The glass furnace set up by the duke,' he says. 'The bastard bought off the best artisans from Murano.' He laughs at the bold fact.

'Will you set up a meeting?' I ask, wanting him to keep to the subject so I can get back to my son.

'You might get a meeting but you won't get a recipe for black glass,' he says. 'Those recipes are ancient as the Phoenicians and quite nearly as silent.'

'I don't want a recipe for black, I want to know what it is that flickers like stars.'

'I'll send word that you're coming,' says Marcello. 'If they're willing to reveal any knowledge of ingredients, don't be swindled by an offer from them to supply any. My raw ingredients are the best. I'll get whatever you need.'

Lucio wakes while I'm worrying over what dress will ensure that I appear respectable, confident. He begins whimpering, then crying. I offer him Padre Renzo's gift of the bells tied with silk.

He bats them away. I try a small carved galleon, from Marcello, and he screeches in frustration. I relent and give him the glass, throw on a cloak in cut velvet and pull him onto my hip. We will travel together.

The Mugello trader sucks through his brown teeth when I walk in with my baby.

'Is that it?' He jerks his head towards the glass bulging from my son's tiny fist.

'It's from my late husband. My son adores it,' I say.

'I must see it,' he says, pulling a lens from a chain around his neck.

I wrap my hand around Lucio's.

'The signore wants to see this,' I say, and his bottom lip quivers. 'Will you hold out your hand, so he can take a quick look?'

His pale umber eyes search mine. I smile to reassure him. He lets me hold out his hand.

The trader leans close with his lens. I watch Lucio watching him, an expression of unmitigated offence on my son's face.

'I can help you,' he says, dropping his lens back inside his shirts.

I want to cry with relief. Want to whoop with joy to the heavens.

'The price is fifty florins,' he says. 'And possession of the black glass itself.'

The old armchair creaks as I sit. My son on my lap. The glass vial in his hand. I take the scrap of cloth with ancient words from its place on my side table, rub the pads of my fingers across it. Quiet tears falling. But not for the trader who demanded more than I could ever pay in three lifetimes. For the fact that I hold my child in my arms. This precious blessing, this warm life in my keeping.

The flax cloth woven by ancient women bears down its grave weight on my palm. Cloth that might have dressed Jacob the Elder and Sarah. That might have swaddled their child, Abdiel. Before he was taken.

28

Beit HaKerem, 5 BCE

From the village comes the keening, the wailing of women. As I draw closer, Yiska falls to her knees, her face filthy with blood and dust. Her tunic is torn from her chest and her breasts hang loose. Three men crouch beside her, consoling her, urging her to hand over the child in her arms. She sees me and stops her wailing. Rising to her feet, she runs towards me. I shift Yoḥanan into one arm and hold the other out to her, expecting an embrace. But she stops short and spits at my feet, grabs a fistful of dust from the ground and pitches it at me. Yoḥanan starts crying.

Yirmiyahu, Yiska's husband, grasps her shoulders with both hands. 'It's Elisheva,' he says, and shakes her as if to bring her to her senses.

'I know who she is!' Yiska says. 'She who is favoured.'

'Her husband is dead,' says Yirmiyahu. 'She suffers too.'

'She knew! She knew to run and save her child. She suffers nothing like us.'

Yiska's face is swollen by rage. She collapses again and the men surround her, lift the child from her arms and wrap it with swaddling. She claws the air for her baby, wailing. A sound not wholly human. The sound of a wound being torn in a mother's soul.

'We will take them all to the Cave of the Families,' says Yirmiyahu to me. 'Before nightfall.'

To lie unburied is dreaded.

Yiska tears at her hair and her mantle, her thin body straining, sinews tight and twitching as if she might snap. I kneel down, reach for her.

'Get away from me. Get away!' Fistfuls of dust in my face, Yoḥanan screaming.

Yirmiyahu lifts his wife from the earth and she buries her face in his chest, sobbing and clawing at her own skin, mewling and then growling, reaching towards the bundled child now in the hands of their nephew.

In a daze I follow Ya'akov the Younger to the home of his parents, Sara and Ya'akov the Elder's. I stop short of their threshold, wondering if all the women of the village will feel as Yiska does. My Yoḥanan, my little boy, alive with me, at my breast. For some a miracle, for others a further injury to their loss.

In their home Sara embraces me and touches her hands to my face, my arms, as if to be sure I am truly here. But there's something that doesn't seem like the Sara I know, a flatness in her expression that disturbs me. The girls, Sussana and Tsipora, stand silent in the corner of the room, Ya'akov the Younger now beside them.

'Ya'akov, come! Hurry!' she calls her husband. 'Yoḥanan is here. It is Elisheva and Yoḥanan. What a blessing!' She takes the child from my arms and showers him with kisses.

'A miraculous blessing,' says Ya'akov the Elder. Sara hands him my son and my body lurches for him, my child. But Sara is upon me, taking me again in her arms, kissing my forehead, my cheeks. I can feel her body trembling against mine.

'Little son of Beit HaKerem.' Ya'akov the Elder holds my son up to *sh'maya*, the heavens, and I feel the urge to seize him back. To return him to the empty, aching space against my breast. Yoḥanan's feet dangle in the air and he frowns down at Ya'akov, a spit-bubble poised on his lower lip.

'Dat?' says Yoḥanan, pointing to the floor. To the white bundle I had not yet noticed. 'Dat one?' he asks again, but I cannot reply.

Wrapped inside it will be Avdi'el.

Avdi'el. Eight months old. Sara's fourth and last child. I don't know where to look. In every set of eyes there is bewilderment, incomprehension. A bundle on the floor that should not be so still.

'Dat?' says Yoḥanan, insistent now.

Sara's legs begin to buckle and Ya'akov the Elder is beside her.

'A stool,' he commands his son. 'Sit, *ḥavivta*, sit.'

'She's not wept, she's in shock,' Ya'akov tells me, handing my son to his eldest girl, Tsipora, and again I want to snatch him back to myself. Perhaps this is how it will be now. My child as everyone's child to love or loathe, never again entirely my own. Scorned or cherished because he has survived the sword of King Herod.

Ya'akov the Elder clears his throat. I know he will tell me of my husband. 'Watch over your mother,' he says to his son. Then to me, 'His body has been taken home.'

I want to refuse what he has said. *His body.* My mind reels around everything I have been taught about life and our inevitable death. But all learnings seem to have left me. How I struggle with the words that now replace my *b'el*, my husband. My living, breathing Zakhariya. *His body.*

'Was it swift?' I ask. And wonder why it matters. Why we ask such things. As if the pace of death can somehow outwit the fact of it.

'The first blow,' he replies.

'Go on,' I say. Knowing that I could prepare a lifetime for this moment and never be ready.

'Take Yoḥanan to the courtyard,' says Ya'akov the Elder to his daughters.

Keep him where I can see him. I want to scream my objection. But I also know that Ya'akov the Elder will speak frankly. Yoḥanan, growing restless, will distract my attention.

Then he leads me to the far corner of the room and begins.

'The soldiers grew more frenzied with each splash of blood. Even after the tenth infant was slain, Zakhariya implored them.

But they were here on Herod's orders. They would not leave until each boy was dead. Yiska's husband told her to stay hidden. But in the confusion, she tried to run for the terraces. She'd seen you head that way and you hadn't returned. Zakhariya saw her first, but the soldiers a close second. He defended her with his body and the soldier was incensed. "Stand down or be struck!" he demanded over and over. "Stand down, stand down!" But Zakhariya remained as protector, his eyes not on the soldier but appealing to *sh'maya*, the heavens, calling on Ribon Alma for intervention. I swear I saw *sitra ahara* in the soldier's face. The turning to evil. Deaf to the screams of the children and women. He cleaved Zakhariya through the navel, but still he would not stand down, using his last breaths to defend.'

'Enough,' I say.

I would have torn at my mantle if my hands had the strength. The room shifts around me. The tiny bundle blurs through my tears.

'How many women?' I ask.

'No women.'

'And the daughters?'

'All spared but one, Agathe.'

Talitha, only new to her bleeding. Betrothed and exultant.

'She was running for her young brother, and a horse reared and charged.'

'How far did Herod send his horsemen?' I ask.

'When they first arrived, the guard commander demanded that any relations of Maryam, the mother of Yeshu, must come forward. If they did, no other child would be harmed,' says Ya'akov the Younger.

'Yeshu of Natsrat?' I ask, a new anguish passing through me.

I know whose son they sought. It was three moons ago we received news of Yeshu's birth. Of his young mother, my cousin Maryam, recovering slowly.

'For now we must focus on burying our children,' says Ya'akov the Elder. 'See them safely to Alma d'Atei, the world to come. The men are already adding a chamber to the Cave of the Families.'

'How many?' I ask.

'Fourteen children and Zakhariya,' replies Ya'akov the Elder.

My mind struggles to make sense of the number of bodies. So small in our arms, but not enough room in the Cave.

Sickness swells from my core, the room spins and sways.

'Give me Yoḥanan,' I say. The urge to leave this house of my beloved friends, and never return. 'Give me my son.' I can't keep the edge from my voice; I want my child in my arms.

I take him from the girls and, as Ya'akov the Younger sees me home, I push away the gore of the images that reel in my mind, instead worrying about how our village will manage its grieving. It is usual for friends and families to aid those who are in mourning. To bring food and help with chores during *shiv'a*, the seven days of mourning after the burial. But who among us is not mourning? Who among us will bring the meals of consolation?

Bohan waits in the courtyard. Even from here, I can see he has been weeping. Thalia is beside him, clutching his hand. I set a sleeping Yoḥanan on the mat under shade in the courtyard. Without a word, Thalia takes watch.

Bohan walks with me up the stairs, to the room I shared with my beloved. Stations himself by the door. I pause on the threshold. The body is covered, a shape under a shroud that does not seem like my husband. This familiar place where I lay with him over four decades of marriage; now the place where I will begin my time as *avila*, a mourner.

As a woman, I will not be the one to clean his body. I will not shroud his skin. But I will be the one who, night after night and moon after moon, half-wakes and reaches for my Zakhariya beside me, scraping the emptiness his warm body once filled.

We gather at the spring before the sun sinks behind the hills, then walk in procession to the Cave of the Families. All is still. Not even the chittering of the birds or the keening of jackals. All is quiet and still. As if all of life pays its respect to this moment.

The bodies will be placed inside the cave in the niches carved by the men. A year from now, when the flesh has returned to the earth, the bones will be collected and placed inside stone ossuaries carved by each family.

The procession is led by the women, our wailing a deep ululation blended with higher-pitched moaning, the tearing of clothes to show the rupture of our normal lives with the advent of death. But it isn't only grief playing out through our voices; anger too is being pushed from our bellies through our throats. All that needs to be screamed or questioned can be channelled into our hypnotic grief-songs. I throw back my head and keen to the skies.

The four of us arrive home. Me, my son, Bohan and Thalia. She takes the sleeping Yoḥanan from me so I can rest. But the walk across our courtyard catches me unprepared. Near his favourite stool, where it caught sunlight in winter, my husband's footprints are still in the dust. I fall to my knees, press my palms to the earth inside the marks made by his living feet. My mouth gaping in anguish but making no sound, silently wailing an unspeakable grief so I do not wake my son.

In the weeks after *shav'a*, I find little rest or sleep. A constant ache in my stomach means I can hold nothing down. I keep to myself, worried how I might be treated. Will others condemn me as has Yiska? I have spent so many years ostracised as a childless woman, then for being deemed too old to carry. Will I now be condemned for the one child I gave birth to?

In my workshop I have been trying to channel my grief by creating a gift for Ya'akov the Elder and Sara. A gleaming black vessel, like Tsad's, beautifully polished and shaped, and hollow inside to carry a dedication for their baby boy.

Avdi'el bar Ya'akov K'shisha w'Sara.

Avdi'el, son of Ya'akov the Elder and Sara.

I make my way slowly up to my workshop; try to relish the flawless blue sky, the deep valleys, the familiar hills and mountains. But everywhere I look, holds the memory of my husband. The new black piece is not where I left it. I'm too tired to be angry, but I feel I know what has happened. I will deal with it once I am rested.

Later that evening, Thalia and I lie on the roof. She is restive and uneasy, and, for Thalia, too quiet. I wait calmly, knowing she is finding her courage for a confession.

'I must tell you something,' she says.

I hold my silence while she stalls. I already know what her admission will be. She makes it quicker than I expect.

'Matrona-Imma, I stole your black glass. The one meant for Ya'akov the Elder and Sara.'

'When are you planning on returning it?' I ask, thinking that she will pull it from her pouch and we'll be done with the issue.

'I wanted cloth to sew a new tunic for my father, his has so many patches,' she gushes. 'A trader at the market said the Egyptians think black will protect them from chaos. He paid me enough for a mantle as well.'

I pause, let her suffer a little longer. Bohan had worn his new garments so proudly.

'You'll tell your father how you made the purchase,' I say finally. Her punishment, one that would break her heart to see Bohan's disappointment. I will speak with him first.

'I also bought figs,' she admits. 'I meant to share some with Yoḥanan.'

It was an effort not to smile at this more innocent admission. If she'd bought figs from Aḥiya, they were small and succulent, sweeter than honey. I understood the temptation to devour them all.

'Are we done?' I ask, although I sense there is more.

'Can I ask you a question?' she says.

'One,' I reply. 'And then we must rest.'

'Are you lonely, Matrona-Imma?' she asks.

I draw her in close. 'I have you. I have Yoḥanan. I have all that I need.'

Above us the fingernail moon has long set and the dark sky is brushed with stars.

'Your black glass is like a night sky,' Thalia says, her voice soft and sleepy. 'My mother told me the stars are a map. A map for the souls who travel back home.' She rolls over into the crook of my arm. 'I'll never let you be lonely, Matrona-Imma.'

I stroke her head as she sleeps.

The next morning, I awake on Bayla's old sleeping mat. I remain quiet, praying that Yoḥanan stays sleeping. I hear Ya'akov outside and will that he leaves. I've been avoiding the weekly meal shared with him and his family. My world for so long was my husband, and some days it's too hard to be among other families.

Ya'akov the Younger calls softly, so I know he is waiting. Yoḥanan stirs, rolls towards me. I keep my eyes closed and Yoḥanan presses his fingers to my lips. Wanting me to whistle. But I have no will to purse my lips and whistle the flute notes of the hoopoe.

'Not yet,' I say to both my son and Ya'akov.

'My parents are now insisting,' says Ya'akov.

'Dat one?' asks Yoḥanan, sitting up and pointing his finger towards the door. 'Imma, dat one?'

'Ya'akov,' answers Ya'akov from outside the door.

'Ya'akov, come,' says Yoḥanan.

'I'll wait until nightfall if I must,' says Ya'akov.

I know that he will.

I rise, wash and dress. My routine joyless but familiar.

When I open the door, Yoḥanan squeals with delight to see Ya'akov.

On the road into the village centre, a man walks towards us. When he sees us he seems startled and halts for a moment, blinking hard against the morning sun at our backs. As he continues uphill, I can see his face better. His strong features familiar. It is Binyamin. One of the men who came to visit with my brother.

'*Sh'lama*,' he says to me and Ya'akov.

'Dat?' asks Yoḥanan.

'Binyamin,' I reply. 'He's a friend of your uncle, Tsad.'

'Tsad come?' says Yoḥanan, and Yehudah's wide hand is on my son's head.

That's when I see it. The gravity in his expression. And a terror rips through me because I already know the news he has come to deliver. I begin to shake my head. I won't hear it. I can't. Ya'akov hears it for me and pulls me into his arms.

'*Ta'heh,*' says Binyamin. But I don't care to hear his apology.

When he offers me the wrapped package he withdraws from his knapsack, I want to throw it down into the valley. I want to tell him to take it with him and return instead with my brother. Ya'akov extends his hand to accept it, and I scream and beg him not to take it. This terrifying package wrapped in a tattered pouch. Inside it, the black glass that I made for my brother. That he pledged to carry with him, safe and unbroken until the end. The end has now come. It is no longer whole.

The year passes. The seasons blur, seamless. I am numb to whether the air brings heat or a chill. I keep myself busy, but do not visit my workshop. When Ya'akov the Younger calls for me, his voice is now that of a young man. His scrappy whiskers become a beard and his arms and legs thicken into those of his father. I look forward to the hour each day when he stops by to check on me and Yoḥanan. To offer gossip or, after harvest, some newly pressed oil. We find strength in the routines of our village life. The seasons and rituals that bind one moon to the next. Each of us moving further from grief and closer to this day, when the bones of our loved ones can be collected from the Cave of the Families and placed into the stone boxes carved through the seasons. They have become *our* children now. Each of us a parent, in some way, to those who perished.

I meet Ya'akov at the gate to our courtyard, to walk to his parents' home for our weekly meal together. When we reach the spring, we hear the men yelling.

Yassin, Elḥanan's son, stands rigid like a confused child. He's been sent to the Cave of the Families to roll back the heavy stone in preparation for our ritual of collecting the bones and setting them with reverence into carved ossuaries.

'The stone was already shifted,' he says, breathless. 'Everything is gone. Every last bone.' Some of us gasp, some mutter distraught prayers. Women are wailing. All of us shocked by the vile desecration.

'The Romans took our children, what more can they want after death?' says Yiska, her face sagging with despair. 'Our bodies still hunted.'

'I will fix this,' I say, and when Yiska's face flickers hope, I am determined to make sure I do. 'I know where the memories of our children will be safe.'

Since the day of the soldiers and the loss of her newborn, Yiska has turned from me in the streets. 'May I walk with you?' she asks.

I move away from the crowd and she follows.

When we are some distance from those gathered, Yiska reaches for my arm. 'I never said sorry,' she says, her shoulders wilting.

'You can't say sorry for what you haven't done,' I say.

'I let Herod's madness afflict me,' she says, her face crumpled with the self-recrimination I know all too well. The madness of Herod leaves no one untouched.

I have missed Yiska's company, her once easy laughter. The grief I buried seems to grip every muscle.

'I wished you and your child dead, Elisheva,' she says.

'What woman wouldn't wish another's death in the place of their own child's?' I say.

'You,' says Yiska. 'You would never wish that.'

I am unprepared for her words. Unprepared for what they stir up inside me, the shuddering of my body against hers as we embrace. The sincerity of her regret opening my heart without reservation. Our faces are wet with tears, pressed cheek to cheek. Sharing that most precious and silent language of forgiveness between women.

At dawn, I take Ya'akov the Younger and Yassin up through the terraces along the slopes of the high mountain, then into the steadily narrowing gorge. Their eyes are wild and excited as we reach the first pool and I tell them to follow me. I dive under the surface and squeeze through the hole in the rock. We emerge, panting, in the hidden pool.

The boys gape at the world within rock walls, a hole to the sky. I point to the glittering seam of quartz through the rock.

As Ya'akov hoists himself from the water and into the cavern marked by the quartz, it appears as if the mountain has opened up and swallowed him into a whole other world. A world that from one angle is as sheer as any scarp, but from another is a doorway inside the earth.

'Fifteen ossuaries won't fit,' he calls from inside the cavern. 'The boxes will be too big.'

'We have no bones for ossuaries. I will make small glass vials, a dedication inside each one,' I reply, handing him the sharp bevel I have tucked inside my belt. 'Chip out the quartz,' I instruct him.

I'll need enough quartz to fill my pouch and achieve my new vision.

The next morning, I return to my workshop with zeal. It will take all I have left to complete the task. All the wood, all the *gifta*. All the raw glass to produce the black vessels, to shape each secret stopper to perfection to hide what's inside. With such a small batch of glass, there can be no mistakes. The first one, sold by Thalia, was shaped by hand; it took too long, and did not have the symmetry these special vessels deserve. I've been up all night making and testing a tapered wooden mould to help shape each vial quickly.

Find your peace with the flame, taught Avner. My body remembers and I find my breath, my pace, the steady rhythm of creation. The swell of the glass, each time a small miracle. Each gleaming piece a miniature memorium, a treasure in my palm. A doorway between worlds.

By afternoon Thalia has joined me to help stack wood and add fuel to the furnace. When we are done, I peer into the cooling alcove, impatient. The first new piece has been in there since midnight and will be cool enough for me to show her.

I press the piece into her palm. 'Go to the window. Hold it up to the light.'

She does as I say, twisting the black vial. It winks and glimmers like stars as it catches the light.

'How on earth did you do it?' Her delight is a thrilling reward for my work.

I'd ground down the quartz until my arms ached, making two sizes of grains, one of coarser flecks and one of fine powder. Then I sprinkled the flecks sparsely over the slab, rolling the first gather carefully across it. Then layered another gather to roll through the fine powder. This layering makes the piece trick the eye, giving the sense of sparkling worlds within worlds. A bottomless depth of celestial magnificence.

'If the stars are a map, then our children will travel fast to the Alma d'Atei,' I say.

Thalia turns the sparkling vial back and forth in the light.

'It's like holding an entire night sky of stars in my hand.'

Again I take up my pipe. Fourteen glass vials for fourteen children, and one for my husband. Our limestone ossuaries are often engraved with the name of the deceased and their family, so I will scribe a dedication for each soul onto linen that, folded and rolled, will fit tightly inside. Each vial will be sealed with a stopper and invisible join to ensure that what is inside is protected. Then the pieces will be taken to the hidden cave by the boys. Set into their carved niches beneath chittering swallows. Surrounded by the mountain that opened for me and my child, away from harm, away from Herod's soldiers and thieves. Safe passage for each child.

The one Thalia holds is the new vessel for Sara and Ya'akov the Elder's son, Avdi'el. The name that means Servant of God. His parents' prayer that he would one day serve at the Temple.

29
Florence, 1529

My prayer to Elisheva is always the same. Please help me keep my child safe. Once possible with disciplines of curfews and chores and consequences for misbehaviour. But Lucio is no longer the boy who would sleep with his head on my lap in San Michele alle Trombe. He is a thirteen-year-old young man wanting to protect his city and help keep our republic.

The double-dealing Pope Clement has formed an unholy alliance with the brute emperor, Charles. The same man who sacked Rome, leaving streets piled with slain bodies. Who burned palaces, plundered monasteries, tortured monks for relics and sold nuns off to soldiers, and who has now summoned Spanish troops to siege upon Florence.

'I won't leave without fighting,' says Lucio. He is calm, but determined.

Tall for his age, and as composed as a cardinal, Lucio sits in the carver chair spinning the black glass vial around in the palm of his hand. The glass he has carried and treasured since he was a child. That Bianca teased she would creep in and steal after she'd lost her own. That he has been told came from his father.

He, Michel and I sit in the loggia, the *pock pock* of gunfire from outside the walls making us all ill at ease.

Michel glances at me and says nothing. He'd returned to Florence, work halted on the vast Medici Chapel so he could be the architect of fortifications for the city. The worry shows in his body, his lean strength replaced by a wiry hollowness. For the first time in years, I wish Mariotto was here. He would know what to say. Some joke or glib affront to set his friend's mood at ease.

'You understand all this war mongering, boy?' Michel asks Lucio of the explosions that continue outside our walls day and night.

'Pope Clement hopes to crush our new republic and reinstall the Medici,' replies Lucio, taking on Michel's test of his knowledge. 'No faction in power can reach an agreement and Florence's government flounders with confusion.'

'You remember in Rome those who didn't die by the sword were struck down by disease that blew from the corpses?' says Michel. He tries to install the gravity of what Lucio wants to be part of, but my son is unmoved.

An explosion sounds in the distance.

'If they take Volterra, then Florence's fate is sealed,' says Lucio.

'As our supply centre, it would mean certain ruin,' Michel agrees.

He stands and paces the floor. A new terror clutches my heart to see that a man like Michel is brought to despair. He thrusts his hands towards me, calloused palms exposed. 'These hands have brought a man to life from marble.' He balls his fingers into fists. 'And now they participate in a war that will turn men to dust.'

For as long as I have known him, Michel has set his jaw against colleagues and patrons, slabs of stone, a chapel roof, a pope and now a city, to perform his work. And I see what it costs him.

Another explosion, louder.

'Will you come with us to San Michele alle Trombe? Share in our prayers?' I ask Michel.

'If the walls are breached, you stay inside, do you hear me?' he says, a fleeting fierceness returning.

'While they stand, there is hope,' says Lucio.

Michel doesn't argue.

'I, too, stop to admire it. The painting you pine over,' he says, not looking at me, but seeing all the same. 'You can see that he loved them. Women, I mean. For better or worse.'

His tone holds none of its usual contempt.

'You've spent so many hours in the church contemplating that painting. Weeks or months if put back to back,' he says, a finger pointed as if this is a culpable fact. 'Maybe your husband's painting was easier to love than your husband?' He scoffs. At me or my husband, I'm not sure. 'What did you learn from all this time? Gazing, thinking? One cannot study so hard and have nothing to say about what one has learned!'

'Go easy, old man.' Lucio stands, is protective. 'Not every painting has to carry a lesson.'

So often I had watched Michel reduce an ambitious young painter. 'What mess is this? Did you bring in a mongrel and let it shit on your canvas?' he'd roared at a hopeful young artist who'd brought a drawing into the loggia. Who'd never returned. But this is the first time Michel's interrogation has made me feel shrunken.

He regards me, gentler now. 'But still you don't offer an answer,' he says. 'What do you think when you sit, all those hours, before Santa Elisabetta and the Virgin, Maria?'

I stall. Unsure if I want to ignore him or answer the question.

'I'll tell you what you think,' says Michel. 'You think these women have something you never can. That together they share a secret that you burn to know, but can only imagine. You visit and visit them again, not for the beauty but for the torture of everything they have that you do not. You yearn for the torture of it. What is past and can never be. If you are already afflicted, nothing more can hurt you.'

'They might call you *il Divino* for your creations, but you can't think like a woman,' I say.

'*Allora!* Let me be more precise. It should not go unsaid that your husband left work to be proud of,' he says. 'But the dead are dead. If we cannot understand them, let us be satisfied with what has passed.'

'Only some things do not pass as quickly as others,' says Lucio.

'Do they still come for money?' asks Michel.

'They are owed it,' I reply.

'By your husband, not you. How much?'

'More than I can pay. Every year that passes I get further behind.'

'Why don't you marry?' asks Michel.

'Why don't you?' I reply.

'If I fight, I'll get paid,' says Lucio, his frustration growing. 'We need the money.'

'Don't be fooled!' says Michel, raising his voice. Lucio appears taken aback. 'You're smart enough to know you'll only be paid if the pope keeps his promise, and if you survive it.' Then to me, 'Your merchant friends, the war has ruined them? Can they not take you in?'

'Marcello has a big family; their house is already crowded with relations who lost their homes in the north,' I say, too embarrassed to mention the barn in Prato that Bianca has offered me.

His ceaseless fretting is exhausting. *Who else but Michel can make a room spin while he thinks?* Mariotto once said.

For the briefest of moments, he is still.

'Finish what you started,' he says.

'What I started?' I say, twisting my hands through my apron.

He seems to ignore my discomfort. But of course he ignores nothing.

'Your husband had talent,' says Michel. 'But I knew him too well to believe he had the patience for invention.'

He falls quiet, regards me. And perhaps it is with more than the usual suspicion with which he views the world. Or perhaps it is my guilty eye for which the world becomes a mirror. I had not spoken up when Mariotto stole my recipe. And likewise, I had remained silent when the recipe was found to be lacking, when the bright white began to fade from the paintings as they dried over time, becoming translucent so the lines of underdrawing behind it began to show through. I thought I had prevailed over the common problem of white paint that begins to turn black. But a paint that reveals the artist's scratchings beneath? This was a failure that brought on both fury from the patron, and disgrace for the artist.

'Any dullard can obsess over colour.' Michel is animated again, slicing the air with his sinewy hands. Hands that themselves appear hewn from marble. 'It is the figures of a painting that show its spirit, its movement. Now, if a white could do something different …' His thoughts wander off, his eyes casting around the room, left and right, right and left.

'Mariotto said a white should dance off the page,' I say.

'A dancing white? That would be something!'

His enthusiasm surprises me. Mariotto and Michel had based their rapport upon hearty debate and a cordial heckling had peppered their exchanges.

'There are patrons who will pay good money for the perfect white paint, Antonia. The kind of money that would help pay for your home here in Florence. Somewhere safe for the boy.'

'I've tried every ingredient,' I say, surrendering to what Michel already knew. That I'd created the white Mariotto had sold as his own.

'The chalks and the marbles?' he asks.

'And the gesso and cuttlefish. Alumen and Tivoli travertine, calcined hart's horn, bones.' I reel off the list. '*Terra di cava, terra da boccali*. Even Venetian glass ground into fine dust. Nothing catches the light the way I imagine,' I say. 'It might take a genius.'

'Genius is eternal patience,' says Michel. 'You were married to Mariotto, so I know you have patience.'

What I don't have is fifty florins for the Mugello glass merchant. To learn what has been used to make the white glimmer like stars from the black glass would, at the very least, relieve me of wondering if it's something I haven't yet tried. But it would shame me to say this out loud to Michel. He might think I am asking him for the money.

'Zio Gee says she's making undue work for herself,' says Lucio. 'That a decent white at a good price is better than a perfect one that might not exist.'

Zio Gee, the name that has stuck since my son was a child unable to get his tongue around the four syllables of *Eugenio*, and so adopting only the second..

'Your uncle is smart, but has no mind for painting,' says Michel. 'The perfect white is about grind and clarity.' He looks at me, then back at my son. Lowers his voice. 'Your uncle has been a good parent.' He fixes his gaze back on me. Rubs at a blister on the fleshy webbing near his thumb.

'When this nonsense is over, bring the boy to Rome to sit for me. I have a pale umber that will render the rare colour of his eyes.' Michel is still holding my gaze. I dare not withdraw from it. And even if I wanted to speak I could not. For both Lucio and Eugenio share this unusual eye colour, and I know Michel's point is to make it clear that he knows the secret I've not told my son.

He pushes a hand through his oily hair with a great sigh. 'I've outstayed my welcome.'

'You're the Son of Florence! You're always welcome,' I say, kissing his cheeks. He scuffs his feet with disquiet. 'Are you afraid, Michel?' I ask. 'Of war?'

'I am a man most at home with a hammer and chisel,' he replies with unusual composure. 'I cannot view destruction as wholly perverse.' He loosens a chip of white stone from under his thumbnail. 'War cracks things open,' he says. 'I neither welcome nor approve it. But from what spills out, we must make something new.'

In San Michele alle Trombe, Lucio kneels beside me, spinning the black glass vial in his hand. Shifting shadow and light turn dust motes into angels. A bright sliver of sunlight is sifting through the milky alabaster pane on the north transept wall.

Then, something different. A movement in the painting. As if she turned briefly, Elisheva, towards me. But, no. She is there, as always, her eyes on Maryam. But I saw something. A flicker. A flutter. A moth brought inside the dusty pleats of a cloak? Or perhaps, like all of Florence, the war has brought on fatigue. Our senses muddled by explosions, only dozing, never sleeping. Our minds always fuzzy.

Elisheva.

I pray in the name given to her by her mother.

Elisheva.

The name that would turn her veiled head in a crowd. Is she weaving? Is she grinding grain for bread? Is she praying? Are her fingers testing the ripeness of figs? Is she walking alone? The harsh light of the desert casting her shadow across dust? Does she feel unease in her heart for the fate of her son?

I keep my gaze upon her. This feeling, this sense of her attention on me, brings with it a wash of embarrassment, of self-consciousness. What would she see in the woman I've become? In the girl I once was? Of the refuge I've sought here? Fleeing my mother, rage burning in my hand. Cursing my husband and his endless betrayals. My disgust at the man who dared kneel beside me, now the father of my son. The hours spent in silence behind Signora Ottolini, thumbing through her rosary after her confession. What sins did she have, this old widow? I'd often borne out long sermons by trying to guess. When she passed away I'd felt hollow with despair. We'd shared more silence than conversation and I hadn't been prepared for the unsettling emptiness left in her wake.

'Xiamara,' she told me when I asked her the name she had not been called since her childhood. The name given to her by her mother and soon changed to Marta to protect her from those who wanted Jews banished from Florence.

The altar step before me is empty.

My heart swells to bursting, for I know I must honour my son in this way. To give him knowledge of his family name, the one of his father.

I recite the brief line from Bianca's scroll like a wish, even though it is a lament.

עבדיאל בר יעקב קשישא ושרה

Abdiel, son of Jacob the Elder and Sarah.

Again I rest my gaze on the painting.

There's a chill in the church, the stone hard on my knees. I draw Lucia's bright yellow-gold scarf around my shoulders. An eerie break in the detonations, the *pock-pock* of gunfire has ceased. Then an explosion that makes the ground tremble. I imagine the walls of our city collapsing like Jericho.

I reach for Lucio's hand and squeeze it. Hands like his father's.

Are there two kinds of truth, as Lucia once said? The one that you know and the one that you tell? Zia Lucia, not really an aunt. Zia Lucia, who cast light into shadow. Who threw shadow upon light. Whose lie broke my heart and whose truth brought me Bianca. Who brought me this moment of grey, this fog of excuses that what was done to me is somehow different, less justifiable, than what I have done to another.

'Lucio,' I say. 'Please remember that you love me when I tell you what I must.'

Lucio, son of Eugenio and Antonia.

I speak and he listens. His beautiful eyes, a clarified umber. A colour seen by artists as conflicted between shadow and light. But not here in my son. Here, a colour of luminous intelligence. He takes it all in, maintaining his composure. And when I am done, we fall into silence.

'I can't help but feel that Mariotto and I might have clashed, as father and son,' he says. 'Zio Gee is easy to love. And he loves in return. Now, I will tell you something important.' He takes my hand. 'One mother is worth one thousand teachers.'

His words steal my breath. Not for the ease of understanding they reveal, but for the young man they show him to be. Not the child I forever want to keep under my wing. What would it cost to deny him his fierce loyalty to Florence?

I take in every detail of his face, his expression. Committing this precious moment between us to memory.

He turns from me and looks down at the glass vial in his hand.

'"You can't know what's inside and keep it", remember you told me?' he says. And I nod.

He rises to his feet and I think he will leave me here, again alone in this church. Instead, he climbs up to stand on the top step of the altar. Extends his arm, fingers wrapped tight around the glass vial.

'Maybe now there is more to be gained than lost,' he says.

A rumbling explosion, a nail clangs to the floor, on the wall the painting of the women swings sideways.

Lucio raises his hand higher. 'What the Venetians wouldn't tell you, we'll find out for ourselves.'

Another silence between explosions.

He opens his fist.

A black night sky of stars winking, slipping through space.

The sound of glass hitting stone. Of war cracking things open.

A rolled piece of linen, specks of sparkling crystal, spilling from broken pieces.

30

Beit HaKerem, 6 CE

'They want to know the ingredients; how the white sparkles through black,' says the trader Aquila. 'The glass vessel alone, is not enough.'

He hands me back the night-sky vial I have perfected.

'Always the Romans to want what is not theirs,' I say.

Ya'akov the Elder and Yosephus murmur their agreement. They are here to help negotiations with Aquila, who arrives weekly from the Holy City's markets.

Yoḥanan observes us with his usual keen interest. The fine auburn hair on his top lip and chin has come earlier than a change in his voice. I know that, too, will come soon.

'If they work it out for themselves, the recipe holds no value,' says Yoḥanan, already able to voice a clear-cut opinion. 'The real question here is: how smart is a Roman?'

Ya'akov and Yosephus chuckle and pat my son's back.

'Maybe soon, maybe not; their artisans will deduce it,' says Aquila. 'Better a living profit than a dead loss.'

I feel kicked. For his innuendo relates to my age and a profit my son might not see.

My vessels are bought by the travellers who flock to the city. They are not acquired for function: they are bought for their beauty. Glimmering trinkets that will sit among others in the homes of Amamei. But the income means I can send Yoḥanan for lessons. I can only teach him so much. Maryam has already sent Yeshu to Kumran and my son is begging to join him.

'See what they would be willing to offer each year, as a fee, for the use of my recipe,' I say.

Aquila seems wearied by the idea, wanting a fat deal done so he can gain his commission. He leaves us, disgruntled.

'Your recipe is worth more than they'd pay,' says Yoḥanan.

'Thieving Romans, always plundering one way or another!' Ya'akov the Elder pounds his fist on the table. 'Have we all forgotten that they slew three thousand Yehuda'ei in one morning? The Sanhedrin stripped of their power? What next? Pagan statues inside our temples?'

The men of the village grow careless with their opinions. They claim to pray for the Hand of Ribon Alma to guide Rome, but I can see in their eyes they don't mean what they say. It's evil they wish to come down and strike evil. To vanquish, not guide; to punish, not pardon.

I also see a desire for Yehuda'ei to crush Yehuda'ei. Divides have appeared among divides so that no thought seems clear; every eye looking twice, expressions clouded with suspicion. I've seen for myself how despair twists the mind and stirs up a violence to strike out with fists or arms where threats are perceived. But never have I seen one hatred cancel out another.

'Let's climb up to the high peak,' says Yoḥanan on the walk home.

He takes off before I can agree. Knowing I will follow.

He bounds and springs like an ibex over the rocky terrain. His calves are beginning to fill out like his father's, angular and taut, and a recent growth spurt means he is now a full hand taller than other boys his age. Ahead of me he freezes, then crouches low, transfixed.

'No tail on that lizard,' he says, when I catch up to him.

He's on his hands and knees following a crosshatch of tracks in the dust, reading the marks left behind as if they are words on a scroll.

This child, happier with his bare feet on the earth than food in his belly and, since a toddler, intent on roaming and exploring. Scratching through rubble for things most others disregard. A carapace of a bush beetle, the sun-bleached jaw of a hyrax. Every feature and detail of creatures living or perished is committed to memory that he can recall in an instant.

I lay out the goatskin and sit.

'Touch it, Imma.' He guides my fingertip across the tiny black veins lacing the clear sheath of a dragonfly wing. 'It looks smooth. But it's not.'

I marvel at both the invisible corrugations of a dragonfly's wing and my son's capacity to discover them.

Yoḥanan picks up a stick and scratches letters into the earth.

Yoḥanan.

I take the stick from him and write my letters next to his.

Yoḥanan bar Zakhariya v'Elisheva.

Rumours flare often that Maryam's child, Yeshu, is still sought by the Romans. They have come once for our sons. Will they do so again? What value do I leave to this world if I can't leave my son?

'You could write out the stories, like the priests do,' he says.

As an only child for the first eighteen years of my life, my own father had not been able to resist teaching me the letters. 'To be used with discernment,' he said. And I understood that I wasn't to show off my grasp of our language. To this I remain loyal. But it stirs a great pleasure and satisfaction within me to write for my son.

'Your writing is better than theirs. The way you curl the ends of the strokes.'

I pass him the stick and lie back on the skin. How quickly, these days, I seem to grow weary.

'Imma, wake up.' Yoḥanan's hand is on my shoulder, gently shaking me.

I sit up, startled, sleep-addled. A flush of shame, for dozing and leaving my child without someone to watch him. His ever-serious expression triggering a guilt that I should help him be more carefree, like other children. That I should be a younger mother, a smarter mother.

'You cried out,' he says. 'Were you dreaming?'

His eyes meet mine and we are locked in an exchange that takes place without speaking. I hear what he knows, what he sees. Images flickering in my mind's eye. In a breath, it is over.

'I'm not frightened,' he says. A softness washing over his usual intense expression. A wisdom of acceptance I want to reject.

I pull him to me and hold him for longer than he enjoys. I lick my thumb to clear the dirt from his face, and he scrunches his nose against the imposition, pushes my hand away.

Then, he rolls away, and as he does, in one swift move, collects the dragonfly wing that has slipped from my fingers and places it in the pouch tied to his waist, then springs to his feet. He points and I turn.

The dust cloud swallows blue sky as it moves fast towards us. It is not unusual for these desert storms to blow in, coating our cities and villages with dust, choking those caught in its thickness, grit clogging their lungs.

'You'll need to keep up, Imma,' he says, taking charge. 'Are you ready?'

He takes off and I follow.

The stable door is wide open and we sprint in, slamming it behind us. We stand against the door, heaving and laughing while the dust storm hurls grit against the wooden door at our backs. The livestock bray and bleat, disturbed by our noisy entry. And this makes us laugh until tears slide down our cheeks.

'You're fast,' says Yoḥanan.

'Or you're slow,' I say, challenging him, knowing he has not run his fastest so I could keep up.

Although the competitions between boys take place in a world hidden from their mothers, I know Yoḥanan's fine speed to be an agreed fact in our village. He is never far behind Ya'akov the Younger in a race through the streets.

'He belongs with the Greeks,' said Ya'akov. 'He'd win all their games against men twice his age.' Ya'akov is a good sport and meant it as a joke, but his father's face turned crimson.

'Guard your tongue!' said his father. 'We belong to no Greek, to no Roman! We belong to each other.'

'It's a jest,' said Sara, trying to calm down her husband.

'Forgive me, Abba,' said Ya'akov. 'I didn't mean to upset you.' He placed a gentle hand on his father's shoulder.

'You were born to upset me,' said Ya'akov the Elder, throwing off his son's hand. 'Roman rule, Greek thought. All defying our tradition. And pagan women ...' The latter under his breath, his face mottled by rage.

By pagan he meant Thalia. All our hearts shrank to hear her insulted.

A possible pairing between Ya'akov the Younger and Thalia had been forbidden, and an argument exploded between Ya'akov the Elder and Bohan. When Bohan and his daughter left one night, as the village slept, Ya'akov the Younger came to me and sobbed in my arms, swearing to follow her against his father's will. But I knew he would not. Even he, in this stricken state, would choose his father's approval over his love for Thalia.

'I will be more careful, I promise,' Thalia said, holding the night-sky glass I pressed into her hands as a parting gift. 'And I'll try not to rush.'

'You are welcome anytime to rush back to me,' I said.

'Will you remember me, Matrona-Imma?' she asked.

And I drew her into my arms, pressed my lips to the fierce heat of her forehead. 'As long as there are stars in the sky,' I replied.

In the stable, Yoḥanan and I catch our breath while the animals settle. I notice a donkey, not mine, set to feed. I walk towards the pen and the beast lifts its head from the bag of grain it is devouring. My heart races now, more than when I ran down the mountain. Its forehead is draped with a woven net set with tiny glass beads. And hung around its neck is a sky-blue glass pendant. A beast with such a magnificent medal could only belong to one man.

'*Sh'lama*, Elisheva.' Avner stands at the stable door that leads into our courtyard.

My skin prickles to hear his voice say my name. I try to greet him in return, but my voice is lost to a swell of emotion.

'Greet Avner, Yoḥanan,' I say instead, and my son takes Avner's hands, accepts a kiss to each cheek.

'I met you when I was a baby,' he says.

'You did indeed,' says Avner, ruffling my son's hair.

'We outran the storm,' says Yoḥanan. 'Imma kept up.'

And Avner laughs softly, the sweet-pungent scent of ginger grass smoke wafting with the heat of his skin.

'Will you stitch until I sleep?' asks Yoḥanan after we bid Avner goodnight. A request that hasn't been made since the night he turned ten and declared that the time had come to fall asleep on his own. That is, as he explained, if he was going to learn to sleep in caves in the wilderness by himself. Which, he'd assured me, was something he must do, and that I must learn not to worry.

I kiss both his cheeks, his forehead and chin. Run my fingers through his auburn curls. Take to my sewing while my child falls asleep. My eyes are gritty and heavy, still specked with dust. I squeeze them tight, try to focus, but the stitches blur. It might take me a moon to recover from keeping up with my son to outrun a sandstorm.

When he sleeps, I go to the rooftop. I tremble, light-headed, as my foot falls on each rung of the ladder, hoping Avner is up there. He is not. I console myself that I will see him in the morning. Perhaps I will ask his advice on my business with Aquila. On what it might mean to sell off my secrets of glass. The mere thought of writing it down for another fills me with regret. All I have created in their indifferent hands.

Then I smile at the idea of sealing it safely inside a glass vessel, the men trading and dealing, not a clue they hold the answer right there inside the vessels whose secret recipes they so wish to conquer. How Yoḥanan would laugh to share in the secret.

I lie back on the mat.

A blast of stars lights the sky. Like grinds of white quartz that dance from my black glass. I lift my finger to the heavens. Draw imaginary lines between stars to make out the letters. Avdi'el. Matia. Ḥalafta. Ḥashmonai. Nehunya. Tarfon. The names of our children taken by Herod. Dahabay. Yo'ezer. Dossa. Levitas. And as I write them, they disappear. How I ache for them to remain etched on the sky for eternity. Nakdimon. Tuviya. Kisma. Talitha. Zakhariya. My *ḥaviv*. My darling. My husband.

One name, not there. Still here, still mine.

'Imma, here I am.'

I wake, hot. My mouth dry. My son is beside me, a goblet of water in his hand. He has felt my distress. He tips water into his palm and bathes my forehead, my throat. Then presses the cup to my lips so I can drink.

I pull him into my chest and he is a child again in my arms, lets me hold him. Lets my hands feel the shape of his face, my fingers through the curl of his hair, the strength filling out in his arms. I press my forehead to his, to convey all the things I cannot say. This boy, the light of my brightness, the safe depths of my darkness. I breathe in his smell. Moss and wood. Scents of the earth. Committing every detail of his aliveness to memory.

I take it all in, cherishing his closeness, His presence a glinting quartz vein in the mountain before us.

31

Adelaide, Spring 2018

The stone in my hand is from Jonathan's childhood box of treasures. Its perfect equator is an unbroken vein of white quartz. Only those where the quartz vein exactly divided the stone earned the title of *wishing stone*. I keep it in my hand as I drive to the coast south of Adelaide, tracing the vein of quartz with the pad of my thumb.

On Kaurna Meyunna country, northerly gusts scatter surf foam across Second Valley Beach. I am the only one here. Raindrops light as pollen drift downwards, sideways. Near invisible, misting my face. I shrug on my rain jacket, tramp through high walls of seaweed to the small-pebbled shore and begin filling my bucket with items for the beach art. This ephemeral artmaking tempers the overwhelm that has arisen with two recent decisions. I will accept the invitation from the Israel Antiquities Authority in Jerusalem. I will find a way to break the news to my mother.

The beach art will be a triptych, three sections set into the sand. On the left, pebble starfish. The right, a series of serpentine lines made with fragments of shells. And, in the centre, a spiral made with stones like the one in my hand. I pocket the stone and forage through rubble and seaweed. It takes me two hours to find enough wishing stones for the art.

Without other beachgoers, the canvas of low-tide sand is untrammelled. I upend the bucket and the stones clatter into a pile. I collect various-sized ochre-stained pebbles. Then I fossick for shell fragments, unearthing white and blue chips from wet sand, prising them from between rocks. Cars pull up and then leave. The roiling clouds promise a storm.

With a piece of driftwood I draw three window-sized rectangles in the sand and begin on the left section, forming four starfish with ochre pebbles. Largest pebble for the heart of the starfish, grading to smallest at the ends of their five legs. I curve the lines of each leg to depict the motion produced by its thousand-tube feet. For the right panel, I stripe the sand with twisting, serpentine lines in alternating white and blue shell pieces. The effect is like a Grecian mosaic. Pieces glint and flicker. I glance up. The asphalt sheet of the sky has greyed to a low veil of light.

In the centre panel, I press wishing stones into sand. The beginning of a spiral.

Under this overcast sky, the white vein of quartz glows as if lit from within. As I touch each one, set it in place, I think of my son kneeling beside me. His painstaking process of finding and selecting the stones to produce the result he intended.

I press wishing stones into sand. Memories find me. I don't try to hide.

Jonathan's determined toddling through seaweed, pockets weighed down with stones. The boy whose school show-and-tells would later recite the ancient story about molten rock heating and cooling too quickly, the stone shrinking and causing a crack where hot brines seeped in, turning to crystal. Then the young man whose wishing-stone story travelled with him, emailing me photographs of beach artworks from work postings all over Great Britain.

When they'd returned his camera bag to me, it was months before I could look at the data chips tucked inside its hidden pocket. Not just photographs but short videos too. The frame wonky, like his writing, where he'd perched the camera on some uneven surface. Him holding newly found stones close to the camera. Pebbles of all shapes and sizes in slate, grit and dolerite, but all with perfect equators of quartz. Him barefoot in a UK winter, in only a T-shirt, building great snaking rock lines at Chippel Bay and St Ninian's Cave, England. Making ancient five-coiled labyrinths along Scotland's Fife Coastal Path. And the last video he made, at Oxwich Point in South Wales: him explaining step by step how the stones must be laid. The last frame, a yellow-gold sunset lighting up a great spiral.

Across the water, the golden sun drops into a sliver of pale blue. The sea gilt with light. I sit back and study the spiral like I do a gallery work of art. I shift angles, attentive. I've followed Jonathan's instructions. Setting the stones side by side so that each vein of quartz, in each stone, appears to connect to the next in one continuous line. The line twists and coils and catches the light. I trace it round with my finger. Not a rope to hold onto, but a single bright stitch holding pieces together. Fragments of the past held in place by the present. Connected by one illumined thread.

The incoming tide laps close. My creation will soon be dismantled, dispersed, some pieces dragged inside rock holes and into seaweed. Others drawn into the deeps of the ocean.

When he was little, Jonathan would applaud as the ocean swept away his beach art. And I'd fretted. What child doesn't shed tears or tantrum when what he's built is destroyed? But there was my five-year-old, jumping and clapping, the water circling his ankles.

The moment I put him into the car, he'd fall asleep. A wishing stone clasped in each fist.

I take his box-of-treasures stone from my pocket, turn it over in my hand, trace the quartz vein with the pad of my thumb. Its myriad glinting crystals filling cracks made under pressure.

In the glow of sunset the water laps liquid gold. I bend down with the final piece for this ephemeral art. Kiss it to my lips and press it into the damp sand, completing the spiral. His treasured stone at the centre.

At home, I shower, braid my hair and put on the dress I have made for the exhibition opening. An elegant *crepe de chine* shift in soft, dusty gold. The boat-necked bodice embroidered with silver acorns and pale blue forget-me-nots. The full skirt with the same crimson ellipses found on Elisheva's cloak, shaped like long seeds with pale yellow kernels. And on the wide belt, a silk-shaded pattern of swirling azure and scarlet clouds. The dress ripples like liquid and glows as it catches the light. Tris will likely be the only one to appreciate its source of inspiration.

As always, I'm ready early. I sit and file through the documents stacked near my bag. Two copies of e-tickets, itinerary, contact numbers in Jerusalem, the letter of offer from the Israel Antiquities Authority, passport, travel insurance details. The flight isn't until next week, but having these in hard copy in my hand makes me feel that it really will happen. I fold each piece of paper and put them inside my satchel. Slide my international driver's licence inside my passport, a small act that cements my resolve.

It's still an hour until the event starts. I have time to visit my mother.

She is at the old laminex table, stitching pearls to a bodice.

'Pass me the snips,' she says as I enter her kitchen. She clips stray threads with deft micro-movements.

'The IAA have invited me to help with garments found in a cave near the Dead Sea,' I say. 'Two thousand years old. At least. The colours still so rich, crimson and indigo. Glass artefacts too. Kohl jars, twisted glass necklaces, earrings. Some small black glass objects that have everyone talking. A rare glass for the period.'

A fleeting glance my way. Her violet eyes study my face, then my dress. She returns her attention to fastening pearls to the neckline.

'The mayor's daughter is turning twenty-one,' she says.

And so begins the dance of non-sequitur conversation that takes place when my mother feels threatened.

'It's a six-month residency,' I continue, undeterred. 'Assessment, cataloguing. Some conservation with their curator of organic materials. Here, I have photos.' I bring up the pictures and hold out my phone to show her, scroll through photos of fragments of finely woven tunics, of sophisticated glass pieces. One glimmering vessel of black glass nestled in the palm of an archeologist's hand.

Without looking up, she sets the bodice aside and installs a new thread for a hem.

The sewing machine chug, chug, chugs. My mother's fierce concentration is on the fabric passing underneath her manicured nails, the same pearl-glaze nailpolish she's used all her life. 'You've stopped seeing your psychiatrist,' she says, unlocking the foot and sliding the fabric out. 'I can always tell.' She stops her sewing. Looks up.

In every moment before this one, what she's said, how she's said it, has reduced me. Why have I never seen this fear now so clear in her face? This ache that consumes her.

I pull out a chair at the table. She flinches, as if I've transgressed a boundary.

'I keep wanting the story to have a different ending,' I say. 'And each time I tell it, I lose him all over again. The only thing I can change is what I do next.'

She takes off her glasses; she is trembling.

'He was mine too,' she says. 'They both were.'

Her face warps and contorts, the confused fury of grief.

'You want me to replace them,' I say. 'I can't. I don't want to.'

'But you have a chance to start again, another marriage, and you're too stupid to see it.' She spits out her insult. But all I feel is pity.

I wait for a moment.

'Why did you put up with Dad?' I can hardly breathe as I speak it.

'He wasn't always like he became.'

'He was in my memory.'

'He tried. Hard.'

'How hard can it be not to raise a hand to your wife?'

I shouldn't push it. But a piece of me still cowers every time I'm back in this house.

'My father needed help.' I don't raise my voice. 'He wasn't right in the head.'

She leaps to her feet; scissors fall to the floor.

'How *dare* you.' Her eyes are squeezed tight, her hands pushed to her ears. If she can't see or hear, then she is saved.

'He's dead and still you pad around as if he will leap from his armchair and strike you. I can't believe you still have his damned chair.' I snatch the scissors from the floor and stride to his old armchair, score the blade through the leather. Shredding its cushions while my mother screams *stop!* But I don't; I draw the blade through it until the stuffing explodes from inside.

She is sobbing, her hands still over her ears.

I go to her, try to hug her, she pulls her hands from her ears and pushes me away.

'Selfish. You always were. Selfish and judgmental.' Her tears have left white tracks in her makeup. 'And of course you'll never remarry, because you're wed to your story of the poor, stricken widow and her pathetic ghost of a life.'

I feel my hand twitch, ready to slap her, but she does it for me. Slaps her hands to her mouth. Stands heaving before me. Her eyes wide with shock, confusion, at the venom in her own words. I can see the regret bleeding through her expression. To watch her diminishment is more unbearable than what she has said. Then, she looks so small. Her eyes clouded with sorrow, with every regret that steeps in her marrow.

'You're leaving me behind,' she says, her body shuddering as she cries.

I try to take her in my arms, but she shakes her head. Refuses to let me.

'I don't know how you do it,' she says. Her perfect eye makeup is smeared, rivers of kohl. 'How you keep going.'

I try to hold her again. This time she lets me. Wraps her arms around me like this will be our last hug.

'I'm so angry that you know how to move on,' she says, sobbing. 'I didn't even have the guts to tell your father to pick up his own fucking socks.'

I hold her.

Like I've yearned to be held. Like no one has ever held her; I hold her. I kiss her rose-scented skin.

'We did nothing wrong, except that we stayed. But not me. Not now.'

'I love you, Mum.'

'I don't deserve it,' she says.

And in her voice I hear my own. So I am careful to make the truth clear. 'The only thing that keeps me going is the talents you've taught me.'

Tris is waiting at the gallery door.

'Thank god you called,' she says, hugging me. 'I got stuck with Herb.' She pulls back, surveys my dress and mouths *oh my god*. 'We could frame it! But I'll swoon over it later. I have someone I want you to meet.'

She leads me through the gathered crowd. The warm buzz of laughter, excitement as people mill around the exhibition artworks. Women are gathered around *The Head*, some standing back, some leaning close with grave expressions. One is dabbing at tears, hand to her chest. I know how she feels. I can't take my eyes from these women who are enamoured, horrified, entranced by the carving.

'Doctor Reed! At last we meet!' A woman throws her arms out and then sweeps me inside them. 'The exhibition is marvellous!' Her smile fills the room and she hugs me again. I have a feeling of floating, of burning, inside the embrace of Caterina Sirani, the artist who crafted the piece I yearned to hold for so long.

'Surprise,' says Tris, having lost the moment to Caterina's exuberance.

Caterina moves close; her breath smells like musk. Her gaze is both tender and fierce.

'I know why I made it,' she says. 'But, tell me, why does this head matter so much to you?'

I always envisioned this public moment with terror. A waking nightmare where I'm falling. Losing my stomach. Nowhere to anchor, nowhere to hide. Bloated by anguish, shrunken by fear. Collapsing, dismantling, flesh falling off bone. Decomposing, decaying. Every filthy, revolting process of death as those before me look on with disgust. But this does not happen.

'Is there somewhere we can sit?' I ask Tris, and she ushers us through the crowd to her office.

Caterina fills the space like a giant. There is no hidden corner her light does not touch. Every place of stuck grief, of thick shadow, is lit up by her presence. I speak without stopping, without faltering. Every dark word burning up in her brightness.

Then I am done.

The mellow *tick* of a desk clock.

'Death is not clean. Not neat.' Caterina's words pierce me, enter me, but I do not flinch. 'The challenge of the past lies in being aware of the present. It's why we must create!' She sits back in her chair. 'When we create, we stop chasing the past or pursuing the future. We are here. We arrive.' At this she throws back her head and laughs like a goddess.

'I think of my ancestors, women with little means, hours of their day grinding grain for their bread. But together! You see? Not alone, like us. Talking, laughing, gossiping. I often wonder how and why we must create, so often, alone?'

Tris comes closer, sits on the arm of my chair.

'When did women forget the power of creating together?' asks Caterina.

We are quiet. Tris looks at her watch.

'The patrons will get restless if we don't get this started,' she says.

'Two minutes,' I reply, digging my phone from my bag. 'I want to show Caterina the textiles they've asked me to work on in Jerusalem.' I tap the black face of my silenced phone. There's fifteen missed calls.

'Everything okay?' asks Tris, as I frown at the screen. I hit play on the first message, push the phone to my ear.

'My mother's been taken to hospital.'

Tris is calling me an Uber but I'm already running. Royal Adelaide Hospital is close by; it will be quicker on foot.

She is sitting up in her bed, a steaming cup in her hands. I can see she's been to the hairdresser and the nail salon. And she's bought a new lipstick.

'See what happens when you shock me?' she says, sipping at her tea.

The 'S' word coils like a wound spring on my tongue. The baggage of blame I'm expected to carry. I will not say sorry for what I have not done.

'What happened, Mum?' I ask.

Her bed is so narrow that can't sit beside her. I pull a chair covered in peach bouclé close to her bed.

'She's clean as a whistle,' the doctor says behind us. A young olive-skinned woman with a gold ring through one nostril. 'I'm Doctor Cherry. Your bloodwork is perfect.' She takes the teacup from my mother, sets it down, pushes the scope against my mother's chest. 'Lovely.'

And it occurs to me that the sound of a heart beating is indeed that.

'And you say you're not taking any anti-anxiety medication?' Doctor Cherry asks my mother.

'Why would I?' My mother pales at the suggestion.

'You did the right thing calling an ambulance. But what you've had is an anxiety attack,' replies the doctor. 'How often do you get them?'

'What nonsense,' says my mother. 'My heart is not coping with the fact that my daughter wants to flit off to the Middle East.'

'I understand,' says Doctor Cherry, while my face burns with shame. 'I'll borrow your daughter for a moment; we need a next-of-kin signature.'

'She's the only kin I have,' says my mother.

Doctor Cherry leads me down the hall. 'Before you ask,' she says, 'your mum is fine. Better than most half her age.'

'It's okay, I'm not really going,' I tell Doctor Cherry, anticipating her suggestion.

'Was it intended as a permanent move?' she asks.

'A six-month residency,' I reply. 'But it's fine. There'll be other rare woven textiles to work on.' I laugh and wonder if I'm coming off as hysterical.

She doesn't respond for a moment. I can see she's being cautious. Mulling it over.

'While I'm not qualified to give opinions on rare textiles, I can suggest a registry of home nurses to help you and your mother. Whether you go or you stay.' She hikes a perfect eyebrow. 'My husband and I went back to Myanmar. An extended stay with our families. I got so many updates from my nurse, my mother singing her praises in every conversation, all I could think of was the impossible standard she was setting for when I returned.'

We laugh quietly together.

A nurse runs towards us. 'Doctor Cherry, room six.'

'You can take her home in the morning,' she says, and leaves before I say sorry. Before I say thank you.

Mum is sleeping, open-mouthed. She would be horrified to know it. I dab the spittle from her chin and settle into the peach-coloured, uncomfortable chair. I text Tris and Mum's neighbours then stare at my phone. When did I stop having people to tell things?

I thumb through the old editions of *Women's Weekly* stacked by her bedside. Then I take out the travel documents and flick through each one. Departing Adelaide in four days. Arriving London twenty-six hours later. Two nights with Priscilla, who insisted. Then car hire for ten days. My intention had been to drive to Chippel Bay and Saint Ninian's, down to Oxwich Point. Then up to Scotland to walk some of the Fife Coastal Path. To take my shoes off on the beaches; collect wishing stones of all sizes. To know that he'd been here, his bare feet, his wholeness, on this same earth.

It's not important whether or not you go. It's a victory you booked it! my last shrink would have said.

I take the passport out and flick through the pages. The last stamp is from New Zealand. We went together. Me, my husband, our son. My husband in what they thought was remission. My son old enough to manage his first zoom lens, as big as a lighthouse against his small chest. I know the country was spectacular, but I have little memory of the landscapes they fixed their sights on with zeal, with precision. My eyes were on them. Committing to memory them standing together.

In the conservator's studio, I roll out the trays of Maori textiles bequeathed from a private collection. The traditional black dye used is made from Manuka bark and iron-rich mud, and, over time, its acidity can cause the cloth to fracture and split. It is my opinion that these pieces should be returned to New Zealand, but I do agree they should be stabilised first. It's a delicate process that will take time and patience. If the textile is bent, it will snap.

The studio door clicks and swings open. 'What the hell?' says Tris, who should herself be on a week's leave. 'Why didn't you call me?' She throws up her arms, lets them slap back at her sides. Her face is bare of makeup and she looks like a tattletale child, ruddy cheeked and defiant. She is wearing old jeans and sandshoes. A crumpled blue T-shirt.

'We're shifting my father into care,' she says, explaining how she is dressed, under-eye circles darkening. 'More crap in that shed than in the Bolivar sewer.'

'More's the question, why are you here?' I ask.

'Maisie called me,' she replies.

'So now I'm under surveillance?' I'm only half joking.

'You can't stop others caring,' she says.

'I'm a talent at packing boxes,' I say, changing the subject. 'I can help pack up your dad's shed.'

'You can help me by getting on that plane,' she says. 'Once Dad settles in, I might even visit.'

'Mum needs me,' I say.

'Oh come on!' she says. 'Your mum is fine, for God's sake.' There is something in the way she is looking at me that makes me feel nervous. 'Don't hate me,' she says, a loud exhale. 'But I went to see her.'

A sense of transgression, like a stick in my eye.

'Please hear me out,' says Tris. 'I can bring her with me, in November. I'm in Florence, at the Uffizi. They're offering a preview of the Del Monte Mappa. Surely you'd love to see it? Both of you? We'll visit together.'

She knew it would seduce me. The Del Monte Mappa is silk embroidered with spun silver. Mount Sinai blooming with flowers, the tablets of Law surrounded by clouds and musical instruments. The sacred cloth intended to protect a Torah scroll.

I stay silent.

'For fuck's sake,' says Tris. It's the first time I've heard the 'F' word from her mouth. 'You made me say it.' She points her slender pale finger.

My body shakes with the tension of biting my tongue. Of not saying something I'll regret, like my mother. I turn my back on her, start unpacking the box I'd brought back in with my things. I fumble the stack of printed-out images I've collected, and they fall to the floor.

'Don't be *that* girl,' says Tris. 'The one who can't look herself in the eye in the mirror each morning.'

Make a new choice.

'It's too late,' I say. The clock on the wall clear that I have no time to go home and pack.

'All you need is your passport,' she says, clapping her hands. A fairy batting its wings. 'You can buy a change of clothes at the airport. I'll ship everything else you need.'

Make a new choice.

Hadn't I already made it?

I pick up the scattered images from the floor, push them inside my satchel. Tris bends down, hands me one I have missed. The Albertinelli.

'Keep it,' I say. 'I'll see it for myself when I meet you in Florence.'

I fish my house keys from my bag, press them into her hand.

The Uber pulls up at my mother's and I ask the driver to wait. She's seated at the table, her sewing machine pushed to one side. A laptop is open before her.

'Tris left it,' she says. 'Don't look so surprised. She put *zooming* on it. She'll teach me to use it.'

I kiss both her cheeks.

She takes out a handkerchief I've long forgotten. One I embroidered for her when I was a child. Blue forget-me-nots, red butterflies and yellow-gold tulips. I'm shocked that she's kept it.

She flattens the handkerchief on the table, then swivels the laptop to face me, the before and after images of the embroidery on the screen. 'Don't you find it strange this embroidery has so many of the symbols you sewed onto this?'

'They're common symbols …' But all I can see is my child self's inelegant stitching.

'But still …' she says, running a finger across the gold-thread petals of a tulip. 'You spent hours unpicking the thread from an old curtain tassel you found in a church op-shop. Remember?'

I laugh. 'I was resourceful.'

'You were four years old,' she says, her finger touching every image. I cringe, stomach knotted at their imperfect stitches.

'You were gifted,' she says. '*Are* gifted.'

At the door, I hold her close. She won't let me go, her arms encircling me.

She's still waving from the letterbox when the car turns out of the street.

Inside the airport, I grab sleepwear and two shirts. Toothpaste and toothbrush and rose spray for my face. I hover over the pashminas. I select navy, to use as a scarf and a blanket.

'Did you see all the colours?' asks the young girl as she rings up the items. As if the navy pashmina was chosen because I didn't know there were others.

I stall for a moment. Then take it back to the shelf and grab the one in warm yellow-gold.

The screen showing my flight flashes *Closing.* The flight attendant sees me running and smiles as I reach her. On her tooth is a fleck of red lipstick. I hand her my boarding pass.

'Welcome, Doctor Reed,' she says, directing me to a now-empty aerobridge. 'Front doors, row two on the right.'

I sink into my seat.

A young male steward offers a tray with half-filled glasses of champagne.

'I'm James. I'll be looking after you.'

'If I took two, James, would you judge me?' I ask.

He lays out two napkins, lowers his voice as he sets down the glasses. 'Barely enough to pickle an onion.'

The attendant from check-in kneels down beside me. 'You dropped this, Doctor Reed.'

'I prefer Elisabeth,' I say.

She hands me the white handkerchief I stitched as a child. Indigo blues, deep crimson and gold thread unpicked from a tassel. The one my mother has somehow slipped inside my pocket, the soft scent of roses.

'Is there anything else I can get for you, Elisabeth?' asks the attendant.

And my mind starts to checklist.

Items I don't have. Things that I should. So much of it still packed in boxes stacked in my hallfway. The stuff that I once mistook as my life.

She is waiting, expectant. My thumb traces the texture of an embroidered gold petal. I smile at the feel of its imperfect stitches.

'Thank you,' I reply. 'I have all that I need.'

GUIDE TO ARAMAIC LANGUAGE USED

A note on the translation

The Aramaic in this novel was translated from English by Nahum Ben-Yehuda, a graduate of the departments of Talmud and Jewish history respectively at Bar Ilan University, where he is currently completing his doctorate. He is also an ordained orthodox rabbi. The fields of research in which he is engaged include Hebrew Bible, Talmud and Targum – with special focus on Hebrew, Aramaic and non-Semitic loanword linguistic aspects.

In Judea, during the period in which this story is set, a certain dialect of Aramaic was the common spoken language. The following translations have been identified with academic rigour, in accordance with contemporaneous literary sources.

The historical Aramaic word for mother is *emma* (pronounced *EE-mah*). However, given the problem of potential confusion with the common English name, I have opted for the Hebrew word, *imma*.

Due to the significance of the name Hanna, Nahum has advised to keep it in its Hebrew form. All beautiful names, so we are spoiled for choice.

At the time of printing, the guide to pronunciation was still being devised. Please visit sallycolinjames.com for these details.

A note on the typeface

The typeface used in this book is Bembo Standard, designed by the punchcutter Francesco da Bologna around the turn of the sixteenth century for the Venetian printer Aldus Manutius the Elder. The first book printed in this typeface is by the poet Pietro Bembo, who appears as a character in this book, and for whom the typeface is named. Unfortunately, neither da Bologna nor Manutius included within their typeface the pharyngealised diacritic ˤ that is common in many Aramaic words. That diacritic has been included in the table below for proper translation, but within the text itself has been replaced with an apostrophe. This is not academically ideal, but we have taken all due care to ensure an easier reading experience for this English edition.

Aramaic Glossary	
Abba	Father
Aḥata d'Em	Aunt (mother's sister)
Akara	Barren/infertile
Akh'n'shuta	Autumn/harvest
Alma d'Atei	The World to Come
Amam Amamei (pl)	Gentile
Anak	Pendant
Avil (m) Avila (f)	Mourner/one who grieves or is grieving
Aviva	Spring
Aviya	Abijah (priestly order/lineage)
B'rati	My daughter
B'rei	Son of
Baˤla	Wife
Bar	Son
Barta	Daughter
Bˤel	Husband
G'zura	Circumcision
Gifta	Olive pressings used to fire the crucible in a furnace for glass making
Ḥalit'ta	Necklace
Ḥavivta (f) Ḥaviv̇ (m)	My darling

Aramaic Glossary	
Hodaya	Thanks/thank you
Imma (Emma)	Mother
K'tem	Stain
K'tubta	Contract of marriage
Kafrisin	Cyprus
Kayta	Summer
Makva	Mikvah (Jewish ritual purification bath)
Malʾakh	Angel
Matrona	Aunt as term of respect for non-blood female elder
Mazala tava!	Good fortune!
Melḥa	Salt
Milut	Chickpeas
M'shugaʿat (f)	Crazy
Nedda	Menstruation/menstruating
P'rishay P'risha'ei (pl)	Pharisee
Paraḥta	Bird
Pinikaya	Phoenicians
Pinikiya	Phoenicia
Ribon Alma	Lord of the World
Sava	Grandfather
Savta	Grandmother
Sh'lama	Peace!
Sh'maya	The Heavens
Shavʿa	Shiv'a
Shawsh'na	Lily
Shʾerin	Bracelets
Sitwa	Winter
T'he (f) Ta'heh (m)	Sorry
Tawarei Yehuda	Mountains/Hills of Judea
Tsadukay Tsaduka'ei (pl)	Sadducee
Tsar	To form, to shape
Yehuda'ei	Jew(s)
Z'gugita	Glass
Zagag	Glassmaker

Aramaic Names	
Avdi'el	Abdiel
Avraham	Abraham
Avshalom	Absolom
Dahveed	David
Elisheva	Elisabeth
Hanna	Hannah/Anna
Maryam	Mary
Sh'lomo	Solomon
Y'hoyakim	Joachim
Yaʿakov	Jacob
Yirmiyahu	Jeremiah
Yiska	Jessica
Yoḥanan	John
Zakhariya	Zachariah

Aramaic Place Names	
Azotus	Port of Ashdod
Beit HaKerem	Ein Kerem
Beit Leḥem	Bethlehem
Ḥevron	Hebron
Kesari	Caesarea
Kumran	Qumran
Moav	Moab
Natsrat *(Modern Hebrew, probably from old Arabic)*	Nazareth
Pamias	Banias
Sart'ba	Sartaba
Shomron	Samaria
Suria	Syria
Yard'na	Jordan
Yehuda	Judea
Yeriḥo	Jericho
Yerushalayim	Jerusalem

GUIDE TO ITALIAN LANGUAGE USED

Babbo is the term I have chosen to refer to Antonia's father. While *papà*, a French derivative, became the popular term for father in Italy in the seventeenth century, *babbo* has been part of the Tuscan vernacular since medieval times and is still used today. Papa Leone was the vernacular title for Pope Leo X.

AUTHOR'S NOTE

While *One Illumined Thread* is a work of fiction, it was born in an unexpected and exhilarating moment when I found myself standing before Mariotto Albertinelli's Renaissance masterpiece, *La Visitazione* (*The Visitation*). The life-sized painting depicts mothers-to-be Elisheva and Maryam (the Aramaic names for Saint Elisabeth and the Virgin Mary), both pregnant with their miracle sons. I was transfixed and transported. Amid the crowds at the Uffizi Gallery, Florence, it felt as if only the three of us stood there: myself, Elisheva and Maryam. Around me, the space pulsed with the silent sense that I was not simply viewing a painting but standing witness to a moment between women that I had long yearned to experience myself. The strength in Elisheva, who, without words, delivered a magnitude of grace, of conviction, of unassailable dignity to her apprehensive young cousin, lit a spark in my heart.

When I discovered that, upon Mariotto Albertinelli's early death, he left his wife, Antonia, with sizeable debts to the artist Raphael (Raffaello Sanzio da Urbino), a story began to emerge. Like holding a mirror to a mirror, so began the tale of Antonia and her husband's painting, and the women in the painting from whom she sought inspiration and refuge. Parallel lives that would intersect. For the better. Just as mine did with the painting that day in the Uffizi.

I once read Albert Camus' musing that 'a [wo]man's work is nothing but this slow trek to rediscover, through the detours of art, those two or three great and simple images in whose presence [her] heart first opened'. While I had been inspired and touched by many works of art at that stage of my life, I knew, deep down, I had not yet experienced the type of 'heart opening' of which Camus spoke. Until I stood before *The Visitation*.

One Illumined Thread is not a story about religion or religious figures. It does not purport to understand the complexities of Judaism nor the complications of Christianity. It is not a story about a painting. It is my way of expressing and sharing the way it felt to stand in the presence of female eldership, the collapsing of time and space that morphed the world around me. The exhilarating cracking open of my heart. It is also my paean to female endurance and creativity, written with a reinvigorated understanding of why we must, at all costs, continue along our brave voyages of creativity. For in one day – or one millennium – we may pass on that heart-opening gift to another and, forever, for the better, change their world.

Notes on the research

The production of a work of historical fiction is a demanding curiosity, an endless confrontation of indecisions that argue story or fact. Here's my clear decision: where technical knowledge disimproves the character's journey or the reader's experience, my choice is story.

In this regard, there were many painstaking moments of indecision. A neighbour once asked me: do you want to be right or happy? I wonder if my characters have tired of the same persistent query.

Given how savvy readers of historical fiction are, I have set out below a select few of what I feel might be the first questions that are asked. Please visit sallycolinjames.com for further details, annotations, citations, links to artists, artisans and academics, and an extended bibliography.

Anachronisms, events out-of-time and detail quirks

As someone who loves to 'imagine', I was constantly surprised by the pain and anguish it caused me to bend, flex, change or (in rare instances) ignore what history and text-book knowledge professed. However, this novel is indeed an imagining, an imagination. A creation seeded in an exhilarating non-thinking moment. One that, despite the gravity of all we think we know, pushed with all the Newtonian force a sprout needs to breach the earth towards the sunlight.

If you have specialist knowledge in any relevant field, you may spot some or all of these anachronisms and quirks. For example, Antonia's recipes drawing on Vermeer's idea of finely ground quartz. Apparently, a better choice than cristallo (ground Venetian glass) for its refractive qualities. Or Antonia's experience with 'the physician', where I have conflated what would have been quite a different method of consultation regarding pregnancy, one I felt was more universally relatable in this all-too-common way. Or Herod's landing at Ptolemais, which probably happened the year before it did in my novel. As mentioned below, the existence of black glass has an academic argument all of its own. There is also the entire 'story of glass' and everything that is known to date. In this regard, my humble and earnest thanks will always go to those specialists who have been so very patient with my fictional pursuits. Other quirks include the dress of the woman who likely sewed the embroidery *Embracing Figures*. I have her in an outfit that would have been better suited to hosting company than embroidery. As Cristina Balloffet Carr pointed out, she would likely have worn 'a simple but of most excellent quality clean chemise of thinnest linen; they were often embroidered along cuffs and neckline with silk thread'. A lovely outfit indeed, but in this instance I made a choice for a more contemporaneous but decorative dress. Although I do accept that lace flounce sleeves are not ideal for the act of embroidering! There are quotes from Aristotle borrowed by Lucia. And Michelangelo sometimes speaks in his own words.

On women, history and religion

Let me be clear: I am neither an expert, nor a minor scholar, on Judaism and Christianity. Furthermore, I will never in this lifetime be such. After the first two years of research, I realised the folly of any goal that sought a comprehensive grasp on monotheism. Chastened, I accepted my place as literary pilgrim. However, the constant humbling I experienced in traversing the complexities and complications of faith has served to bring me a depth of human understanding that I will forever cherish.

Within the scope and worlds of this novel, my core intention is to render with respect and transparency my willingness to walk in another's shoes. I grew up with Greek and Italian migrants whose industry, familial loyalty and Christian faith instilled in me a reverence for their beliefs. Likewise, I have participated in numerous conversations with lay, non-observant and orthodox Jews, who – in my humble opinion – at least concur that discussion, debate and conversation are essential. I have also deferred, with great academic relief, to Sarah J Tanzer's notion that 'The picture that has emerged is of multiple Judaisms, distinct Jewish religious sytems, yet with connecting threads, indicators that they share a common legacy.' Tanzer goes on to say, 'The primary literary sources for the Judaisms of the first century provide only a limited picture. Those preserved are those which were important to the victors of history.'

All in all, this leads me to feel satisfied – convinced – that there is a place in the realm of human potentiality for the dreaming of an Elisheva in ancient Judea, or an Antonia in Renaissance Florence. A dreaming that conceives of the space, the creative pathway, for our Elisabeth.

As a writer and researcher, I cannot wholly reject what has come 'before' – in whatever conjectured or proven form – and aims to preserve an earlier tradition. Equally, neither can I turn away from the uncommon, the rare or the exceptional. For me the interest in this relates with particularity to women. Brilliant women. Who have inhabited our world for millennia.

Mariamne and Maryam

To ease confusion I have kept Princess Mariamne as the Hebrew spelling, and Maryam, as in Virgin Mary, in Aramaic.

Mariamne's hanging

Josephus doesn't say how Mariamne was executed. However, there are sources that speculate strangulation. One suggested that Herod's offensive golden eagle was torn down from the Temple using the rope that he used on Mariamne. Regardless of how it took place, the death of Mariamne is brutal and deeply affecting, and deserves attention.

'Aunt' as blood relative and term of respect

For ease of plain English I have referred to Hannah, Elisheva's blood relative on her mother's side, as Dodah, although the full term of respect is Dodah Min Ha'em.

Ahata d'Em-Imma

While the independent words are conveyed in accurate Aramaic (that is, Aunt and Mother respectively), the conflation is my invention as Thalia's way of referring to a non-blood-related female whom she considers a respected elder.

Glass: history, archaeology and production

Zakharya's enthusiastic recounting of how glass was discovered was documented by Pliny the Elder in 100 CE. However, he must have heard it from somewhere. Maybe from the same source as Zakharya.

The experts of glass have been humble and generous in more ways than I can express. They have tolerated my urgency for anachronisms, and patiently suggested technical amendments. I can only assure them of one thing: any failure in accuracy is in support of the human endeavour of these characters. This I know they understand. They are the tireless seekers of truth among rubble and ruin. They are those who divine our past with the sweat of their brow.

Black glass

The black glass vials are my invention in every way. The opinion of experts like Dr Yael Gorin-Rosen is that this type of black glass did not exist in Judaea during this period. However, it is included here as part of a fictional story in order to represent everything we do not know.

Tools used for glassmaking

Blowpipes and jacks are more modern inventions. I decided to include reference to these tools as a way to convey the process of Elisheva's work. According to Dr Gorin-Rosen, early pipes were more like tubes. However, I decided, for the sake of comprehension, to stick to terms that caused the least confusion for readers. Although during the period in which Elisheva is perfecting her glassblowing scholars are uncertain if wooden panels were used, I felt it was easier for the reader to understand the shaping process if I gave Elisheva wooden tools that have been made by her teacher, Avner.

The scroll in the vial

Those who understand antiquities will know that the scroll in this vial would probably have been leather or even metal. Dr Naama Sukenik from the Israel Antiquities Authority also confirmed a leather scroll would have been more likely used. The leather she showed me was so beautiful and finely made it was almost like paper. However, given how well the vial was sealed and the presence of other scrolls and documents on various materials, it seemed important for me to link the tactile nature of woven cloth to Elisheva and Antonia. I hope you agree that the sensory point of this helps better convey what is transferred between women across time. Rather than something like leather, from a beast, or metal, which requires forging and other aggressive constructions, linen is evocative of the themes of this book.

Antonia, Amadeo and Biagio

Antonia Ugolini was Mariotto Albertinelli's wife. In the writ ordering her to repay her deceased husband's debts, her father is listed as Amadeo and her son as Biagio. In the novel, Antonia's father is cast in a role that led me, out of respect for the real-life Amadeo, to change his name to Franco. I know nothing of Antonia's father, so this seemed only fair. Lucio, named after Zia Lucia, seemed the right fictional name for Antonia's son.

Paintmaking

Those of you who know the history of paintmaking will quickly see that Antonia is experimenting with ideas that came both before and after her time. This is purposeful on my behalf because this is the very nature of an inventive mind. And who among us truly knows what was discovered and never recorded, or recorded and lost, only to be rediscovered centuries later. If you would like to further explore the extraordinary world of paint making please visit my website for suggested reading.

Lead white

The basic lead white recipe was taken from the Bolognese Manuscript, dated to around 1450. Antonia's recipe for using Alberese white came with the help of Robert Gamblin in a somewhat extraordinary coincidence. He was reading a book on the subject as I was asking him about his expertise in paintmaking. The reason for the white failing came from marvellous discussions with Dr Gregory Smith.

Alberese stone

Those familiar with the geology of Italy and/or winemaking will know that Alberese stone is not a bright white but can vary in colour from brownish-grey to a more creamy colour. My choice was whether to invent a name that carried pure white (like the famous pebbles, or cogoli, from the River Ticino), or invent a white but keep the term 'Alberese'. I chose the latter, for the reason that I felt this humble stone deserved a place in this novel. As Piero Antinori says in his book *The Hills of Chianti*, '[Alberese stone] has played an important role in Tuscan history … Its white veins enliven the Tuscan landscape.'

Ultramarine as described by Bianca

The recipe for ultramarine is taken from the manuscripts of Jehan le Begue.

Painter's colic

Caused by lead poisoning, painter's colic wasn't really properly diagnosed until the nineteenth century, but I felt creative licence was appropriate to make the point about the reality of the dangers of working with lead, and other ingredients, important to this story. I was born in a city famous for being host to the 'World's Largest Lead Smelters'. I have my own opinions on how this has affected my life. Enough said.

Choice of words and language

As often as possible, I have used Aramaic or Italian names of people and places, and peppered the text with colloquial exchanges. However, where I felt such choices affected comprehension, I chose from the work of Josephus or plain English.

San Michele alle Trombe

Based on the initial advice of, and subsequent discussions with, Elaine Ruffallo, I chose to locate Albertinelli's painting in the church of San Michele alle Trombe (Saint Michael of the Trumpeters), even though it was reported, in some places, to have hung elsewhere. It seemed fitting that this church was the place, given that the hotel that has replaced it stands in the Piazza Sant'Elisabetta. It's also worth noting that the alabaster windowpanes in the church would more likely have been *impannata*, starched canvas. However, alabaster panes were afforded in more lavish churches, and I felt this little church deserved the best.

Michelangelo as Michel

It was pure instinct that lead me to want to refer to Michelangelo as 'Michel'. Michelangelo's name is so powerful that I needed a way to, somewhat, integrate him as a man among many, and to somehow present him in a way that could explicate his friendship with Antonia. Some Renaissance scholars love the idea of 'Michel', some do not. But it was just one of those moments when, for me, the name felt right. Ludovico Ariosto, I later discovered, must have felt likewise. In *Orlando Furioso*, Canto 33, stanza 2, he proclaims: 'Michel, more than mortal, divine Angel'.

Signor, Signora and Italian names

In Antonia's time it was not the practice to address people in the way that many of us in the English-speaking world have come to recognise as Italian vernacular, that is, Signor and Signora. For example, Signora Ottolini is addressed by Signora and her last name. But historian Anatole Tchkine advised me it would most certainly have been Monna, along with her first name. For example, Monna Maria. I agonised over this decision. However, having grown up among Italians, I felt that Signor/Signora may be more familiar to most readers and connotes a rhythm of language both delightful and immediately recognisable. It was rare for people to address each other by surname. Again, in balancing the depth and breadth of the novel, I have made choices that serve to render both known and unknown characters in the work in a clear and consistent manner. And hopefully I have done so in a way that most readers will happily take each character on face value. Albertinelli would most certainly have been called Maestro Albertinelli. However, I've retained that use for Leonardo and Michelangelo, since Albertinelli, to most readers, would not be as well known.

Featured artworks

La Visitazione
1503, Mariotto Albertinelli
Oil on panel
232 x 140 cm
Inventory 1890 n.1587, Uffizi Gallery, Florence

Embracing Figures
Early to mid seventeenth century embroidery
Glass beads, metal threads, silk floss (please see my website for extensive details)
26 x 28 cm
Ashmolean Museum of Art and Archaeology

Description of the embroidery 'Embracing Figures' (accession number WA2014.71.38, Ashmolean Museum, Oxford).
Permission to use explicit details from the Micháel and Elizabeth Feller catalogue (*The Needlework Collection* pp 56-57) for *Embracing Figures* has been granted by the author Dr Mary M Brooks, PhD MA DMS DipTexCons FSA FIIC ACR. Besides her impressive achievement of having more letters in her qualifications than her actual full name, Mary's contributions to the world of textiles both technically, academically and in raising awareness of the importance of textile collections make her (along with her international associates Dr Cristina Balloffet Carr and Patricia Nguyen Wilson) a global treasure in the textile world. Conferring with, and being guided by Mary, Cristina and Patricia – as well as the textile conservators here in Australia – has been one of the highlights of my extensive research.

Dr Patricia Nguyen Wilson has granted permission to put her recent, and as-yet unpublished, revelations that provide a different argument to the dominant 'cage theory' into the mind of my character Dr Reed. See pp 60–61 of the novel. I absolutely love where Tricia is headed with this thinking, and humbly thank her for sharing it with us. In essence, she is asking us to think more laterally about the value of skills like embroidery, and the contribution it makes to problem solving in general.

Death, Third of the Four Sights seen by Prince Siddhartha
1890–1910, Burma
Wood, pigment, metal, fibre
90.0 x 38.0 x 48.0 cm (body with crows)
24.0 x 36.0 x 16.0 cm (vulture)
Gift of Barrie and Judith Heaven, 2010
Art Gallery of South Australia, Adelaide

Study of Head (John the Baptist III)
1992, Ana Maria Pacheco
Polychromed wood
31.8 x 50.8 x 74 cm (excluding base)

Acknowledgment of Country

Much of this novel was written from my rainforest home. I would like to acknowledge the Arakwal Bumberlin people of Bundjalung Nation who are the Traditional Custodians of this land which I live, work and stand on. I acknowledge and extend my respect to Elders both past and present, and upcoming future leaders.

A final thought

If you, like me, are a reader who all too often allows the pursuit of facts to hamper a good story, then there's plenty more detail available on my website. However, perhaps we might all do well to, more often and with more reverence, recall Einstein's sentiments on imagination and knowledge in a 1929 interview with George Sylvester Viereck for the *Saturday Evening Post*: 'For knowledge is limited, whereas imagination embraces the whole world.'

Indeed, the worlds within this novel, and the one in which it was written, are better for this embrace of imagination.

ACKNOWLEDGEMENTS

The journey to write this novel has pushed me, daily, to step beyond myself. However, in doing so, it has brought me into contact with some of the world's most uniquely talented, intelligent, creatively exceptional and humble women. Many whose generosity, grace and enthusiasm for this project offered me, more than once, a rope to hold on to. To them I say this: in showing up to do my work, what a fortunate twist of fate that I have found in you what I first saw in that painting. Thank you.

The research has taken place across continents. Covid, of course, affected this; sometimes in the most harrowing ways. However, I feel we have prevailed if only by virtue of our kindred connections, our shared patience, our voyages of creative work, and our continued kind words.

To all of you, both women and men, listed below: thank you. Not only for the part you have played in this novel, but for showing up on this elaborately peopled blue planet and gracing us with your gifts.

My heartfelt gratitude to:

Australia

My husband, Darren. Your magnitude of heart and mind continues to leave me breathless with the sheer good luck that not only are you my husband, but that you are my friend, my ally and the loyal cheerleader of my creative spark.

Margaret Connolly, my tender, erudite, wise, prudent, ever-courteous, advice-rich agent. I think my husband coined it best when I was relaying some guidance you offered and he asked: 'Does Margaret know she is the Keeper of All Knowledge?' She doesn't. Which makes her all the more extraordinary.

Catherine Milne, it's a rare human able to combine supreme professionalism with infinite duty of care. And you do so while offering perspective, creative insight and equanimity. Catherine, you would excel at anything you chose to do. What an honour it will always be that you chose to take this dear-to-my-heart novel under your ample wing.

The HarperCollins editorial and design team: Hazel Lam, whose persistence to encapsulate the soul of this complex novel delivered a meaningful and magnificent result. Wow. Shannon Kelly, fleet-of-mind, clever and calm. Shannon, your generosity of spirit and keen editorial eyes have provided guide ropes and essential mental sustenance to climb the mountain of the intense final weeks. Your allegiance has been impeccable. Down to the last diacritic. Rebecca Sutherland and Jo Butler, your poignant understanding and astute story-eyes helped amplify and refine the clarity of my vision. Graeme Jones, thank you for your handling of dots and diacritics, Aramaic and Italian alike. Your selection to set this book in Bembo is a spectacular synchronicity.

Suzanne Leal, what a gift from the stars you were during our shared writing time at Varuna. Your bright mind is one to be reckoned with! That you wield it for so much good in this world – we are all the luckier for it. Your introduction to Margaret is treasured. Thank you.

Dr Kathryn Heyman, Australian Writers Mentoring Program, whose resolute opinion of the value of this novel helped tether my vision to writing confidence and whose literary acumen encouraged me to say 'yes' to the incredible opportunity to reinstall the modern narrative when Catherine's narrative radar detected a missing voice.

My first readers, from every comma in the text, to every last question mark in the margins, your contribution to my clarity is treasured. In order of who read the longest-winded versions first: Belinda Lyons-Lee, Tim Crawley, Jillian Tierney (my Aunty Mum); Kate McCabe, Pamela Crocker (my actual Mum), Simon Tierney, Felicity Finlay, Daxine Waterman, Heather Anders, Jacqui Hooper, Ian Dowler, Julie Smith, Jacqui Cookes OAM, Terry Tierney (my Uncle Dad).

Belinda Lyons-Lee, author, educator and fluent speaker of wisdom. Thank you for your friendship. B, you are one powerhouse of a woman.

Varuna, the National Writers' House for hosting me as a PIP Award winner, and for their tireless loyalty to writing and writers.

Elisabeth Storrs and Diane Murray from the Historical Novel Society of Australasia (HNSA), not only through the HNSA Colleen McCullough Residency Award, but their ongoing advocacy of historical fiction and its authors.

Mary-Jo O'Rourke AE, my first and last pages editor for the last decade. Reliable, sincere and consistent in all the very best professional ways.

Rowena and Michael for your ease of love and loyal friendship. Tim and Emma and Rachel and Al who always asked and always listened. Jessica Vander aa Kennedy for walking beside me as we traverse our glittering beaches, spot pied oyster catchers, and speak on all matters spiritual; then laugh and laugh and laugh at everything we will never know. Ryan Hollingsworth, for sending me Richmond Birdwing butterfly photos that lift my heart. Chip Richards, long-time writing ally, who encouraged me in a challenging moment: the writer's life is quiet, at best. But who also is a brother to my husband in all the best ways my husband deserves.

Margot Duell for our many writerly chats, and for connecting me to Suzi Rosedale, whose warm words were so needed and who, in turn, connected me to Carol Ann. Dr Michael Trainor, whose suggestions for my Middle East research trip were reassuring.

Ischbel Johnstone and Christine, for sharing their table with us that lovely evening in Whispers Wine Bar, Fremantle, and who told me of the quartz in King Solomon's treasures.

Dr Tim Johnson, Director of Treenet, and Gregory Moore, Senior Research Associate, University of Melbourne, Burnley, for their assistance with the trees of North Adelaide. From the Art Gallery of South Australia (AGSA): Rebecca Evan and Rusty Kelty. This novel's gallery, Adelaide International Gallery, and its staff are entirely fictional. My character's textile conservation work has been inspired by an amalgam of the brilliant conservators from ArtLab and curators from the AGSA.

My Australian and American family

As a novel about women and connection, every female in my family has helped inform my own rich knowledge about what it means to be a woman in connection with other women. What a wild ride we have chosen to share!

To my parents, Pam and David, my brothers, Jason and Toby, and my sisters, Esther and Lucy. If only I could find a way to show you the countless solo walks where, in the presence of the trees and surf and sky, my love has beamed towards you. How I stand, arms outstretched, until I see in my mind's eye a radiant, glimmering thread connecting our hearts. Caileb, Gaige, Jesse, Luke, Lewis and Dakota: I believe in you. I love you.

During the writing of this novel – and after searching all my life – I finally found my American family. Overnight, a dark void in my heart became its own illumined thread, as the Badours, Fords, Pagels and Charlestons and extended families welcomed us into their lives. Just knowing they are out there makes my world a better place.

To Tony, Val, Kerri, Emily and Abbey, may your lives be lit with love.

In my humble opinion, South Australia's spectacular artisans in textile conservation and glassblowing are unique in the world.

Finding my way into the homes, studios and lives of these humble and talented artists has been a highlight of my research. My respect and thanks to:

Glass artists Clare Belfrage and Tom Moore, who offered so much to this novel, both technically and imaginatively. They pretty much make the world a better place by waking up and doing what they do. Not least of which is their truly exceptional – and globally acclaimed – art. Through spending time with them in their respective Adelaide studios, and at Adelaide's arts hub JamFactory, I was taken into an Alice-in-Wonderland world of glass, where any sense of fixed materiality is defied by inspired vision and painstaking industry. Both Clare and Tom are known nationally and internationally for their art, and you'll see exactly why when you seek them out online, and in their respective galleries.

Artlab Australia conservators: Mary-Anne Gooden, A/Principal Conservator Textiles, and Kristin Phillips, Senior Textile Conservator, who both read the chapters relating to my fictional textile conservator and whose work is literally mindboggling. Mary-Anne's and Kristin's humility is astounding, given the ongoing contribution their work makes to the global story and legacy of the fabric of who we are, both metaphorically and literally. And Victoria Thomas, Textiles Conservator, whose talented mind helped design Dr Reed's gorgeous opening-night dress.

Mary Jose, Textile Conservator, Fabric of Life whose training as a textile conservator at the Textile Conservation Centre, Courtauld Institute of Art, Hampton Court Palace in the UK and previous management of ArtLab brought intricate and fascinating insight; Kate McLaren, Textile Conservator.

Israel and Palestinian Territories

Dr Yael Gorin-Rosen, Head of Glass Branch, Israel Antiquities Authority, Jerusalem. Where do I start with the woman who is Yael? Perhaps with this question: who among us could sense, by smell, the origin of a newly excavated ancient glass vessel?

Who among us could be so gracious as to allow us to view with trembling awe glass artifacts fresh from the earth? Yael lives her work with a dedication and commitment that make it clear why she stands at the helm of Glass at the IAA. She is also a woman with tender and fierce love for her family and friends. That she shared both these worlds with me in Haifa and Jerusalem is more than I could have dreamed.

Dr Naama Sukenik, Curator of Organic Materials, Israel Antiquities Authority, Jerusalem. The privilege Naama afforded me to see, study and know the ancient materials that may have been exactly like those touched and worn by Elisheva was an acutely emotional and revelatory experience. Naama (like my fictional curator Tris), is an effervescent, fairy-like woman but with a powerhouse of experience in the textiles that help tell us about our past, and help inform our future.

Nahum Ben-Yehuda (please see the note on translation within the glossary) has endeavoured to provide words that not only reflect the language of the period, but the sense of the people by whom it was spoken. Nahum's integrity, efficiency and prodigious mind are all too rare. Nahum: my humble thanks is not enough, but it is the beginning of honouring the miracles you have performed under our shared high-pressure timeline. The glossary provides Nahum's work along with any of my own variations brought about by the constraints of time and typesetting.

Hana Bendcowsky, Rossing Centre for Education and Dialogue, our official tour guide in Jerusalem and non-stop on-the-spot for each and every query that arose. Hana, your allegiance and spirit is that of one who 'walks their talk'. Rabbi Kenneth Spiro, whose tours and books and sharp wit were so helpful in navigating the sheer volume of Jewish history. Itai Lavee, Shelly Eshkoli, researcher of femininity in the biblical era and tour guide and author.

Carol Ann Bernheim, tour guide, Holy Land expert, global traveller and voice of reason, whose knowledge and wisdom and spirit of adventure is fathomless. What a marvellous coincidence that she hosted my Aunty Mum and Uncle Dad in her beloved land. The sign above the door to her balcony says 'Wild Witch', a title that serves as both quaint understatement and valiant two-word poem to her supreme individuality. How thankful I am to have crossed Carol Ann's path. And felt her expanded soul.

Alex Stein, Israel tour guide, who was willing to navigate the crushing Covid issues and help me find ways to conduct field research in a shutdown world. And who also connected me with the marvellous Hana.

Miriam Feinberg Vamosh, author and translator, whose commitment to and aptitude for vast research across faiths and eras make her books and articles a must-read for those seeking to understand the history of the Holy Land.

Professor Amram Eshel, scientific editor of wildflowers.co.il, whose willingness to answer all things flora from the biblically vast to the thorny microscopic was sheer delight. His ability to deliver brief answers packed with knowledge and humour was a skill I continue to appreciate.

Ilana Stein, artist and wild plant forager, who took me on a wild plant foraging tour of Ein Kerem valley, and with partner, Davidi Maller, introduced me to grape honey and to their artisanal ceramics made in, and inspired by, the heart of Ein Kerem.

Pnina Ein Mor, longtime resident of Ein Kerem, and self-proclaimed wanderer of Ein Kerem's paths, who was awarded Jerusalem's 'Worthy Citizen' prize for contributions to tourism in Ein Kerem and whose gracious time brought me to precious local details. Her cookbook/history lesson is a love letter to this beautiful region.

Hebron Glass and Ceramics, and the entire Natsheh family, who nurture a centuries-old tradition of glass blowing and a modern workshop in Hebron, Palestine, that will forever be remembered as a once-in-a-lifetime experience. Hamzeh Natsheh, Tawfiq Natsheh, Hamdi Natsheh, Emad Natsheh and family, thank you for sharing an insight into your world with me. I urge readers to explore the Natsheh history and work. The Natsheh family heart beats strong.

Gila Yudkin, pilgrim guide, photographer and research consultant, who provided early, thoughtful and robust research perspectives; Yoav Druyen and Simon Young; Nosson Shulman, CEO and senior tour guide, VIP Israel Tours, speaker; Rabbi Elhanan Miller for guidance on key Jewish passages; Rabbi Geoffrey Black, whose help over several weeks to address many issues of Judaism was efficient and appreciated; Alice Ahearn for the Latin translations.

Italy

It was on a PhD research trip many moons ago that I found myself before Albertinelli's painting. During this time, there were some key people who helped begin my Florence research journey: namely Professor Graziano Baccolini, his daughter, Licinia and Dr Romano Romali, whose family fabric shop Casa dei Tessuti more than deserves its fleeing mention in this novel.

With Covid preventing my return to Florence, there are many academics, artists, historians and guides who contributed their clout and years of experience to fact-checking, sensitivity perspective and experience to the Florence chapters: Christina Mifsud, Dr Nicholas Baker, Dr Elaine Ruffalo, Elaine Ruffolo, Art Historian, Art History Encounters, Florence, who helped me flesh out San Michele alle Trombe, both locationally and speculating on what it might have looked like inside.

Elizabeth Wicks, who, through Elaine, helped me with the pigments that may have been used in Albertinelli's painting; Professor Carlo Falciani, Accademia di Belle Arte, Florence; Hector Ramsay, fresco artist, whose verve for invention was a breath of fresh air; and Sally Tucker.

United Kingdom

Dr Mary Brooks, whose first-hand knowledge of the embroidery *Embracing Figures* and whose assessment and recording of the embroidery on behalf of the Ashmolean Museum, along with the fact that she took such time and care to help me understand the piece, was a gift.

While Caterina Sirani is a fictional character, Ana Maria Pacheco is the actual artist behind *Study of Head (John the Baptist III)*, one production of genius among her exceptional list of artworks in various media. See her work. Because she sees more than most. Ana Maria's agent and owner of Pratt Contemporary Art, Susan Pratt, whose warm-heartedness and generosity, along with her fine eye for art made for a connection of intelligence and shared appreciation.

David Hill and Mark Taylor, 'The Glassmakers', UK. I urge you to view their incredible work. David's willingness to deliver beautifully articulated responses to my novice questions over two full years offered me fascinating insights into the always-mystifying process of glassblowing. He also bolstered my courage for creativity. This mattered, a lot.

Professor Sir Ernst Gombrich, for my very first lessons in art history, but also for teaching me the fine art of the 'walk and talk', as we strolled the streets of Hampstead.

United States

Dr Patricia Nyguen Wilson, owner of Thistle Threads, polymath and inventor, whose ongoing ability to combine arts, technology and textiles makes her a rare talent; Cristina Balloffet Carr, Conservator, Department of Textile Conservation, The Met, NY.

Katharine Duiguid, independent artist, scholar and educator, an angel of the embroidery world! Kat's pieces are literally divine. As is her gentle nature. Her explication on the embroidery featured in the modern narrative was truly a magnanimous gesture.

Roy Saper, Saper Galleries, Michigan, once the keeper of the largest Hebron glass display outside the Middle East. Roy's gentlemanly demeanour, early enthusiasm and experience in exhibiting glass pieces were pivotal in helping me feel I could render the world of glassmaking. It was Roy who connected me with the Natsheh family in Hebron. A connection that will stay with me for the rest of my life.

Dr Alysia Fischer, whose rigorous and thoughtful work, both archeologically and artistically in glass, is proof that the academic world and the arts world can intersect in an educational, lively and inspirational way. Alysia is also an artist, whose suspended sculptures, wearables, wall pieces and metalwork demonstrate her bona fide talent.

Carol Meyers, Mary Grace Wilson Professor Emerita of Religious Studies at Duke University, whose specialties of the Hebrew Bible, archaeology of the southern Levant, and gender in the biblical world, offered rigorous insight into subjects of ancient Israelite women including household and socio-political activities, relationships and reproduction, gender and society. And much, much more.

Sharon Strocchia, Professor of History, Emory University, Atlanta, has written impeccably researched books on nuns, nunneries and women healers. Her work should be on the reading list for every avid reader, not purely for their historical illumination but for their elegant and accessible lyricism.

Professor George Bent (Florence As It Was project); Dr Gregory Smith, Indianapolis Museum of Art, Conservation Science Department, whose brilliant mind and willingness to think creatively helped me invent paint processes to support Antonia's journey; Yona Sabar, Emeritus Professor of Aramaic, UCLA, who first took time to take me into the world of Aramaic. You are a *ma'alakh*, Yona.

Anatole Tchikine, Curator of Rare Books at Dumbarton Oaks in Washington, DC. Anatole came out of the clouds like a bright slant of sunshine, and with fierce intellect and overwhelming compassion, offered technical guidance to the many complexities of rendering an exotic world into plain English. His sensitivity and insight towards my vision for this novel was overwhelming. And, at the time it was conveyed, a tonic for my soul. If there is an argument for cloning, Anatole's humanity is the resolution.

Crystal King, author, culinary enthusiast, professor and marketing expert, for being generous and responsive in all my questions about food and associated subjects; Stephanie Storey, author, TV producer and artist advocate, who I wish I'd met earlier, but luckily who I met (through Crystal) just in time to reassure me that calling my character 'Michel' was an instinct to follow.

Robert Gamblin, artist and founder of Gamblin Artists Colors, whose patient conversation helped me to begin understanding the history of paint making. And whose incredible coincidence of reading a book with a fleeting reference to Alberese stone sparked Antonia's first idea on white.

Dr Cynthia Shafer-Elliot, Associate Professor of Hebrew Bible and Archeology, William Jessup University.

As I complete these acknowledgements, I was about to add herein a dedication to my dear friend, Cherry, whose sparkling nature and role as a doctor and surgeon inspired the fictional Doctor Cherry in this novel. I had also begun a heartfelt note to her, her fiancé, Jeremy, and Cherry's family for the loss of their beautiful sister and daughter, Dahlia, and Cherry's father, Gordon, last year. As I began to write, I received word that Cherry's beloved Jeremy died suddenly of a heart attack. She, and we, are heartbroken. Since this is a novel that does not shy away from loss, I take a moment to say this: My precious Cherry, you are my treasured friend of twenty-seven years. I enfold my arms around you now to let you know I am here always for you. For now. For tomorrow. For next year. For the years after that. And I will always be the one who never backs away from your agony of loss. But I will always be the one who reminds you that your value on this planet is immeasurable.